D0859399

THE SEVENTH TRUMPET

**Also by Peter Tremayne
and featuring Fidelma of Cashel**

Absolution by Murder
Shroud for the Archbishop
Suffer Little Children
The Subtle Serpent
The Spider's Web
Valley of the Shadow
The Monk Who Vanished
Act of Mercy
Hemlock at Vespers
Our Lady of Darkness
Smoke in the Wind
The Haunted Abbot
Badgers Moon
Whispers of the Dead
The Leper's Bell
Master of Souls
A Prayer for the Damned
Dancing with Demons
The Council of the Cursed
The Dove of Death
The Chalice of Blood
Behold a Pale Horse

Tremayne, Peter.
The seventh trumpet : a
mystery of Ancient Irela
2013.
33305228262469
mi   07/26/13

The Seventh Trumpet

A Mystery of Ancient Ireland

Peter Tremayne

Minotaur Books ✠ New York

This is a work of fiction. All of the characters, organizations, and events portrayed in this novel are either products of the author's imagination or are used fictitiously.

THE SEVENTH TRUMPET. Copyright © 2012 by Peter Tremayne. All rights reserved. Printed in the United States of America. For information, address St. Martin's Press, 175 Fifth Avenue, New York, N.Y. 10010.

www.minotaurbooks.com

Library of Congress Cataloging-in-Publication Data

Tremayne, Peter.
  The seventh trumpet : a mystery of Ancient Ireland / Peter Tremayne.—1st U.S. ed.
    p. cm.
  ISBN 978-0-312-65862-5 (hardcover)
  ISBN 978-1-250-02611-8 (e-book)
  1. Fidelma, Sister (Fictitious character)—Fiction. 2. Nuns—Fiction. 3. Women detectives—Ireland—Fiction. 4. Murder—Investigation—Fiction. 5. Ireland—History—To 1172—Fiction. I. Title.
  PR6070.R366S48 2013
  823'.914—dc23

                                                                    2013010681

Minotaur books may be purchased for educational, business, or promotional use. For information on bulk purchases, please contact Macmillan Corporate and Premium Sales Department at 1-800-221-7945 extension 5442 or write specialmarkets@macmillan.com.

First published in Great Britain by Headline Publishing Group, an Hachette UK Company

First U.S. Edition: July 2013

10 9 8 7 6 5 4 3 2 1

For Dorothea who has shared the best of times and the worst of times
is feidir linn

Et septimus angelus tuba cecinit: et factae sunt voces magnae in caelo dicentes: Factum est regnum huius mundi, Domini nostri et Christi eius, et regnabit in saecula saeculorum.

And the seventh angel sounded his trumpet; and there were great voices in heaven, saying, 'The kingdoms of this world are become the kingdom of Our Lord, and of His Christ, and He shall reign for ever and ever.'

Revelation 11:15
Vulgate Latin translation of Jerome, fifth century

PRINCIPAL CHARACTERS

Sister Fidelma of Cashel, a *dálaigh* or advocate of the law courts of seventh-century Ireland
Brother Eadulf of Seaxmund's Ham in the land of the South Folk, her companion

At Cluain Mór
Tóla, a farmer
Cainnear, his wife
Breac, his son

At Cashel
Colgú, King of Muman and brother to Fidelma
Finguine, son of Cathal Cú-cen-máthair, heir apparent to Colgú
Ségdae, Abbot of Imleach, Chief Bishop of Muman
Gormán, a warrior of the Nasc Niadh, bodyguards to the King
Caol, Commander of the Nasc Niadh
Enda, a warrior of the Nasc Niadh
Drón, Lord of Gabrán
Dúnliath, daughter of Drón, Lord of Gabrán
Ailill, a warrior, foster-son of Drón, cousin of Fidelma and Colgú

At Fraigh Dubh
Saer, a carpenter
Brother Ailgesach
Fedach Glas, the innkeeper
Grella, his wife
Brother Biasta

By the River Suir
Torna, a bard
Echna, the ferryman

At Durlus Éile
Gobán, the smith
Leathlobhair, the half-leper
Gelgéis, Princess of Éile
Spealáin, her steward
Daig, Bishop of the Éile
Brocc, Gelgéis's Brehon
Áedo, Chief Brehon of Muman
Étain of An Dún

At Liath Mór
Abbot Cronán
Brother Anfudán, the steward
Brother Sillán
Ségnat, a hostage

In Osraige
Canacán, a shepherd

At Baile Coll
Coccán, a smith

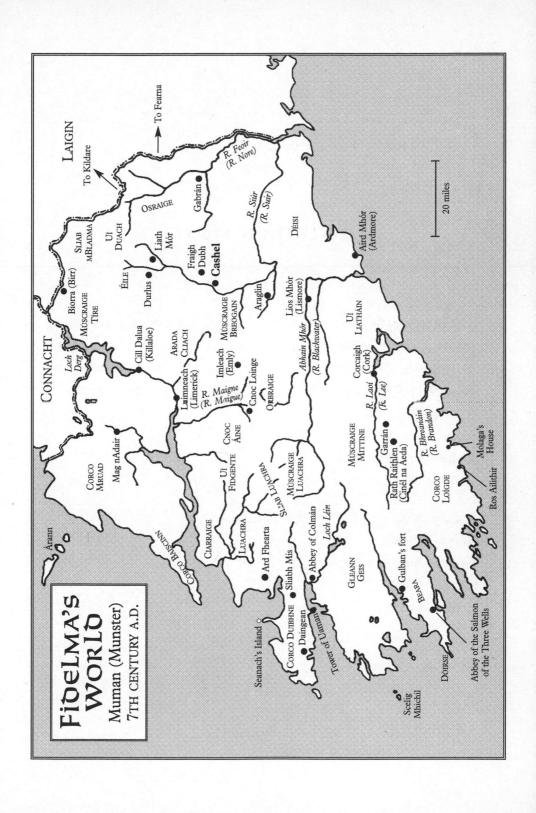

FIÐELMA'S WORLÐ

Muman (Munster)
7TH CENTURY A.D.

LAIGIN

To Kildare

To Fearna

CONNACHT

Arann

CORCO MRUAD

Mag nAdair

Loch Derg

Cill Dalua
(Killaloe)

ARADA CLIACH

MÚSCRAIGE TÍRE

Biorra (Birr)

SLIAB MBLADMA

UÍ DUACH

ÉILE

Durlus

Liath Mór

OSRAIGE

Gabrán

R. Feoir
(R. Nore)

Fraigh Dubh

Cashel

R. Siúr
(R. Suir)

DÉISI

Aird Mhór
(Ardmore)

20 miles

MÚSCRAIGE BREOGAIN

Araglin

Líos Mhór
(Lismore)

Luimneach
(Limerick)

Imleach
(Emly)

R. Maigne
(R. Maigue)

Cnoc Loinge

OSRAIGE

Abhain Mhór
(R. Blackwater)

UÍ LIATHÁIN

CORCO BAISCINN

CIARRAIGE

UÍ FIDGENTE

CNOC ÁINE

LUACHRA

SLIAB LUACHRA

MÚSCRAIGE LUACHRA

MÚSCRAIGE MITTINE

Corcaigh
(Cork)

R. Laoi
(R. Lee)

Garrán

Rath Raithlen
(Cinél na Aeda)

R. Bhreanáin
(R. Brandon)

CORCO LOÍGDE

Seanach's Island

Ard Fhearta

CORCO DUIBHNE

Sliabh Mis

Daingean

Abbey of Colmán

Loch Léin

Tower of Uaman

GLEANN GEIS

Gulban's fort

BEARA

DÓIRSE

Scelig Mhichíl

Abbey of the Salmon
of the Three Wells

Molaga's House

Ros Ailithir

AUTHOR'S NOTE

The events in this story follow in chronological sequence after those related in *The Chalice of Blood*, and are set during the season known as *Fogamar*, the harvest season AD 670, in the last days before the autumn equinox.

THE SEVENTH TRUMPET

CHAPTER ONE

Tóla paused on the threshold of his farmhouse, looked towards the black mounds of the eastern hills, standing out sharply against the white bar of light that heralded dawn, and breathed in deeply before exhaling in a satisfied fashion. It was an action that had become a regular ritual each morning over many decades. He stood for a moment, gazing at the sky and estimating what sort of day it might bring before turning his attention to the dark, undulating land that spread southward before him. The light of the new day was spreading rapidly towards the thrust of rock which dominated the southern skyline just a few kilometres away. The grey-white buildings of The Rock of Cashel, which constituted the capital of the rulers of Muman, were already sparkling in the dawn light.

Tóla took a step forward and stretched languidly. He was a thickset and muscular man; a man whose very frame seemed to proclaim that he was a son of the soil; a man used to working the land and caring for the livestock. The rising sun glinted on his blue-black hair, enhancing his tanned skin and pale eyes. His features had been coarsened and aged by his outdoor life, but they were neither ugly nor unkindly. He stood like a man content with his life and all he surveyed.

There was a rustle from nearby and a large, rough-coated hound trotted round the building and whined in greeting, accompanied by quick movements of its tail. Its quiet, easy nature belied its intimidating appearance. The man bent and petted the heavy head, making a soft grunting sound as the dog gave another whine. Then Tóla turned back to the door behind him and called out: 'It will be a good day today.'

A woman appeared, framed in the door, rubbing her hands on an apron and glancing towards the eastern hills. She was as tanned as Tóla; a pleasant, well-built woman, used to hard work.

'Good enough to finish the harvest?'

'Good enough, Cainnear. We can finish the small field today and then all the grain will be in.'

'You had best check the heifer that's still in calf before you do so,' the woman advised.

'She's been slow, that one,' agreed her husband. 'The rest of the calves are already out to pasture. I'll go and see how she is. She was down by the stream last night – she's probably given birth by now.' Then he paused. 'I suppose that our lazy son is not yet stirring? Better get him out of bed – there is a great deal to be done.'

'I will so, and join you in the small field later,' Cainnear replied with a smile.

The farmer nodded absently and, with his dog trotting at his heels, he went to the shed at the back of the *bothán*, the stone-built cabin in which they lived, and collected a scythe and rake. Balancing them easily over one broad shoulder, he began to stroll across the fields towards the distant dark line of trees which marked the path of the little stream that was the southern border of his farmlands. The stream flowed west to join the great river called the Suir, which provided the western border of his land.

It was fully light by the time he had reached the small area of wheat that still needed to be cut. Soon it would be the moon which was called *Gealach na gcoinnlíní* – the moon of the stubble. This marked the time when all the grain crops should be cut down to their stalks and harvested. He paused and cast an eye over the field and then pursed his lips in a soundless whistle as if in approval. It would not take long to complete the harvest now. Thanks be; it had been a good harvest and a good year, for he had not lost one cow, pig or chicken to ill-fortune nor to predators. That thought prompted him to peer towards the treeline to look for his heifer, which had been waiting for her first calf. It was late. He hoped the calf had come during the night for, if it had not, the animal would be in difficulty. It was still too shadowy to make out much among the dark treeline. Placing the scythe and rake by the cornerstone of the field, he strode across the stubble towards the trees, his dog panting behind him.

He was nearing the trees when the dog suddenly halted, raised its head, as if sniffing the air, and gave a soft growl.

'What is it, Cú Faoil?' Tóla spoke quietly, unable to see anything untoward. Then he spotted a dark shadow at the far end of the field: it was a heifer no longer, for the smaller shadow of a calf stood by it. He smiled in relief before he realised that his dog was not looking in that direction – and the growl was still rumbling in its throat. Tóla looked cautiously in the same direction, but could see nothing. He advanced slowly, the dog obediently following, head up, alert and wary. Tóla knew that Cú Faoil, his loyal protector, was able to perceive danger before any human could. Tóla also knew that if there was scent of a predator, the animal would be more vocal in its warning. Indeed, if there were an immediate danger, then the cow, with its newborn calf, would not be standing docilely at the other end of the field. Yet something was not quite right.

The gushing of the stream behind the trees was loud at this point. This was because the waters frothed over a series of stepping stones which people often used as a pathway to the far bank. Unless travellers moved along the eastern bank of the Suir, or had access to a small boat, they had to turn along the path by this stream, called the Arglach, and make their way to this crossing through the shallows in order to continue south. On the southern side they could join the track that eventually led to the fortress of Cashel and its surrounding township. Tóla had lived all his life in this area. He expected the waters of the stream to resound against the stepping stones at this crossing-point. But his sensitive hearing picked up a different note – that of a stream in flood. He was aware that Cú Faoil had heard it too, and again the low rumble came from its throat.

Tóla walked through the trees and on to the path by the stream. At once he could see that the stones of the crossing were blocked by something which caused the waters to gush around and over them. What he saw made the breath catch in his throat.

Lying in midstream, as if fallen from the stepping stones, was a body.

Tóla moved swiftly, the cold waters coming up to his knees, and reached down to take a firm grip of the body's clothing. Tóla was a strong man, befitting one who had worked the land all his life. Even so, it was a burdensome task to pull the body back to the bank, fighting the clawing pressure of the water which tried to press it against the stepping stones. Soon, however, the body was out of the water and stretched on the bank.

Having taken a few deep breaths to recover, Tóla examined it. The man, who had not been long dead, was young and good-looking. Moreover, the clothes he wore were of good quality and they were embroidered with fine needlework. A gold chain was still around his neck and a large ring with a semi-precious stone sparkled on his finger. The man was clearly someone of rank. He wore a short, brightly coloured cloak, pinned at one shoulder with a brooch of fine workman-ship crafted in the form of an emblem. His bejewelled dagger still rested in a sheath on the left side of his belt, and his sword remained in its scabbard on the right-hand side.

Tóla raised a hand to the back of his head and rubbed it in puzzlement as he gazed at the corpse. His first thought was that the young man must have slipped and fallen from the wet stepping stones, possibly hitting his head in the darkness. But what would a young man of position be doing, travelling in such a place as this and without a horse? It was all very perplexing, not to say worrying. For a youth of rank to meet his death, even by accident, on Tóla's farmlands could mean big trouble for him. Tóla vaguely remembered something about liability under the Law of Compensation.

He knelt to see if he could find the wound, but there were no signs of cuts or abrasions to the young man's head. It was as Tóla was turning the body over to see if there were any wounds on the back of the head that he noticed the rents and tears in the man's clothing. At the same time, he became aware that his hand was not just wet with water but stained faintly pink. Blood. He swallowed hard. It was now obvious to him how the young man had met his death. He had been stabbed at least three times in the back.

When Tóla realised the significance of his discovery, he was alarmed: this did, indeed, mean trouble for him. It was only the whimper and the cold muzzle of his dog, the animal sensing that all was not well with its master, that caused Tóla to finally stir. The young noble, whoever he was, had been murdered on his farm, albeit on a right-of-way that was frequently used. The big man rose unsteadily to his feet and tried to control his apprehension while he considered what he should do.

He realised that he was unconsciously staring towards the Rock of Cashel, no more than a short ride to the south. There would be Brehons at Cashel; lawyers and judges. They would know what should be done. They would investigate, they would advise. Tóla had been raised with an implicit belief in the wisdom of the Brehons. He glanced down again at the body, and noted the strange design of the brooch, fixing the cloak at the shoulder of the young man. Perhaps it was an emblem of his clan? Anyway, it would surely induce a Brehon to come here to investigate. Kneeling down once more, he undid the clasp. Then, with a swift glance around, he hastened back towards the farmhouse, with his dog loping along at his side.

Cainnear saw him coming and realised immediately that something must be wrong.

'What is it?' she demanded.

'Is the boy up?' Tóla asked breathlessly, not answering her question.

'He was getting the ass ready to move the—'

Tóla turned towards the stable building, shouting, 'Breac! *Breac!*'

A boy, not long past the age of choice, emerged from a nearby barn and came running over, a worried look on his freckled face.

'What is it, Father?'

'I must go to Cashel immediately, so I will need the ass,' Tóla told him. Then: 'I want you to take a weapon and go down to the crossing on the stream. There is the body of a young man there.' He ignored the gasp given by his wife. 'Don't touch it – and don't let anyone else touch it, or go near it,' he ordered. 'I am leaving Cú Faoil with you while I am off to Cashel to bring a Brehon back.'

Breac knew better than to start asking questions. Instead, he hurried to the stable and finished saddling up their ass. Meanwhile, Tóla had exchanged a few swift words of reassurance with his wife, and then, having placed the dog's collar in the hand of Breac as an indication to Cú Faoil that he must stay, uttering the word, 'Guard' several times to the animal, Tóla swung up on to the ass and, with a quick wave of his hand, set the beast in an ambling trot towards the palace of the King of Muman.

chapter two

Gormán stood at his ease outside the dark oak doors that led into the private chambers of the King of Muman. The kingdom was the largest and most south-westerly of the Five Kingdoms of the land of Éireann. Gormán was a youthful man, fair of skin with thick, raven-black hair, dark eyes and pleasant features. He wore the gold band, or torque, at his neck with a degree of self-conscious pride because it denoted that he was a member of the Nasc Niadh, the Warriors of the Golden Collar, who were the élite bodyguard of the Kings of Muman. Gormán had a right to be proud of his position for he had won it by his own strength and dexterity against many odds. Usually, members of the élite bodyguard were the sons of chieftains or of great warriors. Gormán had been the son of a *bé táide*, a former prostitute, but his abilities, not just those with weapons but his intelligence, had caused him to be singled out for a position of trust in the household of the King.

A figure appeared at the far end of the corridor and came towards him. He stiffened a little and then relaxed almost immediately as he recognised the King's sister. He was still not used to seeing her dressed in anything other than the robes of a religieuse. Today she wore a tight-fitting upper garment in the manner of a short, bright blue coat that reached to the middle of her thighs. It had no collar but, from the shoulders, fastened by brooches, hung a *cochnull*, a short cloak also of bright blue but with designs in gold- and silver-coloured needlework. She also wore tight-fitting *triubhas*, trousers from the hips to ankle, so that they showed perfectly the shape of her limbs. Such trousers were held in place by a slender strap passing under the foot. They were also patterned in many bright colours. Her leather boots came above the ankles, and she carried her gloves in one hand.

Her long red hair was carefully combed, separated and plaited in three braids, wound and held in place by silver circlets. This fashion denoted someone who was leading an active life. The fact that the top of her head was covered in a small silk scarf of matching colour to her coat, provided the information that she was married or of mature age. At her waist she wore a girdle, a *criss* or belt, from which hung her comb bag, the *ciorbholg*, which all women carried, containing the articles needed for toiletry.

'You are abroad early today, lady.' Gormán allowed a smile of greeting to spread across his features. 'Are you going riding?' The manner of her dress, the fact that she held a pair of leather gloves in one hand, needed no intense thought to reach such a conclusion.

Fidelma of Cashel, sister to King Colgú, returned his smile. She had once helped defend his mother, Della, from unjust charges and since then had been a friend to both her and Gormán. The young warrior had acted as her bodyguard many times.

'It is going to be a fine day. Better not to waste it by lying a-bed,' she told him. 'Anyway, I was roused very early by the sound of horsemen leaving the fortress. Was anything amiss?'

'That was Finguine and a few companions,' replied Gormán.

Finguine mac Cathail was the *tánaiste*, the heir apparent, to Fidelma's brother.

8

'What takes him away from Cashel so early in the morning?'

'I believe that the Cenél Lóegairi are behind in their tribute to Cashel and, as the harvest is now over, the *tánaiste* decided it would be prudent to visit their chieftain and remind him of his due.'

The Cenél Lóegairi was a clan in the south-west of the kingdom which had a reputation for being reticent in fulfilling its obligations to the King of Cashel. Finguine was Fidelma's distant cousin from a branch of her family known as the Eóghanacht Áine. He had become heir-elect to the kingdom four years before, after the death of the former heir-apparent, Donndubhán, who had unsuccessfully plotted to assassinate Colgú and take over the kingdom. Finguine was known for his conscientious attention to administrative work on behalf of the King.

Fidelma indicated the closed doors behind Gormán with a gesture of her hand. 'Has my brother arisen yet?'

'He was also up before dawn, lady, but Abbot Ségdae is already with him.'

Ségdae was Abbot and Bishop of Imleach, the premier prelate of the kingdom.

'It's early for the abbot to seek a meeting with my brother. I did not even know he was in Cashel.' Disappointment crossed her features. She had been hoping to entice her brother to accompany her on her morning ride. 'Why are there such early-morning stirrings?'

'Abbot Ségdae arrived with the dawn, lady. He must have ridden through the night and was accompanied by only one of his brethren. He had a troubled look and demanded to see Colgú immediately.'

'That does not bode well,' Fidelma responded with a frown. 'Have they left word not to be disturbed?'

Gormán shook his head. 'None that I have been told.'

'Then I shall enter.'

Gormán moved to the doors, rapped twice before opening it to allow Fidelma to pass through.

Inside the large chamber, where King Colgú usually received only special guests, Fidelma's brother and his visitor were seated in chairs before a log fire. Colgú glanced up as his sister entered and greeted her with a smile. The elderly figure of Abbot Ségdae was rising to his feet from the other chair but she gestured to him to remain seated.

'A good day to you, Sister Fidelma,' the prelate said.

'And to you, Abbot Ségdae,' she replied, slipping into a vacant chair. Then she added softly, 'Although you may recall that I have now formally left the religious so I am no longer "Sister" but once more plain Fidelma of Cashel.'

The abbot regarded her protest with humour.

'You will always be Sister Fidelma to us,' he told her. 'Your reputation is already fixed throughout the Five Kingdoms so that no one can speak of Fidelma without the prefix of Sister.'

'I am hoping that people might come to know another prefix,' she replied undeterred.

'Ah yes,' sighed the abbot. 'My regrets that the Council of Brehons of Muman did not see fit to approve your application, but the role of Chief Brehon of this kingdom is one requiring many years of application.'

Fidelma's eyes sparkled dangerously for a moment, wondering if there was some hint of sarcasm in his voice. Then she relented.

'I concede that Brehon Áedo does have much more experience than I do.' Her tone was without enthusiasm. 'Doubtless the council chose wisely in appointing him as Chief Brehon to my brother.'

Colgú stirred uneasily. He knew well that Fidelma had set her ambition to be appointed to the position of Chief Brehon of Muman. When Brehon Baithen had died, Fidelma had declared her intention to leave the religious and seek the position. However, the choice of the appointment of Chief Brehon was in the hands of the Council of Brehons, and they had chosen the elderly and more conservatively minded Brehon Áedo.

'So what now, Fidelma? What does the future hold for you?' queried the abbot.

'The future? I shall carry on as before. I see no change in my life.'

'But having left our religion . . . ?'

'I have not left the religion, only the religious,' replied Fidelma crisply. 'And since I left the Abbey of Brigit at Cill Dara, several years ago, I have acted independently of any Rule or religious authority. To be honest, and I am sure you will admit it, my recent leaving was a formality only. So that is why I see no alteration in my life in the future. There are plenty of matters that require the ability of a *dálaigh*, an advocate of the law, and I can still sit in judgement in minor cases.'

'That is true,' Colgú said reflectively. 'But perhaps this is also an opportunity. You hold the degree of *anruth*, which is the second highest degree in the land. Why not take the opportunity to return to your studies and become an *ollamh*, the highest degree? That would surely improve your future chances when you go before the Council of the Brehons?'

Fidelma did not reply but her expression showed that her brother's suggestion found little favour with her.

'And what does Brother Eadulf think?' the abbot pressed. His question made no attempt to disguise the fact that he knew of the tensions that had existed between Fidelma and the father of her son, little Alchú. Indeed, when she had announced her decision earlier in the year, Brother Eadulf had left to seek solitude in the community of the Blessed Rúan not far from Cashel. He had returned only at the request of King Colgú to help Fidelma resolve the matter of the murder of Brother Donnchad at Lios Mór.

'Eadulf has now accepted the choice that I have made,' Fidelma informed him coldly. 'But if you need further information about his thoughts, it would be better to ask him.'

Abbot Ségdae's cheeks reddened a little and he smothered a cough while Colgú shook his head in disapproval.

'Abbot Ségdae has only the good of our family and the kingdom at heart, Fidelma,' he rebuked in a soft tone. 'Indeed, that is what brings him here so early in the morning.'

It was obvious to her that her brother was trying to guide the conversation into other channels. Fidelma obliged him, for she was wondering why the abbot had ridden through the night to seek him out.

'Is there some matter that affects the well-being of either?' she asked innocently. 'I thought it might be arrangements for some more pleasant occasion that brought Abbot Ségdae hither?'

Her brother actually blushed. Drón, Lord of Gabrán in Osraige, and his daughter, Dúnliath, had been guests at Cashel for three days now and Colgú had confessed to Fidelma that he was going to discuss the terms of a marriage contract with him. Fidelma had tried to put aside the fact that she had taken a dislike to the arrogant noble and regarded his daughter with indifference. She was trying to rationalise what she saw as her prejudice and accept that what would make her brother happy would be for his good and, therefore, the good of the kingdom.

'There is news of unrest coming out of the lands of the Uí Fidgente,' said Abbot Ségdae. 'That is what brought me here.'

'That is nothing new,' Fidelma replied lightly. 'The Uí Fidgente have always caused trouble to our family and to the unity of the kingdom.'

The princes of the Uí Fidgente in the north-west of the kingdom had long claimed *they* should be in the line of the rightful rulers of the kingdom – and not the Eóghanacht, descendants of Eóghan Mór. They even claimed their line descended from Cormac Cass, the elder brother of Eóghan, and hence they called themselves the Dál gCais, descendants of Cass. Beyond their clan lands, however, they found little support for their claims. It had not been many years ago that Colgú had to take the field with his loyal warriors against Prince Eoghanán of the Uí Fidgente and his allies to quell their insurgency. For as long as Fidelma could remember, if there was any plot or mischief in the kingdom, it was usually inspired by the discontent of the princes of the Uí Fidgente.

'I thought,' she continued, 'that since Donennach became their ruler, and agreed a treaty with Cashel, there had been peace among them?'

'This time we cannot be sure that the Uí Fidgente are behind this unrest,' the abbot sighed.

'What unrest do we speak of?' Fidelma asked.

After a glance at the King, as if seeking permission to speak, the abbot explained. 'We hear that several villages and farmsteads around the territory of the Uí Fidgente have been set ablaze and many killed. The news only reached Imleach yesterday morning. That is why I set out to bring the information to your brother.'

'What is the specific information that you have received?' pressed Fidelma. 'Burning villages and farmsteads – who reported this to you?'

'The first account came by way of a merchant who had seen several homesteads in ashes. He then saw an entire settlement that had been torched.'

'Where was this?'

'A settlement on the banks of An Mháigh.'

'As I recall, that is a fairly long river. Was he more specific?'

'The settlement that was destroyed was near a crossing called the Ford of the Oak, Áth Dara.'

'That is certainly in Uí Fidgente territory,' Colgú confirmed, 'but if memory serves, it is on the very border of their territory, for the eastern side of the river is the territory of our cousin Finguine of the Eóghanacht Áine.'

'Did this merchant make enquiries as to what had happened at this ford?' Fidelma asked.

'Alas, there was no one left other than corpses. The men, women and children had all been cut down or fled. The merchant felt it wiser not to tarry there but carried straight on to our abbey at Imleach. He was very fearful about what he had seen.'

'You gave the impression that he was not the only person bearing such reports,' Fidelma remarked. 'You said this merchant gave the first account?'

The abbot nodded slowly. 'It is true. Not long after the merchant had brought his news, a band of our Brothers arrived from the Abbey of the Blessed Nessan, at Muine Gairid. They came with a similar story, for they too had seen several churches and farmsteads burned on their journey south and people's bodies lying unattended.'

'Churches burned?' Fidelma was astonished.

'And religious killed,' confirmed Abbot Ségdae.

'Muine Gairid is north of Áth Dara,' observed Colgú, 'so these killings and burnings are mainly located in the territory of the Uí Fidgente. Did these brethren encounter anyone who knew what was happening, anyone who could identify those responsible?'

'No one,' said the abbot.

'If the territory of the Uí Fidgente is under attack, then we should have heard something from Prince Donennach,' Colgú pointed out. 'When he became ruler over his people, under the peace settlement, we agreed that he should notify me of any dissension in his land.'

'And this is all the information that you have?' Fidelma glanced from the abbot to her brother. There was a silence. She waited a moment and then said to Colgú: 'What is it that you intend to do?'

'There is little action I can take without more facts about the perpetrators of these attacks. Apart from the reports that the abbot has brought us, there has been no word or request for assistance from the Prince of the Uí Fidgente, nor from any of the surrounding clans and settlements.'

'Maybe Prince Donennach has been unable to send for assistance,' Abbot Ségdae suggested.

'Perhaps.' But Colgú did not sound convinced. 'The only thing to do is send some of my warriors to Prince Donennach and see what they can find out about this matter.'

Fidelma was quiet for a few moments and then she said, 'I too see no other path that can be taken at this time. But it is curious that we have heard nothing before this. We must be careful, lest we send our warriors into a trap.'

'A trap?' Colgú raised his eyebrows. 'What makes you say that?'

'Recent history. The Uí Fidgente have a reputation for plotting. I do not have to remind you of the assassination attempt on you. We should have a care, brother.'

Colgú understood the dangers only too well. 'I shall instruct Finguine to deal with the matter. He is of the Eóghanacht Áine and is acquainted with the territory.'

Fidelma frowned. 'I was told that Finguine and some warriors had left before dawn to remind the Cenél Lóegairi that it was time to pay their tribute to Cashel.'

Colgú was momentarily surprised.

'He did not—' He caught himself and shrugged. 'Finguine is far too conscientious. I was not told he had left. In that case, I'll appoint Dego to command.'

'Not Caol?' Fidelma enquired. 'He is more experienced.' Caol was the commander of Colgú's élite bodyguard and one of the best military strategists in Cashel.

'Dego has experience enough for this matter,' her brother said firmly.

'Perhaps he should be accompanied by someone legally qualified to ask pertinent questions?' Fidelma mused.

Her brother chuckled cynically. 'Meaning you, I suppose? The answer is no. I know that you have been bored and with little to do since the meeting of the Council of Brehons, but I am not going to send you into a situation which may prove dangerous.'

Fidelma was indignant. 'Why not? Have I not been in dangerous situations enough times?'

'Until we know who these raiders are and what their purpose is, then I agree that caution is needed,' intervened Abbot Ségdae. 'If religious are being slaughtered in the land of the Uí Fidgente, then your rank and position may not protect you.'

'The abbot is right, Fidelma,' her brother agreed. 'Anyway, I shall not allow it. Dego will command a *céta* and will go north-west to investigate. That should be sufficient to deal with the matter.'

A *céta* was a company of 100 warriors. Unless the kingdom was engaged in a full conflict, the King maintained only one full-time *cath* or battalion of warriors consisting of 3,000 men. The battalion was divided into small companies of a hundred men, and further sub-divided into units of fifty and squads of nine men. Should the services of more men be needed in time of war, a *sluaghadh* or hosting was called and all free clansmen, under their chieftains, were expected to come forward. Such hostings were confined to the summer months, the season for warfare, if warfare ever erupted. Throughout the year, the *cath*, or battalion, lived in a permanent and well-ordered encampment. There they trained in the art of warfare as well as being instructed in music and poetry, and were provided with other entertainments to amuse them as if they were in their own villages. Their commanders were usually members of the Nasc Niadh, the élite bodyguard of the Eóghanacht kings. Therefore, at any season of the year, the King was able to call upon warriors in time of need without waiting for a call to the clans to gather in a hosting.

'I would like to start back to Imleach now,' the abbot said. 'I am expecting Bran Finn to arrive back at the abbey soon and would not like to miss him.'

'Bran Finn? Who is he?' asked Fidelma.

'The new Prince of the Déisi Muman, who is returning from a trip to the west. But I thought he came here first to Cashel as courtesy to you, Colgú? Did you not meet him then, Fidelma?'

'My sister was visiting someone at the Hill of Rafon that day,' Colgú intervened. 'Bran Finn did not stay very long before travelling on to Imleach. In fact, only long enough as protocol dictated to pay his respects. He seemed in a hurry and I was surprised to see that he travelled alone.'

'I do not know him,' confirmed Fidelma. 'Surely it is unusual for a prince of the Déisi Muman to visit Imleach and the west?'

'The abbey administers to the unfortunates in the Glen of Lunatics, as you know. The Prince has a distant relative under the care of the abbey. He came some days ago to ensure his relative is well sustained, and brought gifts to the abbey before going on into the Glen of Lunatics.'

'He promised to return to the abbey on his way back to the territory of the Déisi,' the abbot explained. 'I wanted his assurance that he approved our work. His patronage would be welcome, you understand. It is difficult caring for those whose minds are unbalanced and—'

Abbot Ségdae was cut short by an urgent knock on the door. Even before Colgú could answer it, the door opened and Caol, the commander of the Nasc Niadh, entered. It was clear to Fidelma that he had important news to impart, but Colgú spoke first.

'Why was I not told that Finguine had left Cashel?'

Caol blinked at the abruptness of the question.

'He told me not to disturb you while you were with Abbot Ségdae, and said he would return within a few days. I did not think it essential that you be informed.'

'Well, I have a job for Dego . . .'

'I think Caol has something more urgent on his mind,' Fidelma interrupted. 'Let's hear what he has to say.'

Her brother turned to Caol. 'You have some other news?'

'A farmer has arrived here to report the finding of a body on his land,' said Caol. 'He seeks a Brehon's advice.'

Fidelma was curious. 'Then why come to bother the King about it? There is a choice of Brehons even in the township.'

'I thought that Colgú should see this first,' Caol said, holding out an intricately worked brooch. 'It was found on the body, and the farmer thought it might help identify the corpse. The body was that of a well-dressed young man.'

Colgú took the metal object with its inlaid semi-precious stones and turned it over in his hands a few times, his frown deepening. It was obvious that he recognised it but he handed it to Fidelma, saying only, 'What do you make of it?'

Fidelma took it and her eyes widened slightly. 'It's a brooch bearing the emblem of the Uí Máil,' she said immediately.

Colgú's expression was grim.

'Exactly,' he said. 'That is the emblem of a member of the Royal House of Laigin.'

CHAPTER THREE

Abbot Ségdae leaned forward in astonishment. Fianamail mac Máele Tuile of the Uí Máil was King of the neighbouring Kingdom of Laigin. They all knew the significance of the emblem. Fidelma was examining it more closely. She had noticed a small catch on the side of the brooch and pushed it open. There was a tiny recess but it was empty.

'Where is the farmer who found the body?' she asked Caol.

'Outside, lady,' replied the warrior. 'His name is Tóla. His farmstead is at Cluain Mór just north of the stream called the Arglach.'

It was such a short distance to the north-west of Cashel that she knew it well.

'Bring him in and let us hear his story,' Colgú instructed.

Caol left the room, to return a moment later with the nervous-looking farmer, who appeared awed at being in the presence of his King, the King's sister and the senior prelate of the kingdom.

Colgú motioned him forward with an encouraging smile.

'Come in, Tóla. Come closer, and be at your ease.'

The farmer took a few hesitant steps, bobbing his head shyly as if in greeting to everyone.

'We are told that you have found a body,' Fidelma prompted, after the man had stood silently for a while with downcast eyes.

'I have, lady.'

'Tell us the circumstances of how you did so.'

Tóla, after a few false starts and the clearing of his throat, told them what had happened to him that morning. They listened attentively until he had finished speaking.

'What made you think that he was a noble?' Colgú asked.

'His clothes, weapons and jewels proclaimed him so.'

'You brought us this brooch,' Fidelma said, indicating the item still held in her hand. 'Do you know its significance?'

'I do not. However, I have seen such emblems used to mark the identity of noble families and their clans. I imagined from that, and the dress and appearance of the body, it was someone of not inconsiderable position.'

'You considered him a stranger to this territory?'

'I knew only that he was not from one of the clans of this area because I see most of the chieftains at the great fairs and markets and would have recognised him.'

It was obvious that Tóla was no fool.

'And you are certain that it was no accident which caused his death at the ford?' interposed the abbot, speaking for the first time since the farmer had entered.

Tóla actually managed to summon a nervous smile as he shook his head. 'I fought in my clan's muster at Cnoc Áine, lord. I know enough of wounds to understand when they are inflicted by accident or design. But it is not for me to venture my opinion when a physician's word would be better informed. My son has been left to guard the body until someone qualified should examine it.'

'You have acted in a correct manner, Tóla,' Colgú said with a smile. 'Caol, take our friend and provide him with some refreshment while we discuss this matter. Leave that emblem with us, Tóla. We shall send someone back with you to view this body and arrange for its removal.'

When the door had closed behind them, Colgú sat back and sighed. He retrieved the brooch from Fidelma and was turning it over in his hands.

'This is the second piece of worrying news this morning. If this person was a member of the Royal Family of the Uí Máil, what was he doing here and why would he have been killed?'

Fidelma grimaced. 'No speculation . . .'

Her brother interrupted her with a groan: . . . without information.' He completed her favourite saying. 'Nevertheless, an Uí Máil killed in the shadow of the fortress of the Eóghanacht is a matter of great concern for us. Our relations with the Kingdom of Laigin have never been of the best, in any case. Unless we can find out who was killed, why the killing took place and who is responsible, reparation might be demanded by King Fianamail. Unlike his predecessor, he is a hard man to deal with.'

'First we must learn the identity of the body,' Fidelma declared. 'Simply because someone wears the emblem of the Uí Máil does not make them one.'

'That is agreed,' her brother said. 'So what do you recommend?'

'It is obvious what we must do,' she replied.

Colgú made a wry grimace. 'You are going to suggest that you accompany the farmer back to the body to investigate the death?'

Fidelma's jaw came up a little. 'Unless you think that there is someone better qualified to do so? You have already ruled that it is too dangerous for me to accompany Dego to the lands of the Uí Fidgente, so surely it will be less dangerous for me to look at this matter?'

Abbot Ségdae stirred. 'What if this new matter has something to do with the unrest among the Uí Fidgente? What if some war band is roaming the country?'

'It is something to be considered,' acknowledged Fidelma. 'But we have little evidence to make such assumptions at this point.' She turned to her brother. 'Am I allowed to undertake this investigation? I can surely meet with few problems within sight of Cashel.'

Colgú saw the glint in his sister's eyes and simply said: 'Who will you take with you?'

'Eadulf, of course,' she replied at once. 'But I was also thinking of Gormán, if he can be spared from his guard duties. It is always good to have a warrior of the guard along with us.'

'A good choice,' agreed Colgú. 'But take another man as well, in case you need someone to send messages back.'

'Very well. Then I am fully empowered to conduct this matter in my official capacity as a *dálaigh* at your command?'

'The council may have given the office of Chief Brehon to Áedo, but you are still my personal adviser and sister,' her brother replied gravely.

'I'll ask Gormán to choose a good companion. I'll send Caol back to you so that you can instruct him about despatching Dego to investigate these reports that Abbot Ségdae has brought.'

'Thank you. As I have said, Dego will command a company to escort the abbot back to Imleach and then they can proceed onwards into Uí Fidgente country.'

Fidelma was rising to her feet. 'I shall start out immediately. I was all ready to go riding this morning, but now this matter gives purpose to the journey,' she said.

Her brother shifted uncomfortably in his seat and glanced at her with an almost embarrassed look.

'If you see the Lady Dúnliath, it would be best if you do not alarm her with these matters connected with the Uí Fidgente.'

'Of course,' Fidelma replied shortly. Then she added more softly, 'Anyway, I doubt whether she will be abroad yet. I understand there was a feasting last night that kept people up late.'

If she were honest, she was concerned for her brother. He had long passed the usual marriageable age and, as yet, no suitable match had been presented. Then the unexpected had happened. Colgú had been out hunting in the eastern part of the kingdom, a territory known as Osraige, when, seeking the hospitality of Drón, Lord of Gabrán, he had met the man's daughter, Dúnliath. She was not the kind of woman Fidelma had expected her brother to find attractive.

Dúnliath was young enough, true. She had corn-coloured hair and dark blue eyes, and a heart-shaped face – which would have been attractive had it not been for the curious combination of a slightly pudgy nose and thin, almost mean lips. She had a sturdy figure, and Fidelma would have said, overall, that her features were plain. She found the girl's almost permanent apologetic smile extremely irritating. However, looks did not matter. It was the intellect that went with them. Dúnliath's interests, however, were few. She seemed to indulge herself only in entertainment, in the songs of the bards, in dancing and the tales of storytellers. She seemed to have no leanings towards more intellectual pursuits or statecraft. And she was hopeless at board games like *brandubh* or *fidchell*. Fidelma felt guilty for even thinking these thoughts. After all, it was what her brother, Colgú, saw in the girl that mattered and not what she felt. Colgú had helped her when she had decided that she wanted to marry Eadulf, a stranger not only to her clan and her kingdom, but to her entire culture. There were many among her people, the Eóghanacht, who had disapproved of the 'Saxon' as they called Eadulf. Her brother had stood up for her. Now it was her turn to stand up for her brother.

She tried to hide her thoughts from Colgú as she bade farewell to him and Abbot Ségdae; however, she realised he was sensitive enough to know that she had reservations.

A short while later, she stood impatiently watching Eadulf choose items to pack in his saddle-bag. Even though he had now fully accepted that Fidelma was no longer of the religious, Eadulf himself continued to maintain the robes of a religieux. He still felt a commitment to the organisations of the Faith.

'Have you given instruction to Muirgen about little Alchú?' he asked, not for the first time.

Alchú was their three-year-old son who, during the times they had to be away from Cashel, was looked after by their faithful nurse, Muirgen, whose husband, Nessán of Gabhlach, herded sheep for Colgú.

'Of course,' Fidelma replied, suppressing the urge to tell Eadulf to stop fussing.

When Fidelma had entered their chambers and asked him if he would come with her to Cluain Mór, explaining the purpose of the trip, Eadulf had actually felt a sense of relief. He had seen the sparkle of exhilaration in her eyes; a change from the dark and unyielding expression that she had worn during these last few weeks since the meeting of the Council of Brehons. He had come to realise, more than anyone, how important her ambition was to become Chief Brehon of Muman. Right from the start, during the six years of their often tempestuous relationship, Fidelma had always insisted that her first duty was to the law, and that she had only joined a religious community for the sake of security, on the advice of her cousin, Abbot Laisran. Her father and mother had died when she was a baby and, at the time, her brother had not even been heir-apparent to the Kingdom of Muman.

When Eadulf and Fidelma had first met at the great Council of Streoneshalh, he discovered that Fidelma had already left the community of Cill Dara and was employed by individual prelates to give them legal advice or counsel. For many years she had lived separate from religious communities and their Rule. Indeed, Eadulf could hardly consider himself as involved in any one community. He, too, had acted for some years as an emissary between kings and prelates.

While the Faith did not forbid marriage among the religious, in spite of a growing number of ascetics who advocated celibacy, their relationship had often been a cause of some friction. Fidelma had always placed the law first. He had often thought that life in a religious community was the answer to the problems that beset them. He had even tried to live for a short time in such a community, before King Colgú had ordered Fidelma and himself to go south to the Abbey of Lios Mór to investigate the death of its famous scholar, Brother Donnachad. That had been when Fidelma had announced her firm intention to leave the religious in name as well as practice. The rest was left to him to make his choice.

Eadulf had considered carefully and made his choice. What did he want in life? He wanted to nurture and support the woman he had fallen in love with. He wanted to protect and raise the son they had given birth to. He wanted to use what talents he had for the good of the people around him, those people who had taken him in, a stranger in a strange land, and been kind to him. When reason combined with emotion, there had been no choice for him to make. He supported Fidelma, but not by always giving in to her. He knew that she had a strong will, but he was sensitive enough to realise that it was borne of her insecurity, having lost both her parents when she was a baby.

The case in point was the recent meeting of the Council of Brehons, the judges of the kingdom. Their decision to elect Brehon Áedo as the Chief Brehon instead of her had hit Fidelma hard, although she did not show it in public. Not that she ever said anything, even to Eadulf. When he ventured on to the subject, she would merely say that the council had made the logical choice. Áedo was older and wiser than she was, she would say. But he saw the bleak expression; indeed, the disappointment and hurt in her eyes. It had cast a deepening gloom over their lives for the last week or so. Eadulf realised that his wife needed his steadfastness, his quiet support and his optimism. She needed the emotional stability that only he could give her.

Seeing her entering the chamber with an animated expression, for the first time in weeks, was a relief to Eadulf. Here was the distraction that she most needed; a distraction which would call on the use of her talent and capabilities so that she did not have time to be bored, nor to brood.

'You say that this ford, where the farmer found the body, is at Cluain Mór?' he asked as he made a final check through the contents of his saddle-bag.

'It is only a short distance from here,' confirmed Fidelma, giving the specific measurement in her own language. He spent a moment trying to work out a translation of 1,000 *forrach* and realised it was just a few kilometres. Fidelma had already packed her bag and was now waiting for him.

'Then at least it is not a long ride,' he said thankfully. Eadulf was not a brilliant horseman and disliked long journeys, although, during his lifetime, he had probably travelled further than most of his contemporaries would ever imagine might be accomplished. He had twice travelled to Rome itself and once to the Council of Autun in Burgundia.

The second bag that he was taking was called a *lés*, a bag filled with some physician's instruments and apothecary's potions. Eadulf had first come to the land of the Five Kingdoms of Éireann many years ago to study at Tuaim Brecain, the premier school of medicine in the land of Ulaidh, the Northern Kingdom. There he had learned enough of the medical skills to assist in many of Fidelma's investigations. That was after he had been converted to the New Faith. He had grown to manhood in his native Seaxmund's Ham, in the Land of the South Folk, part of the Kingdom of the East Angles, where he had been an hereditary *gerefa* or magistrate. An Irish missionary named Fursa had turned him away from the worship of Woden and the other gods and goddesses of his people.

'I am just going to give some final instruction to Muirgen,' Fidelma said, jumping to her feet. She always found it difficult to sit still, doing nothing, while waiting for him. If necessary, she could induce the meditation exercise called the *dercad*, but now was not the time. So she left Eadulf to finish packing his bag and went in search of the nurse.

She was hurrying across an interior courtyard when she became aware of two figures blocking her path.

'You look absorbed with some weighty matter, lady.' The speaker was the smaller of the two, a man who spoke in a thin, hesitant voice as though he had some speech impediment.

She noted his pale skin and close-cropped, untidy grey hair. He gave the impression of being emaciated; his eyes were so deeply set under bushy brows that, at first glance, they appeared as black hollows. The red lips were thin and cruel, drawn into a permanent sneer. It was Drón of Gabrán.

Fidelma found herself, not for the first time, musing on the fact that he bore little resemblance to his daughter. And yet . . . there was something about that mouth, the thin lips, the expression . . . that marked their relationship; something indefinable. She had heard that Drón had been married twice and there were stories that he kept women in his household. It was rumoured that his daughter, Dúnliath, had actually been raised by his *dormun*, or concubine, and not by her own birth mother. Fidelma wondered how a man she found so repugnant had been able to attract women to him.

The second figure was her cousin Ailill. He stood deferentially behind Drón as befitted a foster-son. Ailill's grandfather, Fingen, had been Fidelma's father's brother. Until Ailill had arrived in Drón's retinue, she had not seen him since he was a child. He had been sent to be fostered at Drón's own fortress at Gabrán, as was the custom to strengthen bonds of kingship in her culture; a practice from remote times followed among all classes of society. Children were sent away to be reared and educated, and those who undertook the task became foster-parents of the child. Now Ailill had grown into a handsome young man of twenty; very tall, with dark, red hair that bespoke his Eóghanacht inheritance, and light blue eyes. He smiled shyly at her in greeting.

'You seem preoccupied, lady?' Drón repeated, and Fidelma realised she had been dwelling so deeply on her thoughts that she had not responded.

'Excuse me, Drón. I am, indeed, preoccupied. I have a commission from my brother which is going to take up my time.'

'I am sorry to hear that. I was looking forward to inviting you to join Ailill and myself for a hunt today. I thought we could organise a party to see if we could find red deer to compensate for his wasted day yesterday.'

'Wasted day?' queried Fidelma absently.

Ailill said sheepishly, 'I went out hunting on my own yesterday and tracked a magnificent deer all afternoon and evening but, regretfully, had to return to Cashel empty-handed.'

Drón smirked at the discomfiture of his foster-son. 'He returned well after last night's feasting and so had to make do with cold meat and cheese. That is why we have taken pity on him today and will organise a hunt as recompense for his failure. Are you sure you cannot join us?'

Fidelma shook her head. 'I am afraid it is not possible.'

'A pity. I was hoping to get better acquainted with those who will be my daughter's new family.' Fidelma felt the irritation rise in her as the noble continued, 'Although your cousin, Ailill, here, is as much a son to me as foster-son, so the rights and privileges of your family are not entirely unknown to me and my daughter. After all, Ailill's own father was once King of Cashel.'

Behind Drón's shoulder, Ailill gave her a grimace, expressing his disapproval at the impropriety of the remark.

Fidelma needed no reminder that Ailill's father, Mánach, had succeeded to the kingship and ruled for over twenty years following her father's death. Mánach had died eight years before, after which another cousin had succeeded, only to succumb to the Yellow Plague. Thus, her brother Colgú became King. Succession was often a tangled skein which was not merely passed through the bloodline but, by the consent of the family, through the electoral processes of the *derbhfine*, a council usually consisting of three generations from the last King, who then appointed the head of the household according to his ability to fulfil the demands of office.

'There will be plenty of opportunity for us all to get to know one another in good time,' she replied distantly.

'Let us hope so,' Drón said. 'When my daughter is installed in this grand fortress I shall doubtless be a frequent guest at Cashel.'

Fidelma fought madly to think of some polite, neutral response.

Thankfully, at that moment, Eadulf appeared. He greeted Drón and Ailill briefly before addressing Fidelma. 'Apparently Muirgen is in the courtyard with Alchú. Gormán has taken our bags down.'

Drón's smile was thin. 'So you are both leaving Cashel? It sounds important, this commission of your brother's.'

'A matter concerning the law,' Fidelma said briefly, not answering his implied question. 'So if you will excuse us . . . ?' Without waiting for a response she turned, with Eadulf following her, and made her way down the flight of stone steps that descended into the main courtyard.

As they neared the body, Eadulf whispered: 'I am afraid I don't like Drón any more than you do. What is it about people that makes you know instinctively that you cannot trust or make friends with them?'

Fidelma glanced at him and sighed. 'I feel sorry for my young cousin. Ailill is made to follow Drón about as if he were a servant.'

'He is over the age of choice,' replied Eadulf, 'and is supposed to be Drón's bodyguard. He seems a pleasant enough young man, anyway.

I am sure if he felt things were bad, he would simply leave Drón's service. The choice is up to him.'

Muirgen, the nurse, was waiting to bid them goodbye, holding little Alchú by the hand. In spite of their journey only being a short one, Fidelma had insisted that Muirgen be prepared, just in case they could not return for a long period. For a few moments they paused to say goodbye to Alchú, who stood with a stubborn look on his features, for he knew what this ritual portended. The set of the little boy's face seemed to say that he would not give way to the welling unhappiness he felt. Eadulf still experienced guilt at seeing his son clinging tightly to the hand of Muirgen.

Fidelma was about to say her farewells when she noticed that Dúnliath had joined them. The girl's smile was apologetic as usual.

'Are you going riding so early, lady?' she asked, gazing round at them in wonder. 'Or is it some hunt? My father was talking about a hunt earlier.'

'Not a hunt, lady,' replied Fidelma, hoping she would not pursue the question. 'I have duties to fulfil as a *dálaigh*.'

'Of course, I forget that you are so clever,' sighed the girl without guile. 'I am not clever at all. On a day such as this, I prefer to sit in the garden and listen to tales of wonder and magic and love. I have found that one of your bards knows the tale of the courtship of Étain, a beautiful tale of immortal love. My mother was named Étain. Do you know the story, lady?'

'I have heard it,' replied Fidelma irritably.

'Étain the wife of Midir was turned into a fly and—'

'I know the story!' Fidelma repeated. 'I am glad that you have found someone to tell it to you. But I must depart immediately.'

The apologetic smile spread. 'Of course, I am sorry to delay you. It is so wonderful being here in Cashel that I . . .'

Fidelma felt the girl would have gone on chattering obliviously and so, in spite of feeling guilty, she simply turned away. On the far side of the stone-flagged courtyard, Gormán and a warrior called Enda stood with four horses already saddled. With them was the farmer, Tóla, seated on a patient ass. Rider and beast looked incongruous next to the horses, especially next to Fidelma's favourite mount, Aonbharr. An ancient breed, he was short-necked with upright shoulders and a body with slight hindquarters and a long mane. The beast recognised Fidelma as she came into the courtyard for it gave a slight whinny and stamped one of its forefeet on the stone flags, causing sparks to fly. Fidelma called it 'the Supreme One', after the magical horse of the pagan Ocean God, Manannán Mac Lir, which could run across land or sea and not be killed by man or immortal. Enda was holding the mount reserved for Eadulf, which was the roan-coloured cob that he had been riding recently. Eadulf now had a fondness for the horse because it was of a docile and willing nature.

Fidelma and Eadulf were pleased that Gormán had chosen the warrior Enda to come with them because they had several times been together in dangerous situations. There was the time he had accompanied Fidelma to save Eadulf from execution from the evil and malicious Abbess Fainder in Ferna. He was another of Cashel's élite bodyguard, not quite as reflective or intellectual as Gormán. Indeed, he was quick to flare up, but was both loyal and trustworthy, and his sword hand was ever steady in any tight corner.

After the farewells to Muirgen and Alchú, and a quick nod towards where Dúnliath stood, still smiling at them in her vacant fashion, they had all mounted and trotted out of the gate of the fortress and down into the township that lay huddled below the ancient Rock of Cashel. They skirted the base of the Rock, turning west through the streets. There were several people about, a few who greeted them, but otherwise the place was quiet apart from the sharp blow of a smithy's hammer on his anvil in the forge. They joined the track to head northwards, measuring the pace of their horses to match that of Tóla's ass because the small beast was far slower. There was no need to hurry for it would not take them long to cover the distance to the ford across the Arglach.

Eadulf had been right in his assessment. Fidelma could hardly suppress her excitement. For the last few weeks she had found nothing to challenge her. She had been more than simply bored: she had felt as if her mind was being withered by inactivity. After the decision of the Council of Brehons, it seemed even her fellow lawyers had avoided her. No one offered her work, not even sitting in judgement on very minor cases. She would have preferred anything rather than letting her mind lie fallow as it had been doing since she and Eadulf had returned from Lios Mór. Now the adrenalin increased as she contemplated the few facts that Tóla had been able to give her.

If the victim was, indeed, a noble of the Uí Máil of Laigin, slain within sight of Cashel, then her brother was absolutely correct. It meant trouble.

CHAPTER FOUR

Tóla's young son, Breac, had been relieved of his guard duty and sent back to the farmhouse with the dog and ass while the farmer remained with Fidelma and her companions to show them exactly how he had found the body. Gormán and Enda stood to one side holding the horses while Fidelma and Eadulf approached the corpse.

The finding of a murdered youth in this beautiful little glade with its gushing stream produced a curious feeling of unreality. The frothing of the water around the stepping-stones, the rustle of the leaves in the trees and even the musical warble of the *smólach mór*, a missel thrush, high above them in one of the trees, added to the chimerical scene. It seemed so peaceful, and yet – yet here was the corpse of someone whose life had come to a violent end, shattering the serenity of the place.

It was Eadulf who knelt to examine the body first.

'There are no wounds in the front of this young man's body,' he announced, echoing what the farmer had already told them.

Fidelma cast her eyes quickly over the body and its clothing, paying particular attention to the hands, which were fair-skinned and delicate, with slender, tapering fingers. The hands and nails were carefully manicured, which was a sure sign of nobility. The long hair was neatly trimmed and the young man was cleanshaven. There was no mistaking – the clothing was of good quality, even had the jewellery, which enhanced it, not proclaimed a person of some status and wealth. Of particular interest was the fact that the man still wore his sword and dagger in their bejewelled sheaths.

'One thing is certain from this,' Fidelma observed softly. 'He was not attacked from the front and did not have time to draw his weapons to defend himself.'

Eadulf nodded absently before glancing up at Tóla. 'You said that when you turned the body over, you found rents in his clothing, and blood?'

'I did,' replied the farmer, feeling apprehensive. It was still uppermost in his thoughts that the body, being that of a noble – and a murdered noble, at that – was on his land and he would be liable, under law, for payment of compensation.

Fidelma guessed what was in his mind and smiled encouragingly. 'Do not worry, Tóla. You have done well in bringing news of this to Cashel. And you also did well in realising that this unfortunate young man was someone of status. The responsibility is now ours, so just tell us everything you did, no matter how insignificant.'

Tóla compressed his lips for a moment before he replied in a slow, considered tone: 'I had dragged the body from the stream, where it had been blocking the waters against the stepping-stones of the ford . . .'

'So it was lying across the stream, but facing which way?' interrupted Fidelma.

'The head was towards the southern bank, towards Cashel, and it was face down in the water.'

'So you dragged the body on to this bank?'

'I did. Then, as I have said, not seeing any wound on the front, I turned the body over to examine the back of his head. At first I thought the young man had slipped on the crossing-stones and hit his head. Then I saw the cuts in his short cloak and jacket. And there was still blood there. I laid the body back down . . . it seemed an insult to leave it face down. I left it face up, as you see it now. Then I removed that brooch, which I took to be an emblem and means of identity, and went back to the farm to get my ass. I left my son and my dog to guard this place and came straight to Cashel. That is all I know.'

'You did well, Tóla,' Fidelma repeated. Then she turned to Eadulf and gave a nod.

Eadulf unfastened the short cape and the man's upper garment and linen shirt. Then, with the help of Tóla, he turned the body over and finished removing the upper clothing. The cause of death was immediate to see. There were three jagged wounds in the back, all fairly close together between the shoulder-blades. They matched the jagged tears in the garments that the young man had been wearing. Eadulf examined them with pursed lips.

'Fairly deep,' he reflected. 'Any one of them might have been the fatal blow.' He glanced at Fidelma. 'Would you say he was a tall man?'

Fidelma followed his gaze, examining the corpse from poll to feet.

'He is certainly not short. I would say that he is slightly above average height. What makes you ask that?'

'Whoever inflicted these wounds was taller than he was. They must have stood behind him, and even raising their dagger for the blows to descend into the area of the wounds, they would need height to gain the strength to make the cuts so deep.'

'A good point,' Fidelma agreed. 'But there is another possibility – that whoever did this could have been standing on an elevated piece of ground or a rock behind the victim.'

Eadulf looked round at the muddy bank and the stream. 'Nothing I can see fits such a theory.'

'Perhaps his attacker was on horseback while his victim was on foot.'

Fidelma began examining the muddy ground of the bank. She then turned and nimbly crossed the stepping-stones to the far bank and repeated her search. She returned without saying a word.

Tóla was helping Eadulf put back the upper clothing on the corpse.

'We will have to remove the body to somewhere in preparation for burial,' Eadulf stated.

'There is a little chapel and burial-ground not far from here at Fraigh Dubh – the Black Heath. It is on the highway that leads south by the heathland into Cashel,' said Tóla. 'There is a new priest there, but I do not know him.'

'It would surely be better to learn the victim's identity before the burial – especially as he seems to belong to the nobility,' Eadulf observed.

'But that will take time, and we cannot leave him unburied,' Fidelma argued. 'It is a practical matter.'

Eadulf acknowledged that she was right. He bent to rearrange the clothing on the corpse. Suddenly, he withdrew his hand, uttering an exclamation, and put his fingers to his mouth.

'What is it?' Fidelma demanded.

'Something sharp,' he replied. 'A prick from a splinter, probably.' He knelt to find out what it was that had hurt him. Something was protruding from the sword sheath. 'Curious,' he muttered. 'It's a broken piece of wood in its own little leather sheath, tied to the sword belt.'

Fidelma carefully unhooked the small leather sheath and removed the broken piece of wood. It was a short wand of white wood – rowan, she thought. The top had been snapped off but there was some evidence of gold binding on the lower part.

She breathed out sharply as she recognised it.

'Does that mean something to you?' Eadulf queried, seeing her expression.

'It means that this man was an envoy or of equivalent rank,' she said. 'Not only was he wearing a brooch with the emblem of the Uí Máil, the Kings of Laigin, but he was carrying the wand of office of an envoy. Sometimes even chieftains of high rank carry such wands to proclaim their office.'

Eadulf knew that this was the custom of Fidelma's people. He also knew that, under the law, the life of a herald or an ambassador was inviolate, even during warfare. Neither harm nor injury could be visited on such an official for, if harm was done, blood feuds could carry from one generation to another until reparation was made. It was a heinous crime, and the punishment for the perpetrator was great.

Gormán, who had been standing a short distance away with Enda holding their horses, now took a step forward, having overheard the conversation.

'But what would an envoy from the King of Laigin be doing alone and on foot in this place?'

'That's a good question, Gormán', Fidelma said. 'One that needs an answer, and very soon. It seems inconceivable that such a noble or an ambassador was travelling alone here on foot in the darkness. That is why I was looking at the muddy banks of this stream. I am afraid our horses must have obliterated any signs of tracks at this point. So, if this ambassador came here on horseback, which way would he have come?'

The question was addressed to Tóla. The farmer immediately pointed to the west.

'This stream flows into the great river, the Suir, not far from here. As you know, lady, this crossing is usually used only by local people who travel on the track along the east bank of the river and then turn inland along this stream to cross at this ford and continue their journey to Cashel. From the east, there would be no reason to come in this direction since there is a good highway there which leads all the way to Cashel.'

'So if this man came from the Suir, he could have ridden down along the eastern bank to turn along this stream to cross here on his way to Cashel?' asked Eadulf.

'That presents other questions,' interposed Gormán after Tóla had agreed. 'A man of this elevated rank would surely have an entourage or a companion and, as such, would have taken the main highway where there are hostels for such travellers. So he would have followed the road to the east of here, not the west.'

'Whichever way he came, lady,' Tóla said, 'the paths to this point from both west and east are on my farmlands, and my livestock wander freely. The mud is always turned, as you see. I doubt whether you could trace any individual horses along it. And as you said, lady, why would an ambassador, on his own or with an entourage, be coming through this place after nightfall?'

Fidelma suddenly let out an exclamation which caused everyone to start. 'What a fool I am!' She turned to Tóla. 'You say that you found the body this morning?'

'It was exactly as I told you, lady. It was just after first light that I had come down here to find whether my heifer had produced her calf.'

'When were you at this spot before that?'

'As dusk approached last night. The heifer was in the field behind us. I was worried for her as she was overdue with her calf and so I came to look at her.'

'Did you look at this crossing at that time?'

'I did not. However, the body was not here.'

'How do you know that?'

'Because the stream was running freely.'

'I do not understand,' Eadulf said.

'I was alerted to the body being in the stream by the fact that it was being pushed by the current against those stepping-stones and thereby forming a dam. The water makes a different noise when it is allowed to flow freely. Also, my dog, Cú Faoil, was at his ease when we were here last night, whereas this morning he was nervous and showing signs that something was untoward. His behaviour prompted me to find the body.'

'So there is yet another conundrum,' breathed Fidelma. 'The logical conclusion is that this ambassador came here alone in the darkness or with a companion who was his assassin. If they were both on horseback, then the young man was obliged to dismount at the crossing while his companion, still seated on his horse, stabbed him from that superior height. Afterwards, the assassin must have led both horses away without alarming anyone. Not even your dog was awoken during the night, Tóla.'

'If there had been any disturbance, however slight, Cú Faoil would have surely raised an alarm,' agreed the farmer. 'There is nothing that escapes his attention.'

'There is another answer to that conundrum.' It was Eadulf who spoke.

Fidelma turned to him in slight surprise. 'Another answer?'

'What if the man was killed elsewhere and then brought in stealth to this place? The body could have been dumped here by someone thinking it was an out-of-the-way spot where it would not be discovered.'

There was a pause while Fidelma considered this. 'It is a good point,' she conceded. 'But if the murderer brought the body here, thinking it a good hiding-place, surely the stepping-stones across the stream would have warned him that it was not so remote, and that people used the crossing. There are plenty of better places around here to hide a body. And why leave so many clues behind, like his Uí Máil emblem? Why leave part of his wand of office, showing he was an envoy? Indeed, why not just remove all his valuable jewellery, the dagger, sword and so on? In fact, why not strip the body entirely, which would have made the task of identification almost impossible?'

'Of course, if the murder was done here, perhaps the killer left these things on the corpse because they heard someone coming and had to flee,' Eadulf suggested.

Fidelma shook her head. 'If so, why was the body not reported by the person who disturbed the killer?'

'It seems,' Eadulf reflected, 'that we are engaging in speculation when we have no information.'

Fidelma glared at him before noticing the amusement in his features. The corners of her mouth turned down with a wry expression.

'So now we must start in pursuit of information,' she said in a firm tone. She turned to Tóla. 'We need trouble you little. Perhaps we can fodder our horses and obtain some refreshment for ourselves when we have finished here? It would help if we could also purchase a linen sheet for use as a *racholl* – a shroud – for the body. We shall take the corpse to the chapel you spoke of, at Fraigh Dubh and make use of the burial-ground there. We may have to travel all the way to Laigin to establish the identity of this young noble: the body cannot be preserved during such a long journey and must therefore be interred here.'

'You are welcome to what hospitality we can provide,' Tóla said politely.

'Then we will not interrupt your harvesting any further. We have a few things to do here first.'

The farmer left them while Fidelma began to give instruction to the others.

'Secure the horses to those bushes, Enda. Then I want you to walk a distance along the bank of this stream towards the east. Watch out for any sign of the passage of horses. Gormán, I want you to examine the bank to the west.'

The two warriors moved off immediately.

Fidelma stood for a moment looking down at the broken rowan wand that she still held in her hands, and wondering where the top was.

'It is usually the top part which bears the emblem of the holder of the office. See if you are able to find it, Eadulf. Search the body thoroughly, if you will. It may have broken off as he fell. I am going to check the stream, for if it fell in there, the gold mounting from the top will have caused it to catch on the bed of the stream.'

There was a silence as they both bent to their tasks. Eadulf not only carefully checked through the clothing on the corpse but thoroughly searched the muddy bank nearby. There was no sign of the splintered top piece of the wand of office, and when he glanced at Fidelma, she was wading out of the stream looking disappointed.

'Nothing,' she said. 'No sign of it.'

A few moments later, Gormán came along the bank of the stream.

'I went as far as the point where the stream empties into the Suir,' he reported. 'Along the path there were long stretches of hardened earth, but where there were also muddy stretches with signs of horses' tracks, these were obscured by the passage of sheep and cattle. Is Enda not back yet?'

As if on cue, they saw the warrior trotting towards them along the embankment.

'Anything?' Fidelma asked hopefully.

'A short distance from here, there is a bend in the stream and a muddy stretch of ground by it. There are signs that two horses emerged from the stream at that point. However, it is difficult to say how long ago the prints were made. I would estimate that it was not long because the ground is soft and muddy. There has been no time for the tracks to dry.'

'Any sign of footprints?'

'Whoever was on the horses did not dismount. I only saw prints of cows and wolves, but nothing else of significance. The prints of the horses led eastwards. I followed them as far as I could, but soon lost them when the ground became hardened. They were heading towards the highway that leads north to Durlus Éile or south to Cashel.'

There was a brief silence as Fidelma and Eadulf absorbed the information. Then Fidelma said: 'Well, there is little more we can do here. Eadulf, can you and Enda remove all the valuable items from the corpse, the sword and dagger as well as anything else that might provide a means of identity? We'll go to the farmhouse and get the winding sheet. Then we'll take advantage of Tóla's hospitality to feed the horses and refresh ourselves before moving on.'

It was after midday when Fidelma and her companions recommenced their journey from the farmstead of Tóla where his wife, Cainnear, had fed them, and his son Breac had tended their horses. The body of the unknown envoy had been wrapped in a linen sheet and strapped across the back of Enda's horse. The four of them had then set out due east along the banks of the stream. A short time later, they recrossed the stream and turned a little southward on to the edge of a rough stretch of uncultivated land called Fraigh Dubh.

Here was the burial-ground to which the people of the area took their dead, and the small chapel where they went to receive blessings. The chapel lay close by the main highway that eventually connected Cashel to the northern township of the kingdom, Durlus Éile, the strong fortress of the Éile, whose territory bordered the lands of the Osraige; beyond this was the covetous Kingdom of Laigin.

They crossed the highway along which merchants and pilgrims travelled in both directions; although it was usually very busy, it was not classed as one of the five great highways that united the Five Kingdoms, such as the Slige Dála that connected Cashel to the Palace of the High King at Tara. This smaller highway was classed as a *bothar* – a cattleway – for it was along earlier tracks in ancient times that people herded their cattle to market and, indeed, still did so. At this hour, the highway was deserted, for most people liked to travel early in the mornings and then halt to take refreshment at midday when the sun stood at its zenith. By the time the day became cooler, their refreshment had usually influenced them to delay their journey until the following morning. Therefore it was not surprising that the small party encountered no one as they joined the highway and crossed to the little wooden chapel that stood on the edge of the wild heathland.

Surrounding the construction was the burial-ground, each grave aligned east to west. It was to the west that people believed the souls of the dead were taken, even in the earliest times before the coming of the New Faith. It was obvious to Fidelma's eyes that this was a poor, rural burial-ground, for there were but few wooden crosses, some weathered in the passing of the years. From the time of the coming of the Faith it had become customary to erect a cross over the grave of a Christian. But those of rank would have a flat slab or a pillar stone erected on which was inscribed a name, sometimes in the characters called Ogham and sometimes in Latin. She noticed that there were no such stone grave-markers here.

As they approached the chapel, they heard the sharp blows of a hammer, striking hollowly, and saw the figure of a man on the roof, securing some roofing boards. A ladder leaned against the side of the building.

Fidelma gave a quick nod to Gormán, who leaned back in his saddle and called up, 'God bless the work, Brother.'

The man paused and looked down before he removed a couple of nails that he was holding between his lips. He carefully replaced them, and his hammer, in a sling in his belt, before he returned the greeting. 'He does bless this work, indeed, warrior. But I am no Brother. Just an *ailtirecht*.'

Eadulf had to think for a moment, confusing the word with *ailithir*, a pilgrim, before realising that *ailtirecht* meant a craftsman in wood.

Fidelma edged her horse forward and looked up towards the workman. 'What is your name?' she asked.

The man peered down and then, appearing to recognise her, he left his position and slid down the ladder with surprising dexterity before coming to stand at her horse's head. He was a weathered-looking man of medium height with greying hair and light blue eyes, obviously used to heavy work. He bowed his head in respectful acknowledgement to her.

'I am called Saer, lady. I maintain this building for Brother Ailgesach and, indeed, the other buildings of our little settlement.'

'Where might we find this Brother Ailgesach?'

Saer hesitated and then gestured with his chin in a northward direction.

'At this time of day, lady, you may well find him in the *bruden*, the tavern run by Fedach Glas. It is but a short distance along the highway.'

'Brother Ailgesach?' Even in the circumstances Fidelma could not help the smile that came to her lips. 'He sounds a truly pious man.' The name meant 'servant of the saints'.

Saer caught her humour and muttered sourly, 'Neither pleasant nor pious, lady. But that is not for me to condone or condemn.'

'You will not get into trouble for giving your opinion,' Fidelma reassured him, interested by his response. 'In any event, we intended to go to the tavern even if this Brother Ailgesach had not been there.'

Saer had noticed the burden that Enda's horse was carrying. 'Has one of your party come to harm, lady?' he asked.

'Not one of our party,' she replied. 'The dead man is a stranger whom we found. We do not yet know who he was or what he was doing in this area. So we have brought his body to this chapel as it would be unlawful to leave a stranger to the mercy of the wolves, crows and other scavengers.'

'Then, in the absence of Brother Ailgesach, I would say that you should bring the body into the chapel and we shall lay him out there. Come, warrior,' this was addressed to Enda. 'I will help you down with your burden.'

Between the two of them, they took the body and carried it into the small, dark chapel. Fidelma swung down and followed them.

'Perhaps you can help us further, Saer?' she said, after a thought had occurred to her. 'Unwrap the winding-sheet from the face, Enda. Saer, look on the man's features and tell us if you have seen him before. Perhaps he passed recently along the highway here?'

The carpenter gazed on the face of the corpse and then shrugged. 'There are always strangers passing along this highway from Durlus to Cashel and in the other direction.'

'Look closely, if you will. This was a young noble and of rich and striking appearance.'

Saer peered closer at the pale bloodless features. 'He does bear a resemblance to someone who called to see Brother Ailgesach many days ago. But I can't swear to it.'

'A resemblance?' pressed Fidelma eagerly.

The carpenter shook his head. 'I can't swear that it was the same person. I was passing by here when I saw Brother Ailgesach entering the chapel with a young man. He was richly dressed. This could have been that man. I walked on without further interest. I was on my way to the tavern.'

'You saw nothing else? Did you notice whether the man had a horse?'

To her disappointment the carpenter shook his head again and repeated, 'I am sorry, lady.'

'And you never saw Brother Ailgesach's visitor again?'

'During the last several days I have been at my hut in the woods cutting planks for this job.' He jerked his thumb towards the chapel roof. 'New planks were needed because the roof was letting in water.'

'I suppose no one else has spoken of any such person to you?' enquired Fidelma.

'As I say, I have been at my hut in the woods cutting timber. I spoke only briefly to Brother Ailgesach when I came to fix the roof earlier. He did not mention any visitors.'

Fidelma nodded thoughtfully. 'Well, we shall go to the tavern of Fedach Glas and speak with Brother Ailgesach. You have been very helpful, Saer.' She reached forward and placed something in his palm, at which he raised a hand to his forehead in thanks. They left the interior of the chapel, remounted their horses and Fidelma led her companions back to the highway, where they turned north.

'Well, if the carpenter says this Brother Ailgesach is regularly at the tavern, then it seems he believes in taking the advice of the Blessed Paul to Timothy,' Eadulf commented, breaking the silence.

Fidelma frowned absently. 'What?'

'"Take a little wine for thy stomach's sake",' Eadulf joked. This did not, however, raise a smile from Fidelma who had been deep in thought.

The *bruden* of Fedach Glas lay only a short distance along the highway. Gormán knew the place, saying that it was not one of the higher class of hostels that were to be found along the main highways of the kingdom. These hostels or taverns could be run by either men or women. The higher classes of hostel were, in fact, provided by the landowner, sometimes a chieftain or even the king of the territory himself. The laws proclaimed that these hostels were required to entertain guests without asking questions or payment. The bigger ones would employ men on the approaching roads to advise travellers of their locations and to extol the comforts of the facilities they provided. And after dark, each *bruden* had at least one lantern on a tall pole to advertise itself to travellers.

The smaller hostels were more like wayside inns where charges were made and questions asked. One thing all *bruden* had in common, as Fidelma well knew, was that they were a place of refuge. A suspected murderer could claim sanctuary from summary arrest and punishment in a *bruden* until they were assured of a fair trial before a Brehon. The system of the *bruden* had been carried abroad by the missionaries of

Éireann, providing accommodation and food for those pilgrims travelling to Rome, along the roads through Gaul, Frankia and the other Germanic lands.

Fedach Glas's hostel was a series of rough-built log cabins surrounding the main house, and with stables for the horses. As they reined in before the entrance, a man came hurrying towards them. He had grey hair and a full beard, a sallow skin and dark mournful eyes. His gaze ran over their mounts and manner of dress. It was obvious that he quickly made up his mind what manner of travellers they were.

'Welcome lady, welcome sirs. We are no *brugaid-lethech* but only a poor *bruden*. Do your honours wish to alight here?'

It was a polite way of pointing out that the tavern of Fedach Glas was not used to catering for people of rank. Gormán assumed the lead. 'We do not intend to stay, but will refresh ourselves inside with your ale.'

They dismounted and tied their horses to the wooden hitching-rail.

The host, for such the man who greeted them turned out to be, went to the door and ushered them inside. It was gloomy, although a smoky wood fire was crackling in the hearth over which a cauldron was simmering; the pleasant aroma of meat and vegetables filled the place. A thin-faced, elderly woman with her hair tied back in a scarf but still showing wisps of grey about her forehead and neck, was stirring the contents with a long wooden spoon. She glanced up at them with surprise and then returned to her task. The man took his place before a crude wooden counter.

'Welcome again, your honours,' he greeted with a smile. 'How may this humble tavern be of service to you?'

This time it was Fidelma who stepped forward. 'My companions wish for refreshment, your finest ale. As for myself, do you have wine?'

The man shook his head. 'Wine, lady, is for the nobility and the clergy of rank. We cannot afford to import it here for we rarely have such distinguished guests. All we have is *corma* or *lind*.'

Corma was a strong intoxicating spirit distilled from barley while *lind* was weaker ale.

Fidelma realised her mistake and quickly said: 'Then we will all have ale.'

They turned to some benches by a table and seated themselves, watching as the *brugaid*, the tavern-keeper, filled a jug of ale and set it before them, together with four clay drinking vessels.

'Can I serve you further?' asked the man, obviously used to his guests pouring their own drinks. Gormán decided to fill the mugs for all of them.

'I presume your name is Fedach Glas?' asked Fidelma.

The man moved his weight uneasily from one foot to the other. 'That it is,' he answered.

'Then I am told that in this tavern we might find Brother Ailgesach. He is the religious who is in charge of the nearby chapel.'

Fedach Glas frowned, and his eyes flickered to a dark corner of the tavern before returning to meet her gaze. 'Why would you seek him?' he countered.

Enda snorted indignantly. 'It is incumbent upon you to answer the questions of a *dálaigh*, especially—'

'Especially when a hosteller is responsible to his guests,' Fidelma interrupted, annoyed that Enda had revealed her rank.

Fedach Glas's eyes widened a fraction. 'A *dálaigh*?'

'Is Brother Ailgesach here?' she repeated loudly.

A figure stirred in the gloom at a far corner of the tavern, then rose to its feet somewhat unsteadily. It moved forward a pace, supporting itself for a moment with one hand on the table at its side.

'I am Brother Ailgesach,' it intoned wheezily.

Taking another pace forward, the figure was revealed as a very rotund and short man clad in worn brown woollen robes. A wooden cross hung on a leather thong about his neck. The wood and the leather denoted that the wearer was not of a wealthy Order. His head was like that of a baby, plump and fleshy with red cheeks, but whether the lack of hair was due to baldness or due to his choice of tonsure was difficult to discern. The lips were so thick and red that the mouth could be described as ugly. Only the eyes were striking by being tiny pinpoints of black almost hidden in the folds of flesh around them.

'Come forward, Brother Ailgesach,' invited Fidelma. 'We would speak with you about God's work.'

The rotund religieux stopped, his fat features screwed into an expression as if he were trying to recall something.

'I am . . .' Fidelma began.

But the man suddenly raised an accusing finger at her.

'I know you. I know you! You are the Whore of Babylon.' His voice was rasping and breathless. 'The Whore of Babylon – mother of harlots and the abomination of the earth!'

ChAPTER FIVE

There was a shocked silence in the tavern, broken a second later by the thud of the woman's ladle falling to the floor. Enda sprang to his feet with a suppressed oath and took a threatening step towards the rotund religieux. But even before he had finished that step, the man swayed before him, staggered sideways and collapsed on to the floor. Enda was on his knee beside him in a moment, turning him over to examine him. The others had risen to their feet and were gazing at the recumbent form with incredulity. Enda stood up with a sour, disapproving expression.

'The man is drunk, lady.'

Fidelma looked at Fedach Glas with raised brows. The man understood the silent question and shrugged. 'Brother Ailgesach has been known to indulge his taste for *corma*,' he muttered defensively.

'And is he also known for his insults? Insults *to the King's sister*?' snapped Enda.

Fidelma frowned, but it was too late to warn him. She had not wanted her rank to be known, other than her being a lawyer. The tavern-keeper stepped back a pace and they heard a gasp from the woman at the cauldron.

'Forgive us, lady. I did not recognise you. You should have announced yourself. P-please . . .' the tavern-keeper stammered.

Fidelma made an impatient gesture. 'Intoxication to this degree,' she indicated the prone form of Brother Ailgesach, 'is reprehensible in one who aspires to be a religieux.'

The tavern-keeper looked nervous. 'I am afraid Brother Ailgesach has been here since midday. He asked for a jug of *corma* and sat in the corner there. To be honest, I had almost forgotten that he was here until you asked for him, lady.' Then, remembering she was both a *dálaigh* and the King's sister, he asked: 'Why were you looking for him?'

'We came to ask him to perform a burial.'

Fedach Glas was surprised. 'A burial, lady? Who is it that is dead? I have no knowledge of anyone from our local community who—'

'A body has been found near here and we have left it in the chapel. We were told by a carpenter called Saer that Brother Ailgesach administers at the chapel and simply came here to ask him to make the arrangements.'

'But, surely the Brother that you travel with,' he indicated Eadulf, 'could perform the necessary ceremonies?'

'If needs must, then my husband will say the offices for the dead. But it is not our intention to linger here.'

Fedach Glas's eyes widened a little; he glanced at Eadulf then back to Fidelma. 'I had heard it said that you are married to a Saxon Brother,' he murmured.

Eadulf sighed. 'I am an Angle from the land of the East Angles,' he told the man, knowing that to all the people of the Five Kingdoms he would be classed as a Saxon whether he was Saxon, Angle or Jute.

'Is there a place where this man may sleep off his intoxication?' asked Fidelma, as the Brother lay snoring loudly from his prone position on the tavern floor.

'He can do so in one of the guest cabins. May I ask for someone to help carry him there?'

Fidelma looked at the heavy form of Brother Ailgesach and then at Enda and Gormán. 'It will take both of you to carry the man,' she said.

Gormán and Enda picked up the dead weight of the unconscious man. The tavern-keeper moved ahead of them to open the door. After they left, the woman who had been stirring the contents of the cauldron retrieved her fallen ladle and placed it to one side. Then she came nervously forward and bobbed awkwardly to Fidelma. 'My husband is a conscientious man and fulfils his duties as a *brugaid* with diligence,' she said. 'He should not be blamed for Brother Ailgesach's behaviour. Truly, lady, I am sorry for this transgression of the laws of hospitality.'

Fidelma had resumed her seat with Eadulf and motioned the woman to join them at the table. She hesitated before shyly seating herself opposite them.

'I fear Brother Ailgesach will be even more sorry when he comes back to consciousness.' Fidelma smiled thinly. 'What is your name?'

'I am Grella, wife to Fedach Glas.'

'Then be assured, Grella, the behaviour of Brother Ailgesach will not reflect on you or your husband, nor on your tavern.'

'But the strange words that he shouted at you, lady. It was a terrible insult.'

'It would have been, had the words been meant for me. However, they were from the Holy Scripture. Does he often quote from the Scriptures when he is in his cups?'

'He often raves as if troubled and calls out that we should all beware.'

'Beware? Of what?'

'Something about the sound of a trumpet.'

Fidelma was silent for a moment or two, pondering on this, before turning to the more pressing subject. 'I was wondering whether you could supply me with some information. The body that we have found is of a stranger and cannot be identified. I would like to know if you have seen any strangers on the highway in the last day or so.'

The woman was thoughtful. 'There are always strangers travelling on the highway. What sort of stranger was this, the one whose body you have found?'

'He was a young man of rank.'

'We have seen no such traveller recently. But then a young man of rank would hardly be likely to choose our poor tavern to break his journey.'

'If not here, then where would he stay?'

'If the man was travelling from Durlus Éile to Cashel, or in the other direction, then those are the only two places where he would find the sort of hostel to cater for the likes of him. North to south or south to north, he would not halt here. We are not grand enough.'

This was probably no more than the truth. Fidelma, knowing the body carried the emblems of an envoy, had not expected such a person to have stopped here for refreshment.

'No other travellers passed by here recently, to your knowledge?'

Grella glanced round, almost in a conspiratorial manner. 'I did hear something.'

Fidelma waited a moment or two and then prompted: 'Well?'

'I heard that some travellers had stayed last night with Brother Ailgesach.'

'Brother Ailgesach told you this?'

'Not him. One of the woodsmen saw them arriving last night and departing about midday today. They were heading north towards Durlus Éile. The woodsman said they were riding fine horses.'

'Who is this woodsman?' asked Fidelma with quickening interest.

'His name is Sétna, lady.'

'And how did he come to observe this?'

'Sétna was crossing by Brother Ailgesach's cabin at the back of the chapel. He had been helping Saer take wood to the chapel when the visitors arrived just after dark.'

'Was Saer a witness of their arrival then?'

'Saer had already left and Sétna was on his own. He said that one was a man, who looked like a warrior, and the other was a finely dressed woman. A noble.'

'How did this woodsman see so much if they arrived after dark?' asked Eadulf.

Grella turned a pitying look at him. 'One of them carried a lantern to light their path and there was a lantern lit outside the door of Brother Ailgesach's cabin.'

'Very well.' Fidelma gave her a smile of encouragement. 'And he also saw these two leaving about midday?'

'He was making a journey to see his mother who farms at the place called "the Field of Stones" beyond the Suir. He spends most of his time working the woods on the heath beyond the chapel. Anyway, he was passing, as I said, when the man and woman came out of the cabin with Brother Ailgesach. Sétna was close enough to hear what they said. The woman was saying that should Brother Ailgesach receive news, he was not to delay but to contact them immediately. Their horses were already saddled outside and they mounted them and took the road north.'

'How did you come to hear of this?' Fidelma wanted to know.

'Because Sétna came here to break his journey and told me. Is he not my own nephew and his mother my own sister? He felt it strange that two such fine people would be staying at the cabin of a religieux.'

'And they turned north?'

'That is what he told me.' Her features suddenly lightened and she added, 'I have just remembered what it was that Brother Ailgesach used to mumble in his cups. It was: "Beware of the seventh trumpet!" That was it.'

The main tavern door opened and Saer, the carpenter, entered. He was followed by a very tall figure clad in the robes of a religieux. The latter was well-built, with pugnacious features that made him appear almost ugly. His thin red lips and dark, nervous eyes did not enhance his appearance. He wore grey robes with a cowl, a hood that almost covered his head.

Grella moved forward to welcome the newcomers and was surprised when Saer greeted Fidelma. 'So you are still here, lady? Did you find Brother Ailgesach?' He glanced about the empty tavern room. 'Is he not here?'

'We found him,' Fidelma answered gravely. 'Alas, we were unable to talk with him.'

Saer frowned. 'I don't understand.'

'He was inebriated and passed out,' explained Eadulf.

The ugly religieux let out a deep sigh. Saer's expression was one of awkwardness. 'This is Brother Biasta. He is a cousin to Brother Ailgesach and has come to visit him.'

'You must forgive my cousin, lady,' the newcomer said. 'He has not been himself recently. Some illness seems to assail him.' He spoke with a curious whispering tone, a sibilant voice that oozed with ingratiation.

Fidelma regarded the man carefully for a moment. 'I am sorry to hear it, Brother Biasta,' she replied. 'Is the matter of his illness related to anything specific?'

'I cannot tell you, lady. He sent word to his family that he was not well and so I have only just arrived at his chapel to find out what ails him.'

'That is why I brought Brother Biasta directly here,' said Saer. 'But I have never seen Brother Ailgesach pass out from the drink before.'

'He never used to indulge in drink . . .' began Brother Biasta.

'When was the last time you saw your cousin?' Fidelma asked.

'A year or so ago.'

'Well, a lot may happen to a man in such a period,' Eadulf said quietly. 'A lot may happen to change a man.'

'You work at the chapel.' Fidelma addressed her next question to Saer. 'Would you know how long it has been since Brother Ailgesach indulged in drink?'

The carpenter hesitated a moment, glancing at Brother Biasta. Then he shrugged. 'I thought he had always indulged. Anyway, I have not known him long. Only since he came to administer the chapel here.'

'Which was when?'

'No more than two weeks ago.'

'Only two weeks ago?' Fidelma was surprised. At that moment, Fedach Glas re-entered with Gormán and Enda.

'We left him sleeping like a baby,' reported Gormán in a cheerful tone to Fidelma. 'I doubt whether the clap of doom will awaken him before tomorrow morning.'

Fedach Glas then greeted Saer, and gave his companion a questioning look.

'This is Brother Biasta, the cousin of Brother Ailgesach,' Fidelma introduced them. 'I have told him of the condition of his cousin.'

'I am sorry that you have arrived to find your relative in such a state,' the tavern-keeper said uneasily. 'It is in the nature of a tavern-keeper to speak the best of his guests, but . . .' He shrugged.

'Saer is right, of course,' added Grella. 'Ever since Brother Ailgesach arrived to administer to the chapel, he has come here each day to drink his fill. However, he has always managed to return to his cabin without assistance. Today is the first day that I have seen him become insensible.' She looked at her husband with an expression of disapproval. 'Fedach Glas should not have served him that last jug of *corma*.'

'He must be ill,' interposed Brother Biasta. 'He never used to drink.'

'You say that you have not seen him for nearly a year,' Fidelma said. 'And he has been at the chapel here only a couple of weeks.'

'Indeed, lady,' interposed Fedach Glas. 'He came here when poor Brother Tressach died.'

Gormán frowned. 'I remember Brother Tressach, an elderly and kindly man. He was here when I last passed this place.' He turned to Fidelma. 'I think I mentioned that I had ridden by here before. So Brother Tressach is dead?'

Grella sniffed. 'He was a good man. He had served here since I was a young girl. Indeed, he blessed our union – the marriage of Fedach Glas and I.'

Fedach Glas nodded agreement. 'We had to make representation to Abbot Ségdae of Imleach for a new priest, for he has authority over the chapel. Finally, he sent Brother Ailgesach to us. Alas, even during his short time here, Brother Ailgesach has spent less time in chapel than he has in our tavern.'

'Would the death of Brother Tressach have distressed my cousin?' Brother Biasta asked quickly.

'Not at all.' It was Saer, the carpenter, who offered the opinion. 'As far as we knew, he had never met the old man. As I said, he arrived here to replace Tressach.'

'So, as far as you knew, Brother Ailgesach's behaviour has been the same since the day that he first arrived here?'

'As far as we knew him, he always had a fondness for *corma*,' said Saer, looking towards Grella for support.

'Where did Brother Ailgesach come from? Where was he before he came here?' Fidelma aimed the question at Brother Biasta.

'We are originally from the north of the kingdom,' Brother Biasta replied. 'We both studied at the holy abbey of Brendan of Biorra. After that we went our different ways.'

'How was it that you came to know your cousin was ill and where to find him? You said you had not seen him during the last year,' Eadulf said.

'A traveller brought me the message,' Brother Biasta replied, but he sounded unconvincing.

'So Brother Ailgesach knew where you were even if you did not know where *he* was?'

'The contact was made by chance, for I was visiting my old mentor at Biorra a week or so ago. Ailgesach's message had been sent to the abbot, asking him to pass it on to our family.'

The answer seemed glib to Eadulf, but Fidelma appeared to let it pass. Eadulf was wondering why Fidelma should be so interested in Brother Algesach's failings when it had nothing to do with the finding of the unknown body.

'So you have journeyed all the way from Biorra? That is nearly on the border of the Kingdom of Connacht. Surely it is a long way to travel on foot?'

'Along roads such as this, there is often a merchant's cart that will give hospitality to a wandering religious,' Brother Biasta replied. He turned to the company with a pathetic expression. 'I would like to see my cousin now, even if he is in a state of intoxicated sleep.'

'I hope you will be able to discover what ails and distresses him,' Fidelma answered. 'Our only concern and business with him was that I needed to ask him if we could use his office for a burial. We discovered a body . . .'

'This man, Saer, told me about it,' Brother Biasta said quickly. 'I saw the body in the chapel while in search of my cousin, and there met the carpenter. The poor fellow has no identity, I am told?'

'None at all,' returned Fidelma.

'That is sad. I hope you are able to give the corpse a name before you bury him. Now, may I go to see my cousin? Perhaps I can sober him up enough to get him back to his own bed.'

Fidelma glanced at Fedach Glas and nodded. The tavern-keeper offered to take Brother Biasta to the cabin in which they had laid Brother Ailgesach.

Grella served Saer with ale while Gormán and Enda joined them, leaving Fidelma and Eadulf together.

'Well, what now?' Eadulf prompted after Fidelma had been silent for a moment or two.

'A difficult choice is to be made,' she replied.

'Do you think the two people who stayed with Brother Ailgesach last night have some connection with the murdered man? Why would they stay with Brother Ailgesach?'

Fidelma turned to Saer and called him over.

'I am told that you and Sétna, a woodsman, were at the chapel last night?'

The carpenter looked surprised. 'We were,' he agreed. 'Sétna helped me carry some roofing planks for the chapel.'

'Did you see Brother Ailgesach's visitors?'

Saer's face was blank. 'Visitors?'

Fidelma tried another tack. 'You and Sétna took the wood to the chapel. Was it dark when you both left?'

'I had to leave before dark. I left Sétna marking the planks for use.'

'Ah,' Fidelma let out a soft breath. 'So Sétna remained behind. And what time did you go to work on the chapel roof today?'

'I suppose it was after the sun reached its zenith. I had to do some work on my own cabin before I went to the chapel. In fact, I had barely arrived when you and your party came by, lady.'

'So that makes sense,' muttered Eadulf after she had thanked him for the information. 'Brother Ailgesach's two visitors had already left. So now we have to wait until Brother Ailgesach sobers up and tells us who they were.'

'That is one choice,' Fidelma agreed.

Eadulf stared at her. 'You propose to wait here until that time? Why, it will be tomorrow at least. It would be just as easy to set out after the two and follow them north, trying to overtake and question them.'

Fidelma ignored the sarcasm in his tone. 'That had occurred to me.'

'Maybe they were simply relatives. Being religious does not exclude one from coming from a noble family. Mind you, that would mean they were also relatives this Brother Biasta.'

'This is true,' agreed Fidelma. 'There is one thing that troubles me about Brother Biasta. How did we come to miss him on the highway?'

Eadulf was unsure what she meant.

'The chapel is within walking distance to the south,' she said. 'Do you agree?' When Eadulf conceded the fact, she went on: 'We rode our horses north up the highway until we came to the tavern – but saw no sign of this Brother Biasta, who says he came down from the north. We have not been in here long enough for him to pass by the tavern, reach the chapel, speak with Saer and then return here with him. He was not on the highway nor have any merchants' carts passed.'

Eadulf thought about the matter. 'The logical conclusion is that he did not come down the highway but rode across country or came up from the south.'

'Yet he *said* that he came from the north,' Fidelma emphasised.

'Then we will ask him to explain how that was possible when he comes back.'

At that moment the door opened, but it was not Brother Biasta. It was Fedach Glas who returned by himself.

'I pointed to the cabin and left Brother Biasta to make his own greetings with his cousin. Not that they will be able to have much of an intelligible exchange.' The innkeeper went to the bar and poured himself a small beaker of ale and swallowed half of it in one gulp.

'So long as one of them is ready to perform the services for the burial of the unknown corpse by midnight,' Saer reminded them.

Eadulf had nearly forgotten that corpses were usually interred at midnight on the day of death.

'I presume that Brother Ailgesach has not endeared himself to this community since he came here?' Eadulf rose and went to join Fedach Glas.

'We hardly know him,' the man replied. 'Though I suppose he has been a good customer in my tavern during these past two weeks. But he has never spoken properly to any of us. He mumbles curious phrases, that is all. As to his background, he is very secretive.'

'But you, Saer, you have worked for him, during the time he has been here. I am sure that you must have picked up some knowledge about him.'

Saer shrugged. 'Only that he is very fearful of people, particularly of strangers. Perhaps fear has caused him to indulge too freely in drink. I can certainly add nothing more.'

'Could you tell me what manner of man he is?' Eadulf asked. 'Is he well-read? Does he come from a noble family? Do you know anything at all?'

'How could I tell who is well read or not?' countered Saer. 'He was always quoting some text or other, so I suppose he has read the Holy Book, but I had no understanding of it. He has said strange things; sometimes frightening things.'

'Such as the words he cried before he fell into unconsciousness?' Eadulf suggested. 'Have you heard such words before?'

'Similar words, I suppose,' admitted the tavern-keeper.

Eadulf was thoughtful for a moment, but before he had time to frame his next question, the door burst open.

Brother Biasta stood on the threshold looking dishevelled, his pale face even whiter than it had been before. It seemed that he was unable to form any coherent sentence and for a moment or two he just stood with his mouth opening and closing like a fish newly caught.

'My cousin –' he began; then he paused and swallowed, peering round at them in a distraught manner. 'My cousin . . . he is dead!'

CHAPTER SIX

Everyone was moving towards the door when Fidelma's sharp tone of command halted them.

'Stay where you are, please. Eadulf and I will examine the body. Fedach Glas, you will come with us to show us where Brother Ailgesach is.'

'But . . .' began the tavern-keeper.

'I am taking charge as a *dálaigh*,' Fidelma said with quiet authority. 'Eadulf has been trained in the apothecary's art. I shall need his advice. Gormán, you and Enda will remain here.'

Outside, Fedach Glas conducted them towards one of the small log cabins which apparently provided overnight accommodation for the tavern guests. He pushed open the door and went inside with Fidelma and Eadulf following. The small dormitory room contained four wooden cots arranged along the walls on either side. They could see the rotund form of Brother Ailgesach stretched on the cot nearest the door.

The tavern-keeper waited by the entrance while Eadulf went forward to examine the corpse.

The body lay flat on its back, the hands slightly clenched as if they were trying to form fists, but both arms rested in a straight line on either side. Eadulf saw traces of vomit around the mouth and across the front of the robes. The eyes were closed although the mouth was slightly open. The body appeared to be in repose.

Eadulf immediately searched for any signs of life, but the body was already growing cold, the skin slightly mottled. He noticed dried blood around the nostrils. Then Eadulf, wrinkling his nose in distaste, bent forward and tried to ease the mouth further open, peering inside. He sighed and rose, turning round to face them.

'Brother Ailgesach is certainly dead,' he announced.

'And the cause?' asked Fidelma quietly.

'To all appearances, it would seem that he went to sleep in a drunken stupor and choked on his own vomit.'

Fedach Glas, standing behind them, was looking anxious.

'Am I responsible for this?' he muttered.

Fidelma turned to the tavern-keeper. 'In what manner do you mean – responsible?' she asked.

'I am a tavern-keeper. I served him with the drink. And now he has died in my tavern. Isn't there some law . . . ?'

'As I understand the laws relating to drunkenness, you have no responsibility in this. Only if you had forced the man to drink against his will would you be culpable. As this was clearly not the case, then you are exonerated from any recompense to his family.'

Fedach Glas looked relieved.

'I would go back to the others,' Eadulf suggested to him. 'I need to speak with Fidelma so that we can clarify the matter.'

Eadulf opened the door of the cabin for the tavern-keeper and watched him for a moment as he hurried back to the main building.

'What is wrong?' Fidelma asked, after he had closed the door.

'I believe Brother Ailgesach was murdered,' replied Eadulf as he turned back to the corpse. 'It is unusual that the eyes are closed, for someone who has just had a seizure and choked on their own vomit.'

'Perhaps Biasta closed the eyes. That is something I have seen people do automatically when confronted with death.'

'Well,' continued Eadulf, 'for one who goes to sleep full of alcohol and is seized by sickness, choking on his own vomit, the corpse is quite composed. If you were choking, even when almost incapable with drink, you would move your hands upwards, fighting for air, striving to clear your mouth and throat. The hands, as you observe, are calmly placed on either side of the body.'

'But there is vomit on the front of his clothes,' observed Fidelma. 'Surely that is indication enough how he choked?'

Eadulf raised the man's head carefully from the pillow. The cloth underneath was stained with vomit and flecks of blood.

'That is the point. Perhaps Biasta came in and found Brother Ailgesach choking on his own vomit *face downwards*. Then he turned the body over, put the pillow neatly under the head and composed the corpse . . . *requiescat in pace*.' Eadulf was rarely given to sarcasm.

Fidelma stood for a moment gazing sombrely down at the corpse of the rotund religieux before saying, 'It still does not point to the conclusion of murder, Eadulf.'

'Then I think this will prove it. You will notice that, unusually, there are two pillows behind his head. The soiled one and one that is only a little soiled. And look at the other cot.' He pointed. 'It has no pillow.'

'What are you suggesting?'

'My suggestion is that someone came in here and held a pillow over the man's face. His struggle for air produced a paroxysm of vomiting and bleeding from the nose and mouth. The result was that he asphyxiated. The killer then rearranged the body, laying the arms by the side, closing the eyes and putting the pillow behind the head, hoping it would not occur to anyone that if he had choked on vomit while lying face upwards, there would hardly be vomit and blood on the pillow behind his head.'

'And I suppose Brother Ailgesach was too drunk to stir when the killer came in and calmly removed the pillow from behind his head and commenced to suffocate him?'

Eadulf shook his head. 'A pillow is missing from the next bed.'

'And so?'

'The killer grabbed the pillow from the next bed to smother him with. That is the soiled one. After the deed, the killer realised that the pillow on his victim's bed was also soiled. So he could not put either pillow back on the next bed. They were both soiled and this would be noticed. So he left the two pillows on Brother Ailgesach's bed and hoped no connection would be made.'

Fidelma nodded slowly in approval. 'You've touched the thing with a needle,' she said, using an old saying, meaning that he had spotted matters correctly. 'And the suspect has to be Brother Biasta?'

'Who else? The only other choice is the tavern-keeper.'

'We must tread this path with care, Eadulf,' she said thoughtfully and suddenly sat down on the edge of the other cot, still staring at the dead religieux.

'But his guilt is almost beyond question,' protested Eadulf.

'"Almost" is a word that contains many questions.'

'But . . .'

'You forget that we came here to find out who the dead envoy was and why he was killed. There are so many questions I would have dearly wished to ask Brother Ailgesach. You see, instinct tells me these matters are connected.'

'We have a case against Brother Biasta which also needs to be answered,' said Eadulf. 'Why, he might even be the killer of the noble as well as his cousin.'

'Oh, we will ask him questions, have little fear of it,' Fidelma promised. 'However, I do not want to put Biasta in a corner so that he sees no way out. Not yet anyway. I want to find out what else he knows. Maybe he can identify the people who stayed with his cousin last night.'

'So how shall we approach this matter?'

'We will pretend that we have noticed nothing untoward and that we accept the theory that Brother Ailgesach has choked on his own vomit. We will express curiosity about him, which is natural, and see if Brother Biasta will lead us anywhere.'

Eadulf smiled without humour. 'Like playing a fish with a line,' he sighed. 'But remember, fish can be elusive and slither off your hook.'

Fidelma smiled reflectively. 'Since we talk in fishing similes, Eadulf, I remember what an old mentor of mine once told me about the art. When you have a strong fish that wants to run, let it run. Let its fear and strength work for you. Then, when it is weak and exhausted, only then do you haul it in.'

Eadulf shrugged. 'I'll be surprised if this fish will lead us anywhere.'

'Well, let us start the fish running,' Fidelma said, moving to the door.

There was quiet in the main tavern room when they re-entered. Brother Biasta was seated, sipping at a beaker of *corma*. Saer was also drinking and did not look at all concerned at the events around him. Fedach Glas and his wife Grella stood together, their expressions strained, while Gormán and Enda had taken up positions near to the door, almost as if they were sentinels.

Fidelma and Eadulf seated themselves in silence before Fidelma turned to Fedach Glas, who started nervously when she called to him by name.

'I think we might all be the better for some of your *corma*.'

He hurried to fulfil her request while she turned to Brother Biasta and said: 'It seems as though your cousin unfortunately choked on his own vomit, having drunk himself into a state of unconsciousness.'

Did a look of relief pass across the man's features? It was gone too quickly for Eadulf to be sure, yet he was watching the man very closely.

'Tell me what you found when you went into the hut,' she invited.

'I found the body, of course,' replied the bewildered Brother Biasta.

'I mean, in what manner and circumstances did you find it? A report of this matter must be made to Abbot Ségdae, being also Chief Bishop of this kingdom.'

Brother Biasta frowned. 'You have to report this to the abbot?'

'It was he who sent Brother Ailgesach to this place,' Fidelma affirmed. 'Let us start with what more you can tell us about your cousin. You told us that you were both trained at the Abbey of Biorra. From what clan are you?'

Brother Biasta hesitated. 'Are these questions relevant? My cousin is dead and, sadly, from an indulgence in his own weakness.'

'You know well that if it is deemed that his own weakness killed him – that it was self-inflicted it is classed, in law, as suicide. And how is suicide classed?' Fidelma asked, then answered her own question. 'Brother Ailgesach would be named a *fingalach*.'

Fidelma used the legal term which indicated that a suicide was classed as a kin-slayer, and as the horrendous crime of *fingal* or kin-slaying struck at the very heart of the kin-based society of her people, the law could apply heavy sanctions.

'But he had no control over his actions,' Brother Biasta protested.

'That is not a good defence,' replied Fidelma. 'He *did* have control and he chose not to exercise it, in drinking more than he knew was good for him. All else follows – but there may be mitigating circumstances. So let us try to discover them.'

Brother Biasta grimaced helplessly. 'What can I tell you? I had not seen him in such a long time – I have already told you that. I can offer no explanation as to what ailed him.'

'Then answer my question to the best of your ability and we will see how far we can progress.'

The religieux stared at her for a moment almost in defiance and then he relaxed with a sigh, realising that he could raise no other protest.

'What was your question?'

'To start with, where did he come from and what clan? And I mean *before* he entered the Abbey of Biorra. You say that you are his cousin.'

'We are of the Muscraige Tíre.'

Fidelma knew that the Muscraige Tíre inhabited the north-west of the kingdom and were one of six Muscraige sub-lordships that were widely separated but subscribed to one overlord. They had long ago accepted the authority of the Kings of Cashel. From the north-east, the Muscraige stretched almost in a diagonal line south-west to the Muscraige Mittine in the Valley of the Laoi, one of the great rivers of the south-west.

'So you are of the race of Cairbre Musc?' she asked quietly.

For a moment Brother Biasta looked lost, and then he repeated defensively: 'We are of the Muscraige Tíre.'

'I know your territory,' Fidelma replied. 'When I was a child I went for my initial education to the Abbey of Inis Celtra in the Red Loch. That was before I went to study law,' she added for Eadulf's benefit.

Brother Biasta said quickly: 'We came from the territory of the two streams, Tír Dhá Ghlas, to the north of the loch.'

'Indeed a beautiful country. And your family – who are they?'

'Just farmers, but my cousin and I went for our education at Biorra, as I said.'

Once again Fidelma had the impression that Brother Biasta was not going to tell her much, if anything, about his own background or that of Brother Ailgesach.

'What was your cousin's name before he adopted his saintly servant's name?' she tried.

Brother Biasta blinked. Then he said: 'It was his real name. His parents were devout and intended him to join the religious.'

Once more Fidelma suspected that he was blocking her questions.

'So you last saw your cousin . . . where and when?' There was sharpness in her voice as she ended her question.

'Why, as I told you, about a year ago and at Biorra before he came south.'

'To the Abbey of Imleach?'

Brother Biasta's eyes narrowed. 'I told you, I do not know, only that he was coming south.'

'And you remained at Biorra? Serving in the abbey?'

Brother Biasta seemed to be gathering confidence. 'I went back to Tír Dhá Ghlas . . .'

'To the abbey?' interposed Fidelma, for she knew of the Blessed Brendan's foundation there.

'I crossed into the country of the Uí Maine and preached there awhile.'

'And you said that you received a message from your cousin?'

'A week ago I returned to Biorra and found a message waiting there for me. It said that he was ill and would like to see me.'

Fidelma's expression was implacable. 'Indeed, you told me as much but I am still curious.'

'Curious? About what?'

'Your cousin would surely have sent the message to his family at Tír Dhá Ghlas. And you say that you had gone into the country of the Uí Maine . . . that is in Connacht. You had both left Biorra, so why did he think his message would find you there?'

Brother Biasta hesitated and then simply shrugged. 'I have no idea. I can only say what happened.'

'Very well. His message said no more than that he was ill and wanted to see you?'

'No more than that. So I came here straightaway.'

'Forgive my inquisitiveness, but by what means did you come here?'

'What means . . . ?' Brother Biasta was looking suspicious.

'What road, what means?' demanded Fidelma.

'There is only one road from the north and you can see the means.' The man gestured towards his feet.

Fidelma's expression hardened. Now she knew he was lying but she did not comment on the fact.

'So you came here . . . and found matters thus?'

'Exactly.'

'Just a few points more,' Fidelma said, as the religieux began to rise from his seat. He sank back sullenly.

'There is nothing more to tell,' he grumbled. 'I should go to the chapel and start making arrangements for the burial of my cousin and the person who you found.'

'Indulge me for a moment more.' Fidelma smiled thinly. 'Fedach Glas took you to the guests' hut. Did he enter with you?'

'He did not. Only I entered.'

'He remained outside?'

'Excuse me, lady,' Fedach Glas intervened. 'I told you that I left Brother Biasta to go in alone. I saw that one of the horses was nervous and went to attend to it. An old wolf was sniffing about and I threw a stone to chase it away. Sometimes you can encounter an old male wolf that has been driven from the pack by a younger animal. They can resort to scavenging.'

'So you went inside on your own, Brother Biasta. Tell me what you saw.'

'I found my cousin dead.'

'I asked what you *saw*, not what you found,' she prompted him quietly.

Brother Biasta frowned as he tried to work out the difference. 'My cousin was lying on the cot.'

'On his back?' queried Fidelma.

'Of course. I saw that he was choked on his own bile and vomit. I felt for signs of life and seeing none, came straight to tell you. That is all.'

'Very well. Did you touch anything apart from checking that Ailgesach was dead? Did you move anything, for example?'

'I did not,' snapped the man.

She stood up abruptly. 'Eadulf and I will go to the chapel and examine Ailgesach's cabin. Gormán, you will come with us. Everyone else will stay here until our return. Enda, you are in charge and will see that my wishes are carried out.'

Brother Biasta had also risen. 'I am my cousin's nearest relative. I demand to come with you, if you are searching his cabin and belongings.'

'I thought that I had made my instructions clear?' Fidelma's eyes flashed a little.

'By what right do you issue orders?' blustered the religieux.

It was Gormán who answered. 'By the right of being a *dálaigh* of the courts of the qualification of *anruth*, as well as by the right of being sister to King Colgú. Is that enough?'

Brother Biasta sat down again, looking sullen.

Fidelma led Eadulf and Gormán out of the tavern to where their horses were tethered. As they were mounting them, Eadulf commented: 'I am not sure what information we have gained from that.'

'We know that Biasta is a liar and that he smothered Ailgesach.'

As they moved down the highway towards the chapel, the afternoon held a strange quiet, broken at intervals by the deep, harsh voice of the omnivorous *feannóg* or hooded crow.

'Carrion birds,' muttered Gormán in disgust. 'Maybe they can smell the bodies in this place. And speaking of bodies, lady, what do you mean about Brother Biasta?'

Fidelma told Gormán of the evidence behind their suspicions about Brother Biasta.

'As for the rest, we know that Biasta is not of the Muscraige. I suspect that he is not even a cousin of the inebriated Ailgesach. Biasta was lying about journeying from the north along the highway on his own two feet. Had he done so, we would have seen him as we came up from the chapel.'

'What makes you so sure that he is not of the Muscraige Tíre?' Eadulf asked, having thought the matter through.

'It is from Cairbre Musc that they took their name. Any member of the Muscraige Tíre, even a farmer, would know and be proud of their progenitor. Yet when I mentioned the name, Biasta did not appear to know it.'

As they turned into the grounds of the chapel, the sky was still cloudless and the afternoon was warm for an autumn day. At the rear of the chapel they found a sheltered wooden cabin with some outbuildings. Fidelma remained on her horse for a moment, surveying the surrounding terrain before dismounting. Then they tied their horses to the wooden rail outside the cabin. Gormán insisted that he should enter first to ensure all was safe. Almost at once an odour assailed them. They did not need the sight of the discarded earthenware jugs to recognise the smell of stale alcohol. The odour permeated the room. In spite of the fact that the sun was still warm outside, it was dark and cold within the cabin.

'I'll light the oil lamp,' Gormán said, moving across to the table and taking from the bag at his belt his *tenlach-teined*, containing his flint, steel and kindle. This was the *tenlam* or hand fire which every warrior was taught to use so that they could ignite a fire quickly. It was a few moments before the oil lamp was lit, throwing dancing shadows over the interior of the room. They stood just within the door and looked about. The place had certainly not been tidied in a long time. There were two rough wood cots with straw mattresses and discarded blankets. A bundle of clothes, immediately identified as religious robes, were dumped in a corner. A wooden crucifix hung from one wall and on a small table a free-standing wooden cross was balanced. It was splintered as if ill-used.

Eadulf looked around in disapproval.

'So here is another thing that Brother Ailgesach did not believe in,' he muttered.

Gormán raised a quizzical eyebrow. 'I don't understand. What do you mean?'

'Did not the Blessed Paul adjure the believers in Corinth to cleanse themselves from defilement both of flesh and spirit?' he replied. 'We have seen how he drowned his spirit with alcohol, and now we see that he did not believe in cleansing his flesh. I have seen pigs living in much cleaner circumstances.'

Gormán grimaced in agreement. 'I have to admit, the odours and mess do not indicate the home of a religieux or clean man. There is an old proverb that cleanliness is part of glory. Obviously, Brother Ailgesach did not have an ambition for glory.'

'The sooner we commence our search, the sooner it will be finished,' Fidelma said curtly, 'and the sooner we can remove ourselves from the foul odours of this place.'

Gormán held high the oil lamp and peered round. 'Where shall we start, lady?'

Fidelma had caught sight of a wooden box in one corner. It seemed the only object in which anything could be hidden. She pointed to it without speaking, and they moved towards it. The light of the oil lamp revealed the lid was coated with dust and the iron lock seemed quite rusty. There was no key and Fidelma instructed the warrior to use the handle of his sword to break it. The lock splintered away easily and she threw back the lid. A smell of must emerged and, at first, it seemed only to contain clothing; the robes of a religieux. She picked them out one by one.

'They are rather long for Brother Ailgesach,' remarked Eadulf.

'Then we may suppose this trunk belonged to Brother Tressach, his predecessor,' she replied. 'I doubt if this box has been opened for years.'

Under the clothes, Fidelma found some vellum texts but they were of little interest, only sections of the Scriptures. There was one bound book. It was fairly small, with its vellum pages bound in polished boards of oak. Fidelma had seen similar books before. She frowned as she remembered that a scribe had come to Cill Dara when she was there and brought three such treasures to the abbess. They were the special work of the abbey from which he had come. Her eyes widened suddenly. It was the Abbey of the Blessed Ruadhan at Lothra. Lothra! An abbey situated between Tír Dhá Ghlas and Biorra. Was it merely a coincidence that these places were beginning to feature in this investigation?

'What is that?' Gormán asked, as she stood quietly turning the pages over.

'It is called in Latin a *Missale*, a book of liturgical instruction for the celebration of Mass throughout the year. It is rare for a poor religieux in such a spot as this to possess such a valuable book. Usually, a man of wealth, an abbot or a bishop, would have one, but a simple Brother . . .'

'I heard that Brother Tressach was well-respected and something of a scholar,' Gormán offered.

'He certainly served here for several decades, as we have heard from Grella,' Eadulf commented. 'That does not reflect any influence or power.'

'Not all talented people are interested in power or influence,' reproved Fidelma. 'However, the book and manuscripts should go to the Abbey of Imleach.'

'Then the book itself is valuable?'

'It is. I shall make sure that Abbot Ségdae receives it. He should decide what to do with Brother Tressach's belongings.'

Eadulf had turned his attention to a pile of old clothes on a chair and absent-mindedly gathered them up. Something fell from them and he picked it up. It was a small sheet of paper with some spidery writing on it, in Latin. He read it aloud.

'"Brother Ailgesach, I send this by a trusted courier who will be passing your chapel. I shall be leaving this place soon and will be with you before the time of the last quarter moon. I have proof of conspiracy. A philosopher once said that if you want something hidden, then place it where everyone can see it. I shall follow that advice. I think I am suspected. If I have not joined you and our friends by then, know that I am discovered and you must act on your own."'

Fidelma took it from his hand and read through it silently. Then she added: 'There is no signature, only the letter "B".'

'The last quarter moon was three or four nights ago,' Eadulf pointed out.

'But does this message refer to *that* quarter moon?' she pondered. 'There is no knowing when this was written.'

'It looks new,' Eadulf replied. 'And it seemed as if Ailgesach was hiding it from prying eyes, since he tucked it among those old clothes. He did not agree with the writer's advice to hide it where everyone could see it.'

Fidelma did not want to appear over-enthusiastic about the find. It raised many questions that could not be answered at that moment. 'We will keep it with us.'

'The word conspiracy sounds serious. A conspiracy about what?'

Fidelma placed the paper in her *marsupium*, the bag she carried slung from her shoulder, and made no further comment, ignoring Eadulf's disappointed glance. She then renewed her search, going slowly through the contents of the cabin until she was sure there were no other hidden surprises. There was little else in the cabin that caught their attention.

'I'll place the *Missale* and vellum texts in my saddle-bag,' Fidelma announced as she made for the door. 'They can be delivered to Abbot Ségdae when we have a chance.' She paused and glanced back at the darkened hut. 'We have done enough here. Let us see if there is anything more of interest in the outbuildings or in the chapel.'

They tried the closest outbuilding first. It bore a resemblance to a stable, although there were no animals inside. However, there were signs of recent occupation. Gormán pointed to the straw-covered floor.

'Those droppings were made by horses – and recently. Perhaps as recently as last night. I'd say that two horses were stabled here, according to the dung.'

'So there is further proof that Sétna did not dream up the story he told Grella,' Fidelma remarked.

They walked across to the chapel and buildings. Clouds were beginning to form in the west and the day was turning cold; the afternoon was drawing on. The chapel stood in gloom and the body of the envoy that they had brought to it earlier was still stretched out before the small wooden altar. Agreeing that nothing would be revealed by any closer search of the buildings, they returned to their horses and set off back to the tavern of Fedach Glas.

As they turned into the tavern yard, Enda came running out to meet them. It was clear that something was very wrong, from his anguished expression.

'What is it?' Fidelma demanded without dismounting. She had a premonition of what he was going to say.

'Lady, I have failed you. It is my fault. Biasta has fled – he used my horse to get away. Fedach Glas has no other horse here so I could not ride after him. The scoundrel tricked me and escaped.'

CHAPTER SEVEN

'What exactly happened?' Gormán demanded, the suppressed anger clear in his tone.

'He said that he needed to go to the privy,' replied Enda unhappily. 'I suspected nothing. He went outside, and the next thing I heard was the sound of my own horse galloping off. By the time I ran out, he was vanishing along the road.'

'How long ago did he leave?'

'Long enough not to be overtaken if you set off after him now. The tavern-keeper had no horse to chase him, unfortunately.'

'He went north, otherwise we would have seen him,' Eadulf commented.

'One thing I noticed,' the unhappy warrior said. 'As he galloped off, I saw that his cowl had been flung back. He wore no tonsure. I don't think he was a religieux.'

'That doesn't surprise me,' Fidelma replied.

'It is my fault,' Enda said dispiritedly.

'Truly, it *is* your fault,' snapped Gormán. He turned to Fidelma. 'What now, lady? Do we chase after him?'

'We must certainly find him,' she said. 'He has many questions to answer.'

78

She swung down from her horse and hitched it to the rail. Her companions followed suit and she led the way into the tavern. Saer was still seated with a mug of ale before him. Fedach Glas and his wife Grella faced her nervously. Fidelma spoke directly to the tavern-keeper.

'I am told you have no horse. Do you have any animal at all, even a mule or plough horse, that you can let us have?'

Saer looked up from his ale and gave a chuckle. 'If you could run quickly, you could have secured yourself a good horse on the Black Heath.'

Fedach Glas stared at the carpenter. 'What nonsense is this?'

'I tell no lie,' the carpenter responded. 'At dawn this morning I saw a good stallion running wild on the heath. I had half a mind to try my luck to catch it. But I don't have the skill.'

Fidelma was impatient. 'We do not have time to indulge ourselves in fantasy. Is there nothing that you have, Fedach Glas?'

'I do not, but my cousin has,' answered the tavern-keeper. 'He runs the farm on the hills behind us and has two good horses – but they are there to work the farm, not horses such as you ride.'

'Then we must borrow one. Will you go and bring it back here and, if possible, obtain a saddle of some sort.'

'A plough horse would not be able to overtake a warrior's horse,' protested the tavern-keeper.

'I do not mean it to do so. I merely want it to transport this warrior, Enda, back to Cashel, that is all.'

Enda was chagrined. 'Are you sending me back to Cashel, and on a plough horse?'

Fidelma waited until Fedach Glas had set off on his errand and then turned to the disconsolate warrior.

'I am not doing it as a punishment, Enda. There are important messages to be taken back to Cashel. Tell Caol and my brother what has happened here. That we believe the body is, indeed, an envoy from King Fianamail of Laigin. We suspect that Brother Ailgesach had something to do with this matter, but he has been killed by someone calling himself Brother Biasta. Also, I want you to go on to Imleach, taking some documents and a *Missale* that I shall give you. They are valuable, so put them into the hands of Abbot Ségdae. I also need to find out from the abbot whether he knows anything about these two religieux – Ailgesach and Biasta.'

Enda repeated the instructions. 'And where will I find you, once I have gathered such information?' he asked.

'We shall be heading north for Durlus Éile to see if we can pick up Biasta's trail. If we have moved on, we shall leave instructions at the fortress of the Éile so that you may follow us. Is that clear?'

'It is indeed.'

'Then wait here until Fedach Glas returns with the horse and do your best to return to Cashel quickly.' She turned to Saer the carpenter. 'I have to leave you with two unpleasant tasks but there is no alternative.'

The carpenter set aside his ale and gazed at her with a frown. 'Tasks?'

'We saw and heard crows around the chapel. You must try to find someone to help you bury the bodies – the one left in the chapel and that of Ailgesach. We cannot tarry any longer to help you in this.'

Grella intervened. 'My husband will give him a hand. But what of the burial blessing? A religious should bless the grave.' She glanced with meaning at Eadulf.

'That I know,' replied Fidelma. 'However, we cannot wait. Perhaps, Enda, you could ask that a religious be sent here to fulfil this task?'

'I don't like it,' sniffed Grella. 'Things should be done according to ritual, otherwise the spirits of the dead will not lie at rest.'

'It must be, until we can do otherwise,' Fidelma told her. 'Better a delay in a ritual than a murderer escapes justice.'

It was apparently the first time that either Grella or Saer understood the reason for Biasta's flight. Their eyes widened and they exchanged a nervous glance.

'We will carry out your wishes, lady,' Saer said in a subdued manner.

Fidelma thanked them, turned to her companions and simply said: 'Let us set off.'

They bade farewell to Enda, mounted their horses and within moments were cantering northwards along the highway that led to the fortress of the Éile. Fidelma did not really believe that they would overtake Biasta. Indeed, the sun was already well on the rim of the western mountains. She actually began to question her decision to start out so late, for it would soon be dark. It might have been better to spend the night at Fedach Glas's tavern and make an early start in the morning.

She glanced to her left at the lowering sun. Eadulf, riding alongside her, caught the movement and said, 'It will not be long before nightfall.'

'We can cover a lot of ground before then,' she replied, almost irritated that they had shared the same thought.

Gormán, who was riding in front of them, twisted in his saddle.

'If we can maintain this pace, before nightfall we will arrive at a place where we can stay. The river comes close to this highway soon, and there on the left is a track that leads to a little chapel and another tavern on the banks of the Suir.'

Fidelma vaguely remembered the place from previous travels.

'Maybe that is where Biasta is making for,' Eadulf offered hopefully.

'I doubt it,' Gormán grunted. 'I think he will want to put as much distance between Fedach Glas's tavern and himself as possible. He will surely realise that we will give chase. I have a feeling that he would have left this main highway as soon as he was able.'

'You may be right,' Fidelma agreed. 'And with the head-start that he had, he will probably have made it to Durlus Éile. Enda's horse is fast and if Biasta is a good rider . . . And Durlus is a large enough township that he could be more anonymous than in an isolated country tavern.'

'Do you agree with Enda that this Biasta is not a genuine religieux, lady?' asked Gormán. 'Enda says that he doesn't wear a tonsure.'

It was Eadulf who answered for her. 'Even if he did, anyone can cut their hair to create the right appearance.'

'All we know for certain is that he killed Ailgesach, whom he claimed was his cousin,' added Fidelma. 'There are many questions that must be answered before we start speculating.'

Eadulf suddenly turned to Fidelma in a burst of excitement. 'I have just realised! Saer said that he saw a good stallion running wild upon the heath. It could have been the missing horse of the murdered envoy.'

'It could,' she said. 'However, we now have other matters to concern—Wait! Someone is approaching.'

A cart, being pulled by an ass, was creaking round a bend in the road ahead of them. Seated on a pile of sacking and cursing volubly at the animal straining in the shafts was a fat, balding man, whose dress proclaimed him as a merchant. The back of the cart was filled with farm produce and sacks of wheat and corn. He eased on the reins as he approached them.

'Are you bound for Durlus?' He greeted them with an apprehensive smile, having noticed Gormán's weapons. Lone merchants travelling on isolated roads so late in the day sometimes had reason to be ill at ease. 'You'll not make it before sunset.'

'We are aware of the position of the sun,' replied Gormán dryly. 'Have you seen any other travellers on this road?'

'Only a few,' said the man, realising that the warrior's party were not dressed as he imagined bandits might be, and thereby relaxing a little. 'A lady and her companion stopped me earlier and asked where they could find a boatman to transport them to Imleach. Of course, I said the river didn't go there and it was best to get to An Ghabhailín, the fork of the river, and—'

The fat merchant was garrulous but Fidelma interrupted him. 'A lady and her companion? From what direction were they travelling?'

'Coming from the south, as you are.'

Fidelma glanced at Eadulf in surprise. 'How long ago was this?'

'Some time after midday,' the man said with a shrug.

'After midday? But that is a long time ago,' Gormán pointed out suspiciously.

'Indeed, that was before I pulled off the highway to Cill Locha. I had some trading to do there. I have only just rejoined the highway to the south but I am not going to make even Fedach Glas's tavern before dark. I wanted to be in Cashel before sun-up.'

'The man and woman,' Fidelma said musingly. 'They were looking for a boat to take them to An Ghabhailín . . . Where would they get that from?'

The man shrugged. 'Hard to say, and they would have had to abandon their horses. No boats are going to take horses downriver. As a matter of fact, I suggested that they might try Mugrón's tavern . . .'

'That is where I was suggesting we might halt, lady,' Gormán intervened. 'It's a ferry crossing on the Suir. We have to leave this highway and take a small track to the west.'

The merchant nodded. 'You have the place correct. The lady did not seem happy and I think that she would have preferred to travel on to Durlus. But I'd be surprised if those two were able to pick up a boat today. Even if they abandoned their horses, they will find little traffic on the river. There is some festival or other, I think, which most boatmen are attending. Anyway, I left them to the joys of the day.'

Fidelma was thinking. 'How long ago was it that you say you directed this woman and man to Mugrón's tavern?'

'Oh, it was quite a while ago.' He suddenly chuckled. 'As I said, I had to go to Cill Locha. I trade with the farmer there. Funny thing . . .' He paused with a smile and shook his head.

'What is funny?' demanded Eadulf.

'Well, I had only just rejoined this highway, a short while ago, when a religieux on horseback came riding up behind me. He asked if I had seen a man and woman on horseback, saying that they were friends and he wanted to catch up with them. He described them and so I told him what I have told you.'

'A religieux on horseback?' queried Eadulf, trying to suppress his excitement. He gave the man a brief description of Brother Biasta and Enda's stolen horse, but the merchant shook his head.

'That wasn't the man or the horse, which was a roan mare. This man was young, had black hair and features that were best worn with a scowl. A curious fellow. He turned and made off back northwards at a gallop. When I watched from the brow of the hill, I saw him miss the turning along the track leading to Mugrón's tavern.'

They watched in silence as the merchant cracked his reins and his cart trundled off down the road. Then Fidelma smiled at Eadulf's disappointment. 'The merchant did say that when he turned back on to the highway and was heading south, this religieux came up *behind* him. So the man came south along this highway and was not riding north as Biasta was.'

Eadulf heaved a sigh. 'Well, we might be in luck in catching up with the mysterious couple who stayed with Brother Ailgesach.'

The sun had sunk completely below the western mountains, and twilight was spreading long dark shadows from the east by the time they heard and saw the rippling waters of the Suir. The great river rose on the slopes of the mountain of Beanán Éile to the north-east and pushed in a great semi-circular route through the kingdom, around Cashel itself, almost in the shape of the blade of a sickle before joining two other great rivers, the Bhearú and the Fheoir, in one giant estuary which emptied into the sea beyond. Merchants used the river for trading, bringing large vessels as far up as the 'honey fields' south of Cashel, while smaller vessels could navigate the river as far as Durlus Éile. It was in the Suir that Fidelma had learned to swim with her elder brother and where they both had learned to fish for brown trout and salmon.

On a bend of this river, in the gloom of the early evening, they could see a group of wooden buildings, one of which had the outline of a chapel. The others seemed to be a curious mixture of half-finished living cabins. They slowed their horses to walking pace as they approached.

'Curious,' observed Gormán, peering around.

'What is?' asked Fidelma. 'Apart from the fact that this place looks unfinished.'

'That is just it, lady. This is Mugrón's tavern. When I was here last time, it was a substantial building with a flourishing business.'

It was Eadulf who had been sniffing the air and who finally pointed beyond one of the newer buildings. 'There has been a fire here. It looks as though part of this place was burned down.'

They moved forward cautiously and examined the buildings. Now they came closer, the signs of fire were obvious. None of the buildings had escaped and not one possessed a complete roof. The structures that had once housed the tavern and quarters for the guests and horses were certainly unusable. They could now see the ash covering a lot of the site. Even the chapel was derelict.

'Is this recent?' Eadulf asked.

Gormán regarded the remains with a keen eye before answering. 'I'd say it was fairly recent. No longer than a couple of weeks.'

'Someone careless with their cooking fire?' mused Eadulf. Such accidents were not unknown among these types of wooden buildings, especially in the dry summer months. But no one bothered to answer him.

'Talking of fire . . .' Gormán was pointing towards the remains of another derelict building further down by the riverbank. A plume of smoke was rising into the darkening sky behind it.

The warrior dropped a hand to his sword-hilt and nudged his horse gently forward. The others followed him without speaking. Turning the corner of the ruined structure they came on to the bank of the river, a broad area of flat grass looking almost as if it were cultivated. The object that held their attention was a small fire – a cooking fire, for above it was placed an old iron firedog on which a large brown trout was gently roasting. There was no one by it, but signs showed that someone was nearby. A platter lay on the ground ready. There was a kettle of water in which two more brown trout were immersed. And they could see a wooden board on which someone had cleaned the fish before putting it on the spit.

Gormán eased his sword from its sheath and glanced swiftly about him.

Then a voice cut through the silence. It came from a copse, beyond an area of undergrowth a short distance along the bank. It was a man's baritone, raised in melancholy song.

'Dark and grim is this life
No soft bed to lie on.
Just the cold, frosty earth
And the harsh, icy wind.

Even the birds now refuse me their song
In the shade of the cold, unfriendly sun . . .'

The voice suddenly halted as the singer appeared through the bushes, his hands full of green shoots and fungi which he had apparently been gathering.

He was a young man with a mass of fair, curly hair, blue eyes and regular features. The tumble of hair came to his shoulders, where it mingled with a full beard which, unlike his hair, was well trimmed and combed. While his clothing was somewhat worn, it was of good quality and one would have pronounced him a person of quality even though he wore no jewellery or emblems to mark his clan or rank.

He stood still, gazing up at them, noting their clothing and Gormán's half-drawn weapon.

'No need for a sword, warrior,' the young man greeted him. Then he moved forward, ignoring them, to put down his forage by the cooking fire, before turning to face them again. 'Welcome, strangers, to my poor fire. You are all welcome to share my frugal meal.'

'Frugal?' sniffed Eadulf, indicating the large brown trout on the spit and the two others in the kettle.

'I admit I have been lucky with the trout that obligingly leaped from the river on to my hook,' laughed the man. 'But apart from that, I can offer little else, not even a jug of ale.'

'How long have you been encamped here?' snapped Gormán, his hand still on his sword.

'Since late afternoon,' replied the young man, lifting an eyebrow slightly at the tone in the warrior's voice. 'Have I offended anyone by doing so?'

'No one that I am aware of,' replied Fidelma. 'We just wondered how came you here. I see no sign of a horse other than our own mounts.'

'That is because I travel on foot, lady.' He pointed to his feet. 'I have to confess that it is not by preference but by necessity. I came here expecting to find a boat to take me downriver, not a deserted tavern and chapel. So I am stuck here for the night until I can find a better means of transport.'

'Have you seen anyone else around here?' enquired Fidelma.

'You are the first people I have seen since I arrived.'

'You have not noticed a couple, a man and woman on horseback?' When the man shook his head, she pressed: 'Nor a religieux, also on horseback?'

The young man pointed to Eadulf with a broad smile. 'Do you mean other than this one?' Then, seeing Fidelma's scowl he immediately assumed a more serious expression. 'No, I have not. Why are you looking for them?'

'Perhaps we should introduce ourselves,' Fidelma suggested. 'What is your name?'

The young man turned his blue eyes on her. 'You seem very curious about these people,' he countered, ignoring her question. 'Does something concern you?'

'Your name!' rapped out Gormán, his eyes narrowing and his sword hand tensed.

The young man held up his hand, palm outwards. 'Hold hard, I am not hiding my name. It is . . . Torna.'

'And where do you come from, Torna?' Fidelma asked, hearing the slight hesitation before he gave his name.

The young man shrugged. 'I am from an insignificant clan to the north and am merely following this river as I believe it will take me to the rich townships of the King of Muman.'

'And why would you wish to go there?' said Fidelma.

'Because I am told that the King is appreciative of good verse and will be generous to a wandering bard.'

Fidelma smiled, perhaps a little grimly. 'And are you a wandering bard, Torna? Do you have good verses to sell?'

'Modesty prevents me from boasting but since you ask, lady, my verses are well regarded.'

'Well, you bear a good name for a bard. Torna Eigeas's verses are still sung today while he lived long ago.'

'As I say, modesty forbids me from comparing myself to such a noble ancestor.'

'That is wise,' Eadulf observed dryly. 'Because someone's ancestor did something well, it does not mean that they are just as good.' He had taken a dislike to the young man's attitude.

The young man flushed. 'Are you a philosopher, my Saxon friend?'

'Neither philosopher nor Saxon,' replied Eadulf curtly. 'I am an Angle.'

'Angle or Saxon, they are both the same,' dismissed the young bard. Eadulf knew that in the eyes of the peoples of the west, this was true and he would never change their opinion. Now and then, when irritated, he would still try to correct them.

Fidelma was dismounting, with Gormán and Eadulf following her example.

'Well, Torna the Bard, I am Fidelma of Cashel. This is my husband, Eadulf of Seaxmund's Ham, and this is Gormán of my brother's bodyguard.'

Torna's eyes widened. 'Then you are related to the King of Muman?'

'I am his sister.'

'Then forgive my manners, lady. I did not expect to meet with such exalted company on this riverbank.'

Fidelma indicated the roasting spit. 'I think your fish might be in need of attention.'

The young man hurriedly removed the trout and placed the other fish on the spit in its place. Gormán took their mounts and tethered them nearby while Fidelma found a log for a seat and continued her conversation.

'So you are a wandering bard intent on selling your songs in Cashel?'

'That I am, lady.'

'Why did you stop here?'

'I was told in Durlus Éile that there was a chapel and a tavern at this spot where I could get a boat to take me downriver. When I reached here I found the place deserted, indeed, most of it burned down. Nor were there signs of passing boats on the river. I could have carried on by foot, but I was not sure how far I would have to go, to find another place to sell my poems for a night's repose. Nor did I think it wise to travel down unknown roads in darkness. So I decided that I would wait until daylight before journeying on.'

Gormán had returned and was looking at the young man with a suspicious gaze. He glanced at Fidelma and said: 'You may want to check your horse, lady, to ensure that it is tethered correctly.'

When Fidelma joined him at the spot where the horses were tethered, he whispered: 'I have done a thorough check, lady. There is no sign of any other horses, nor of a woman or a religieux. Perhaps they all moved north when they saw this place was ruined and deserted. Even so, I do not trust this one.' He indicated the poet with a slight movement of his eyes.

'Well, we will have to spend the night here anyway,' she replied. 'Continue to be watchful.'

When they returned to the fire, Gormán asked the young poet: 'If you were travelling south along the river, then you would surely have passed a ferryman's cabin a short distance up from here. Why didn't you stop there? He might have known of a boat going south.'

'Had I been coming along the river then I might have done so,' returned the young man easily. 'However, I tried a short cut across land at the place where the river bends. I must have missed the ferryman's place.'

Gormán frowned. 'Then how did you know it was a short cut?' he demanded.

The young man chuckled. 'You are a very suspicious person, my friend. I did not know it was a short cut until a farmer advised me to take it.'

'How far have you come?' asked Fidelma.

'North of Sliabh Bladhma,' he replied, indicating the direction where a group of mountains formed the northern border of her brother's kingdom. 'I decided to see what fortune held for me in the Kingdom of the Eóghanacht.'

The young man then returned to his cooking. He bent over his fish again and began to put the cooked fish on to wooden platters that he had produced.

'I found the jug and platters here and cleaned them up as best as I could,' he explained as he set the dishes. 'The water is fresh and clean, for there is a little spring on the rise behind those trees. Probably that was the reason why this tavern was built here. It is such a beautiful spot. A pity it has been destroyed.'

With the fish and the mixture of herbs and fungi, he put pieces of dry bread, taken from his bag that lay nearby, on the platters. These platters he distributed, and then he also passed round an earthenware jug full of water, apologising for the fact that it did not contain ale.

'We are grateful for your hospitality, Torna,' Fidelma acknowledged on behalf of her companions, as they spread their cloaks around the fire. There was a contented silence as they fell to eating, hardly noticing the change from twilight to darkness.

'Why do you seek these people?' Torna suddenly asked, re-opening the conversation. 'I mean this man and woman?'

'To ask them some questions,' replied Fidelma shortly.

Torna was interested. 'To question them?' he asked, inflecting the word. 'That sounds ominous. About what?'

'That is not your business,' Gormán said firmly, and added with a note of pride: 'Fidelma of Cashel is a *dálaigh*, an advocate of the law.'

Torna's eyes widened. 'Fidelma of Cashel – of course! I should have known the name. Fidelma, sister to King Colgú. I have heard you spoken of as a great lawyer, lady. When Sechnussach, the High King, was murdered in his bed, were you not asked to solve the riddle of his death?'

'I was,' Fidelma admitted. 'And Eadulf and Gormán were with me.' The last thing she wanted to talk about was her own experiences and so she decided to deflect the conversation, since it seemed clear that the young man had no information of consequence to give them. 'But what stories have *you* collected on your journeys? What songs? Sing us a good song and I will commend you to my brother, so that you may earn your keep.'

'That would be truly welcome, lady. But what songs would you like? Songs of adventure, of love, of visions, of inescapable fate or of battles? I have a whole repertoire that I can sing.'

'Let us have something new. Let's hear one of your own songs.' She turned to Gormán. 'Stoke up the fire and we will hear our young poet.'

The warrior gathered a number of branches that lay near and built up the fire as they stretched themselves around its warmth. Torna, it seemed, had chosen the spot well for his encampment, for the wind was blowing from the north-north-east, and they could see little wisps of froth on the southward-flowing river where the wind was causing tiny wavelets. But they were sheltered by the woods to the north and the buildings behind them.

As soon as they were settled, Torna cleared his throat and began his song in soft, sad cadences.

> 'What greater fortune on the sea of life,
> To find the girl you crave to take for wife?
> This love has lit a tempestuous fire
> No clan rebuke can quench your hot desire.
> A girl to share one's dreams and all one's hopes

Against a despot's harsh, constraining ropes,
That forced you both to leave your homes behind
And cast your fortunes on the wild west wind.
The fates are blind, it seems, alas, alack
For what the sea brings in,
The ebbing tide takes back.'

There seemed a slight catch in the young man's voice as he ended and Fidelma gazed at him thoughtfully. 'A song of experience?' she asked.

'A song of bitter experience,' he confirmed with a shrug. 'You want something merry, not melancholy. I am sorry, lady. I was not thinking.'

'I believe you *were* thinking, Torna,' Fidelma corrected. 'Or rather, I think that you were remembering.'

'I did not mean to sing that song. When asked to perform there should be no place for personal recollection. It just came unbidden to my tongue.'

'On the contrary, my friend. Where else can you express feeling than from the well of personal experience? Did she die, this girl that you loved?'

Torna hesitated for a moment. 'She did, lady.'

Fidelma glanced to where Eadulf already lay asleep huddled on his cloak and beyond him Gormán seemed to be dozing.

'Can you tell me about it?' she invited.

Torna seemed to think about it for a moment or two before responding. 'It was not so long ago. Two full moons have passed and still my grief is strong. My clan . . .' He paused. 'I will keep that to myself. My life was not privileged. I met a girl. I fell in love. It is as simple as that.'

'But her family did not agree with you marrying her?' interposed Fidelma. 'You indicated as much in your song.'

'That is right enough, lady. You see, I was of the class of the *daer-fuidir*.'

Fidelma raised an eyebrow in surprise. The *daer-fuidir* was the lowest of the social classes in all the Five Kingdoms. They were usually criminals, unable to pay fine or compensation, or sometimes they were even captives taken in battle from other lands.

Fidelma knew that a *daer-fuidir*, if he showed remorse and industry, had the ability to progress to the level of *saer-fuidir*. That meant he could be allocated land from the common wealth of the clan and be allowed to work it in order to pay off his debt to society. Some *daer-fuidir* could accumulate sufficient wealth and status to move forward to become a clansman, a *céile*, with full rights.

'How did this come about?'

'How did I become a *daer-fuidir*? I was taken captive during warfare when my clan was accused of cattle-stealing. It was a lie; an unjust accusation. The powerful chief of our territory hated my family because once we had been as powerful as his family. So he saw this as an excuse to crush us. We fought to defend our honour and I was taken captive. We were slaves in his fortress.'

'So there was no chance of you progressing from this class?'

Torna shook his head. 'None at all, lady. I was set to work labouring, building the fortifications for this evil despot. That was where I met . . . met the girl. I approached a fellow captive who had once been a Brehon. I thought I could trust him because of his oath to pursue truth and justice. I asked his advice and he told the girl's father in return from more privileges.' He made a helpless gesture.

'So what did you do?' prompted Fidelma.

'Well, I had been working on constructing the vaults of the fortress, and I knew a way out through an underground tunnel. So we eloped in the dead of night. For a while, we were chased, yet managed to elude our pursuers.'

'But they caught up with you?'

'They were overtaking us when we found our route was blocked by a big river in flood. There was a storm that night.' He swallowed, went on in a lower voice. 'What happened was my fault. I insisted that we should attempt to cross it. I was sure that our pursuers would not find us, once we had made it to the other side. She trusted me, my soul-friend. She put her life in my hands and I failed her.'

'What happened?'

'I am a good swimmer. I told her to hang on to me. We were not far from the other bank when she lost her grip. I heard her cry out – then she was swept away in the swirling waters.' His voice cracked. A moment passed before he recovered himself. 'I made a desperate effort to find her but was nearly pulled under myself. I made it to the bank and the people there hauled me out more dead than alive. They nursed me back to health. Her body was washed up sometime later.'

'And since then?'

His expression was bitter. 'Since then I have been a wandering bard, singing my songs, telling my stories, and hoping that—' He suddenly stopped.

'Hoping?' Fidelma said gently, after a moment or two of silence. 'Hoping for what?'

The young man shrugged. 'That, I do not know. My life would be that much simpler if I did.'

'Did you ever go back to your parents, your family and clan?'

'I cannot!' The words were harshly said. 'They are dead to me while the chieftain who held me captive still lives. The sorry remnants of my clan have to pay tribute to him. I could not find sanctuary with them because he would send his warriors to punish them further. That is why I wander; still hoping people will buy my mournful melodies.'

'I understand.' She realised how useless all the platitudes were about time healing. She could have used his own imagery that, however high and strong the tide, it always ebbed away. But it would not have been appropriate to add anything to what had been said.

The young man leaned across to the fire and put more wood on it. An owl hooted softly in the trees behind them. Fidelma saw that both Eadulf and Gormán were still sound asleep.

'It grows late,' she said. 'Sleep well, Torna.'

The young man answered with a soft grunt and sat staring into the flickering flames of the fire. She turned and wrapped herself in her cloak, then lay down near Eadulf, and was soon asleep.

Eadulf came awake, his eyes flickering open. He wondered what had disturbed him, then realised it was the horses, which were moving restlessly. He raised himself on one elbow and suddenly felt something heavy crash against his head, followed by the sensation of floating into a black bottomless pit.

It seemed only a moment before he was aware of a bright blinding light. He blinked a little and raised a hand to feel the back of his throbbing head. Then he remembered the restless horses and the blow to the back of his skull. He struggled to get to his feet, but could only make it on to his knees. There was a groaning: it was not coming from himself. It took Eadulf a few painful moments to locate it. Blinking and trying to focus, he saw Gormán sitting, trying to massage his head with both hands. Blood streaked down his face. The shock at seeing this had the effect of diminishing the ache in his own temples. Some sudden inner strength came to Eadulf and he peered around him.

The horses were still tethered where they had been when he went to sleep, but they remained restless, particularly Aonbharr, Fidelma's horse. He was jerking at the reins that secured him, swinging his head from side to side; his eyes rolling and nostrils flaring. Eadulf turned back, rubbing his forehead to ease away the pain. The fire, with the firedogs over it, was just grey ash and it had obviously died some time before. Then he realised there was no sign of the young man, Torna. Eadulf's mind was working too slowly. Shaking his head to clear it, he turned to his side: 'Fidelma . . . ?'

Then an icy coldness swept through him.

Her discarded cloak and *marsupium* were lying on the ground where she had been sleeping. There was no sign of Fidelma.

CHAPTER EIGHT

Eadulf came unsteadily to his feet calling, 'Fidelma!' and peering myopically about. Moaning, Gormán began to realise that something was amiss and also rose to his feet, swaying, with one hand nursing his cut head.

'What happened?' he muttered thickly.

'Fidelma is missing,' replied Eadulf, his voice hoarse, his mind still in a haze. Then he added: 'And that poet has disappeared as well.'

'My head is aching,' Gormán said in a rasping tone.

'There is blood on it,' Eadulf confirmed.

The warrior focused on his hand, seeing the blood on it. He blinked several times and then looked at Eadulf. 'You have a lump on the side of your head,' he finally commented, before stomping over to the river, kneeling by it and splashing his head and face. Eadulf stood looking about him. The riverbank was deserted.

'We must find Fidelma!' he exclaimed, his voice full of anxiety.

'Friend Eadulf,' replied Gormán, speaking slowly, 'we cannot do anything until we have recovered our faculties and are able to think straight. I suggest you bathe your head and take a drink.'

Reluctantly, Eadulf accepted the logic of this advice. It was clear that something had struck Gormán's head, breaking the skin and causing it to bleed. He examined the bump on his own head. It was swollen and tender but the skin was not broken. He crouched by the riverbank and began to bathe it. The cold water was soothing. He was more concerned with Gormán's wound, which still seeped blood.

'I have a salve in my bag,' he said. 'I should dress your wound, Gormán.'

The warrior returned to the fire and stirred the grey ashes. Some of them still glowed and, placing dried twigs on them, he soon had the fire alight again. By this time, Eadulf had found the little jar he was hunting for and instructed the warrior to sit down while he applied the ointment.

'What is it?' demanded the warrior.

Eadulf said impatiently, 'It will not hurt you. It is a lotion made from an infusion of the petals of the marsh-marigold; it will help prevent the wound from becoming infected. It's the best I can do.'

He applied the salve carefully to the other's head. The blood had made the wound look worse than it actually was and Eadulf reckoned that it would soon heal naturally, provided no infection set in.

Gormán himself had been viewing Eadulf's wound with a critical eye. 'You certainly received a hefty blow, my friend.'

'We both did,' agreed Eadulf.

'What happened?'

Eadulf replaced the little jar of ointment in his bag and sat, staring into the fire, for a moment.

'I have been trying to remember. I know I woke up during the night. The horses were fidgety and they disturbed me. I recall wondering if anything was wrong, whether some animal had disturbed them. Then everything went black. I think I was struck from behind.'

The young warrior's lips formed a grim line. 'We were both hit on the head from behind. The lady, Fidelma, has been taken. But who did this? The poet – what was his name? Torna? – he is gone also.'

'He must have had accomplices to do this.'

'There was no one else nearby when we fell asleep.'

'But one person alone could not have overcome Fidelma,' said Eadulf. 'And even if they had, she would have alerted us with her outcry.'

'If only my head would stop throbbing, I would start a search. There must be signs of her struggle.'

Eadulf sighed. His own head was just as painful. Then his eyes narrowed as he caught sight of some plants at the edge of the nearby woods.

'Clean that pot in the river,' he instructed, pointing to one of the small cooking pots that the poet had been using the previous night. 'Then put in some water – not too much, mind – and heat it over the fire.'

Gormán carried out the instruction without comment. Eadulf had risen and taken out his small knife before walking towards the edge of the wood and the plants that had attracted his interest: plants with broad leaves and purple flowers on upright, hairy stems. Bending down, he cut two of the plants and returned to the fire. Gormán watched him curiously as Eadulf trimmed the leaves and stem from the rest of the plant, and put them into the bubbling water.

'What is that?' he asked.

'Something that will help chase away the pain,' replied Eadulf. 'It is a favourite healing plant among my people: we call it betony.'

Gormán glanced at the discarded flowers and then said approvingly, 'It is *lus beatha* – the Plant of Life.'

Eadulf was a little impatient as he was preparing the infusion. He was anxious to start looking for the signs that would lead them to Fidelma, fearful of what harm might have befallen her. Gormán noticed his agitation.

'Friend Eadulf,' he said, 'the Lady Fidelma is fond of a Latin saying: *festina lente* – hurry slowly. The more we hasten, the more we may miss something important.'

Eadulf was about to utter an irritated retort but realised that was precisely what Fidelma would say in the circumstances.

'Anyway,' Gormán continued, 'wherever they went, they cannot have gone far.'

Eadulf stared at him in surprise. 'How so?'

For answer, Gormán pointed towards the still-tethered mounts. Eadulf cursed himself for an unobservant fool.

'Others might have come along on horseback,' he suggested defensively.

'Indeed, but had they done so, we would have been roused by their din. They must have come by stealth on foot to have knocked us out as we slept or as we were just awakening.'

'They might have tethered their horses a distance away,' said Eadulf.

'That is true, and if that is so, they will have left their tracks from here to wherever they left the horses. The tracks will not disappear before we are ready to follow. But there is another matter to consider, which is: why leave the Lady Fidelma's horse behind, if their journey necessitated travel by horse? We were unconscious and could not have prevented them from taking our horses if they needed them.'

The infusion was ready and Eadulf returned to his immediate task, pouring it into a beaker to cool so that they could swallow it.

'So what do you think has happened?' asked Gormán as they sipped at the mixture.

'It is obvious that Fidelma has been abducted and that we were both knocked unconscious to prevent our interfering.'

'And this poet, Torna?'

'I think we may conclude that he was involved, otherwise he, too, would have been hit on the head and left.'

'That's logical,' admitted Gormán, rising to his feet and rubbing his forehead once again. 'But I think we should make sure. They might have killed him and put his body in one of the ruins behind us.'

'But if they did so – why just leave us unconscious?'

'Stay there, friend Eadulf. I am better trained, so I will look through the ruins first.'

It was true. Albeit impatient, Eadulf accepted that Gormán's warrior training made him the better qualified to look for tracks and signs around the area. Curbing his anxiety, he sat waiting, hoping the infusion would work quickly so that he could concentrate on the problem. It seemed an age before Gormán returned, shaking his head as he approached in answer to Eadulf's unasked question.

'No sign of any tracks or anything in any of these ruins,' he stated.

Gormán began circling round the encampment where they had slept. Then he seemed to spot something and moved cautiously along the riverbank. It was not long before he came to a halt on the muddy shoreline of the river and stood staring down.

'Have you found something?' called Eadulf.

In answer, Gormán beckoned him forward and, without a word, pointed down to the mud. There was a deep furrow in the bank and footprints nearby.

'So the abductors came from the river,' Eadulf said.

'The deep furrow is where the prow of their vessel ran into the bank,' Gormán replied. 'It was a heavy riverboat, by the depth of that indentation. It's hard to guess how many the boat contained. A vessel with a prow like that might take six or seven men and even carry a sail.'

Eadulf stood gazing out across the river. On the far bank, the land consisted mainly of fields of stubble where crops had been harvested. Beyond that, not far away, was a small hill; its bald rounded top was hardly higher than surrounding trees. Gormán followed his gaze.

'There is not much across there but grainfields and grasslands for the cattle,' he said dismissively. 'They belong to a few isolated farmsteads.'

'And what of the hill?'

'It is called Dún Bán, not because it is a fortress or white in colour. It is just a small hill of grey rocks which might produce a light shade when the sun shines on it. But no one lives near there.'

Eadulf returned his thoughtful gaze to the river, saying, 'So which way did these abductors go?'

'I suggest they went with the flow of the river. To the south,' Gormán said.

'Southwards towards Cashel . . .' Eadulf shook his head. 'I disagree.'

'Why do you think they went north? That's against the flow of the river.' Gormán was sceptical.

'Because that is where they came from.' Eadulf's voice sounded so definite that Gormán was surprised.

'Tell me your reasoning, friend Eadulf.'

'If they came from the south, they would have had to fight their way upriver, against the current. Their coming would doubtless have woken us. They would have been struggling with their oars against the prevailing current and the wind. Remember how the wind was blowing from the north last night? So we would have heard the movement of their oars.'

'They might have muffled them,' said the warrior.

As answer, Eadulf pointed to the furrow in the mud bank. 'Perhaps, but this proves my argument. You agree that this indentation was made by the prow of their boat, ramming hard into the bank?'

'I do.'

'Then look at the angle of it. The prow struck into the bank from the north, and to make that deep indentation it needed both propulsion and weight. That is what the current and wind gave it. It would not have been so deep, had the rowers been forcing the boat against the tide and wind; nor would it have been able to strike the bank at that precise angle.'

Gormán regarded Eadulf with admiration. 'No wonder you are considered a worthy partner for the Lady Fidelma, friend Eadulf. I thought that I could read all the signs, but this did not occur to me.'

'So they allowed the wind and current to carry them here in silence. In silence they were able to render us unconscious and carry away Fidelma. But why? And where? If they were using the river, where would they head for, remembering they are now rowing against the current?'

Gormán glanced up at the sky, especially noting the rustling tree-tops.

'The north-east wind has dropped. This is a mild breeze from the west, not enough that they could use a sail to good effect, but with a good bank of oars they could progress well. But as you say, where? Not far distant from here, the river swings eastwards and finally it turns again and follows the valley to the north and north-east where it rises in the mountains behind.'

'Are there any settlements along the river?' Eadulf asked.

'The next big fortress and township by the river is the principal seat of the Éile, Durlus Éile.'

'That was the very town we were making for in our pursuit of Biasta,' Eadulf said. 'Do you think these abductors could have come from Durlus?'

Gormán gave an eloquent shrug. 'I would not put it beyond the realms of possibility. The territory of the Durlus Éile has always been seen as an easy door into Muman. Who controls Durlus Éile controls the ways into the Kingdom of Muman.'

'But isn't Durlus Éile part of Muman?'

'It's true that they hold allegiance to the King of Cashel. That might not be the same thing.'

'Are you saying that we might find danger in Durlus Éile?'

'I am merely saying that we should be on our guard if we do go into that township.'

For a few moments Eadulf was silent, regarding the flowing river as if seeking inspiration from the grey, pushing waters. Then he uttered a sharp exclamation and went to a bush near the indentation that the boat had made.

'What is it?' asked Gormán.

'Blood,' returned Eadulf. 'There is blood splattered here on the leaves.' He rose quickly and glanced around. 'Whose blood? Victim or abductor?'

Eadulf remained silent for a moment and then he hastened back to the campfire.

'Do we have a plan, friend Eadulf?' asked Gormán, following him.

'There is only one plan – to follow them. I wish we had a better one,' replied Eadulf. 'We must follow the river north to this Durlus Éile and keep our eyes open for any sign of a likely landing-place along the bank which the abductors might have used. Agreed?'

'Agreed,' Gormán replied solemnly. 'But what if, by the time we reach Durlus Éile, we have discovered no trace or found no lead – what then?'

'Let us hope that we do,' Eadulf said with fervour. 'This is a big country and there are plenty of places where Fidelma might be taken. Remember, as a *dálaigh*, she has many enemies – and who is to say this may not be a mission of revenge that has taken her from us.' He thought for a moment before adding: 'The first person we meet heading south to Cashel, if we think that they are to be trusted, must take a message to her brother Colgú to tell him what has happened.'

Gormán nodded slowly, before suddenly realising, with some surprise, that the throbbing of his head no longer bothered him. The infusion that Eadulf had mixed seemed to have worked, even though the wound was still sore. He began to pick up their belongings, tie them together and take them to the horses, ensuring that their mounts had a drink at the river first.

Eadulf went to where Fidelma had been sleeping and collected her cloak and *marsupium*. Her personal *cíorbholg*, or comb bag, was also there. She usually had it belted around her waist or in her *marsupium*. It was a sign of how swift the abduction had been. She would scarcely move without it. He also realised that not all of Gormán's belongings had been collected.

'I think you have forgotten something, Gormán,' he called, pointing to where a blanket still lay near the fire. By it was a leather bag which had a long strap to sling it across one's shoulder.

Gormán stared for a moment. 'I thought they might belong to you or the Lady Fidelma,' he muttered, 'but . . .'

'They must belong to the poet, Torna,' Eadulf said, bending down and picking up the satchel. There were a few items of clothing in it and some pieces of vellum and two quills, a knife in a sheath but nothing else. The vellum had some writing on it, but it was in the old form of writing, Ogham, which was named after the ancient God of Literacy and Learning, Ogma. Eadulf groaned. *'Ego senito bardus!'*

'What?' Gormán was puzzled.

'I am stupid!' translated Eadulf. 'This changes my conclusion about Torna. Had he been part of this abduction plan, he would not have left his bag and sleeping blanket discarded in this manner. He has been carried off as well.'

Gormán shrugged. 'It still does not bring us any nearer to what happened, or why, friend Eadulf. Nor does it give us any further information as to where Fidelma's abductors have taken her. In fact, it adds further questions.'

'Which are?' grunted Eadulf, still displeased with himself for not noticing Torna's belongings before. 'Aren't there enough to answer already?'

'Why would Fidelma's abductors be content to leave us behind but take the poet – unless he was a victim of the abduction?'

Eadulf gazed thoughtfully at him. 'We have been assuming that the object of the abduction was Fidelma.'

'Of course, she is sister to the King and a prominent Brehon who has made many enemies. It is a logical assumption that she would be the object of the abductors,' replied the warrior. 'But what if she was not?'

'Hmm, so if it was this young man, Torna, who was the intended victim, what if they, whoever *they* are, came for him – and when we awoke they were content to knock us unconscious. But because Fidelma was a woman and a witness, they decided to take her as well.'

'But who would want to abduct a poet?' sighed Gormán.

It was not long before they were riding northwards along the river-bank, with Gormán leading Fidelma's horse, Aonbharr, behind him. Some sections of the way were muddy; mostly the land was flat and open, while drier parts led through woodland. They had been travelling some way before Eadulf broke the silence.

'What's that hill?' he asked, indicating a small rise immediately to the east of them. Apart from the distant hills ahead and those beyond the great River Suir to the west of them, this was the only high ground along their path. Eadulf knew that high ground could often be dangerous, supplying a hiding-place, a sentinel post, a point for ambush. The mysterious attack and abduction had left him jumpy, and he constantly examined the ground around them as they rode.

'That is Feart Éanna – the grave of Éanna,' said Gormán. 'There is nothing there but a cairn to mark the grave. I think a small farmstead lies just beyond it by a small river which flows into the Suir, but I know little else about it.'

Eadulf continued to peer at the round hillock. 'And who was this Éanna?'

'Éanna Airgethech was a King of Muman, so long ago that we cannot count the years. He was called Éanna of the Silver Shield and he reigned for three times nine years, but was slain in battle. That was in the days long before Eóghan Mór, the founder of the race of the Eóghanacht.'

At any other time Eadulf would have been interested, but now he was only concerned as to whether the hill hid any dangers for them.

'Is it worth checking this farmstead?' he asked.

'Not if we are following a boat. We should keep to the river.'

They pressed on again in silence. They could see no boats on the water. The countryside too seemed deserted. There were no farmworkers in the bare fields because all were now stripped of crops. The harvest was over. Nor did there seem any sign of herdsmen or boys attending to the cattle or sheep that they occasionally caught sight of in the distance. It was a clear day with only a few wispy clouds very high in the bright blue canopy over them. The sun was reflected in a milliard of winking bright sparks over the surface of the river.

'We are coming up to the point where the river bends towards the east soon,' Gormán broke the silence. 'There is a ferry there, and if, as you say, the abductors have passed along that route, then we might get information from the ferryman.'

'Perhaps we should be careful?' suggested Eadulf. 'If the abductors came by boat, then the ferryman might be involved.'

Gormán shook his head. 'It is only a small ferry-crossing and it has been there since I have known it. As I recall, the ferry is run by a man and his wife, and they have a son who helps them.'

Eadulf knew that ferryboats were common on the rivers throughout the Five Kingdoms. Each ferryboat and owner were subject to strict laws and regulations on ownership and management. Sometimes the ferries were owned by individuals; at other times they were owned in common by the people who lived in the settlements along the banks of the river. Churches and religious communities also had the right to own their own ferry, but on condition that people wishing to cross the river were allowed free right of passage.

The ferryman's house was soon revealed as a log cabin almost hidden among the trees that grew close to the riverbank. They could see, as they approached, that the *ether*, or ferryboat, was only a small one that could be pulled by two oarsmen and seat four passengers. It was tied to a small wooden jetty which was a short distance away from the cabin. There were no other dwellings in the vicinity. Obviously the sound of their approach had been heard inside the cabin, for the door opened and a short, muscular man with greying hair came out.

'I cannot take horses to the other side,' he told them, gazing at their mounts.

'We do not come seeking the use of your ferry,' replied Gormán. 'A beaker of *lind* and the answer to a few questions would serve our wants.'

The ferryman pursed his lips in disapproval.

'The ferry is the means of support for my wife and my son, who helps row people across; otherwise you would be welcome to my hospitality.'

'Then you shall be rewarded for your hospitality and your time,' Gormán declared, swinging off his horse and leading it to a wooden hitching-post by the hut. 'Do you not recognise me, Echna?'

The ferryman stared at him, suddenly noticing the golden torque. 'Why, it is Gormán of the Nasc Niadh.' The man seemed well-informed and quick-witted, for he turned to Eadulf and said, 'Then you must be the Saxon named Eadulf, husband to the Lady Fidelma, the sister of our King?'

Eadulf felt the time was not right to be pedantic and point out that he was an Angle, not a Saxon. He simply acknowledged the fact.

The ferryman was already calling into the cabin for his wife to bring a jug of *lind* and beakers. He indicated a wooden bench overlooking the jetty by the river.

'Be seated, Gormán. Brother Eadulf, also. My name is Echna and I run the ferry here,' he added for Eadulf's sake.

'Is this a busy crossing?' asked Eadulf as he seated himself.

At once Echna shook his head. 'Were it not for my fields and live-stock, we would be starving. We are some way from any settlement. The main track to Durlus Éile passes further to the east of here. Of course, there used to be a chapel, tavern and ferry just to the south of us, but they were destroyed less than a week ago.'

'What happened?' asked Gormán. There was no doubt the ferryman meant the place where they had camped for the night and confirmed their estimate of the time it had been burned.

'A strange raid from the west of the river,' continued Echna. 'We were told that a dozen bandits crossed the river, attacked the chapel and set fire to it. The tavern which stood near it, also caught alight.'

Eadulf asked: 'Was anyone killed?'

'The chapel was only attended by a visiting priest and he was not there at the time. Unfortunately, the tavern-keeper, who also ran the ferry, was killed and his family have fled to the Abbey of Ros Cré in the land of the Éile. Now the place is derelict; just a pile of ashes.'

'What was the purpose of the raid?'

'Do bandits and thieves need a purpose?' Echna asked, then added cynically, 'The destruction of that ferry has not helped us by way of business, because merchants now make for safer crossings further north. There are bridges there as well as ferries.'

A homely-looking woman came from the cabin with a pitcher of *lind* and beakers to drink the ale from. With a quick smile she placed the tray within reach of her husband and disappeared back to the cabin.

'It's not often that travellers come to this nook of the river unless they wish to use my ferry. Are you on your way to Cashel?'

'To Durlus,' replied Eadulf.

'I see — in which case you have taken a long route,' the ferryman pointed out. 'But surely you know that, Gormán.'

The warrior smiled thinly. 'We were interested in following the course of the river. Is there much traffic along it these days?'

Echna gave a dry laugh. 'It is still a main trade route into Durlus Éile. North beyond Durlus it is scarcely navigable for traders.'

'There do not seem to be many boats on the water today,' Eadulf observed. They had seen no river traffic since leaving the spot where they had camped.

'Today?' The man shook his head. 'Today there is a feast in Durlus to celebrate the end of a good harvest, and many of the farmers and merchants will be attending. That is why you will not see much traffic along the river.'

'I suppose that you know the river well?'

'I know the Suir like the back of my hand, Brother Eadulf. I know the sound of her waters, the way the current gushes over the stones on her bed; I can tell when she is running in flood or when the water is drying upstream. Indeed, I know her very well.'

'You keep account of the vessels moving up and down?'

The question surprised the ferryman. 'I take note of them, as most river men are my friends,' he explained. 'Often some of the traders will call in at our jetty to rest or take refreshment as they journey downriver.'

'I was wondering if you had heard any vessels passing at night?'

There was a momentary flicker of suspicion in the man's eyes. 'Surely you know that trade vessels do not pass along the river at night,' he said. 'They keep to safe anchorage.'

'In normal circumstances,' Eadulf agreed with a grim smile. 'But do you know of such boats passing at night?'

The ferryman glanced from Eadulf to Gormán, but before he could answer, a sharp voice cut in: 'There was no vessel passing last night!'

They turned at the sound of a new voice. It was the ferryman's wife who was no longer smiling, but who now stood before them in an aggressive manner. Her hands were placed on her hips and her jaw was thrust out. 'No vessel passed here last night!' she repeated angrily. 'Is that understood, my lords?'

CHAPTER NINE

'I did not specify *last* night,' Eadulf said coolly. 'I can now assume that there was, indeed, a boat that passed upriver last night.'

The woman's eyes widened as she realised her mistake. Her husband, Echna, rose and went to her, laying his hand on her arm.

'These are the King's men; we must tell them the truth.'

'Even if we come to harm?' the woman said with a wail. 'Even if our boy comes to harm?'

Gormán spoke firmly. 'You will come to no harm from us, nor from any who is in the service of Colgú of Cashel. Say what you know to be the truth and the truth will protect you.'

Echna turned back to them. 'Are the people you seek, those in this boat, your enemies?'

'They are,' replied Eadulf. 'Now – what did you mean when you said that you or your boy might come to harm?'

Echna patted his wife's arm again and told her to return to the cabin. Then he came and sat down with them, pouring himself a large drink from the pitcher of *lind*.

'Last night we were all asleep; that is, myself, my wife and my son, Enán. It was well before first light. As you know, it is the duty of the ferryman to keep a lantern burning during the hours of darkness, so that travellers who are late on the river might find the place. The lantern was burning low when I awoke.'

'Why did you awake?'

'I heard a noise, the oars scraping in the rowlocks, and a moment later came the sound of a boat knocking gently against the wooden jetty here.' He paused to lick his lips which had gone dry, and take another swallow of the ale. 'As I rose, my wife also awoke. I went to the door. As I say, the lantern outside was burning low and, at first, I thought I would be in trouble for not maintaining its brightness. Everywhere was in shadows but I saw a man standing on the jetty. He turned towards me. Alas, I could not see what sort of man he was. Behind him, I saw the dim outline of a boat.'

'Did you see what type of boat it was or how many were on board?' asked Gormán.

'That sort of craft usually takes four rowers but I had the impression there were others in the boat besides the oarsmen. One of the rowers was leaning forward over his oar and moaning softly. I said: "Do you need help?" The man on the jetty asked me if I was the ferryman. When I confirmed it, he said: "Then you must come with us. We need your skill with the oar. Our companion has had a misfortune and cannot row." I think that he added that I would be well compensated.

'I asked how far they expected to get upriver in the darkness. I said it would be better for them to wait until daybreak. The man, who seemed to lead those in the boat, said it was not far and it would soon be light in any case. He mentioned that they must reach the area of poor land, which we call Cabragh, on the banks of the Suir. That's to the north of here.'

'So you went on board to row?' The hope that rose in Eadulf was quickly dashed.

'As we were speaking,' went on Echna, 'my son, Enán, who had been disturbed, came behind me and heard the last part of the conversation. He said to me: "Your place is with my mother. I will row their craft. Cabragh is only a short distance."'

'Then why is your wife so fearful?' Gormán demanded. 'Has he not returned?'

'The man said that we must tell no one about the boat, neither of its passing nor its passengers. If we did as he bade us, then all would be well. The implication if we did not was that we would suffer.'

'He threatened you?'

'I took it as a threat.'

'But your son went with them?'

'There was no option. They were armed, from what I saw. And that is why my wife fears telling you about it.'

Eadulf looked kindly at the boatman. 'We will not reveal that we have heard anything of this matter from you. However, these people have abducted the sister of the King. That is why we pursue them.'

A shocked expression came over the features of the ferryman.

'Then G-God grant you success,' he stammered. 'You should have told me at once. If Fidelma of Cashel was a prisoner in that boat, and I allowed my son to aid the abductors, then there is great shame on me.'

'You did not know and, if so, what could you have done?' replied Eadulf. 'Can you tell us any more about the man to whom you spoke? Was there anything about him that might distinguish him? Was he round or tall? What manner of man was he?'

Echna reflected for a moment. 'He stood with his back to the lantern which, as I have said, was showing only a poor light as the oil was low. He was in the shadows, so I could scarcely tell what his manner of dress was.'

'Then what manner of speech did he use?' Gormán interposed. 'Was it local or could you place where he came from?'

The question would never have occurred to Eadulf for, as a stranger, he could barely make out differences between the accents of the Five Kingdoms. He gave an appreciative nod at Gormán.

'He was definitely a man from the south-east,' the ferryman replied immediately. 'I would say he spoke like a man of Osraige.'

Eadulf exchanged a meaningful glance with Gormán.

'This river is navigable into Osraige, isn't it?'

'The Osraige claim their land starts on the east bank of the Suir, where it runs through Durlus Éile. But the Éile claim they dwell on both banks at that point. The border agreed by the Brehons years ago was that both banks were the land of the Éile. Nonetheless, the territory of Osraige is very close to the river.'

Eadulf suddenly found himself thinking of their original quarry, Biasta. Perhaps the matter of abduction was a coincidence – but what if it was not?

'From Durlus Éile, would you have to travel far on horseback to the north-west through the mountains to Biorra or Tír Dhá Ghlás?' he asked.

'That would be a long, tough journey,' replied the ferryman. 'Are you saying that these people might abandon the boat at Durlus and proceed in that direction?'

'It would be very difficult, especially if one had unwilling companions to transport,' Gormán pointed out to Eadulf.

'But it might be accomplished?' he pressed.

'Anything might be accomplished with determination,' said the ferryman.

Eadulf sighed softly. It really did not help him form any idea of their quarry's intentions. That the river they were following went north to the capital of the Éile was the only real information they had. They would just have to carry on.

Eadulf stood up and addressed the ferryman. 'The information you have given us is of great help, Echna. Be circumspect with what you tell others, but if a warrior from Cashel named Enda comes by, then be sure to tell him what you have told us.'

'I understand, Brother Eadulf. You can rely on me. And, if you are able, take care of my son, Enán. I will offer a prayer for your safety and for the safe return of the Lady Fidelma.'

It was only a short distance north of the ferry that the course of the river turned almost as a right-angle and headed eastward.

'Do you believe that the abductors would have told the truth about going to this place called Cabragh?' Eadulf asked Gormán, breaking the silence that had fallen between them since they left Echna and his ferry. They were now heading east along the riverbank and passed an islet in the middle of the water. Other than wildlife, there was no sign of movement there and nowhere that anyone with a boat could hide themselves.

'If they were confident that they would not be pursued, they might have told the truth. But I doubt they would be so open about their intentions. I am fearful for the young man they took as the replacement rower. When he has outrun his usefulness . . .' Gormán raised a shoulder and let it fall. 'Once in the boat they could coerce him to row as long as they wanted. A weapon pointed at one's throat is a strong inducement.'

Further on, they had to ford a smaller river that fed the Suir from the south, and to do so they had to move south for some distance before finding a suitable place to cross it. To the east the ground started to rise slightly and they could see some distant hills. They turned north again to find the bank of the Suir and once more follow its course.

Gormán raised his hand and indicated a stretch of low flat country before them. 'This is called Cabragh, the Poor Land.'

Eadulf halted and carefully examined it. It was the same on both sides of the river; low-lying and stretching flat in both directions. There

was a bleakness about it that caused him to realise that it was descrip-
tively named. A poor land, indeed. It was thick with gorse and bracken
and, from what he could see, the earth was very soft, almost bog-like,
land. He presumed it would be liable to flood and that must be why
he could see no habitation anywhere.

'It's a desolate place,' he said. 'I thought that the highway we were
originally following must have crossed this place, yet I see no sign
of it.'

'Remember we decided to follow the river when we left the
highway,' Gormán reminded him. 'The road swings more to the north-
east and it joins another highway leading over a bridge that will take
us into Durlus Éile itself. But that is some way further along this
valley ahead.'

Eadulf glanced round. The land here was uninviting and gloomy.
There would be no place to hide a man, let alone a boat. It appeared
the abductors had lied to the ferryman that their destination was
Cabragh. They could only have been heading for Durlus Éile, after all.

The sun was now high in the sky. It was a warm day for the time
of year. The broad River Suir was reflecting the blue of the sky except
where little white ripples and eddies indicated the current gushing
around stony parts of its bank and across the riverbed.

'We'll have to stop and let the horses drink soon,' Gormán said.
'And it would be no harm to have some refreshment ourselves.'

Eadulf nodded half-heartedly. He would have preferred to press on.
However, they chose a little inlet along the riverbank, which was sheltered by gorse bushes, and dismounted. Gormán led all three horses to
the edge of the bank and allowed them to drink. Then he secured them
by their reins to the roots of the nearby bushes. Eadulf had taken some
dried bread and cheese from his saddle-bag and divided it between the
warrior and himself. A small earthenware pot served to scoop up some of
the brackish water from the river.

As they ate their frugal meal, Gormán remarked, 'Aonbharr is still nervous.' Aonbharr, Fidelma's favourite horse, which they had been leading, had been skittish all morning. 'He knows something is wrong with his mistress.'

Eadulf was certainly no horseman and did not have any knowledge of equine behaviour. He glanced at the animal. It was true that the ears seemed laid back and the eyes were rolling a little as it moved its head this way and that, nostrils flaring as if trying to pick up some scent.

'Horses are intelligent creatures,' continued Gormán, staring moodily along the river.

'I cannot argue with that,' replied Eadulf. 'I just wish *I* had intelligence enough to puzzle out this mystery. At the moment it is like looking at a blank wall and trying to visualise what is on the other side.'

'If they have made for Durlus Éile, then they will have been seen coming ashore in the town,' observed Gormán.

'What manner of place is this Durlus Éile?'

'It's a busy market township. Our task will be to find someone who has made an observation of this boat. The town is overlooked by the stone fortress of the Princess of the Éile, and in front of it is the market and then quays along the western bank of the River Suir.'

'Did you say the *Princess* of the Éile? I think I have heard it mentioned that it is a woman who rules the Éile, but she has never been to Cashel,' reflected Eadulf.

'She is called Gelgéis, the Bright Swan.'

'Is she well thought of?'

'Some have voiced their suspicions of her.'

'Suspicions?' Eadulf asked sharply.

'So far as I know, Gelgéis rules with a firm but just hand and the Éile see themselves as the primary defenders of the gateway into Muman from the north-east,' the warrior replied carefully. 'But some advisers of King Colgú maintain that she is not to be trusted because she is willing to make an alliance with anyone who serves her purposes. I suppose that is natural.'

'Natural?' frowned Eadulf. 'How is it natural? Is there something wrong with Durlus?'

'Not with Durlus but it is on the border with Osraige.'

Eadulf was trying to remember what Fidelma had told him of Osraige, the land of 'the People of the Deer' which was the border area between Muman and Laigin.

Gormán shrugged. 'Forgive me, but my people have long memories. For many years the Éile have been dependable allies of Cashel. Éile sits on the western border of Osraige and that land straddles the easy passes from Laigin into Muman. The Osraige once fought to form their own independent and powerful kingdom. It was only two centuries ago that they submitted to the authority of Cashel. Even so, one feels that if any opportunities ever arise, they will seize them. Beyond Osraige is the Kingdom of Laigin, and Osraige has often sided with Laigin. They did so nearly a century ago when Laigin attacked us and were involved in the killing of King Feargus Scannel of Cashel. True, both Laigin and Osraige were defeated and paid reparation. King Colgú collects his tribute regularly from them, but they are not to be trusted.'

'So what of the Éile?'

'As I say, their small territory lies on the western border of Osraige. We have had no cause to suspect the Éile or their loyalty to Cashel for many decades. However, there is an inherent suspicion among the people of Cashel that the Éile could be intimidated by those from Osraige. The latter are definitely not to be trusted, although they outwardly swear loyalty to Cashel. It is hard to maintain independence when one has covetous and powerful neighbours.'

'How long has Gelgéis ruled the Éile?'

'Not long. I think it was the year that Colgú was acclaimed King of Muman.'

'But she has kept the peace ever since?'

'She has, but as I say, I do not think she is trusted by some of Colgú's advisers. They think Gelgéis would make alliances with her powerful neighbours against Muman, if it was to her advantage.'

'Her advantage?'

'Perhaps I do her a disservice. I am told she always puts the welfare of her people first. So she would make the right choice for their welfare.'

'Knowing this does not actually help us.'

'That is true, my friend,' agreed Gormán. 'But it forearms us in our dealings in Durlus.'

'If, as you say, it is a market town,' Eadulf went on, 'surely there would be boats up and down the river more regularly than we have seen this morning? After all, it is just after the harvest and there is grain to be shipped and produce to be delivered. The river is undoubtedly the main highway for such goods.'

'You forget what the ferryman said. There is some big harvest festival taking place in Durlus – and most people will no doubt be attending it.'

Eadulf glanced up at the position of the sun. 'We should be on our way,' he said.

They rode on in silence beside the broad stretches of the river, moving ever closer towards the rising ground to the east, Eadulf keeping his gaze on the river. They were approaching a slightly elevated ridge running from south to north.

'Another river?' he asked Gormán.

The warrior shook his head. 'That is the highway between Durlus and Cashel: it runs along that ridge. We join it and cross a bridge spanning the Suir and continue into Durlus Éile. Just east of the bridge, the river turns sharply north, passing through the town itself.'

Eadulf had learned that the *droichet* or bridges were usually built where the rivers offered areas for natural fords, and thus those who built them were able to use the existing roadways. The bridge they now crossed was no different, with its supports ranging from natural rocks to artificial piers. Tall broad trees had been cut down and thrust into the softer riverbed, providing strong hurdles on which were laid planks. These timber bridges were very common throughout the Five Kingdoms, so far as Eadulf had seen. The bridge they were crossing was not as wide as some he had observed. It was wide enough for only one large cart to pass at any time, although with plenty of clearance on either side for single horses or people travelling on foot.

Eadulf guessed that the highway leading over the bridge would be classed as a *ró-shét* made for horses, chariots or carts. Their horses' hooves echoed hollowly on the wooden planks as they crossed over. Eadulf noticed appreciatively that the bridge was well kept, and then remembered that the laws of the country were very specific on the main-tenance of roads, causeways and bridges. There was still no sign of any people about and the land on this northern side of the river seemed deserted, although in the distance he could see the buildings of the township.

'That is Durlus Éile,' confirmed Gormán, noting his interested gaze.

Eadulf felt his breath quickening. 'Let us go straightway to the quayside and see if we can trace the boat,' he said.

Gormán disagreed. 'That is not a good plan, my friend. I would suggest that we find a place to stable our horses and then go with circumspection to the quayside. We would not want the abductors to recognise us before we recognised them.'

Eadulf was about to protest when he realised that Gormán was right. Now they were coming to this township they would have to use stealth until they knew whom to trust and whom not.

From its approaches, the place appeared to be far smaller than Cashel.

The main difference was that it was built on one bank of the river. Numerous wooden houses on the west bank constituted the township, and from these rose a small hill whose summit was dominated by the ramparts of a stone fortress. The grey walls stood proud and dominant, facing out over the town and river. Below the fortress, they could see the roof of a wood-built chapel. There were several larger buildings as well. Some distance before the entrance to the main town was spread an area of barns and open fields. They were approaching this area when Gormán reached across and tapped Eadulf's arm, then pointed. A short distance down a track descending towards the riverside, Eadulf saw what appeared to be a blacksmith's forge. At the back of the forge was a small field, with two horses grazing in it.

'That would be an ideal place to leave our horses,' the warrior said.

'Could we trust the smith?' asked Eadulf.

'Only one way to find out.'

Gormán led the way along the short track and halted before the forge. The fire seemed to be dying and the anvil stood silent and unused. But at their call a thin, wiry man with a shock of fair hair emerged from the gloom of the building beyond. He wore the leather apron over his shirtless torso which denoted his profession. His pale eyes glanced over their horses, doubtless assessing the quality of them, before focusing on Gormán. They rested for a moment on his golden torque and warrior's apparel.

'How may I serve you, lord?' he asked, straightening himself in a respectful attitude.

'We seek a place to fodder and stable our horses for a while,' replied Gormán. 'Would this be such a place?'

The smith grinned and nodded.

'It would – and it would be an honour to care for such fine beasts as those that you ride. Especially that one,' he gestured at Aonbharr.

'I have never seen a finer animal. Yet it has no rider. I trust there has been no accident?'

'Who are you?' asked Gormán, not responding to the question.

'My name is Gobán and this is my smithy. I presume from your torque and the direction you have come from, that you hail from Cashel?'

Gormán swung down and faced the man. 'You have a sharp eye, my friend.'

'Your manner proclaims you to be a warrior of Cashel, even if your golden collar did not betray that fact.'

'Then I will admit that is what I am. We come to you to look after our horses because we do not want our arrival or our identity made common knowledge in the township.'

Gobán's eyes narrowed with suspicion. 'Know that I am a true clansman of the Éile, loyal to my people. I will not be involved in any secret plots that bring harm on them or the Lady Gelgéis.'

Eadulf had dismounted and laid a hand on the man's arm.

'Will you take my word, as a member of the Faith, that we are not here to harm anyone but to rescue someone from harm?'

The smith's expression did not change; he remained mistrustful. 'You are a Saxon. I have no cause to accept your word or take notice of you.'

'You *will* take notice, Gobán, smith of the Éile,' Gormán said quietly and confidently. 'Because the Éile claim loyalty to the King of Cashel, and Brother Eadulf and I—'

He did not have to finish.

'You are Eadulf?' the smith exclaimed. 'Then you are husband to . . . ?' He paused, then said quietly, 'Fidelma of Cashel once saved the honour of my sister by her wise counsel and fair judgement.'

'Then know that we have come to this place in search of Fidelma, who has been abducted,' Eadulf responded. 'That is why we do not wish our identities to be made generally known.'

Gobán searched his features closely as if trying to ascertain whether he was telling the truth. Then he replied softly: 'Then God has guided your footsteps to my smithy, my friends, for I am in your service to repay the debt that my family owes to Fidelma of Cashel. I will ask you only one question – how may I help Fidelma?'

'We need to go down to the quays and make enquiries, being as inconspicuous as we can. That is why we need to shelter our horses here.'

'That is easily done.' As he spoke, the smithy took the reins and led the horses into the darkness of the barn behind the forge. 'Once I have removed their accoutrements, I can release them into the field at the back. These saddles and bridles can be hidden until you need them.'

'This is much appreciated, my friend,' Gormán said approvingly.

The smith smiled at the warrior. 'I have to tell you that your attempt to be inconspicuous will not last two minutes, unless you remove your golden collar and perhaps cover your finery with a rough cloak.' He glanced at Eadulf. 'I suppose one more religieux, more or less, will pass unnoticed in this township even if you do wear the tonsure of Rome and not that of the Blessed John. However, one of the élite bodyguards of the King would certainly be noticed.'

'You are right, my friend,' Gormán agreed ruefully. After a moment's thought he removed the golden torque from his neck and placed it in his saddle-bag. Then he unstrapped a cloak and swung it around his broad shoulders, tying it at the neck.

Eadulf looked on with approval before returning his gaze to the smith.

'We were remarking as we crossed the river that there seemed little traffic upon it today and we were puzzled. Someone told us that there is some festival in the town.'

'Indeed, though not in the town,' replied the smith. 'As you say, it is the end of harvest. The Lady Gelgéis has invited farmers, merchants and townsfolk to a great feasting in her fortress to give thanks for a good harvest. That is why the township is so quiet. Most people have gone to the feast.'

'Why have you not gone?'

'I have tasks to be done.'

'Perhaps the absence of townsfolk will work to our advantage?' muttered Gormán.

'Although it might prove to be the opposite when we are looking for people who saw the arrival of the boat and can identify it.'

Having thanked their new host, the two men left the forge to walk through the almost deserted township. There were a few dogs running here and there, and some loose chickens pecking at the dirt track – and somewhere near at hand a cow was bellowing mournfully. The street led almost directly into a central square; while one road turned up the hill towards the gates of the fortress, another ran down the gentle slope towards the river. There were a few people about, mainly elderly, who greeted them courteously enough. A young girl was seated at one corner of the square with a basket by her side in which were some loaves and cheese; she sat alone with tear-stained cheeks. It was clear from the sounds of music drifting down the hillside, accompanined by shouts of laughter, that the majority of people were still at the feasting.

'What's the matter, little girl?' Eadulf asked kindly.

'I need to sell my mother's produce before I can go to the feast to see the gleemen,' complained the girl. 'My mother says I must do so or she will not allow me to go. There is good cheese and do you want bread?'

Eadulf shook his head sadly. 'Alas, we are not looking for food at the moment.'

Leaving the dismal child, they made their way towards several large buildings that were obviously constructed as storehouses and barns. They walked between the buildings towards the river, along which were several wooden-built quays where boats could load and unload. This area still seemed entirely deserted, apart from the empty boats. They walked out on one of the jetties and stared about them in dismay.

There were numerous boats of all manner and sizes, and many that could have fitted the description of the type they were searching for.

'So much for our hope of finding someone who might have spotted our quarry!' Gormán said forlornly. 'So where do we start now?'

'Let us try some logic.' Eadulf considered for a moment. 'We need to find a boat that came here this morning. Perhaps if we started to examine all the boats that fit the description, ones that need four men to row it, and work our way along, we might find something which could give us a clue of some sort.'

'That is a long shot and I am better with a sword than with a bow.'

'It's better than doing nothing.'

'Very well, my friend. Let's start here and work our way along.'

They walked along the quays and began to scrutinise the boats, but found nothing in them to provide any information. It was as they were making towards the next jetty that a cackle of laughter from nearby caused them to halt.

A bundle of rags lying on the ground moved, and a wizened little man sat up and stared at them with a gap-toothed grin.

'You won't find many good pickings here, friends,' he wheezed. 'The merchants are a tight-fisted bunch. They made sure their produce was taken and locked in their storehouses before they went up to the fortress. They haven't left even a stalk of wheat lying about. Don't I know it?'

Eadulf regarded the wreckage of the man in disgust, telling him: 'We are not scavengers, my friend.'

The old man chuckled again, which brought on a fit of coughing.

'A leper,' muttered Gormán, spotting the decaying flesh of the man's arm sticking out from the rags that covered him.

The man immediately tried to conceal himself.

'Have I not got the right to exist, the same as you?' he hissed. 'These are my pickings, when the fat merchants leave them.'

'We are not searching for any pickings, as you call them,' replied Eadulf firmly. 'We are looking for a boat newly arrived here.'

'What's in it?' gabbled the old man. 'What's in it? I want a share.'

'I doubt there is anything in it that you would want a share of, unless it be several inches of steel driven in you,' snapped Gormán, clasping his sword as if to draw it from its scabbard.

'I meant no harm, meant no harm,' cried the old man in alarm, making to scuttle away.

Eadulf laid a hand on Gormán's arm and forced a smile at the leper.

'My friend is not known for the mildness of his manners and his temper is quickly roused. However, you could be rewarded in some fashion if you can show us such a boat.'

The old man's eyes gleamed. 'Rewarded?'

'But first you must prove that we can trust you. Did such a boat arrive here this morning?'

'Several.' The smile was positively a leer. 'Many river craft came here for the feasting.'

'We are looking for a boat that came upstream and was rowed by four men. There were passengers.'

There was a silence before the man said, 'What if I was to tell you that there was such a boat? Five men, one injured, and some queer sacks in it.'

Eadulf and Gormán exchanged an excited look.

'Was there a woman with them?' Eadulf demanded.

The leper shook his head but, seeing the disappointment on Eadulf's face, added: 'They carried queer sacks, as I said. Large enough for someone to be inside.'

'Where is it? Where did they land?' pressed Eadulf.

'Didn't I hear you say something about a reward?'

Eadulf reached into his leather purse and produced a piece of copper. To his surprise the old man spat in distaste.

'What would the likes of me be doing with that? Who would take copper from a leper?'

'Then what do you want?' demanded Eadulf, puzzled.

'Food is what I want. Give me food, and then I will tell you.'

Eadulf turned to Gormán with a helpless expression. 'Where can we get food now?'

But Gormán had grabbed the copper from his hand and run off without a word. He was back almost within moments, with two loaves and some cheese. Eadulf realised that he had gone back and bought it from the little girl. The old man's eyes lit up.

'That's more like it. Hand it over, fellow.'

'Firstly we want the details of the boat,' Eadulf said. 'Tell us.'

The old man shrugged. 'It is not moored along here.'

Eadulf drew in his breath angrily but before he could say a word the old man went on, 'It berthed on the far side of the river. You see those sheds over there? There's one with a small jetty in front of it. That's where they landed.'

'But there is no boat there now.'

'Not now there isn't, but that's where it landed. Five men. One had an injured arm. The others helped him out and then there seemed to be an argument with one of the oarsmen. I couldn't see from where I was because they hurried into the shed. I only know that the argument stopped quickly. They lifted two heavy sacks from the boat and carried them into the shed. Oh yes, and someone had been awaiting their arrival. He was a religieux by the manner of his robes, with one of those cowl things covering his head, so don't ask me what he looked like.'

'What?' cried Eadulf. 'A religieux in robes? Are you sure that he was waiting for them?'

'What else have I to do but sit here unobserved and watch the river, just in case someone comes along and leaves something unattended? I am sure of what I saw.'

'And what happened to the boat?'

'Everyone left the shed, climbed back into the boat and they rowed off.'

Eadulf actually groaned. 'They rowed off? Where?'

'Back downriver. Five of them came out and climbed back into the boat with the religieux who had been waiting for them. Two took the oars, one in the bow while the other three sat in the stern.'

'And these sacks that they took from the boat? What happened to them?'

'They must have left them over there in the shed,' shrugged the leper. 'Now, what about that grub?'

Gormán thrust the loaves and cheese at the old man, who gave an almost animal sound and scampered off among the buildings.

'Well?' demanded the warrior, frowning after the bent figure. 'What now, my friend?'

'Could the person waiting for them have been Biasta?' Eadulf asked.

'He certainly had time to reach here,' replied Gormán.

Eadulf was studying the shed across the now-darkening waters. The late-afternoon sun was already obscured by clouds as it sank to the distant western mountains.

'Five men went into that building carrying two bulky sacks,' he mused, thinking aloud. 'Five men plus the religieux who was waiting for them came out and rowed away. We presume that one was the ferryman's son. That means that one of the sacks contained the poet and—' He came to an abrupt halt. 'The other sack contained Fidelma.' He stared at Gormán. 'That means Fidelma is still in there! Still in the shed!'

CHAPTER TEN

They borrowed one of the smaller craft from the many boats tied up at the quays. Gormán took the single pair of oars while Eadulf clambered into the stern, untied the painter and pushed off. It did not take long to cross the river, although the current carried them a little way to the south of the spot that they were making for. Rather than trying to fight it, Gormán was content to let the boat come to rest where the current took it. They left it secured and began to walk along the bank to the small complex of sheds. It was a gloomy place. The sheds were set slightly back from the wooden jetty and surrounded on the other three sides by tall oaks and birch trees. They had seen no signs of life among the buildings as they crossed the river, and now, as they came close, it was clear that they were deserted.

'We should have asked for more information about this place from the old man,' whispered Eadulf, glancing about.

Apart from the one building that the leper had pointed out, two other buildings seemed also constructed for storage rather than habitation. Cautiously, they made their way to the entrance of the main building: the tall double doors were closed and secured with an iron chain and lock. They were basically wooden beams of stout oak planking.

Gormán uttered a quiet oath. There was no need to ask why. Eadulf knew that *glais iarnaidhi* or iron locks were commonly used in households in the Five Kingdoms, but storehouses such as these usually had other means to secure them. Gormán led the way around the building, but there were no other doors or means of ingress. They returned to the main door and now Gormán went to the bank of the river and picked up a piece of smooth rock.

'Keep a watch, especially on the far bank,' he instructed Eadulf.

Eadulf did as he was asked. Behind him he heard three sharp blows of stone against metal, which he felt must surely be heard even up at the great fortress overlooking the township on the far side. Apart from the sounds of the music and merrymaking drifting down from the hilltop, however, there was silence, which indicated that they had not been heard. One more blow and Eadulf heard metal fall on the ground. Gormán gave a grunt of satisfaction and when Eadulf turned he was holding open one of the large doors.

'Quick – inside!' he hissed.

As Eadulf hurried in, Gormán pulled the door shut behind them. A faint light drifted into the storehouse through some of the loose boards of the walls. The overpowering smell was of dried hay and rotting vegetation. Eadulf was trying to peer into the gloom when sparks caught his eye; he caught his breath before he realised that Gormán was on his knees using his *tenlach-teined*, his tinderbox. It took him a while to light a handful of straw. They were in luck for there was a lantern on a shelf nearby, and once this was lit they could examine the interior of the storehouse more clearly. At first Eadulf experienced a feeling of intense disappointment and panic. The place seemed completely empty.

Then Gormán pointed to some sacking half-hidden under a pile of straw at the back of the shed. While he held the lantern aloft, Eadulf hurried over and pulled aside the straw and sacking. A body was lying under it. He could not help a surge of relief as it was immediately obvious that it was that of a young man.

It was not Fidelma but he still felt a moment of guilt. He peered closer and realised that neither was it the body of Torna, the poet. He glanced up to Gormán with a grim expression. 'It must be the ferryman's son, Enán. They have cut his throat.'

Gormán let out an oath. Then he pointed nearby. 'Quickly, friend Eadulf; pull aside the straw there.'

Eadulf needed no further urging, and in a short while had uncovered another large piece of sacking. There was a body inside it. Eadulf took out his knife and hacked desperately at the thongs that held it together.

'Fidelma!'

She was not stirring. There was a gag in her mouth, tied firmly so that she could not loosen it, had she been able. Ripping off the sack-cloth, they saw she was bound hand and feet.

'Dead?' Gormán's voice croaked with emotion.

'God be praised, she is not!' cried Eadulf, removing the gag and cutting the bounds. 'Do we have water?'

'I'll get some from the river.'

He left Eadulf with the lantern while he hurried outside.

Eadulf bent over Fidelma's unconscious figure and slapped her cheek a couple of times.

'Wake up! Wake up! You are safe!' he whispered urgently.

There was some movement on her face in response to the slap and then her eyes fluttered open for a second or two. Then she groaned and closed them again. Gormán returned with a broken piece of pottery that held a little water from the river. Eadulf took it and splashed it in Fidelma's face. She blinked again and her eyes opened and focused on him for a moment. A brief smile began to form on her dry lips, and then she started coughing.

'More water,' ordered Eadulf. 'Make it as fresh as possible.'

When Gormán returned, Eadulf poured a little down her throat, causing her to cough and retch.

'We must get her out of here. We'll take her back to the smith's place. At least I can use my apothecary's bag that I left there. If she has been bound like this since last night, it is a wonder she has survived at all. Maybe her captors thought she was already dead and that is why they abandoned her here.' Eadulf glanced at the dead body of the ferryman's son. 'We'll have to leave him. Help me move Fidelma to the boat.'

Gormán blew out the lantern and together they lifted Fidelma. She was moaning softly and drifting in and out of consciousness but could make no intelligent sound.

Between them, they carried her from the storehouse and back to the boat. Once placed in the stern, with Eadulf holding her, Gormán took the oars again. The current pushed the vessel to the south so that by the time they crossed the river they had landed on the southern outskirts of the township.

'This is for the best,' Gormán said as they disembarked. 'We won't have to carry her through the township. Gobán's forge is easily reached across these fields.'

It was twilight now but they could see their way clearly.

'Let's hope no one has released their dogs in this area for night guard,' Eadulf observed nervously.

'It's too early,' Gormán assured him.

They carried Fidelma across the fields that ran at the back of the outlying buildings of the township and, by Gormán's unerring sense of direction, they arrived at the rear of Gobán's forge. A lantern had been lit in the forge and the smith was still at work. He glanced up startled as they entered, and then saw their burden.

'The Lady Fidelma,' he gasped as he recognised her. 'What has happened?'

'We managed to find her, but now we need a place where she can be nursed,' Eadulf panted.

'Follow me,' replied the smith, catching the urgency in his voice. 'My cabin is behind the forge. You can bring her there. Have no fear – I live alone. My poor wife died last year.'

They carried Fidelma through the forge and across a small yard area into the stone cabin beyond. There was a bed in a curtained-off area inside the cabin and it was to this that the smith conducted them.

'First we need some stimulant,' Eadulf said.

'I have some strong *corma*,' offered Gobán.

Eadulf asked the man to fetch it. As he poured a little down Fidelma's throat, she began to cough and tried to push it away.

'Being gagged for so long has probably made her throat very sore,' Eadulf fretted. 'Where is my bag?'

Gobán pointed to a corner of the cabin. 'I turned your horses loose in the pasture beyond, but brought your bags inside where they would be safe from prying eyes.'

Eadulf rose and picked up the *lés*, the small medical bag which he always carried, and peered through its contents, sighing in exasperation.

'What is it?' asked Gormán.

'I was looking for something to help ease the soreness of her throat and act as a tonic.'

'Is there anything I can do?' asked the smith.

'Not unless you have some wild angelica,' replied Eadulf, automatically naming the flower in his own language.

Gobán stared blankly at him.

Eadulf thought for a moment: '*Gallfheabhrán*.' He dredged the name from his memory.

'Ah, but there is some that grows not far from here by the grass on the riverbank. I will go and get some. Is that all?'

'That will be fine.'

As he left, Eadulf went to Fidelma's side and gave her another sip of *corma*. Again she struggled and coughed, but this time opened her eyes and seemed to become aware of her surroundings. There was a moment of panic and then she saw Eadulf. She tried to speak but could not manage more than a rasping sound.

'It's all right,' Eadulf smiled soothingly. 'You are safe. You are with me and Gormán here.'

She blinked her eyes in acknowledgement and gave a weak smile. Then she tried to speak again.

'Plenty of time to speak when you are feeling better,' admonished Eadulf. 'Just be assured that you are safe for the moment. You are in the house of a friend in Durlus Éile. Safe with Gormán and myself.'

This time she managed a nod.

'As soon as our friend comes back with a particular plant, I shall mix a potion for you that will do you good. After that, you must rest.'

A moment or so later, Gobán appeared with a bunch of the wild angelica. Gormán, at Eadulf's instruction, had already started to boil water over the fire that heated the cabin. Eadulf removed the leaves of the plant and then chopped the stem and put both together in the hot water to make the infusion. Gobán offered some honey as he also kept bees, and so Eadulf added it to the mixture before allowing it to rest and cool. Then he washed and cleaned the roots of the plant.

'You can chew these, they can be very refreshing,' he explained to his companions when he put them in a small pile.

When the tonic was cool enough, he took it to Fidelma's side and supported her head and shoulders while she sipped a sufficient quantity to satisfy him. Then he told her to rest.

While he had been doing this, Gobán had prepared a meal for them of cold meats, bread and cheese, washed down with some ale which, he boasted, he had brewed himself. They ate the meal seated in front of the fire. It was devoured mainly in silence except for once, when

Gobán glanced at the recumbent form of Fidelma on the bed and asked Eadulf: 'Will she be all right?'

'I have every hope that she will,' Eadulf replied fervently. 'She has had quite a shock. She nearly suffocated with a gag stuffed into her mouth and confined in a sack. But I have found no external injuries apart from where the bonds cut into her wrists and ankles. So once we have her breathing normally, that will be good. She needs only to know that she is safe and without restriction. She should be well in a little while.'

Gobán arose after the meal and told them that he must close the forge while they could make themselves as comfortable as possible for the night. After he left, Eadulf said quietly, 'Do you think we shall be safe here?'

'Gobán did say that Fidelma had saved some relative of his and he wanted to be of service,' Gormán reminded him.

'I was not thinking of Gobán specifically. But someone will eventually see the broken lock on the storehouse and find the body of the ferryman's son inside. If they are just people who noticed the storehouse is opened, they will raise the alarm. If they are the abductors, who might return to dispose of the bodies, then they will start looking for Fidelma. We should have found out who owns those barns. That leper we met will sell his soul for a handful of food. He could tell anyone we were interested in the barns.'

'All is possible,' admitted Gormán. 'But I cannot think that we will find a better shelter than this for the time being.'

'You are doubtless right,' Eadulf replied. 'I am a little nervous, but we have priorities to attend to. Fidelma's recovery must come first.'

After a little while, they heard Gobán returning.

'How is she?' he asked, gazing at Fidelma.

'You are very anxious about her,' observed Eadulf.

'I have already told you that I am in her debt, for she defended my sister when she was unjustly charged.'

'When was that?'

'It was many years ago.'

'Tell me about it,' invited Eadulf.

'My sister was trained in the healing arts, like you have been, and was a member of the community in Cill Dara. Sister Fidelma was then a member of that community as well. There were some deaths from the administration of hemlock, and suspicion turned on my sister, Poitigéir, because she knew the properties of poisons. But Fidelma used her skill to identify the real culprit and thus exonerated my sister. For that I owe Fidelma much. That is why I helped you today and why I am anxious for her health.'

Eadulf felt embarrassed at questioning the sincerity of the man. 'I apologise for questioning you, my friend. I should have taken your word in the first place. But there are many mysteries here and we are not sure in whom we can put our trust.'

'I have said that I owe a debt to Fidelma and will be loyal to you so long as I am not asked to be disloyal to my own people.'

'We trust that you will never be confronted by that choice. Tell us, do you know who owns the three barns on the far side of the river opposite the township quays?' Gormán asked.

'Of course,' Gobán replied at once. 'This is not so big a place that we do not know who owns what.'

'So who do they belong to?'

'Why, to the Lady Gelgéis.'

Eadulf glanced at Gormán, who seemed about to say something but then closed his mouth. However, Gobán saw the gesture and his eyes narrowed.

'Why do you ask about those barns?'

Eadulf decided there was nothing to lose by being honest.

'Because that is where we found the Lady Fidelma, tied up and gagged. Had we not found her and rescued her, she would surely have died.' Ignoring the shocked look on the face of the smith, Eadulf went on: 'There is still a dead body in the storehouse from which we released Fidelma. It is the body of Enán, the son of a ferryman, who was persuaded to act in place of one of the injured oarsmen in the abductor's boat. I suspect he was killed simply to prevent him identifying the abductors.'

'Perhaps a choice has come to confront you sooner than we thought,' observed Gormán dryly.

'The sheds have not been used during the last summer,' Gobán said, ignoring the implication. 'If the Lady Fidelma was abducted by these people, why was she left there for dead? Would that not be the opposite of what abduction is meant to achieve?'

'There are many mysteries that must be resolved,' Eadulf replied. 'Have you ever heard of a young poet called Torna?'

'The only Torna I know of was the famous Torna Eigeas who was bard to Niall of the Nine Hostages. He lived centuries ago.'

'This young man said he was also a bard.'

Gobán shook his head. 'I know of no other bard by that name.'

'Our Torna was certainly alive yesterday. He might even have been the intended victim of the abduction all along; maybe the Lady Fidelma tried to interfere and was taken, along with the victim.'

'I do not understand.'

Eadulf grinned sadly. 'We have little understanding ourselves. Tell us: what does this Lady Gelgéis use the storehouses for?'

'As I have said, they are mainly disused now. It is only when there is an excess of tribute coming in from the outlying clans who acknowledge her authority,' replied the smith. 'And when there has been a particularly good harvest.'

'So someone might have known that these storehouses were unused?'

Gobán hesitated and Gormán interpreted the pause: 'You are thinking that the storehouses are in full sight of the quays. If they were used in daylight it would have to be noticed and reported to the Lady Gelgéis.'

Gobán shrugged helplessly as he pondered the matter.

'What do you know of a leper who begs along the quays?' Eadulf suddenly asked, changing the subject.

'An old man with scarcely the use of his legs?' asked Gobán, and when Eadulf nodded confirmation he went on: 'That is Leathlobhair, or so we call him.'

'Half-leper?' Eadulf translated the name literally.

'Indeed. He has begged along the quayside ever since I can remember. I think he has a cabin in the rough glen just west of the township. Why do you ask about him?'

'Because it was Leathlobhair who saw Fidelma being taken into the storehouse from the river and alerted us to the fact.'

'In return for . . . ?' The smith smiled cynically.

'For food.'

'He would not be so altruistic as to provide information for nothing. However, neither would he lie. And so this was how you came to find the Lady Fidelma?'

'It was.'

'And did Leathlobhair see where the men who placed her there went after they had left?'

'He said they got back into their boat and let the current take it southwards.'

The smith pursed his lips thoughtfully. 'That would take them away from the township and the fortress. So it is clear they were not of the people of Durlus nor acting for Gelgéis, otherwise they would have gone into the town or up to the fortress.'

'At the moment, nothing is clear to me,' Eadulf sighed. 'We must wait for Fidelma to recover her senses and see if she can enlighten us.'

He rose and went across to the bed where Fidelma was lying. She was now breathing normally, and seemed in a deep, natural sleep.

'That is good,' he whispered in satisfaction. 'Sleep can be a great healer.'

There was but one bed in the smith's cabin, but he had sheepskin rugs to act as mattresses and these he spread on the floor before the fire and, with their woollen cloaks as blankets, the men stretched themselves out to get what rest they could. It was a long time before Eadulf could allow slumber to overtake him. He heard the rising snore of the smith and the deep breathing of Gormán long before he too fell asleep. Even then he dreamed of fast-flowing rivers, of Fidelma drowning, and shadowy figures descending on him with a knife. And then . . .

Then he was aware of the crackle of the fire and movement.

He blinked and sat up with a sleepy yawn. It was daylight and Gobán the smith was cooking something over the fire. Eadulf peered round for Gormán, but the warrior's place was empty. Then he looked at the bed. Fidelma was gone. He was on his feet in a moment, gazing around. Sleep had vanished from his mind.

'Where is—?' he began.

The door of the cabin suddenly opened and Fidelma stood there, wet-haired, with a linen cloth and her comb bag in her hands and a smile on her features.

'Where have you been?' Eadulf rapped out.

'Not quite the greeting I expected,' she replied primly. 'Gobán has a small spring at the back of the cabin where one can wash and recover a sense of being human. Thankfully, you recovered my *marsupium*, Eadulf, and hence I was able to find my comb bag.' Then her features broke into a smile, and she put down her things and turned to embrace him. Gobán bent to his cooking, pretending not to notice them as they kissed. 'For pursuing the abductors and saving my life, thank you is not an adequate phrase,' she whispered.

Eadulf felt a little foolish at his anxiety. 'I was just worried. How are you feeling?'

'Famished. Gobán here is preparing a meal so that I can break my fast – which fast I feel has lasted a lifetime. The soreness has gone from my throat. My lungs are properly full of air, and whatever you gave me has stimulated me into life again.'

'Where is Gormán?' he then asked nervously, changing the subject.

'I saw him checking the horses,' Fidelma replied, seating herself at the wooden table.

Eadulf picked up the sheepskin rugs, rolled them to one side and joined her.

'We have much to ask you,' he told her.

'As I, in turn, have much to ask you. But it can wait until Gormán joins us and we can indulge our appetites over Gobán's meal. He has told me roughly how you came here. It is a miracle that you were guided to this forge of all places. A heaven-sent coincidence that I knew his sister, Sister Poitigéir at Cill Dara, and was able to render her a service.'

The door opened and Gormán entered. He paused to sniff the aromas from Gobán's cooking appreciatively. Breakfast was usually a light meal, for the principal meal of the day was the *prainn*, which was taken in the evening. Usually, at midday the *eter-shod*, or middle meal, was also a light meal. But this morning, in view of Fidelma's hunger, Gobán was basting trout with honey on an *indeoin* or gridiron. There was fresh bread, for apparently Gobán had an arrangement with a neighbour to bring him bread while, in exchange, she could call on his services as a smith. There was also butter, plenty of honey, a dish of apples and hazel-nuts, and a pitcher of cold water from his spring or a jug of ale to drink.

At their enthusiastic comments, Gobán smiled deprecatingly. 'After my wife departed this world, I had to maintain myself,' he said, as he gave them wooden platters and indicated that they should help themselves. There were even basins of water provided, for the custom was to use a knife in the right hand and eat with the fingers of the left hand, cleaning them in the water and drying them with a *lámbrat* or hand cloth.

Eadulf was not as hungry as the others and so took the opportunity to narrate what had happened to Gormán and himself since they awoke to find Fidelma and the young man, Torna, gone. Once more Fidelma regarded him with grateful eyes.

When he had finished, Fidelma had completed her meal and was sitting back sipping at a beaker of water.

'Now it is time for your tale,' prompted Eadulf softly.

'There is little in the telling,' she replied. 'Little, that is, you have not guessed.'

'Better that we hear it from your lips.'

Gormán nodded vigorously. 'Indeed, lady. What has happened to you is a great outrage against the honour of the Eóghanacht. I am responsible to your brother, the King, for your welfare.'

Fidelma smiled briefly.

'We were, as you recall, all asleep on the riverbank. I was disturbed by our horses. Aonbharr was fretful. I woke just in time to see the shadows of men behind you both as you slept. You, Eadulf, had begun to stir but things happened so quickly. The men hit you both on the head . . .'

Eadulf ruefully rubbed his head. 'And a sharp blow it was. However, Gormán suffered the worst.'

At once Fidelma looked concerned. 'I should have enquired about that sooner.'

'It was nothing, lady,' Gormán reassured her. 'I've had a split skull before. Thanks to friend Eadulf's skills, the abrasions have begun to heal and the throbbing of the hammers in my skull receded.'

'Just as I would expect from one with his fine skills,' she said gravely, a smile at the corner of her mouth.

'What did you do then?' demanded Eadulf uncomfortably.

'I sprang to my feet. It was still dark but the moon was up so I could see the attackers, although I could not distinguish their features clearly. I heard a noise behind me, swung round and saw Torna fighting with another man, but a fourth was coming towards me. As you know, I am trained in the *troid-sciathagid* . . .'

The Battle through Defence was an old form of unarmed combat which it was said had first been taught by the Druids in the days before the New Faith had come to the land. However, although many of the practices of the Old Religion had been forbidden, this technique was taught to travelling religious as a means of defending themselves against robbers without resorting to the use of weapons and breaking their religious vows not to take a life.

'And what happened?'

'I let the man come at me and used the momentum of his attack to send him flying into the man who had knocked you unconscious. I heard him scream. Later I realised my attacker had knocked into the man who held a knife and this had cut his hand.'

'So that's why they needed another rower when they reached the ferryman's house,' muttered Gormán.

'Go on,' Eadulf urged, ignoring the comment.

'I heard a cry from behind me; turned and saw Torna falling to the ground. His attacker was holding a club. I made ready to face the man. Then I must have been hit on the head as well. Everything thereafter seems to have passed in a semi-waking dream. I know I was bound and that awful gag placed in my mouth. There were snatches of conversation.'

'Such as?'

'Torna seemed to have recovered and was telling them to leave me alone as I was not his companion.'

Eadulf looked up quickly. 'Not his companion?'

'I know that they laughed at him. Someone else replied that they were paid to capture him and his woman.'

'But it tells us something, surely,' said Eadulf. 'It tells us that you were not the object of their abduction. They did not know who you were.'

'That is true,' agreed Fidelma.

'Why would a poet be worthy of abduction? And who was the companion that they thought you were?' asked Gormán.

Fidelma sighed deeply. 'Torna is the mystery. The only thing he told me was that he had been in love with a girl, her parents had disapproved of him and he and she had eloped. She was apparently drowned trying to escape with him across a river, although he survived. After that, he said he became a wandering bard. That is all he told me of himself. So why did these people appear out of nowhere and attack our party and abduct him?'

'You'll recall that a man and a woman stayed with Brother Ailgesach, the night the envoy was killed?' Eadulf pointed out. 'Maybe they thought that you and Torna were that couple.'

'But they both were on horseback going north. Torna said he was looking for a boat to go south.'

'Are we *sure* that you were not the intended victim?' added Gormán. 'After all, you are sister to the King of Cashel.'

Fidelma shook her head quickly. 'They did not know who I was. They thought I was just his companion.'

'When did they finally learn their mistake?'

'I do not think it was until we reached the place where they left me.'

'They did not find out before?'

'I did come round a few times before then. Once I heard the man, the one whose hand had been injured, moaning and saying that he could not row much further in such strong currents. An argument ensued.

The injured man wanted us thrown overboard to lessen the weight. The man in charge repeated that they had been paid to bring both man and woman. I heard something about picking up another rower who could be disposed of later.'

Eadulf grimaced ruefully. 'They did that, right enough. They killed Enán, the poor ferryman's son whom they persuaded to go along. We found his body in the storehouse with you last night: they had cut his throat. But what you say presents another mystery. Who would know that Torna was on the riverbank that night? Although there was moon-light, it was not that bright, so how did they find us in the dark? They must have known he was there.'

Fidelma looked grim. 'You'll be a Brehon yet, Eadulf,' she said. 'Well, it was darkness that saved my life. I came to again when I was being carried into what I now know to be the storehouse. The sacking was removed from my face. A lamp was lit and held over me, and someone swore violently. "This is not her! Anyway, you have handled this woman too roughly. She is near death."' I should be grateful that the speaker had little knowledge of the physician's art. Another voice said: "Let's slit her throat and be on our way."' Fidelma paused for a moment before continuing. 'Then the man who seemed to be their leader said: "No need for that. She'll be dead soon." The sack was drawn back over my face and, indeed, I lay like one already dead. In fact, I passed out again. And then you came.'

Eadulf uttered a soft whistle. 'Thank Providence that they did not learn their mistake. But so many questions! This web is as tangled as ever.'

'We must resolve this mystery,' Fidelma said quietly. 'Why did they want Torna? Who was he and who was the woman they mistook me for? Were they looking for the couple who stayed with Ailgesach? Why is a wandering bard so important to be thus abducted? Where did they take him?'

'The witness who saw the abductors arrive at the shed said a religieux was waiting for them. After two sacks, which contained you and Torna, were bundled into the storehouse, the four abductors came out with Torna and the religieux, and climbed into the boat. They had killed Enán and left you to die. They all went downriver again.'

'They went south?' queried Fidelma.

'Yes. Perhaps the religieux was Biasta,' suggested Gormán.

'Logical thinking,' Fidelma approved, 'but it brings us nowhere near to solving this mystery.'

'You said that Torna had a problem with the parents of the girl he eloped with,' Gormán pointed out. 'Can that help us? Perhaps there was some blood feud generated by this.'

'You mean her parents hired these people to abduct him?' Eadulf shook his head cynically.

'It could happen,' said Gormán. 'Especially if she was some noble's daughter.'

'I thought your laws have covered such matters so that there is no recourse to vengeance?' Eadulf queried. 'Even if the girl objects to the elopement, if she is forced to cohabit with the man, then the abductor must pay the girl's honour price. If the girl died during the abduction then the punishment is honour price and body price. But if the girl went with him willingly, a voluntary abduction or elopement, then the family of the girl are not so entitled.'

Fidelma seemed pleased with Eadulf. 'That is true,' she told him, and then added, 'Well done. Your knowledge of our law increases by the day. Anyway, it does dispose of that argument.'

Gormán said moodily, 'I can see nothing that fits together. The murdered envoy from Laigin, the matter of Brother Ailgesach and Biasta, now the abduction of a poet and a mysterious woman who should have been with him.'

'We will have to form a plan—' began Fidelma, but she was

interrupted by the clanging of a bell. She glanced at the others in startled fashion.

Gobán rose. 'Don't worry; it is the bell outside my forge. If I am not there, customers ring for me.'

He left them and hurried to answer the summoning of the bell. Gormán also rose and followed the smith from the cabin. He was back within moments looking nervous.

'Warriors,' he muttered. 'Four men on horseback are questioning the smith. One of them is a warrior who wears the colours of Laigin.'

CHAPTER ELEVEN

Gobán returned a short time later, a worried expression on his features.

'What is wrong?' asked Eadulf as soon as he entered the cabin.

'They were merchants from Laigin escorted by a warrior who was concerned about a loose shoe on his horse. I told him that I had not lit my forge fire to be able to attend to it. The fortress has its own smith, so I suggested that if they were going there, they could claim hospitality as travellers. The warrior, being a stranger, will doubtless get it mended for nothing and the shoe will hold out that far.'

'You were a long time talking with them,' observed Gormán suspiciously.

Gobán seemed too preoccupied to notice his tone. 'They came with some strange news,' he went on.

'What news was this?' asked Fidelma, for clearly it had impressed the smith.

'They came from the territory of the Uí Fidgente. As they crossed the Valley of An Mháigh they saw several small churches and communities that had been laid waste.'

'Did they give any further details?' Fidelma remembered the reports of burnings and massacres that had been brought to Cashel by Abbot Ségdae.

'They saw the ruins and devastation but encountered hardly anyone who could tell them what was happening. Those they did meet told of bandits, raiders from the western mountains.'

'I have heard stories of these raiders before,' Fidelma said.

'And we were told by the ferryman that the place where we camped, the ruined church and tavern, had been burned down about a week ago in one such raid,' Eadulf informed her. 'Did these merchants know anything else?'

'The strangest thing was that one religious they spoke to told them that the leader of the raiders was a woman. He described her as a wild hell-cat who led the raiders carrying what appeared to be a religious banner.'

Fidelma's eyes widened. 'A woman, you say?'

'And what sort of religious banner?' Eadulf wanted to know. 'Why would they be attacking communities of other religious?'

'I can only tell you what the merchants told me,' Gobán replied. He then said: 'Forgive me, lady, but I had better start making up the fire in the forge for I have work to do.'

After the smith had left, Gorman commented: 'Probably it is the Uí Fidgente, causing trouble.'

Fidelma had to admit that this had been her own reaction when she had first heard of the raids from Abbot Ségdae. Now she responded: 'I heard similar news before we left Cashel, and Dego was sent with a hundred warriors to discover more. The burnings and massacres were reported across the lands of the Uí Fidgente, so the attacks seemed to be aimed at them as much as anyone else. From what Abbot Ségdae said, there was no apparent reason for the wanton destruction.'

'Curious as this news is, there are more urgent matters that we should be concerned with,' Eadulf concluded.

Fidelma stirred uncomfortably. Eadulf was right. She suddenly felt a new vigour after her ordeal as she looked at her companions.

'We three will proceed to the fortress and speak with the Lady Gelgéis. After all, there is the matter of the body of the poor ferryman in a shed owned by her.'

Gormán raised his eyebrows in surprise. 'Is that wise, lady? Do you mean to confront her?'

'Not confront her but only to ask questions,' she corrected.

'You know that there are many in Cashel, advisers in your brother's council, who do not trust Gelgéis? Those who abducted you might even be working for her. If so, you are putting yourself in harm's way. They could find out that you did not die from asphyxiation and might be able to identify them. Also, if the body of the poor ferryman's son has been discovered, or if we were seen, or even if this beggar, Leathlobhair, reports us, well . . . there are so many things that can present dangers to you.'

'Nevertheless, my intention is clear,' replied Fidelma firmly. 'If harm came to me in Gelgéis's fortress then she would know the consequences. She would have to answer to my brother and the Eóghanacht.'

Gobán had entered and overheard her last words. Now he stood with a harried expression on his face.

'I have told your companions, lady, that I am loyal to the Éile and the Lady Gelgéis. I will not be party to any conspiracy that harms them. I have helped thus far because of what you did for my sister.'

Fidelma rose and laid a hand reassuringly on his shoulder. 'I give you my word that we are not seeking to harm anyone, only seeking truth, Gobán. We are going to see Gelgéis to discover whether she is able to help us with finding that truth. As a guarantee of our good intentions, we shall leave our horses and baggage here with you, and shall walk the short distance up to her fortress. Do you agree?'

The smith looked embarrassed. 'I will accept your word, lady,' he acknowledged.

'The walk will do us good – rather, it will do me good,' she continued briskly. 'It is uncomfortable to spend over a day bound hand and foot in the bottom of a boat and not be able to flex a muscle or limb. I need to take the exercise. So the horses will remain here.'

She turned to Eadulf. 'We are going to meet the Princess of the Éile.' She paused and smiled. 'And you have not washed this morning. Better use the spring at the back and make yourself presentable.' She picked up her linen towel and threw it at him. He caught it and pulled a face at her. It was true, however, that he was feeling in need of a wash. They had bathed in the river when they had all camped by it. But since then, they had ridden all day to Durlus and then spent all night in the smith's cabin. Once more he was reminded of the strict toilet customs of the people of the Five Kingdoms. In the morning, they would wash face and hands, while each evening they would have a bath, a full body-wash. In both washing and bathing they used a soap called *sléic* and Eadulf had become used also to using an *altan*, a razor to shave with. This was a sharp piece of steel that he always carried with him. He had even grown used to using a *cíor* or comb to sort out the tangle of his hair. In a peculiar way he was growing used to the routine and even enjoyed it. During his childhood in Seaxmund's Ham, he was lucky to take a regular dip in the river.

The others were waiting impatiently when he returned. The clang of metal told him that Gobán had returned to his forge and was starting to fire up his furnace.

It was a bright and warm autumnal morning. This time, in their walk from Gobán's forge, Eadulf could appreciate the pleasant approach through the outer buildings of the township. The hedgerow was interspersed with birch trees with their silver-white bark. Among them were groups of elders, their blue-black berries still ripening. The hedgerow was alive. He could see wood pigeons and a shrill, rattling warble announced the presence of wrens somewhere nearby.

'I wonder if they have discovered the body of the ferryman's son yet?' muttered Gormán, gazing tensely about him.

Fidelma seemed to have recovered her dry sense of humour. 'We will soon learn if they have.'

They followed the road leading into the main square of the town, where Eadulf and Gormán had encountered the lonely girl selling her bread and cheese. This time the square was crowded. Various merchants had set up stalls and there was even entertainment from jugglers and tumblers. The noise of the crowd was loud. Everyone seemed to be enjoying themselves and no one took any notice of a few more strangers strolling through the market square.

They halted at the edge of the square and gazed about with interest. There were many merchants and visitors in the town, presumably most having attended the Lady Gelgéis's feasting on the previous day. Fidelma led them up the incline towards the tall wooden gates of the fortress, which gave its name to Durlus Éile. It dominated the jumble of smaller buildings below it. These structures stretched from the quays on the edge of the river upwards until they were halted as if by an invisible border some distance before the walls. Those responsible for the defence of the fortress would be lacking in skill if they allowed buildings to encroach any nearer the walls and threaten their security.

The gates stood wide open with a single warrior planted firmly in the middle of the path that led through this portal. He had one hand on his hip, the other on the hilt of his sword. He watched their approach with an inquisitive expression. They halted before him.

'Fidelma of Cashel demands an audience with Gelgéis of the Éile.' Gormán spoke in a ringing tone of authority.

The warrior stared at Gormán, his eyes falling on his golden torque, which Gormán had now resumed wearing. Fidelma had produced her own emblem of authority from her comb bag. He hesitated, looking from one to another, before inclining his head in acknowledgement towards Fidelma. 'Follow me,' he said courteously, and led them through the gates and across a large stone-flagged courtyard where groups of warriors and servants hurried to and fro. The interior of the fortress gave the impression of a bustling centre with its own on-site smithy. Nearby were warriors busy sharpening their weapons on a grinder. Merchants were loading or unloading their wares from mule carts, and other groups were just standing exchanging gossip. There was an atmosphere of prosperity about the place.

A man with short, greying hair and penetrating black eyes stood on the steps of the main building watching their approach. He was cleanshaven, with sallow skin and a jutting jawline. His dress proclaimed him as someone of rank albeit not a warrior, in spite of a short sword attached to his belt and a gold chain of office hung about his neck.

The warrior halted before him and saluted.

'Fidelma of Cashel seeks an audience with the Lady Gelgéis,' relayed their guide, diplomatically changing Gormán's 'demands' to 'seeks'.

The man's eyes swept over them and then he bowed to Fidelma.

'I am Spealáin, steward to the Lady Gelgéis,' he announced in a pleasant but authoritative voice. 'Welcome to Durlus Éile, lady. We had no word of your approach. You seem to have arrived on foot.'

Fidelma did not respond to this, but introduced her companions instead.

'You are all welcome,' Spealáin told them. 'The fame of Fidelma and Eadulf is known here, as among all the Five Kingdoms. I will announce your presence to Lady Gelgéis. However, it is our rule that armed warriors shall remain outside of my lady's personal quarters unless expressly invited.'

Fidelma turned to Gormán with a tone of apology. 'I am sure you will be able to pass the time usefully while we are within,' she said. She did not need to be more specific, in hinting that Gormán should see what gossip he could pick up that might be of use to them. Gormán acknowledged her wish with a brief nod.

'Come this way,' the steward instructed.

He ushered them up the steps into what was the Great Hall. Eadulf whistled to himself as they entered. It was clear that the place had access to the wealth and the produce of merchants from many quarters. It was also clear that Gelgéis appreciated such wealth. Tapestries and statues vied with shields and swords and such weapons which had never seen a battle but had been made purely for show. Tables and chairs of excellent quality were placed strategically. The steward waved to a female attendant and instructed her to inform the Lady Gelgéis of the identity of her unexpected visitors. The attendant peeped towards Fidelma with something like awe before scurrying away on her errand.

There were a few moments of awkward silence, while Spealáin took up a position just inside the main doors, leaving Fidelma and Eadulf standing alone, waiting. It seemed an overly long time before a door at the back of the hall opened and a woman entered. Eadulf was surprised by her youth. She was of average height and slim. Her hair was corn-coloured, with a faint haze of gold, tightly pulled back from her face in a style Eadulf had never seen before. Her full lips were balanced by fair skin accentuating delicate boned features, and her eyes were azure blue. There was the quality of an innocent child about her. Her garments spoke of richness, the blue-dyed silks well embroidered with numerous coloured threads, the predominant one being gold. She looked exactly what she was – a princess.

The girl, for Eadulf could hardly call her a woman, stopped before Fidelma and inclined her head in acknowledgement. Only after she did so, did Fidelma bow her head, though not as deeply – a subtle reminder that while Gelgéis was Princess of the Éile, Fidelma was sister to the King of Muman.

'You are welcome here, Fidelma.' The girl's voice was soft and musical to match her looks. 'I was not expecting you or I would have made preparations to receive you according to your rank.'

'I was not exactly expecting to come, Gelgéis, but my footsteps led me here. Allow me to introduce my husband, Eadulf of Seaxmund's Ham, in the country of the South Folk.' She paused and added with a smile: 'He is an Angle.'

The blue eyes turned on Eadulf as he bowed slightly. This time Gelgéis did not return the courtesy, for protocol did not demand it. She switched her gaze back to Fidelma.

'I had heard that you had married a stranger, and one of the religious. I have also heard that you have withdrawn from the religious and sought the office of Chief Brehon to your brother, the King.'

The words were softly spoken and Eadulf wondered if they disguised some antagonism.

'Then you will also have heard,' Fidelma replied, equally softly, 'that I was not successful in the matter but remain a *dálaigh* still able to pursue the law.'

'Indeed?' The girl smiled. 'News has a propensity to travel quickly but, alas, it often reaches its destination in a form different to that in which it starts out. I hear that it is said that there will soon be a royal wedding feast in Cashel?'

'I, too, have heard such speculation,' replied Fidelma blandly, 'but I am not able to confirm or deny it.'

'Indeed?' Gelgéis frowned thoughtfully for a moment. 'I believe that the people of Gabrán are already celebrating. But then the clans of Osraige can be impulsive. As they are our close neighbours, we are often caught up in their capricious behaviour. Doubtless, then, you have met the Lady Dúnliath?'

'I have, indeed.' Fidelma felt a momentary annoyance at being distracted from the purpose of her visit.

'A pleasant girl,' sighed Gelgéis, 'but not overly endowed with intelligence. Oh, do not look so shocked, lady,' she hurried on, observing Fidelma's expression. 'I have already met her, since she accompanied her father Drón here on her way to Cashel. She gives the impression that she has little time for pursuits of the mind. However, I suspect that she is far from just stupid.'

'If my brother, the King, does choose her for his wife, I think that it would mean that she is very *far* from stupid,' replied Fidelma coldly. Then she frowned. 'How is it they passed through Durlus on their way to Cashel? It is not a direct route.'

'I understand that the Lady Dúnliath expressed a desire to visit our poor market here. We often get merchants from the north bringing interesting goods to sell.' She paused. 'I trust your brother, Colgú, is well?'

'He is well, lady.' Fidelma wondered if there was anything unspoken that she should read into the query.

Gelgéis turned towards one of her female attendants who were standing in the background and beckoned her forward. 'But forgive me, lady. Let me offer you both refreshments as I hear that you have arrived at my fortress on foot. I hope nothing untoward has happened to your horses, as it is a long way from Cashel to Durlus Éile.'

'Rest assured that we have not walked all the way from Cashel. In fact, I came a good part of the way by boat.'

A puzzled look passed over Gelgéis's features.

'An odd mode of travel and not a safe one,' she said rather coolly. Fidelma realised that Gelgéis's glance had fallen to her sleeve. There was a tear in it which she had not noticed. But Gelgéis was continuing: 'It would increase both the distance and the time, and your rowers must be exhausted for they would be rowing against the current of the river.'

Fidelma's smile broadened. 'I do not think we need fear for the exhaustion of the rowers.'

The Princess seemed a little at a loss, and when Fidelma did not offer any further explanation, she conducted them to some chairs before the hearth and indicated they be seated, saying, 'Well, sooner you than me. I nearly lost my life swimming in a river. These days, I always travel on horse rather than entrust myself to a boat. I hate the water. Anyway, what brings you to Durlus Éile?' she asked, changing the subject. 'It is many a year since I saw you, Fidelma. Usually I hear of you passing on the road to Tara or proceeding somewhere else, but never coming to Durlus Éile.'

'You were invited to our wedding,' Fidelma reminded her.

'Alas, I had an ague at that time. I was assured my envoy explained matters to your brother, the King. But at least I am well enough to attend your brother's nuptials.'

'I am sorry to hear that you were not well enough to attend my wedding. One should be careful of one's health and well-being. Eadulf here has the gift of healing, having studied at Tuaim Brecain. Without his knowledge I might well have suffocated last night.'

Once again a puzzled frown flickered on Gelgéis's features as she glanced at Eadulf but then addressed her remarks to Fidelma.

'Suffocated? Well, I am pleased to see that you have recovered, lady. But you have not spoken of the purpose of your visit. Are you simply passing through Durlus?'

'I am looking for someone.'

'And this someone is . . . ?' She paused while two attendants came in with a pitcher of ale and some freshly baked breadcakes. When they had departed, she repeated: 'Who do you seek?'

'Is the name Brother Biasta known to you?'

Gelgéis immediately shook her head. 'The name means nothing to me. Obviously, he is a religieux. If so, my bishop here might know, He is called Daig. I can call him in, if you like.'

'I would appreciate that,' agreed Fidelma.

Gelgéis gestured across to Spealáin, her steward, who had remained present throughout, at a discreet distance.

'Why are you trying to find this religieux?' she asked when he had hurried off to find the bishop.

'I'll explain further when Bishop Daig arrives. It will save me explaining twice,' Fidelma replied, and immediately turned the conversation to inconsequential matters such as the artwork on one of the tapestries.

Bishop Daig was a small, chubby man, with full red cheeks and tufts of silver-white hair around a bald pate. His eyes were soft blue but one held a slight cast. He looked like someone who should be constantly laughing, but his features at that moment were actually set and wary.

'Brother Biasta? The name means nothing to me. Where does he come from?'

Fidelma countered the question with another.

'Perhaps you know Brother Ailgesach?' This brought an immediate reaction. A startled look was exchanged between Gelgéis and the bishop. 'So you have heard his name before?' she pressed.

'Brother Ailgesach?' It was the bishop who answered for both of them. 'We both know poor Brother Ailgesach. He was here in Durlus Éile only a short time ago, but he has gone south to Fraigh Dubh. Perhaps I know him better than most. You see, we both studied at the Blessed Brendan's community at Biorra.'

'Why do you say "poor"?' Fidelma asked sharply.

Bishop Daig uttered a slight sigh. 'Drink, that is why. But you must have passed his little chapel at Fraigh Dubh if you have come from Cashel?'

For a moment Fidelma did not answer but then asked: 'Can you tell me anything about him?'

'Would it not be more fitting to address such questions directly to Brother Ailgesach himself?' intervened Gelgéis.

'It would be impossible to ask anything of him,' Eadulf said dryly. Then, as they turned to stare at him, he added: 'He is dead.'

There was a sharp intake of breath from Gelgéis. She averted her head so that it was difficult to see her expression. Bishop Daig's eyes had widened in surprise and then he slowly shook his head with a sad expression.

'I suppose the drink was his downfall? Poor man.'

'That is the second time you have used that word,' pointed out Fidelma. 'In what manner do you think he became so poor?'

'You mean, what drove him to drink?'

'Yes, precisely that,' replied Fidelma irritably. 'You say that you studied with him at Biorra. Please – tell us what you know.'

'I know that Brother Ailgesach was a kind and caring person. He had ambition to become a physician but was unable to complete his studies, lacking as he was in the aptitude to wield the physician's knife, which is as necessary as the ability to hand out potions.'

Eadulf, having studied the healing arts, knew well that the ancient laws made clear provision about qualified physicians and there were severe penalties for those who tried to practise without qualification. Eadulf knew of no other people in the lands he had travelled where such detailed laws applied. The lawmakers seemed to know that it was easy to deceive people who were ill and, desperately seeking a cure, would grasp at anyone who claimed that they were able to heal them. Indeed, even qualified physicians were responsible for the well-being of their patients, and if their treatments went wrong, if a wound that the physician treated broke open within a certain time, the physician had to refund his fees, or pay compensation, and allow a better physician to be brought into the case.

'So after he failed to become a physician?' Fidelma prompted.

'He offered to help look after the sick; to nurse them.'

'At Biorra?'

'Initially. Then he left the abbey and wandered to the land of the Eóghanacht Áine in the west.'

'In a religious house?'

'In a house of the territory.'

Eadulf knew that the *forus tuaithe*, or 'house of the territory', was one of the many secular hospitals for common use, governed by strict rules of the law of the Brehons. It was claimed that the great queen, Macha Mong-Ruadh, who had become ruler of all the Five Kingdoms at Tara in the times beyond memory, had ordered the first hospital to be set up in the place that still bore her name – Emain Macha. Now there were hospitals and leper houses to be found in most territories of the Five Kingdoms. They were all under the patronage of local nobles. The laws were very specific. The hospital was to be clean, ventilated, have running water, be accessed by four doors, and have a staff of trained physicians. If people could not afford to pay for the food, medicine and the attendance of the physician, it was provided. The poor had no fear of being refused treatment, for the law stated that the patient's relatives or the clan itself were liable for the *folach-othrusa* or sick maintenance. Anyone who was injured was maintained by those who had caused the injury.

'So he worked looking after the sick as an attendant in a *broinbherg*.' Fidelma used the popular euphemism for a hospital – 'House of Sorrow'. It had been the name of Macha's first foundation. 'Then what?'

'I had news of him from time to time. I heard that he had volunteered to go on to another hospital further west, and lately I was told that he had started drinking while he was looking after the sick at that place.'

'Do you know where that was?'

'He went to serve the unfortunates in Gleann na nGeilt.'

Eadulf frowned at an elusive memory. 'I have heard of that place before.'

Bishop Daig went on: 'It is called the Glen of Lunatics. It is a place among the western mountains where many unfortunates are consigned, those whose minds have passed beyond the reality of our world. Those who have lost their reason.'

Eadulf suddenly recalled where he had heard of it. It was the place where one of the murderers whom he and Fidelma had uncovered at Lios Mór had been consigned when it was clear they were insane.

'Is it not a dangerous place?' he asked.

'The lunatics are guarded not only for their own protection but for that of others,' explained Bishop Daig. 'Those who tend to their needs are volunteers and poor Brother Ailgesach was one of those who took on this task. He was there nursing the demented for many years, and doubtless it was that experience which turned him to an excess of drink.'

'So he eventually left Gleann na nGeilt – what then?' asked Fidelma.

'That was only a short time ago. Abbot Ségdae of Imleach, under whose auspices Gleann na nGeilt is governed, found him a place where it was thought his duties would not be too arduous and would allow him to recover. It was the small chapel at Fraigh Dubh. That was just two weeks or so ago. Now you tell me that he has drunk himself to death.'

'Eadulf said he was dead, not that he drank himself to death,' corrected Fidelma. Before the surprised bishop could answer she went on: 'So having known Brother Ailgesach for so long, and studied with him at the Abbey at Biorra, I do not understand why you say that you do not know Brother Biasta.'

Bishop Daig looked bewildered, replying, 'I have told you that I have never heard the name. Who is he?'

'He told us that he was a cousin of Ailgesach and studied with him at Biorra.'

Bishop Daig was obviously puzzled and he looked towards Gelgéis as if seeking guidance. 'I can assure you that there was no one called

Biasta who studied with us at Biorra. Who did you say this man was?'

'He claimed to be a cousin of Ailgesach and said that they were of the Muscraige Tíre from Tír Dhá Ghlas by the red loch.'

The bishop was regarding her as if she were mad.

'You are clearly mistaken, lady. Ailgesach was of the Éile and from this very town – indeed, as am I. He was not from Tír Dhá Ghlas.'

'Then Ailgesach was not the son of pious farmers?' Eadulf said heavily, knowing what the answer would be.

'Where did you get such false information? Ailgesach was the son of a merchant boatman on the river here. The father was drowned when he was young. We went to the Abbey of Biorra to study together. He had no cousin called Biasta, so far as I was aware, and certainly no one of that name studied with us at Biorra.'

Somehow Fidelma was not surprised at this news but she asked a further question. 'I presume, then, that there is no one called Biasta in Durlus Éile?'

'We have told you that it is a name that neither of us is acquainted with,' Gelgéis said tightly, breaking her long silence. It was obvious that the news of the death of Ailgesach had affected her, for her face was very pale. 'Indeed, no one of the Éile would call a child by that name.'

Fidelma started. She had not realised the connection before. The word *biasta* meant a monster. How stupid of her to overlook the fact.

'You said Brother Ailgesach came here not long ago?' Fidelma went on, trying to pick up a thread.

'Bishop Daig told you, he came here a few weeks ago. What is the meaning of these questions that you are asking, Fidelma? Is there some mystery here that we should know? After all, Ailgesach was from this township. You said he is dead – but you also said that he did not die from an excess of alcohol. What *did* he die of?'

'You are right in that there is a mystery. At the moment, there is nothing I can tell you except that Brother Ailgesach was smothered while in a drunken stupor, and the circumstances point to this man who called himself his cousin – Brother Biasta – as the culprit. That is why we seek him.'

There was a shocked silence. Gelgéis was regarding Fidelma with a horrified expression. She licked her lips as if they had suddenly gone dry.

'Why do you seek this man in Durlus, the man you say killed Ailgesach?'

'He was last seen heading north in this direction.'

'Because he was heading north from Fraigh Dubh, it does not mean to say he was heading for Durlus Éile,' Gelgéis protested. 'Any strange religious passing through or staying in the township would have been noticed and mentioned. Just as we heard that yesterday, two strangers were in the town. One of the strangers was obviously Brother Eadulf. The other was a warrior.'

'That was well observed,' muttered Eadulf, almost to himself.

'I believe that the man calling himself Brother Biasta might well have come here,' Fidelma said.

'What makes you think so? There are many paths that he could have taken.'

'Because I am no believer in coincidence, only the wind of fate.'

There was a concerned expression on Gelgéis's features before the Princess of the Éile shook her head firmly. 'Were I not aware of your reputation, I would say that you are playing games here and wasting our time. I feel you trespass on our hospitality. State plainly what you mean.'

'The storehouses on the far side of the river, the ones just opposite the quays – I am told that they are your own storehouses. Is that correct?'

'I do not deny that they are mine.'

'In one of them you will find the body of a young man. His name is Enán. He was the son of a ferryman called Echna who plies his trade on the river just to the south. He was murdered in your storehouse.'

There was no questioning that the news shocked the Princess. Daig had also sat back with an expression of horror.

'How do you know this?' demanded Spealáin, stepping forward.

'Because I, too, was nearly killed there. I'll come to the detail in a moment, but please tell me when you last used those buildings.'

Gelgéis motioned to her steward, who answered for her. 'They have not been used this summer,' he replied. 'The harvest has not been bountiful enough to fill them as well as my other stores. In fact, we have not used them for well over a year.'

'No one else has permission to use them?'

'Of course not.'

'Then I will tell you how I came to know of this matter.' Fidelma quickly filled them in with the broad details of the abduction of Torna and herself. 'In all these matters, I am acting under the authority of my brother, the King, and will exhort your cooperation and support in my investigation. I believe it is all part of one mystery.'

Gelgéis was silent for a while. Her features were now pale and haggard as she said slowly: 'You have stated your authority and I accept it. You have but to call on me for any assistance you may need.'

'Some assistance I shall need immediately, for I cannot spare my companions,' Fidelma replied straight away. 'I need to ask that the body of the young man who was murdered in that storehouse be transported back to his father, Echna, the ferryman.'

'It shall be done,' Gelgéis said quietly.

'Echna is to be assured that the culprits will be found and compensation obtained for the loss of his son,' Fidelma continued.

The princess inclined her head. 'Very well. How else can we help?

You intend to go in pursuit of this man you call Torna and his abductors?'

'I do. I do not suppose the name Torna means anything to you?'

Gelgéis blinked and then shook her head. 'This is the name of the poet, who was abducted with you? This man . . . er, Torna – was he injured?'

'We were told that when he was removed from the storehouse, he was able to walk between two of the abductors and sat in the stern of the boat that removed him,' offered Eadulf.

'Are you sure that he is unknown to you?' questioned Fidelma.

'I know of no one by that name,' Gelgéis told her. 'The boat went south, you say?'

'It did,' Fidelma replied, rising from her seat. She realised she could not interrogate Gelgéis further but sensed there was some link. 'You will excuse us. There is much to do and little time to do it.'

'Then let my steward know what you want. You have only to ask. But a word of caution, Fidelma. To the east of us, as you must know, lies the territory of the People of the Deer – the Osraige. It is a border territory where not everything is as it seems. Remember that, Fidelma of Cashel. Have a care.'

They took their formal leave and found Gormán waiting impatiently for them in the courtyard.

'Well, any news?' he greeted.

'All of it negative,' replied Fidelma. 'Did you discover anything from people's gossip?'

'Only one piece of news seems to be of relevance to us.' It was clear Gormán felt it was of some importance.

'Which is?'

'I found one of the local farmers who had been on his way here last evening for the festivities. He had arrived by boat just before dusk with his sons from his farm on the other side of the river. They came down the River Dríse, a tributary of the Suir which flows into the river just a short distance south-east of the township.'

'Are you going to tell me that he saw the boat with the abductors?' asked Fidelma, leaping ahead of him.

For a second Gormán looked disappointed that she had guessed his news. 'Indeed, he did. There was a religieux in the bow and two men rowing. Three were seated in the stern of the boat,' Gormán replied. 'The farmers confirmed that the young man who sat in the centre of the two in the stern did not look happy, and his companions seemed to have an unusually tight hold of him. The boat was moving upstream along the Dríse.'

Eadulf grimaced. 'Well, wherever they were going they have a full day's head-start on us, if we are to follow.'

'I know part of that river,' offered Gormán. 'It leads straight into the heart of Osraige territory.'

This information made them think. Then Fidelma asked: 'Was there any other news that you were able to pick up?'

'Nothing that can help us. But I did see those Laigin merchants who stopped at the forge this morning. They were still full of the gossip relating to the strange attacks in the west – the burning of churches and communities. They said that they had even encountered a fellow merchant who had fled from the west and saw part of this band of raiders. He was able to hide in a cave and escape their attention.'

'Was anything in particular noticed, anything that could identify who the raiders were?'

'Only what they told the smith – that the raiders were led by a woman who carried some sort of religious banner. The merchant I spoke to said that the curious thing was that, although she led roughly clad bandits, she herself was dressed in purple with a great scarlet cloak deckled with gold and precious gems.'

'Strange, indeed,' muttered Fidelma, pondering the information.

'It was told at third hand,' shrugged Gormán, 'so perhaps it should not be taken as fact. Stories are embellished the longer they take in spreading.'

'Perhaps,' Fidelma said absently. 'Even so, it is a strange tale to invent if untrue.'

The three walked slowly back to Gobán's forge in sombre mood. The entrance was deserted, although the coals in the fire still burned red-hot. The back of the forge, leading to the man's cabin, was dark and empty. Gormán called out to let the smith know that they had returned. There was no answer. He found the bell which the smith had placed for customers to call him when he was not in the forge, and rang it. There was still no answer to its summons, however.

'He'll be in the cabin,' Eadulf suggested. 'He won't be far away with the fire still alight.'

Eadulf led the way out of the back door of the forge towards the cabin. Then he halted when he saw the smith standing before him. His back was pressed against the wall of the dwelling; his arms were spread out as if in a position of surrender, and he was staring at Eadulf in wide-eyed terror. Eadulf was about to demand what the matter was when he felt a prick against his neck and a voice hissed. 'Throw down your weapons, if you want to live.'

CHAPTER TWELVE

'Put up your sword, Enda!' came Fidelma's quiet voice.
Eadulf heard an audible gasp and swung round. Enda was in the act of lowering his sword in embarrassment. He was apologetic as he sheathed his weapon. 'I would have recognised you a second later, friend Eadulf. You were in no danger. Your tonsure is hard to miss.'

Eadulf sniffed indignantly. 'That is of little comfort to me.'

Enda said to Fidelma: 'I am sorry, lady . . .'

'It looks as though your apologics should be directed to Gobán.' She smiled at the poor blacksmith, who was just beginning to relax, leaning against the wall.

'My apologies, smith – these are my friends.' Enda turned to explain to Fidelma. 'I was about to ride into Durlus Éile to see if there was any trace of you, as you told me to do, when I recognised Aonbharr and the other horses at the back of the smithy. When the smith here refused to acknowledge your existence, claiming the horses were his, I thought that something must have happened to you. I decided to lie in wait.'

'Gobán was merely protecting us,' Fidelma explained. 'Are you all right, Gobán?'

'Your friend did not hurt me, lady,' the smith offered, rubbing the back of his neck. 'While he was none too gentle, it is understandable if he was concerned for your safety.'

'Which I was,' asserted Enda. 'I have heard some wild stories along the way here. There was one panicking merchant on the road with tales of ravening hordes of bandits, raiding and burning.'

Fidelma sighed. 'We have heard those stories also.' She addressed the smith. 'Let us trespass further on your hospitality, Gobán, and use your cabin while we discuss our plans. Will you be our watchdog at the forge and make sure we are not disturbed?'

Gobán gave his assent and Fidelma led her companions into his cabin.

'Now,' she said, finding a seat, 'tell us your news first, Enda. You left us and returned to Cashel. Did you tell my brother what had happened?'

'I did, lady. He was very concerned.'

'Tell us, in your own words.'

'After you left me at the tavern of Fedach Glas, it was not long before he returned with a plough horse, as he promised. I saddled up and rode for Cashel. You can imagine the laughter it provoked among the men when I rode in . . .'

Fidelma waved aside Enda's tale of his humiliation.

'I spoke immediately to the King and told him what had happened. He provided me with a good horse and I set out for Imleach, but soon it was fairly dark so I found a place to sleep at Ara's Well and then I travelled on to Imleach at first light.'

'Of course,' Fidelma encouraged him. 'And then?'

'Abbot Ségdae was surprised to see me. I gave him the items you sent and he was very grateful. I then told him the story.'

'And could he provide you with any information?'

'He knew of Brother Ailgesach's problem with alcohol. Ailgesach was from Durlus and had served in the Abbey of Biorra. He was skilled in tending the sick but could not qualify as a physician. He had come to Imleach and expressed his desire to help in nursing the sick and afflicted. Abbot Ségdae appointed him to go to Gleann na nGeilt, the Valley of Lunatics.'

'It is the same story that we have heard here in Durlus from Bishop Daig,' commented Eadulf.

'Continue, Enda,' encouraged Fidelma. 'When was it that Brother Ailgesach was sent into the Glen of Lunatics?'

'The abbot said it was a few years ago. Brother Ailgesach remained there until some weeks ago when he arrived in Imleach wishing to resign from the task. The abbot told me it was clear that he had been deeply affected by his years attending to the insane. He was much troubled and given to drowning his troubles with strong liquor. Now and then he would hallucinate and utter profanities. He would accost the brethren and accuse them of being in league with the Whore of Babylon. I am not sure who she is, lady, but I recall that these were the same words that he hurled at you in Fedach Glas's tavern.'

'They were exactly his words.' It was Eadulf who confirmed this. 'It is from the sacred writings of the Faith. The Whore of Babylon is a symbol of evil. Presumably something troubled Brother Ailgesach and was set off by his drunken fits.'

'Abbot Ségdae said that he would exhibit instances of terror and cry out something like "Beware of the seventh trumpet!" And: "Blood begets blood!"' went on Enda. 'Abbot Ségdae believed that he would be a disruptive influence if he remained within the Abbey at Imleach, so he had decided to send Brother Ailgesach to Fraigh Dubh because Brother Tressach had recently died. He felt it was a small, fairly isolated chapel and the work would not be onerous. With luck, the place might help him to adjust and cure his drinking.'

'And did the abbot know anything of Brother Biasta?'

'The abbot had never heard of the name, which he felt was a curious one for a religious to have.'

Fidelma sighed deeply. 'It was, more or less, what we have learned here. Were you able to pick up any information about Dego and his attempts to find the raiders we hear so much of?'

'Dego and his warriors had already left Abbot Ségdae at Imleach. There was no news of him but, as I say, there is much gossip abroad about these bandits. Some even tell stories of riders coming through their villages bearing a religious banner carried by a woman.'

Fidelma sucked in her breath sharply. She turned to Eadulf.

'The Whore of Babylon,' she rapped out. 'Do you recall her description from the old Scriptures?'

'I think I recall the passage,' he said. 'It is mentioned in the Book of Revelation. She is described as a woman arrayed in purple with a scarlet cloak decked with . . .' His voice trailed off.

'With gold and precious gems,' finished Gormán. 'That is exactly how the merchant described the woman leading the raiders.'

As Enda was looking puzzled, Gormán quickly explained.

'What can it mean?' wondered Eadulf.

Fidelma thought for a moment and then shrugged. 'It is Dego's task to discover the meaning. We have more than enough tasks to concentrate on.'

'So what is our next move, lady?' asked Gormán.

'We follow the same plan as we were about to embark on when Enda joined us. We try to trace Torna and his captors.'

'Torna?' Enda echoed.

'I'll tell you about him as we go,' Gormán said. 'We have half a day of daylight left. We should start out soon, otherwise we shall lose a day.'

'If the man who observed the boat yesterday was correct, how are we to follow it?' asked Eadulf. 'They were seen on the far side of the river and going east along some tributary.'

'It's easy enough,' Gormán assured him. 'We ride back south across the bridge then ride east over rough ground, eventually reaching the tributary called the River Drise – that was where the boat was spotted. We can then proceed eastwards along it. We should be able to find out if they have left the river at any point.'

'Very well.' Fidelma was decisive. 'Gormán, you and Enda get our horses saddled and ready.'

After the warriors left, Fidelma turned to Eadulf. He was looking thoughtful and she knew what was passing through his mind.

'This is turning out to be more complicated than I expected, Eadulf. I must admit that I do not see any purpose to these seemingly unrelated matters – as yet. My instinct is that they are all connected.'

'Would it help to run through the situation?'

'Very well. We find a body near my brother's palace. It seems to be that of an envoy from the Uí Máil Kings of Laigin. His killer has apparently ridden eastward in the direction of the Black Heath: there we lost his tracks. We start our search for clues, and are led to the chapel of Brother Ailgesach. He has had two visitors staying on the night of the murder, a man and a woman. The woman is said to be of noble appearance. They ride off early that morning.

'We find Brother Ailgesach in a drunken stupor in the local tavern when we arrive. Then someone who claims to be his cousin Biasta arrives. He kills Brother Ailgesach and escapes northward. We try to follow and fall in with a poet named Torna. Abductors arriving from the river attack us. I am mistaken for the poet's companion and am left for dead when the error is discovered. An innocent young boatman is killed. You are told that a religieux was waiting for them. Was it Brother Biasta? I now realise that it could not be, since I would have recognised his harsh whisper when I heard a voice tell the abductors that I was not the right woman. I am rescued by you, but Torna is taken into the Land of the Osraige. To get to Laigin from here you need to cross

Osraige. Is there some connection with the killing of an envoy from Laigin? Have I missed anything?'

Eadulf grimaced. 'Yes – what about the message that was found in Ailgesach's cabin from an unknown person, saying that they would come to him there with evidence of some conspiracy? I am certain that Gelgéis recognised the name, Torna, when you spoke it. What is she hiding? Also, what about the fact that Brother Ailgesach was raving about the Whore of Babylon and these raiders from the west being led by someone who resembles the description in the Scriptures?' Eadulf paused and asked: 'Is that another thread?'

'At the moment, it is a loose one,' said Fidelma. 'There are too many of these loose threads with no apparent connection that I can see at the moment.'

Gormán re-entered. 'All is ready, lady. The horses have been watered and foddered. Shall I tell Gobán that we are going? He is at work in the forge.'

'I will do so,' Fidelma replied. 'I want to make sure that he has not been put out by the hospitality that he has afforded us.'

Within the hour they were crossing the long wooden bridge that spanned the Suir south of Durlus Éile. Gormán rode in front, followed by Fidelma and Eadulf, with Enda bringing up the rear. They rode at a brisk pace, but not as fast as would quickly fatigue their horses, and soon encountered the smaller River Dríse where it flowed into the Suir.

Just beyond a slight bend after some thick woodland, the river narrowed a little and Gormán called on them to halt. He pointed. Someone was swimming in the waters and it seemed that the swimmer was making towards an empty boat that was caught in a log-jam about mid-stream. As they watched, the swimmer reached the boat and was apparently intent on loosening it.

'Let's give him assistance,' Fidelma suggested, dismounting.

'Careful,' warned Eadulf. 'He might be one of the abductors.'

'There's no one else about,' replied Gormán, 'so we stand in no danger.'

They walked their horses down to the bank and Gormán called to the swimmer, asking if he needed help. The man glanced back over his shoulder and waved acknowledgement. He was holding up the painter, the rope attached to the bow of the boat used for tying it, and was trying to ease the bow away from the logs which had held it fast. He began swimming back, and Gormán quickly stripped and entered the water to help him drag the vessel towards the bank. As they neared it the others lent a hand while Fidelma remained on the bank.

She averted her gaze until Gormán and the unknown swimmer had climbed out, secured the boat to a nearby tree stump and resumed some garments. The swimmer was a young man whose clothes placed him as a farmer.

'Did you have an accident?' she asked.

'This is not my boat, lady,' he replied, noting her dress and obvious rank. 'I farm the land beyond this rise and when I came down just now in search of one of my sheep, I saw this boat caught in those logs. It looked a good boat and not damaged, so I thought I would swim out and try to free it.'

Gormán was rubbing his chin as he examined the boat. 'It must have come adrift,' he said. Then his eyes narrowed; a moment later he had climbed aboard and was extracting something from the stern planking.

'What is it?' asked Fidelma.

'There are some blood splatters on the stern seat – and this.' Gormán was holding up a tiny particle of material that he had spotted, caught on a splinter of wood.

Fidelma gasped and her hand went to her sleeve where there was the slight tear.

'This must be the boat we are following,' Eadulf said, stating the obvious.

It was not good news for Fidelma. 'They have abandoned it – and they could have done so anywhere along the river, so that it drifted down and was caught in this log-jam.'

Eadulf smiled and shook his head. 'Not so. They abandoned it here.'

'What makes you say that?' She felt irritated at his confidence.

Eadulf pointed to the river. 'They were pulling upstream, against the current. If they abandoned it before this point, it would have been swept back downstream. So they came here, abandoned it and took to the land.'

She flushed slightly at having forgotten the flow of the river. However, she recovered her poise and said: 'And why would they leave the boat at this point?'

'Easy enough.' Eadulf gestured at the log-jam in which the boat had been trapped. 'That log-jam is so secure that even the current has not dislodged it. I think they came here but could not move beyond the logs. They might have been able to drag the boat out of the river and haul it around to the other side of the dam, but maybe that was too awkward for them with a prisoner to take care of and a man with a damaged hand.'

Fidelma smiled ruefully. There were times when she underestimated Eadulf's capabilities at deduction.

'I suppose you can't tell us which bank they landed on and the direction that they went?' she said in a sarcastic attempt to cover her own shortcomings.

Eadulf's face was expressionless. 'Yes, I can. They came ashore on this side of the river and started walking eastwards.'

Fidelma raised her eyebrows, wondering if he were exchanging sarcasm for sarcasm. But Enda, who had a reputation among the warriors of Cashel as an expert tracker, let out an exclamation of triumph.

'Friend Eadulf is right, lady!' he called. He indicated the ground. 'Six men passed here, one dragging his feet reluctantly. They came ashore and began to move off across the land, taking that path eastwards.'

'So now they are travelling on foot,' Eadulf commented, ignoring Fidelma's irritation. He neglected to say that he had spotted the footprints and made a guess, whereas Enda had provided the detail. 'Is there anywhere near here where they can purchase horses?'

The question was addressed to the young farmer.

'No, your friends will not find any horses around here. I have only one strong plough horse and there are no other farmsteads for quite a distance.'

'Then we might be able to gain on them,' Gormán said with satisfaction.

'Catch them after a night and a day's start?' Eadulf was sceptical.

'If they are heading east, their way will take them through bog land. One has to know the safe tracks. Although the countryside is flat, it is difficult terrain through which to maintain speed, especially on foot.'

'Are there no marks on the boat to show to whom it originally belonged?' asked Fidelma, turning back to the craft.

'None that I saw,' Gormán told her. 'It is fairly typical of the boats along the Suir, having four oars and plenty of space.'

Fidelma addressed the young farmer: 'You do realise that under the law the boat constitutes a *frithe*.' The term meant 'that which has been found' and implied a lost property.

'I have no knowledge of the law, lady,' muttered the young man.

'Who is the chieftain of this territory?' she asked. 'Are we in the territory of the Osraige?'

The young farmer looked indignant. 'This is still the land of the Éile, lady. Our land ends further on when you come to a fork in the river.'

'Then you must travel to Durlus Éile and ask to see the steward of the Lady Gelgéis. Say that it is Fidelma of Cashel who has sent you.'

The farmer was staring at her with wide eyes, very nervous now that he had learned who she was.

'Tell Spealáin the steward that you have found this boat. Say that you have come to proclaim the finding of the boat as it is stated in law, for the finding of all lost property must be proclaimed in this fashion. Do you understand?'

'I understand, lady.' The young man licked his dry lips.

'But this trip will be your gain,' continued Fidelma, smiling. 'You see, you are entitled to part of the value of your find. The more remote the place in which the find is made, then the greater proportion of the value goes to you.'

The farmer was frowning. 'But you came along and helped me bring it ashore.'

'We are not interested in the financial value of your find,' replied Fidelma. 'And you may well have brought it to the riverbank yourself, even had we not been passing. The value will help towards your farmstead. In fact, tell the steward of the Lady Gelgéis that I suggest this river be considered a highway, in which case I recommend that you are to be compensated with half to two-thirds of the value and, indeed, the payment of an *austad*, a storage fee, for as long as the boat remains on your land. If it is not disposed of, then you are entitled to the full value. Say that is my judgement, and when I return to Durlus Éile I shall hope to see that it has been carried out.'

Leaving the farmer stammering his thanks, they mounted their horses and began to move off, this time with Enda leading the way, bending slightly forward to follow the tracks on the ground. It was only a short time before they emerged from a small stretch of woodland to a more open grassy plain and saw that they had come to the fork in the river. One arm flowed directly from the north, continuing on towards the Suir while a smaller arm flowed from the south to feed the Dríse. Although this smaller river blocked their path, it was narrow and easily fordable.

'If I recall, the northerly arm is still the River Dríse while the south-erly one is called the Bréagagh, the Deceitful River,' reflected Gormán. 'Once we cross this river we are in Osraige territory – the Land of the People of the Deer. This whole area beyond is low-lying and very boggy.'

'Which way then, Enda?' asked Fidelma. 'Do we try to turn north along the Dríse?'

Enda glanced down and his keen eyes followed some trail that they could not see on the ground.

'Six men walking and one appears to be stumbling quite a bit,' he told her. He walked his horse slowly to the confluence and then moved along the bank of the smaller southern river, where he halted. 'They decided to ford the river here, lady. It's quite shallow. They are contin-uing to move directly east.'

As if to prove the point, he rode across to the far bank, halted and then peered towards the ground. Then he turned and called them across.

'They came to this point and set off eastward,' he confirmed.

They swiftly joined him and Gormán pointed across the flat plains towards some distant, low-lying hills, saying, 'This way lies the old Abbey of Liath Mór.'

'Will they be able to pick up horses there?' asked Eadulf.

'Perhaps,' replied Fidelma. 'I have not visited the Abbey of Liath Mór before. The community was formed by the Blessed Chaemóc scarcely seventy years ago. He was a good man, by all accounts.'

'So he might assist us?'

'Alas, he died many years ago. I have no idea who his successor is.'

'What are those hills to the south-east?' asked Eadulf. 'Could they be making for those?'

They relied on Gormán, who appeared to know something of the topography of the area, to supply the answer.

'They are called the Sliabh Ardachaidh – the Hills of the High Field.

It is not a tall range of hills but they are the highest hills that stand between the boggy plains of Osraige and the borders of Laigin further east. The men we follow would have to travel further east before they could turn on a safe road through the bogs towards them.'

They continued to ride in silence for a while, with Enda now and then checking the tracks left by the group they were pursuing. Even these tracks had come to an end now, for they had arrived at more boggy land over which, to their surprise, stretched a newly built causeway. There were many causeways of this nature throughout the Five Kingdoms on which to cross the bogs; they were constructed with quantities of timber, mainly birch for the base structure, its long, straight planks used for the supports for the upper timbers of alder, elm or hazels. There were even sections of it paved with stones that had been smashed and laid almost like flagging. Most of this was very new. Indeed, there were piles of materials lying on both sides of the road – clearly not abandoned but indicative of work in hand. It seemed as if the workers had merely left their toil for the day so that they could return home before nightfall.

'I presume the community are trying to build a roadway from the Abbey to the river crossing into Durlus Éile,' Fidelma said.

'But through their efforts I have lost the tracks,' Enda complained in exasperation, since any traces left by the walkers had now vanished.

'Even so, I think they will stick to the easy path along the causeway and not go wandering off into the bog land,' Fidelma replied.

Gormán had turned to her with a puzzled frown. 'Nevertheless, the Osraige have obviously been doing a lot of new road-building here.'

She agreed that she too was surprised at the amount of new work. Eadulf knew that her people classified their roads in terms of size: the laws mentioned seven classes of roadway, starting with the five great *slige* or main highways that linked the Five Kingdoms to the High King's seat at Tara. This new roadway was undoubtedly curious for, as

Fidelma pointed out, it could only come from the old Abbey of Liath Mór. But as they rode along it, it became plain that it was no small by-road of the type that usually led to abbeys. It was what could be classed as a *ramut*, a wide highway with no fencing but open on either side so that war horses and chariots could travel from fortress to fortress. Such a road was usually the main highway from a King's residence, to which all small by-roads led. She noted the structure with interest. This causeway, or *tóchar*, was laid first with branches of trees, earth and stones and bushes placed in layers and pressed down until they were firm enough to cover with the planks. There was room enough for two chariots, drawn by two horses apiece, to pass each other at the gallop without slowing. Four horses abreast and still space to spare . . . What manner of highway was this, and for what purpose?

'It's more like a military highway than a road leading to a religious community,' observed Gormán, articulating her very thought.

'New causeway or not, dusk will not be long in coming. We shall soon have to seek hospitality for tonight or sleep out on this road itself, for we have bog land on either side,' Enda said practically.

The journey across the plain was fairly easy because of the causeway, but it provided no shelter from the wind that was rising as dusk began to show in the eastern sky. Fidelma kept her feelings of unease to herself. Osraige nominally accepted the Kings of Muman as their overlords and, as such, new roadworks of this dimension would have to have the King's approval. However, she could not remember hearing about such new building-work among the gossip exchanged in Cashel. But Enda was right. They would have to find a bed for the night – and soon.

They had been travelling on firmer ground and over small, rocky hillocks, keeping to the newly built highway. This had led them through an unexpected, albeit small, stretch of woodland. It was an oasis in the bog land. As they emerged from the shelter of these trees, Enda, who was in the lead, gave a sharp gasp.

'Look, lady, a fortress! That's where the new highway leads.'

They halted on the edge of the woodland and surveyed a series of grey stone and wooden buildings that were surrounded by a high stone wall. The whole structure seemed newly built, with the roadway running towards its oppressive dark wood gates. There was what appeared to be a watchtower to one side of the gates. The whole structure was quite extensive.

Fidelma stared at the construction in surprise.

'That is no fortress,' Gormán said. 'Or, at least, it should not be. This was where the Abbey of Chaemóc stood. The Abbey of Liath Mór. How has the community grown from the collection of wooden buildings into such an imposing structure? I last passed this way when I was a mere youth, and the abbey was nothing like this.'

'My cousin, Abbot Laisrán of Darú, used to say that this abbey was hardly more than two huts and a little chapel,' agreed Fidelma.

'It certainly appears more like a fortress than the dwelling of a religious community,' Eadulf said.

Gormán was examining the structure with the critical eye of a warrior. 'Those walls are built for defence – a few bowmen there could stand off an entire army. Even the watchtower does not seem a place where the bell is chimed for prayers. If I were trying to plan an attack on the place, I would be hard-pressed to choose any weak point of entrance.'

'My friends,' Fidelma tried to overcome her unease, 'you will observe the surrounding countryside. What is there to defend here? From this small woodland rise, all before you is bog land. Why build a fortress in this desolate place? Why fortify an abbey? What army could march against it? There is no main track through here . . .' She paused when she suddenly recalled the new causeway.

'Well, someone is trying to build one.' The comment came from Gormán even before she could correct herself. 'And surely this is the territory of Tuaim Snámha, the Prince of the Osraige? He has to seek approval from Colgú of Cashel before he can build new roads or improve buildings.'

'Perhaps we are getting a little sensitive?' Fidelma said. 'Let us continue on. We need to find out if there is news of those whom we pursue and, in any event, as Enda says, we need hospitality for the night before it grows late.'

They left the cover of the wood and continued along the track towards the imposing new buildings. As they approached the stern edifice, the dark oak gates swung open. Their approach had been observed from the watchtower.

A group of men clad in grey religious robes had moved forward from the darkness of the entrance and stood watching them, their arms folded in the sleeves of their robes. All had their cowls covering their heads. As Fidelma and her companions halted a short space from them, one of the brethren stepped forward and held up his hand, palm outward.

'*Pax vobiscum*,' he greeted in the language of the Faith. Like his companions, he remained with his head obscured by his hood. Fidelma could just see his lower face and noted that he was a cleanshaven young man.

'*Pax tecum*,' replied Fidelma. 'We come seeking shelter from the oncoming night.'

To her amazement the young man responded with a negative shake of his head.

'Our sorrow, lady, that we cannot extend our hospitality to a woman nor to wandering warriors.'

Fidelma reached over to restrain Gormán as she saw his hand slide to the hilt of his sword.

'Is this not the Abbey of Liath Mór?' she asked coldly.

'It was.'

'*Was?* I am sorry that I have been badly informed. I believed this to be the Abbey of Liath Mór in the territory of the Osraige.'

The young man's expression did not change. 'It is now called Dún Muirne.'

'Dún Muirne? The Fortress of Muirne? That's a strange name for a religious community.'

'I should explain that the Lady Muirne was the daughter of our patron and abbot, who was drowned crossing the Suir. He desires that this place commemorates her life.'

'And who is your abbot?' she enquired.

'Our abbot is Cronán.'

'Then announce us to this Abbot Cronán.'

'I have explained that it is not possible.'

'Not possible?' There was a dangerous rise to her voice. 'Who are you?' The second question was snapped out in the tone of authority that Fidelma had developed as an advocate of the law courts.

'I am Anfudán – Brother Anfudán, the steward of the abbey.' The young man remained defiant in tone.

'Then listen closely, Brother Anfudán. Night is now quickly approaching and inhospitable bog land stretches for long distances all around us. My companions and I wish for hospitality, which this Abbey of Liath Mór is bound to give under both law and custom.'

The young steward drew himself up, thrusting out his jaw aggressively.

'I do not have to answer to you, lady. Who do you think you are, to believe that you have the right to give orders here . . . to a pious community of the Faith?'

'I am Fidelma of Cashel, sister to the King, advocate and judge qualified to the level of *anruth*. Now bring forth your abbot to answer why you have refused hospitality to my companions and me, and are thus not compliant to law and custom and the rights of your King!'

The young man stood staring at her from under his cowl, and then an interesting thing happened. One of his companions hurried forward and whispered in the steward's ear. The latter waited with head bowed for a moment and then nodded. The man who had whispered to him had turned and hastened back through the gates. Then the steward cleared his throat.

'You and your companions may enter our courtyard and dismount while I seek clarification in this matter.' He gestured for the brethren who were with him to stand well back so that Fidelma and the men with her could enter.

Beyond the gates they were in a fairly large courtyard, where some of the brethren were already lighting torches against the approaching night. Fidelma quickly registered the numerous outbuildings, storehouses, a smithy's forge, and what looked like the ornate entrance to a chieftain's hall rather than a chapel. The abbey was unlike any that she had ever seen before. She could now entirely agree with Gormán that it was more like a fortress than a community for the Faithful.

The young steward, Brother Anfudán, was curt. 'You may dismount and wait here.' He then marched away in the direction of the main building.

'That sounded more like a military command than a request,' Gormán murmured.

Behind them, the great oak gates were swinging shut and a bar was pushed into place to secure them. Eadulf shivered slightly. He felt like a prisoner being shut in.

Members of the brethren had not dispersed but stood nearby, almost as if on guard. The newcomers were aware of figures moving along the walkways on the high wall, like sentries patrolling the battlements. Fidelma did not like the situation. Had she been wrong in insisting on her rights and revealing her identity? It was too late now. She had let her irritation get the better of her. They should have ridden on and learned more about how Liath Mór had come into its new existence.

'What now, lady?' whispered Gormán, edging forward. He sensed what was going through Fidelma's mind. 'This is no abbey. Surely, it is the custom of most abbeys to bring water to wash the feet of travellers when they enter?'

'This place has already revealed the fact that it does not share the customs of hospitality common in other abbeys,' she sighed.

'How do we proceed?'

'We continue to behave as any normal traveller would, in their own land,' she said quietly. 'We will wait and see. After all, it is not we who have broken the laws of hospitality but the arrogant young steward, Anfudán. We will see if he really denied us on the instructions of his abbot and, if so, how this is justified by the abbot himself. We must have a care. This place does not inspire feelings of tranquillity.'

There seemed an inordinate passing of time before one of the brethren came back from the hall, without Brother Anfudán. Fidelma thought it was the same man who had given some instruction to the young steward at the gate.

'Will you and your companions follow me, lady?' He spoke in a gruff but respectful tone. 'My men – my brethren – will attend to your horses.' He turned to those nearby and, raising his voice, issued orders. Members of the brethren came forward and took their horses and led them away towards buildings that looked like stables.

Their guide then motioned them to follow him towards the main building. They went up some stone steps and found themselves in a massive hall that would have done justice to that of a petty-king. In the centre of this was a large hearth with a smouldering turf fire. In those areas of the Five Kingdoms where wood was scarce, particularly in the vast boggy plains like the surrounding one, people cut the turf or peat moss, where plants and matted roots combined to present a fuel called *móin* suitable for slow-burning fires. The intensity of the warmth was marked as they entered. Before this fire were several chairs and a table.

A man sat in one of the chairs. At his side and slightly behind his left shoulder stood the young steward, his head still covered by his cowl.

Their guide approached and bowed before the figure in the chair before turning and moving to one side.

It was clear that the man was tall, in spite of being seated. His head was uncovered, showing his bald pate, and his robes were tight upon him as if his entire frame was muscular. His facial features were full and tanned. Fidelma noticed a livid scar on one cheek. It was clearly an old wound. The man stared at them with pale, almost colourless eyes, which seemed to glint, like glass, against the light given by a nearby lamp. They were close-set, with bushy eyebrows, emphasising the long, thin nose that gave a curiously aggressive cast to his appearance. The thin red lips were tightly compressed. Overall, he had the unkempt appearance of a man more used to the countryside than existing within the shady confines of an abbey.

He made no effort to rise to greet them. When he spoke, it was in a sharp staccato tone.

'I am told that you are Fidelma of Cashel, sister to Colgú. What do you want here?'

Eadulf heard Fidelma's slow intake of breath. It was not a good sign.

'Yes, I am Fidelma of Cashel. It grieves me to find you unwell, Abbot Cronán.'

Eadulf frowned, wondering what she meant. The abbot obviously shared the same thought; his gathered brows showed that he was puzzled.

'I? Unwell?'

Fidelma smiled thinly. 'Had you been well, I presume that you would have risen to greet me, as is protocol and custom. For even if I were not the sister of the King of Muman, of which this territory is part, I am also a *dálaigh* of the rank of *anruth*, and thus able to seat myself in the presence of the Kings of the Provinces without seeking permission.'

The abbot stared at her, a range of emotions struggling on his features. Then, reluctantly, the man pushed himself up out of his chair and inclined his head towards her.

'Your forgiveness, lady.' He almost muttered the words. 'There is much on my mind at present. Please seat yourself and I will order refreshment for you and your companions.'

Fidelma turned to Eadulf and introduced him before seating herself and indicating that Eadulf should take the seat next to her. Gormán and Enda took their places, standing warily just behind them.

The abbot then lowered himself back into his chair and ordered their guide to arrange for refreshments to be brought. Brother Anfudán remained close at hand, his expression sullen, judging from the shape of his lips underneath his cowl.

'And now, Fidelma of Cashel, how can we be of service to you?' The abbot tried to sound polite but his tone was strained.

'Has your steward not informed you of what service we require?' Her voice was mild.

The young man shifted his weight awkwardly at the abbot's side.

'As you have seen for yourself, our abbey is but newly constructed and lacks facilities,' the abbot replied, spreading his hands and trying to sound apologetic. 'Perhaps my steward did not explain—'

'No explanation was necessary,' Fidelma replied easily. 'The law and custom is firm on this point. Were this but a lowly shepherd's hut, the law would still be the law. This abbey, I believe, was first constructed by Chaemóc seventy years ago. I see that much building has been done since then, but that does not mean all etiquette is lost nor the law ignored.'

'The rebuilding is not yet complete,' the abbot said with a frown. 'We do not have facilities for a person of rank such as you, lady. My steward was merely thinking of your comf—'

Fidelma cut him short. 'Anyone thinking of the comfort of myself and that of my companions would not have arbitrarily consigned our fate to find hospitality in the surrounding bogs at night-time.'

The abbot appeared to struggle with himself; and then he forced a weak smile.

'Of course, you and your companions are welcome to our hospitality for this night. I regret that there has been any misunderstanding and apologise that my steward was not able to make himself better understood. He is new to the task.'

'So I observe,' Fidelma replied grimly. 'And, as I observe, new to the religious.'

The abbot looked uneasy. 'I do not understand, lady.'

'Your steward is so new that he has not taken cognisance of the rules of a religious community,' she replied. 'That is why he covers his head at a time when the custom of all religious orders dictates that the *cabhail* should not be worn. Can it be that he is so new to the religious that he has not even acquired a tonsure?'

Brother Anfudán expelled his breath with an angry hiss and took a step forward. His head jerked back so that it succeeded in dislodging his hood. Her guess was correct. He had a shock of thick black hair and no sign of a tonsure. But it was the gesture of his right hand that caused a look of satisfaction to pass across Fidelma's features. The hand went to his left side as if seeking a sword.

CHAPTER THIRTEEN

As the young steward took an angry step forward, the abbot raised a hand to stay him. Fidelma had not flinched but remained seated. At the same time, she too had raised her hand – aware that Gormán and Enda were grasping the hilts of their swords. She stared challengingly at the young man's menacing features. Halted by the abbot's movement, Brother Anfudán stepped back, but the fury had not receded from his expression.

'It seems that Anfudán lives up to his name,' Fidelma observed softly, addressing her words to the abbot. The latter actually forced a tight smile. The name meant a turbulent or a tempestuous person.

'You will forgive my young friend, lady. He has not been with us long. In fact, he is the son of my brother and I have agreed to take him under my care so that he may follow the path of Christ. He has not yet taken the vows of obedience. He is, as you say, a little restive and we hope he will be influenced along the path of serenity. There is no need for apprehension.'

'Of what should we be apprehensive, in a house of God?' asked Fidelma gravely.

'We are merely curious, Abbot Cronán, that is all,' interposed Eadulf. 'It is unusual to find the steward of an abbey who has not taken a vow of obedience and service which is marked by the wearing of a tonsure.'

The abbot did not appear concerned. 'I have appointed him steward so that he may learn responsibility and humility.' He turned to his flush-faced nephew with a disapproving frown. 'Now, apologise to the Lady Fidelma for any discourtesy to her rank and then you may leave us and ensure that chambers are set up for her and her companions.'

'But—' the young steward began.

'At once!' snapped the abbot.

Brother Anfudán glowered for a moment and then inclined his head slowly to the abbot before turning to Fidelma.

'I seek pardon, lady, for the discourteous way that I have greeted you. I was trying to do my duty to the abbot and this community.' Before Fidelma could acknowledge his words, the young man strode off.

'Does he know enough to provide us with water to wash in as well as beds for the night?' queried Fidelma.

Abbot Cronán looked far from happy.

'I think you may now accept my word that he will carry out all the rules of hospitality, lady. But, tell me, I had heard that Fidelma, daughter of Failbe Flann, had entered the religious. I also heard that you had married a Saxon.' He glanced towards Eadulf.

'An Angle,' muttered Eadulf.

'Is there a difference?' asked the abbot in a cynical tone.

'To an Angle there is,' Eadulf replied quickly.

'You present yourself as Fidelma of Cashel. Does this mean that you are no longer in the religious?'

'It does,' she replied. 'I was trained, as you may know, as an advocate of our law system. I found that many matters I was concerned with in law conflicted with the tenets of religious life. I therefore terminated my role as a religious so that I could concentrate on the law.'

'So what brings you here to Osraige with your companions? It must be something of great import. This is an isolated place, as you have observed,' said the abbot. 'Bog lands stretch around us, so it is not a place that one moves readily through without purpose. Certainly, it is many years since we saw so distinguished a person as an Eóghanacht of Cashel. In fact, so few visitors do we have here that when the sister of the King of Muman and her companions arrive, I must speculate whether it is by chance or whether some specific purpose brings you to our abbey doors.'

'When this abbey was first built, I was told it was a collection of wooden huts,' replied Fidelma without answering his question. 'These new buildings are most impressive, if not a little awesome.'

'Awesome?'

'In that the walls look more military than religious. Why is that?'

'There is no secret behind the intention. You know that we are in a territory that has long been fought over between Muman and Laigin. During the time when the Blessed Chaemóc guided the affairs of this abbey, it was plundered on several occasions by the Uí Néill from the north and the Uí Máil from the east. And when armies did not do so, then there were bandits from local clans who threatened the peace – clans like the Uí Duach to the north of us. When I accepted the task of being abbot here, I decided to facilitate the building of an abbey in which the brethren could be protected; an abbey which would be respected and which would become a great centre that people would approach with a feeling of amazement and respect.'

'Of course, the Prince of the Osraige, Tuaim Snámha, must be very proud of these new buildings,' Fidelma said in an innocent tone. 'I presume everything was done with his permission and patronage?'

The abbot cleared his throat and then said: 'Tuaim Snámha was indeed a good patron.'

'So the abbey was built in this manner to defend the community?'

'It was. The protective shadow of the Eóghanacht does not always extend throughout all the territory they claim jurisdiction over. We needs must look to ourselves for protection. Sadly, this is why you see a fortress to protect the House of God. But you have not yet answered my own question.'

'Which was?' asked Fidelma politely.

'What brings you and your companions to this isolated place?'

'Would you say that its isolation means that few people travel along your new roads, passing the abbey?'

The abbot frowned suspiciously. It was clear that he thought Fidelma was being evasive. Nevertheless he responded: 'Few people, indeed.'

'So that you would know if anyone passed this way yesterday?'

The abbot shifted in his seat but did not drop his eyes.

'I have heard no reports of horsemen passing this way,' he told her.

'I did not say that they were horsemen.'

'Then how else would they be travelling – by wagon? The tracks through the bogs here are difficult, almost impossible, to traverse.'

'Yet from what we have seen of the new roads around here, they should have no problem with wagons. But you are right: these people were travelling on foot.'

'No travellers on foot have passed by this abbey yesterday or for many days. What business would you have with these elusive travellers?' replied the abbot.

'Oh, it is in my role as a *dálaigh* that I need to speak with them, that is all.' Fidelma dismissed the subject as if it was of little importance. 'It is curious they did not pass this way, as we are sure that they were following the new roads that you have constructed through the bog land here.'

'The tracks have been reinforced to help those pilgrims who want to come to worship at the shrine of the Blessed Chaemóc.'

'He is but fourteen years dead and I had not heard of pilgrims coming to his shrine,' Fidelma observed.

The abbot frowned. 'His fame has spread and many come to hear of his miracles. Was it not his bell that awoke the Children of Lir from their curse and changed them from swans to mortal beings again? Did Chaemóc, of blessed name, not baptise them in the New Faith and bury them? Being mortals, they withered and died from the ages they had missed during the eons that they had been forced to exist as immortal swans.'

'I am surprised that you give credence to these legends of the old gods of our people, for Lir was one of the ancient gods whose second wife had the evil power to turn her stepchildren into swans.'

'I can only repeat that through the intercession of the Blessed Chaemóc this curse was lifted from them and they died baptised in the New Faith. That is the story that has come down to us.'

'Yet the abbey is no longer dedicated to his memory,' murmured Eadulf.

Abbot Cronán flushed slightly. 'It is my wish that my daughter's memory be respected here as well as Chaemóc,' he said shortly.

'I understand her name was Muirne and that she died in some accident?' pressed Eadulf.

'An accident?' The abbot's voice was sharp. 'Yes, she drowned.' He suddenly rose and glanced at the religieux who had brought them into the chamber. 'Your chambers should be ready now. I will hand you over to the care of Sil . . . of Brother Sillán. The bell will summon you for the evening meal and I will ensure that someone is sent to collect you.'

Fidelma thanked the abbot, although the words were simply a ritual for there had been no sincerity in his offer of hospitality. In fact, had not night been upon them and had there been any alternative, she would have suggested that they leave immediately.

As Brother Sillán ushered them to the door, Brother Anfudán approached and the two men exchanged a quick word. Brother Sillán turned. 'Your chambers are ready and water is being heated in the bathing room. Your horses are being attended to and your bags brought over from the stables.'

Their bags were piled outside the door, presumably brought by Brother Anfudán, who had now vanished. As Eadulf took those belonging to Fidelma and himself he saw a deepening frown on Fidelma's forehead. Her head was to one side as if she had been listening to something. Their companions each picked up their own bags. Brother Sillán conducted them through several long, dark stone corridors, lit by oil lamps of the type called *lepaire* placed at intervals on little shelves. The lamps, crude, unglazed earthenware pots with a snout to support the wick, produced a shadowy light and gave off smoke and stifling odours in equal quantity. Eadulf's expression was one of disapproval.

'Some of your brethren need lessons in choosing the rush wicks that are not damp when they are dipped in the oil, and ensuring the oil is clean,' he said. 'That would lessen the fumes and smoke.'

'We are a poor community and as yet have no time for such nice-ties,' Brother Sillán replied over his shoulder.

Eadulf was about to retort that a community that could afford such ostentatious new buildings could afford to light them better, but he felt Fidelma's hand squeeze his arm and he fell silent.

Brother Sillán halted before a door and threw it open.

'This chamber is for the warriors,' he announced, indicating the dark interior with a motion of his head.

'There appear to be no windows,' muttered Gormán, peering inside.

'The chamber is placed facing towards the interior of the abbey. There are candles and oil lamps to provide enough light,' responded their guide.

'And where is our chamber?' enquired Fidelma.

'On the floor above this one, if you will follow me.' He took them to a small wooden stair a little way along the corridor. 'You will find a door further along from your chamber where a *dabach* has been prepared for you and your husband.'

A *dabach* was a large wooden tub or vat and it was the duty of those providing hospitality to have either such a tub or even a stone *long-foilcthe* or bathing vessel ready at this time, for the custom was for a full body-wash before the evening meal.

As Brother Sillán continued to lead the way, Fidelma turned to Gormán, who was about to enter the dark chamber, and motioned him and Enda to follow her.

They climbed the stair behind Brother Sillán and came up into another corridor, but this time one side of it was unenclosed and over-looked a small courtyard. It appeared to be the centre of the main abbey buildings and was open to the sky. In fact, the corridor ran around this courtyard on all four sides. A roof covered the corridor, supported by pillars. All around this flagged walkway were doors which led into various chambers. Dusk had descended but lamps had been lit and Fidelma noticed that one of the doors bore the encouraging inscription *Fothrucad* – bathing – engraved on it.

Brother Sillán had bent to open a door before he turned and saw Gormán and Enda behind Fidelma and Eadulf. He opened his mouth to speak, then clamped it shut as Fidelma moved into the chamber and gave it a quick examination.

'At least there is a window and ventilation on this floor,' she said. Then she regarded their guide solemnly as she moved back out of the room. 'Let us see what this next chamber is like.'

'Lady, this is the best of our guest chambers,' protested Sillán.

'I do not doubt it. Now open this next chamber.'

Brother Sillán stared at her, not sure how to handle this. Before he could frame a negative response, Eadulf had pushed the door open.

'It is a similar chamber with a window,' he announced. 'It looks unused and there are several cots.'

'That will be more suitable for my warriors, rather than allowing them to be consigned to such a dark, odious chamber as the one below,' Fidelma said firmly. 'They can be within call if they are needed by me. I believe the bathing chamber is also for their use?'

'There is cold water for them below,' Brother Sillán grumbled.

'The trouble is,' Fidelma's voice was almost confiding, 'that my warriors are of the élite bodyguard of my brother, the King. They have grown used to more indolent ways. We can all wash in the bathing chamber.'

It seemed that Brother Sillán had given up the trial of wills.

'I shall see that more water is prepared,' he replied sullenly. Then, giving the hint of a shrug, he hurried away without another word.

'Gormán.' Fidelma turned to the warrior with a serious expression, her voice low. 'I am certain that Sillán was the man whom you and Eadulf were told was waiting at the shed for the abductors – the same one who said I was not the right woman who should have been taken with Torna. The timbre of his voice gives him away. He must also have recognised me as soon as we arrived. I suggest that you and Enda do not leave your weapons more than a hand's grasp away.'

'That might be difficult, lady.' The warrior was clearly troubled. 'You will recall, it is the custom that no weapons are allowed into a feasting hall and when we go for the evening meal it would be impossible to take our swords with us.'

'Then take your *gláede* – you can use the excuse that you need it to eat with.' The *gláede* was a sharp dagger. 'But leave your swords and any other weapons hidden in a place where they might not think to look, if your chamber is searched.'

Gormán asked no further questions but joined Enda in the adjacent chamber.

'Is there a bolt on this door, one on the inside?' she asked as Eadulf closed the door.

Eadulf glanced at it and then answered affirmatively. 'Why would there not be?'

'Indeed,' agreed Fidelma. 'Why? Gormán and Enda were shown to a chamber that had the bolts on the outside and none on the inside; no window nor any ventilation. We must be on our guard.'

'Are you sure about Brother Sillán?' he asked. 'You are only going by the sound of his voice.'

'I am sure. Do you not feel the antagonism in this place?'

'I admit that I have had a more friendly welcome in the Tower of Uaman, Lord of the Passes of Sliabh Mis,' Eadulf admitted, remembering Uaman the Leper, who had kidnapped their son and imprisoned Eadulf in his tower.

'Have you ever known an abbey to choose a steward from someone so young and inexperienced and who has not taken vows?'

'The abbot said he had appointed him.'

'You should not forget that it is the fashion of our abbeys to elect both the abbot and his officials in accordance with our custom and law. How could a young – and frankly aggressive – man, lacking knowledge especially of the etiquette of such communities, be put in charge of the daily running of this place?'

Eadulf sighed deeply. 'In our travels we have seen many peculiar things, but the whole demeanour of the abbot and the way the brethren behave are certainly at odds with their calling . . . Therefore I agree. I have never seen religious conduct themselves in this way.'

'If Sillán is here, then at least we know Torna is here as well. Now we have to discover where he is and what the purpose is of this abbey.'

'Anyway, we will have to leave tomorrow morning,' Eadulf pointed out. 'We can demand one night's hospitality but we have no excuse to stay longer, especially if they are already suspicious of us.'

Fidelma nodded thoughtfully. 'Well, before we take any further step, I am going to have my bath.'

As Fidelma entered the *fothrucad*, or bathing chamber, she found a young girl stoking the fire to keep the water hot. She stood up nervously and then, to Fidelma's astonishment, she placed a finger to her lips, crossed to the door, peered out and shut it before turning to her.

'Don't be alarmed, lady. I mean you no harm.'

Fidelma's body had tensed, ready for anything.

'Who are you and what do you want?' she demanded.

Once again, the girl raised a finger to her lips. She was no more than twenty years old, with curly black hair and pleasant features, except that they were now grimy with soot and the robes she was wearing were torn and ill-fitting.

'My name is Ségnat, lady. You and your companions are in great danger here. You must leave as soon as possible.'

Fidelma felt the fear in the other's shaking form.

'So what are you doing in this place, Ségnat? In fact, what manner of place is it?'

'I am a *daer-fuidir*, a hostage brought here when Cronán's men captured me. I am of the Uí Duach, and I have been here for two years. Unless you escape, you too will remain here as a hostage – or even worse. This is the Fortress of Cronán.'

'We realise that this is no abbey and we have been greeted with hostility, but so far no physical threats have been made to us. I have seen no sign of imminent danger.'

'When I went to receive instructions from Sillán about preparing your baths, I heard him talking to his cousin Anfudán. It is their intention to lull you into a false sense of security in order to learn what you know about them and their plans. Then you will be made prisoners.'

'What do you know of their plans?'

'Lady, I am only a *daer-fuidir* – I am not privy to their secrets. I only know that they are evil.'

'If we attempt to leave tomorrow, what then?'

'They will either find an excuse to keep you here, or you will not be allowed to leave.'

'Do you know where they are holding Torna?' Fidelma asked.

To her surprise, the girl looked blankly at her. 'I know of no one by that name.'

'He was a captive brought back here yesterday.'

The girl thought a moment. 'There is word that a prisoner was brought here yesterday, but no one is sure where he is being held. There are many secret places in this fortress.'

'It was in search of him that we came,' Fidelma told her. 'Why does Cronán pretend this is an abbey and he an abbot?'

'He has been trying to hide his activities from the Prince of Osraige, from Tuaim Snámha. But what his intentions are, we do not know.' The girl grew more agitated. 'You must escape before first light otherwise you will never be allowed to leave. There are several Uí Duach who are hostages here; they can show you a way to leave without being seen.'

Suspicion immediately came into Fidelma's mind. 'If you prisoners are able to do this, why have you not escaped yourselves?'

Ségnat's face was grim. 'Because if we do, Cronán has threatened to kill our relatives and friends. That is what keeps us here and praying for rescue from outside.'

Fidelma shook her head in disbelief. 'He could not do that. It is unthinkable!'

The girl's face became contorted. 'He could and he has. A few months ago, one of our number did escape. Five of his friends, including his own cousins, were executed in Cronán's rage.'

When Fidelma had recovered from the shock, she asked: 'Did they recapture him?'

Ségnat shook her head.

'What was his name?' Fidelma asked.

'He was a warrior of the Uí Duach called Tormeid. Please,' she added, 'time is pressing; they might get suspicious. You must escape. We can help.'

Fidelma thought for a moment and then sighed. 'We must make an attempt to find this prisoner first. But even then I can't see how we can escape. Say we managed to get beyond these walls, what then? In the middle of flat bog land without horses, how far would we get?'

To her surprise, the girl said, 'You would have your horses with you. Cronán's men are lazy and it is the *daer-fuidir* who are given the task of looking after the animals. The stables cannot hold all the horses; there is a passage to a paddock just outside the walls where the rest are kept. We have ensured that your horses have been taken there. Cronán's men know we will look after them and won't escape, after what happened to Tormeid's cousins and friends. We will make certain that your horses are saddled and ready when the time comes.'

'But what will happen to you if we escape?' protested Fidelma.

'Cronán wants to instil fear in us by threatening our friends and relatives whom he holds. You have no friends and relatives here and we will simply deny any knowledge of you.'

'Did this Tormeid know that the price of his escape would be the death of others?'

Ségnat shook her head. 'It was because Cronán's own daughter escaped with him and was, so we heard, drowned during the flight, that he went berserk and did this terrible thing; then threatened us with the same punishment.'

'He could do the same to you if we got away,' Fidelma said.

'Lady, we hear that you are the King's sister. If you escape, then you can alert your brother to what is happening in this place. You are our only hope for the rescue of all our people.'

'But how can we walk through the gates, even in the middle of the night?'

'We will help you. There are many of us here who laboured to build this place. We were forced to do so for the Lord of Gleann an Ghuail.'

'That is Cronán?'

Ségnat nodded. 'He is Cronán, Lord of Gleann an Ghuail.'

'For what purpose has this fortress been built?'

They heard a faint noise and the girl stiffened in terror, muttering, 'I will contact you here, lady, after midnight. You must not let anyone know that you suspect anything. You must all be ready so that none of your party is left behind, otherwise they will surely be executed. You and your companions must be well away from here before first light.'

The solemn toll of a bell brought Brother Sillán to guide them to the evening meal. Fidelma had thought that she was past surprising, but then, instead of being led into an abbey refectory, they were taken into a small chamber which appeared to be Cronán's private dining room. There was not even a token pretence that this was an abbey. She had already informed her companions of her conversation with Ségnat, but warned them not to express any surprise or suspicion at anything they saw.

A turf fire smouldered, sending out its aromatic heat, and candles and lamps flickered over the wooden platters and goblets that had been laid. Cronán was waiting for them at the table and gestured Fidelma to sit beside him. She noticed that there was no sign of Anfudán. Eadulf sat opposite while Gormán and Enda were shown seats at the end of the table. Sillán took a seat on Fidelma's other side. Once all were in place, Cronán made a gesture to Sillán, who rang a hand-bell.

A *dáilemain*, or distributor of food, emerged through a side door carrying platters and began to serve the food. Fidelma noted that the abbey did not appear to stint itself on meat, fowl and fishes. A joint of lamb was placed on the table and the *dáilemain*, using the fingers of his left hand to hold it, dexterously cut off a large piece and brought it on to Fidelma's platter. He repeated the performance, moving with the joint by each of them. Each diner held a knife in the right hand and used the fingers of the left as was custom. Fidelma wondered whether these servers were all *daer-fuidir*, just slaves in this curious fortress.

As this was being done there appeared a *deochbhaire*, or cup-bearer, who distributed goblets of ale or cider instead of water. Fidelma recognised the young girl Ségnat, but pretended not to know her.

'Your ale is good,' Fidelma said, turning politely to Cronán. 'I presume the community brews it?' She felt it best to maintain the fiction of being in an abbey.

'We try to be self-sufficient,' agreed the abbot. 'That is the aim of all Osraige.'

'All Osraige?' she queried.

'When Tuaim Snámha succeeded as Prince of Osraige ten years ago, it heralded years of plenty and a promise for our people. We are no longer a small impoverished land between two great kingdoms. One day I shall . . .' He paused and then reached for his goblet.

The door opened unexpectedly and the young steward, Anfudán, hurried in and made straight for the abbot, seeming not to notice anyone else. It was clear that he was bursting with some news.

'Urgent information, my lord,' he gasped, stopping by Cronán's chair. Cronán did not look happy and was rising to usher the young man aside when Anfudán blurted out: 'Our friend has returned from the south. It is confirmed that Bran Finn is dead.'

There was a sudden hush in the room and the abbot sank back into his chair with what sounded like a sigh of annoyance. If looks could kill, then Anfudán would have already been laid out for burial.

'Bran Finn, Prince of the Déisi Muman?' Fidelma could not help her exclamation of surprise. 'I thought he was a young man. How did he die?'

Anfudán suddenly seemed to take in the presence of Fidelma and the others. His face went a deep red.

Cronán's voice was cold. 'Brother Anfudán, you may tell our friend that I will see him in my chamber after the evening meal is finished.'

As Anfudán hurried away, Cronán turned to Fidelma and forced a smile of apology.

'You must excuse him. Our young Brother Anfudán has much to learn. The announcement of a death during a meal is unforgivable. Did you know Bran Finn of the Déisi Muman?'

'As far as I am aware, I never met him,' returned Fidelma. 'However, I heard that he was newly come to office among the Déisi and that he was young. I gathered that he was recently visiting the Abbey of Imleach after he had paid his respects to my brother. That was why I was surprised by the news.'

Cronán examined her features carefully before replying. 'My people like to keep me informed as to what happens along the borders of Osraige. The Déisi Muman are our close neighbours south of the great River Suir. Indeed, my own cousin was once married to a noble of the Déisi. So it is natural that I take an interest in their affairs.'

'A noble of the Déisi? Would I know your cousin or this noble?'

'Alas, the noble died many years ago.'

'And your cousin? Is she still alive?'

'I have not seen her for many years, for she stayed with her children and did not return to Osraige.'

'It is sad news, made sadder by the fact that Bran Finn was so young.'

'Of course, of course,' the abbot said quickly. 'We will remember him in the community prayers.'

'If you hear how he died I shall be grateful to be informed.' Fidelma implied that the matter was of little concern. 'There are still isolated reports of the Yellow Plague in the land. We must always be vigilant.'

'Of course, the plague has taken many from this land. And now,' he glanced towards Brother Sillán, 'we must go and see what news has been brought to us. You and your companions have had a long tiring day, so we will absolve you from attendance at evening prayers and allow you to retire for an early night's repose.'

The excuse actually suited Fidelma well, and she rose with the abbot.

'Tomorrow morning, when we break our fast, you must tell me more about this sad news and, in return, I will give you all the news from Cashel,' she promised, a false smile on her face.

Later, in their room, Eadulf flung himself on the bed. His face was full of anxiety.

'I am nervous,' he began.

'That much is obvious,' she replied, picking up her *cíorbholg* and beginning to rummage through it before extracting her comb.

'This girl, Ségnat, tells you that we are prisoners in this abbey and she can help us escape. Do you trust her?'

She sat on the edge of the bed next to him. 'We are not yet prisoners, Eadulf. But we cannot continue to pretend to be gullible. Cronán is playing with us like a cat with a mouse. He is trying to find out what we know and what my brother knows. Once he discovered that we are alone here, immediately we became vulnerable. And, yes, I do believe what Ségnat has told me.'

'So we have to escape before first light? That sounds easier said than done.'

The soft tapping at the door held an urgent quality and yet it seemed as if the person was trying to rouse them by making as little noise as possible.

Eadulf swung off the bed and strode to the door. He had barely finished pulling back the bolt when Enda pushed his way in with a muttered apology.

'What is it, Enda?' Fidelma kept her voice deliberately calm. It was clear that the warrior was in a state of agitation.

Enda paused to gather his breath and then tried to speak slowly and clearly. 'Lady, I have just seen the man who called himself Brother Biasta!'

CHAPTER FOURTEEN

'Is Gormán in the next chamber?' asked Fidelma. She did not appear to react immediately to Enda's news.

The young warrior looked puzzled but answered, 'I think so, lady. He was preparing for bed when I saw him last.'

'Eadulf, ask Gormán to join us. Wake him, if necessary, but do so quietly.'

When the sleepy-eyed warrior, who was still dressed, had joined them and Eadulf had closed the door so that the four of them were alone, Fidelma asked Enda to tell what he had seen.

'I needed to visit the . . .' he coloured a little. 'I needed to visit the *necessarium*.'

'Go on,' Fidelma said impatiently, not interested in the warrior's embarrassment. 'And what happened?'

'I remembered where it was from when . . .' He saw the frown deepening on Fidelma's brow and realised that she did not like super-fluous information. 'It is on the ground floor, in the main passageway. I was about to return here when I heard a voice which stopped me. Like you, lady, I have a good ear for voices. This one was familiar and I recognised it immediately. It was that unnatural sibilant speech that brought to mind someone speaking with a mouthful of honey.'

'You recognised Biasta's voice?' she asked.

'Not only his voice. Near to the *necessarium* is a doorway which leads into one of the smaller courtyards. I glanced through the doorway and saw the two men standing under the light of a brand torch. One of them was Biasta. There was no mistaking that cadaverous murderer even if his voice had not betrayed him.'

'Who was Biasta talking to?' Eadulf asked.

'It was the young steward, Anfudán.'

'I presumed that Biasta was the "friend" who arrived with news of Bran Finn's death,' Fidelma said.

'It will be awkward for us if we encounter him face to face,' muttered Eadulf.

'He already knows we are here,' Enda said flatly. 'He was asking why Cronán had not imprisoned us already. Anfudán confirmed what the girl, Ségnat, told you: Cronán is going to try to find out what we know about him first, and whether anyone else knows. But it is clear that we will not be allowed to leave here.'

'Did Biasta say anything further?' Fidelma asked. 'Did he say in what manner we would be dealt with?'

'Nothing was mentioned about that. However, Biasta was asking how it was that we had found out about the abbey. Anfudán said that he could only guess that we had followed Sillán. So he confirmed that Sillán was the man who was awaiting the arrival of the abductors at the shed in Durlus.'

Fidelma let out a soft breath. 'And he recognised me. I suspected as much.' She turned to Enda. 'Best continue with your story.'

'The story is simple. I'll tell you the sense of the words rather than try to recall the actual words themselves. Biasta told Anfudán that he had gone to Fraigh Dubh to deal with Ailgesach. He had left his horse at a spot called the Little Fortress nearby . . .'

'There is such a place very near Fraigh Dubh, where Ailgesach's chapel was,' intervened Gormán. 'Just to the east.'

'Biasta then went on foot in search of Ailgesach.'

'So that is why we did not see him on the road,' Eadulf said. 'He came over the heath.'

'He told Anfudán the rest of the story as we knew it. How he killed Ailgesach and how he escaped us. He went back to get his own horse, incidentally, and turned my mount loose.'

'Did he say anything about the corpse we found or the man and woman who had stayed with Ailgesach? Biasta has taken a long time to reach here.'

Enda shrugged. 'I can only tell you what I overheard. It seems that as soon as Biasta was a distance along the highway from the tavern, he then circled round to the heath. From what was said, I gathered that he then headed east towards Laigin on some errand before coming back here.'

'Nothing else?' asked Fidelma in disappointment.

'Biasta merely said that he had completed his task. He went on to say something about Laigin being nervous in case the plans had gone awry. I could not clearly hear this exchange as I heard someone coming along the passage and hurried back inside the *necessarium* until they passed. When I came out again, I could tell that Biasta was not happy. Anfudán was assuring him that the prisoner would be dealt with tomorrow. But he was asking why the prisoner had not been dealt with already.'

'The prisoner? Who else could he have meant but Torna?' Eadulf interposed.

'So we are no nearer finding out the "why" than before,' he sighed.

'As friend Eadulf says, it sounds confusing,' Gormán observed.

'All puzzles are confusing until they are solved,' Fidelma replied automatically.

'Usually, there are some strands in a tangled rope that can be tweaked out and followed,' Eadulf said. 'In this matter, I agree with Gormán:

I cannot find anything to untangle or that will lead us to an under-standing. The only solution I can see is forcing Biasta to talk. And will he do so?'

'Not without some persuasion,' answered Gorman grimly. 'I might be able to persuade him, if we can lay hands on him.'

'At least we are beginning to find out the "how" and "who",' Fidelma returned crisply. 'Did you hear any more, Enda?'

The warrior shook his head. 'Only that Biasta wanted to go imme-diately to question the prisoner. Anfudán said he must not do so until Cronán and Sillán are ready. Then, unfortunately, I heard more footsteps approaching and I came here quickly to tell you.'

'You are sure that you were not seen by anyone?'

'I am positive that I was not.'

'This confirms the necessity of what I was about to tell you. We have until before dawn to find Torna. If we do not, then we will have to leave without him.'

'You trust this young girl, Ségnat?' asked Gormán.

'There is no one else to trust. Firstly, let us make an attempt to find out where Torna is being held and see if there is a means to free him. I am now certain he is this Uí Duach warrior called Tormeid. I have arranged with Ségnat to meet her here halfway between midnight and dawn.'

'Find and free him? In so short a time? Easily said, lady. But where do we start?' asked Enda.

Fidelma leaned forward confidentially. 'You recall the chambers that they were going to put you and Gormán in earlier – windowless and with locks on the outside? If they are to hold a prisoner anywhere in this fortress, then that is the place to start looking.'

'Enda and I will go and look at those chambers,' offered Gormán.

'It is best if we all go together so that we can watch out for each other,' Fidelma demurred. 'We tread on dangerous ground here. There may be guards and we must be prepared for anything.'

'This is not a job for the sister of the King,' Enda protested.

His words provoked a rare mischievous grin from Fidelma. 'But this is exactly a job for a *dálaigh*. Anyway, sleep is beyond question, so what could Eadulf and I do here except sit in anxiety awaiting your return. And if you did not return, then what? Better we should all know how we fare.'

Gormán looked as if he were about to argue and then shrugged. He knew when to accept her authority.

Enda left the chamber first in order to assess whether anyone was moving outside. It seemed all was quiet. The courtyard below was filled only with shadows caused by the dancing light of the torches that were hung on the walls. For a moment he thought it was deserted, but then something stirred and he stood back into the shadow. A sentinel strolled casually across the courtyard. Enda finally turned to the open door and motioned them forward, holding a finger to his lips and indicating that they should keep close to the wall. Gormán came next, followed by Fidelma and Eadulf. Keeping within the shadows, they crept to the stairs that led down to the passage below. The sputtering lamps still lit the long passage, and by their light Fidelma was able to see that most of the doors were unbolted.

She whispered: 'We are looking for a prisoner, so we are looking for a door that is bolted.'

Almost immediately, Gormán pointed to a door set back in the wall and indicated the bolt, which was firmly secure. He tiptoed towards it and listened carefully. Then he turned and shrugged, mouthing, 'I hear nothing.'

Fidelma frowned slightly. There was no grille or any other aperture in the door and it seemed constructed of extremely strong wood. Bending, she carefully eased the bolt back, then gently pulled the door towards her. It seemed that the hinges were well greased, for thankfully it moved without a sound. She peered cautiously into the darkness beyond. She was aware from the dim lights in the passage that she was facing a curved wall. Then she realised that there was a flight of stone steps winding downwards, as if inside a circular tower. Had she taken a step forward, she would have tumbled down them and broken her neck.

'Take the nearest lamp,' she whispered to Eadulf, who was closest to one of the sputtering lights. He carefully lifted it down from its holder.

'I'll go first, lady,' Gormán said, taking the lamp from Eadulf and pushing gently by her on to the stairs.

There was only room to descend in single file. The stone steps were steep and wound down quite a way.

After half-a-dozen steps Fidelma called up to Enda, who was the last to enter the stairwell: 'Draw the door to, so that it does not attract attention.'

At the bottom of the stairwell they found themselves in an area from which passages led in three directions. The passageways were stone-built. While they were not ancient, the fact that this area had been excavated below ground-level and in a boggy area criss-crossed by streams was obvious. Water seeped through the walls and mosses already covered many of them. It was not the cold that sent uncomfortable shivers through them but the dampness. They could feel it permeating their lungs. It was, Eadulf thought, the unhealthiest place that he had ever been in. Already he felt an urge to cough as the malodorous fumes caught at his chest.

'Where now?' muttered Gormán. 'There seem to be no lights along these passageways.'

'Then we shall have to explore them one by one,' decided Fidelma. 'We'll start down this one.'

'Just a moment, lady,' Gormán said. 'Let us wait and listen a while.'

They were speaking in whispers and it was obvious that, had they spoken louder, their voices would have echoed through the curious underground labyrinth. They paused a while but all seemed silent and they were able to relax a little.

'What could this place have been built for?' asked Enda, breaking the silence. 'I have never seen the like before . . .'

'Certainly not for storage,' Eadulf pointed out. 'You could not store anything down here unless it was fish.'

With only the one light between them, they let Gormán lead the way along the first passage to their left. Two chambers led off on either side and both of these had doors that stood wide open and were devoid of any object to fill them. The passage ended in a blank wall. They turned back and immediately entered the second tunnel. This led into a narrow vaulted path, along which drifted an odour of decomposing vegetation, of swampy marsh and animal excreta. The tunnel vanished in darkness in either direction.

At the side, before they entered this tunnel with its nauseous stench, there was a small passage and Fidelma indicated that they should investigate it. This one seemed to turn and twist, and they quickly learned that if they were not careful, they could lose themselves. Enda took out his dagger and began to make marks on the wall at the end of each section with an arrow-shaped sign to indicate the direction in which they were proceeding.

They noticed that the passage they had come to was slightly drier and the rooms off it were not as wet and mildewed as others. Then Fidelma gasped and pointed. They had come across a door to which the two bolts had been rammed shut. This time there was a small grille at the bottom of the door. The idea occurred to Fidelma, who had seen such prison doors before, that it was large enough to pass a plate or a jug through. A feeling of excitement gripped them, but Fidelma placed her forefinger against her lips, before motioning Gormán to draw the bolts. He bent and eased them both back. Then he opened the door and stepped inside, holding the lamp high.

A figure was lying on a stone ledge which seemed to serve as a bed. A thin blanket was covering the huddled form. This was clearly the prison cell they had been looking for. The figure was apparently deeply asleep, for it did not move as Fidelma joined Gormán in the cell.

'Torna,' she whispered, and reached out to touch the shoulder. But her fingers did not make contact. There was something about the stillness of the form that made her step back hurriedly.

Gormán stepped forward and drew the blanket aside.

Cold, dead eyes stared up at them. The movement in them, which caused them to start for a moment, was only caused by the reflected lamplight shining on them.

Fidelma drew her breath in sharply. 'It is Biasta!'

Eadulf pushed by her and bent over the corpse, at the same time asking Gormán to bring the lamp closer.

It did not take long before Eadulf discovered the cause of Biasta's death. He said, 'He has been stabbed twice with a fairly crude knife. It has more or less ripped the flesh to the heart rather than being a clean stab.'

Gormán bent down and picked something up. It was a metal platter with bits of food still adhering to it. There was no need to explain that this was where the prisoner had acquired his knife.

Now they could see the cadaver without the blanket drawn over it, they realised that Biasta was without his outer garments.

'What do you think?' Eadulf asked, drawing himself up.

'I think Torna may have made his own bid to escape,' she replied grimly.

'So Biasta came down here to question him, in spite of Anfudán's instructions. Torna still had the knife from his evening meal and so he used it to stab the man twice, then stole his outer clothing as a disguise before escaping.'

'But how was he able to pass himself out of the abbey?' asked Gormán. 'You've seen the gates and the guards there.'

'Doubtless he escaped in the manner that Ségnat has planned for us,' replied Fidelma. 'And now that we know he has escaped, we'd better get back to our chambers and hope Ségnat will be able to help us.'

'But perhaps Torna has been caught,' Enda suggested.

'If he has been recaptured, surely his captors would have come down here to find out how he escaped, and then they would have discovered Biasta. We are lucky. He has clearly not been missed,' Eadulf replied.

'Then we should get after him right away for, as you say, he holds the key to this conundrum,' said Gormán.

'Wait,' Fidelma called, as the warrior turned to the door of the cell. 'If we go charging off, we will alert the whole abbey. Leave things as we have found them and we'll try to get back to our chambers without being seen. Let's hope the body of Biasta is not found until after we have left the abbey.'

'If Torna is as clever as I suspect, then he will leave no trail that can be followed,' Eadulf said.

Gormán replaced the blanket over the body of the man who had called himself Brother Biasta, then they left the cell, with Gormán almost reverently sliding the bolts home. Thanks to the marks that Enda had made with his knife, they had little difficulty retracing their steps to the main chamber at the foot of the circular stairwell. They paused there for a moment, as if by mutual consent to recover themselves. Then Enda climbed the stairway first and checked the passageway at the top. It was still deserted.

'All clear,' came his whisper. Fidelma, Eadulf and finally Gormán, still carrying the lamp, followed him into the passage. Once there, Gormán replaced the lamp in its holder and Enda pushed back the bolt on the door.

Without a word, Fidelma led the way back to the upper floor and to their chambers. There was a movement in the shadows near the door of the *fothrucad*, the bathing room, and the slight figure of Ségnat emerged. She looked agitated.

'I've been waiting for you,' she hissed. 'I thought they must have taken you away already.'

Fidelma smiled reassuringly. 'We went to track down the prisoner,' she whispered back. 'We found where he had been kept – somewhere in the vaults. But he has escaped already. In doing so, he killed one of Cronán's men called Biasta.'

The girl shivered slightly. 'Biasta? He was a beast, as his name implies. No one will raise a tear for that pig.' And then: 'Are you sure that the prisoner has escaped?'

'Unless he is wandering in the vaults.' Fidelma felt it unwise to mention that she suspected that Torna was Tormeid.

'We will check, just in case. First we must get you away. There is even more urgency for you to leave here now. Do you have all your belongings?'

It was the work of a moment, to fetch their saddle-bags and rejoin her. In silence, she led them down another spiral stair and through a door behind the bathing chamber. A short time later, they had once again descended into the bowels of the fortress. It seemed amazing to Eadulf that no one heard them as they hurried after the nimble young girl. The builders of this fortress had certainly believed in dark vaulted structures. Pausing only to take a lantern, the girl hastened them through a series of dank passageways until they halted before a bolted wooden door.

It was the smell that Eadulf recognised first before the girl unbolted and opened it.

'This is a special tunnel that leads to a spot under the north walls of the fortress into the bog land. You must follow me closely and in single file.'

After a while they heard the muffled whinny of a horse.

'Do not worry,' came Ségnat's voice ahead of them. 'My comrades have saddled your horses and brought them to the entrance just behind here.'

She moved on a short distance, holding the lantern high, and paused before a small aperture in the wall. It was just big enough for one person to squeeze through at a time. She bent and called through: 'It is I. Is all clear?' There came a faint sound of something being removed beyond and then a soft male voice answered, 'All clear.' She motioned them through, one at a time, and then followed.

They emerged under the dark shadows of the fortress walls into the blackness of the night beyond. Ségnat had left the lantern in the tunnel and there were no lights here so as not to attract the attention of any watchful eye. It took a short while to adjust their eyes to the darkness. Two men were standing holding their horses, which were already saddled.

Ségnat said: 'Remember, this is the north side of the fortress. The land is boggy so make sure that you keep to the well-used tracks. My advice would be that you walk the horses along to that far clump of shrubs and trees. The ground is fairly solid to that point. Then you can mount and ride. Keep carefully to the track there too, and go as quickly as you can. We rely on you to persuade your brother, the King, to return with his warriors and destroy this place.'

'Are you sure that you can't come with us?' demanded Fidelma.

'There are about a hundred of us imprisoned here,' replied the girl. 'The elderly and infirm are now locked in and used as hostages for our good behaviour. So we stay to protect their lives. If we could get them all released, then it might be a different story.'

Fidelma felt reluctant to leave the brave girl and her companions. 'Surely Cronán will know that you have helped us?'

'Your horses were taken to the paddock outside the fortress. We were supposed to be retired for the night. We know nothing of who you were or where you were sent. He can say we are lying, but executing us will achieve nothing. Cronán is an evil and vicious man but he does nothing without a purpose. Remember that.'

The night sky seemed a lighter blue with its myriad twinkling silvery stars. No word was exchanged as they fastened their saddle-bags. Their horses stood patiently as their minders handed the reins to each of them.

Fidelma held out her hand to the girl. 'I shan't forget this, Ségnat,' she said. 'You have my promise that my brother will come and this evil place will be destroyed. You will soon see King Colgú's warriors marching through the gates to demand an account from this man Cronán.'

'We will place our trust in you, Fidelma,' she replied. 'Remember, when you leave here, head northwards for a while. Try to keep away from the obvious tracks towards the west because Cronán may well send his warriors after you, and they know this country. And try not to make any noise until you are well away from these walls. The sentinels are usually alert on the south side where the causeway is built, but on this side, because of the impassable marsh, they tend to be lazy – but they are not stupid. It is best not to chance matters. Go swiftly now.'

'Keep safe, Ségnat.'

'God be on every road that you travel,' replied the girl solemnly.

Leading their horses in single file, with Gormán at the head, they moved out away from the dark shadows of the imposing walls of the fortress and up a steep embankment which brought them on to ground level. Although there were some clouds scudding across the star-filled sky, the moon was up and bright. Fidelma hoped there were no sharp-eyed warriors patrolling the walls, for they would surely see the shadowy forms of four horses and riders moving swiftly away from the abbey. She felt an urge to mount up and set her horse into a canter and get away, far away.

It seemed an age until they reached the blackness of the trees and shrubs and Gormán signalled that they could mount up. Then, with him leading the way, bent over his horse's neck so that he could follow the firm ground of the track, they set off. There was a chill on Fidelma's spine as she imagined hostile eyes observing them. It was only after an interminable time, when Gormán increased their pace, that she began to feel a little more relaxed. But she was acutely aware that it would soon be dawn. Cronán was sure to send his warriors after them.

ChapTER FIFTEEN

Gormán led the way at a good pace due north across the flat boggy plain. There was now a faint glow of light permeating the eastern sky. Enda brought up the rear, trying to scan the surrounding country-side behind them. The day had dawned bright and clear when they reached a point where the track they had been following split in several directions. Fidelma suggested they halt for a brief rest while she consid-ered what route they should take. Her main concern was to avoid pursuit from Cronán's men. However, her purpose was also to catch up with Torna. Fidelma supposed that he would try to get out of Osraige terri-tory as soon as possible, but she knew that Cronán would also come to the same conclusion.

To the west, the track was wide enough for two horses trotting abreast, and it would bring them into the territory of the Éile. Leading slightly towards the north-east was a smaller track. The third track seemed to lead due north. In all directions the land was mainly flat bog land, interspersed by streams and wetland. Here and there were little areas of woodland and shrub, and small isolated hills that seemed incongruous in that type of landscape.

'Where now, lady?' prompted Gormán after a while, casting an anxious glance behind them.

'We'll take that track directly north as it leads away from Durlus but is not so blatant a choice as the north-east one. Anyone following would think we might head back for the land of the Éile, while those with a devious mind might assume we will mislead them by going in the opposite direction. So we'll take the middle path. We can change our direction as soon as it is safe to do so.'

Eadulf glanced at the comfortable wider western highway. 'A pity,' he said. 'The sooner we are out of Osraige, the better I shall like it.'

'No less than I,' Fidelma agreed. 'In fact, I would like to have discovered where all the so-called abbot's new roads led to, especially those towards the east and Laigin. They were built for some purpose other than merely bringing pilgrims this way. Our task, however, is to get ourselves out of harm's way and catch up with Torna. If he has sense, which I think he has, he will avoid paths where his tracks will be easy to follow.'

They turned on to the northern path. After a while they breasted a small hill and halted. They were in an area where the ground grew more undulating, rising from the low-lying bog land on to dry stretches of higher ground, connected by what seemed to be man-made dykes. There was a good view to the north across this countryside and they saw a line of low hills in the distance. They stretched along the horizon in a dark line.

'The mountains of Sliabh Bladhma,' Gormán identified them, noticing Eadulf looking at them.

Fidelma added for Eadulf's benefit, 'The River Suir rises among those peaks and comes down on to the central plain. It is said the mountains are the centre of all the Five Kingdoms. See that peak there?' She indicated a tiny point that Eadulf found was almost impossible to discern at this distance. 'That is called Ard Éireann – Éireann's Height – and it's the highest among the ten main peaks of the range.'

'There must be plenty of places to hide in a mountain range like that,' he said. 'Perhaps Torna would make for those?'

'I doubt it,' Fidelma replied. 'I think that Torna would head to Durlus as soon as possible. In spite of what Gelgéis said, I believe he is well-known there.'

Eadulf suddenly made a noise between his teeth, a cross between a hiss and a whistle. 'I am so stupid!' he exclaimed. 'The man and woman who stayed with Ailgesach – those who rode north: if Torna was that man . . . have your forgotten that we found him without a horse and without a female companion, and encamped by the river seeking a boat to head southwards?'

Even as he spoke he felt more stupid still, remembering why Fidelma had been abducted – because she had been thought to be Torna's companion. However, he could not quite place the events into a logical sequence. Fidelma watched him as he tried to reason things through. And asked, quietly: 'Do you recall where Torna told us that he was heading when we met him?'

'He said he was trying to get a boat to the place of the fork in the Suir, the place called An Gabhailín.'

'It is a small market settlement,' Fidelma said, 'and the closest point the river comes to the Abbey of Imleach.'

'I don't see how that helps us. Why would he have been going to the abbey?'

'Because Ailgesach had been sent to Fraigh Dubh from Imleach. Remember that when Biasta arrived last night, he brought news to Abbot Cronán about the death of Bran Finn, Prince of the Déisi Muman?'

'I remember.'

'Before we came away from Cashel, Abbot Ségdae mentioned that he had to return to Imleach that day because he was expecting the arrival of Bran Finn there. He mentioned that Bran Finn had already visited Imleach because the Brothers at the Abbey were looking after a relative of his who was unsound of mind.'

'I am not sure how that fits,' said Eadulf. 'Why would Torna and this unknown woman be waiting for Bran Finn? To assassinate him? He clearly did not succeed, if he was in search of him when we met him.'

'Bran Finn was already dead,' Fidelma pointed out softly.

'I am totally confused.'

'I agree that nothing is absolutely clear. Let me remind you of the note in Latin that we found in Brother Ailgesach's cabin. It was signed with the letter B.'

Eadulf frowned. 'But if you are saying that Bran Finn was due to meet with Brother Ailgesach . . . oh!'

He stared at Fidelma who simply shrugged and did not help him further.

'We should move on,' Gormán intervened. 'The longer we stay here discussing things, the more dangerous it becomes. We should continue to put as much distance as we can between ourselves and the fortress.'

'Then I suggest we continue north for a while,' replied Fidelma.

'North it is,' grunted Gormán, nudging his horse forward over the high and firmer ground.

It was a difficult track to follow, as they had to keep to slightly higher ground; most of the low land consisted of flat, deep green plains that seemed to be fields that could be ridden across with ease. It was a deceptive landscape, for these were in fact dangerous bog lands. Fidelma knew that a horse and rider could disappear into the hungry, clawing mud in the blink of an eye, so she kept to the hilly mounds and slightly raised paths crossing the plains. Now and then they spotted sheep grazing on the low hills, and this reassured them that they were not completely alone in this great isolated wilderness.

'Hoi! Hoi!'

Gormán swung round at the sound of the sudden cry, his hand going to the hilt of his sword.

A man was standing waving to them from a small mound a short distance from the track. He appeared unarmed, apart from a large staff of the type shepherds used, and his dress seemed to bear out that this, indeed, was his calling. He was a burly man, with a weatherbeaten face, and dark hair streaked with grey.

They halted and watched as the man bounded nimbly down from the height, moving from one tuft to another to reach the bottom of the slope, showing that he knew well the boggy patches. It did not take him long to reach the track and confront them. His eyes widened a little as he took in their dress and especially the emblems around the necks of the warriors.

'Sorry to detain you, lords.' He spoke in the soft country accents of the area. 'Have you seen anyone on horseback ride by on this track? Not on steeds like yours but a good workhorse.'

'Not along this track,' Gormán replied. 'We have seen no horses since we left Liath Mór.' Gormán's mouth suddenly clamped shut and he cast a guilty glance at Fidelma, realising that he should not have given away such information.

The man's pleasant features turned hard. 'You have come from Liath Mór?'

'We have ridden from there this morning,' Gormán replied hesitantly.

'Liath Mór?' The man spat at his feet. 'Blood built that accursed place, and blood will bring it down.'

'What do you know of the abbey?' Fidelma prompted, leaning forward.

'Abbey, is it? What should a poor shepherd know of such a place? If you are from there, why do you have to ask? Know this, that I am no slave of Cronán of Gleann an Ghuail! I am only looking for my horse and since you have not seen it . . .'

'Wait!' snapped Fidelma, as the man had started to move off.

'Understand that we are no friends of Cronán. I want to know why you are seeking a horse, and why you are on foot. Did it throw you?'

The man let out a curious barking laugh.

'My horse throw me?' His tone was incredulous. 'Never! We have been together too long.'

'Then kindly explain.'

'The horse was stolen from my field. I have been following the tracks since dawn.'

Fidelma showed her interest. 'Stolen, you say? By whom?'

'That I do not know. It was taken in the dark this morning. My cabin is along the way there. I was awakened by noises, and when I went outside, my horse was gone. As I say, it's not a grand horse, like the mounts you all ride. But it was my only beast which I used to plough my field and take my cart to market.'

'What is your name?'

'Canacán, lady.'

'So you say that this horse was stolen by someone in the hours before dawn this morning. Where is your farmstead, Canacán?'

'North of the abbey, but to the west of here.'

Fidelma glanced thoughtfully at the shepherd. So Torna had acquired a horse. If he wanted to throw any pursuit off his trail, it would be a logical idea to head eastward in the opposite direction to Durlus. He would do precisely what they were doing; move in the opposite direction to where he intended to go, swing around in a semi-circle and head back west, having laid a false trail.

'You followed the tracks to this point, heading eastwards?'

'As soon as it was light enough, I took my staff and began to follow the tracks. At first they were easy to follow. They brought me to this place. I was hoping the man would not know this area and become bogged down somewhere so that I could overtake him. Now the tracks have vanished entirely.'

Fidelma sighed. 'Well, we must continue our journey. But tell us, that path which heads north-east looks like a good one to follow. Where does it lead?'

Canacán shrugged. 'It curves towards the north-east and to the mountains through the country of the Uí Duach. Is that where you want to get to?'

'We wish to go in that general direction,' Fidelma conceded without being specific. 'The land of the Éile is more to the west, I understand?'

'To enter either territory, you'll have to cross the Black River.'

'How good is the road to the west after that?'

'Quite good. There is even a bridge across the Suir which you can cross and then join the highway south into Durlus. You take your choice. Alas, whichever way you go, it is of no help to me. I will never overtake the thief now.'

'I am sorry for your loss. If we hear anything about your stolen horse we shall make an effort to inform you and see that you are compensated.'

The man sighed. 'Alas, Brehons are few and far between in this place now Cronán controls it. Even if one is lucky enough to find a Brehon, they demand an exorbitant sum for their services.'

With that, the shepherd turned back the way he had come, and they all sat watching him bound away and disappear beyond the mound on which he had first appeared.

'Which way now, lady?' Gormán asked. 'I think it is obvious that our friend, Torna, was the thief who took the shepherd's horse and laid a false trail to the east.'

Fidelma sat thinking for a moment, trying to consider the options.

'We'll cross this Black River and move west at the first opportunity.' She added thoughtfully: 'The eastern branch of the road leads to the country of the Uí Duach. Ségnat and most of the *daer-fuidir* in the abbey were of the Uí Duach. But we will then turn west towards Éile territory and cross the Suir. I made a promise to the girl Ségnat and her helpers and I mean to keep it. We will find the answers to many questions in Durlus and not in this bleak land.'

'Who are the Uí Duach?' asked Eadulf. 'They have been mentioned before but I don't know this clan.'

Gormán glanced at Fidelma. 'I know the story well, lady, unless . . . ?'

'You tell it,' invited Fidelma. 'It will help pass the time as we ride.'

'The Uí Duach was once a powerful family who ruled Osraige. The original Duach's son was called Feredach Fionn. He was known to have great wealth and prestige. But the son of a chieftain named Connla grew jealous and coveted not only his wealth but he also wanted to rule the Osraige. The story is that he waited until Feredach Fionn was lying on his sickbed before he burst into his house, slew him and made off with his wealth. That was less than a hundred years ago. Feredach Fionn's son, Colmán, managed to wrest back the kingdom and rule for nearly twenty years in peace, before members of Connla's family seized the rulership after he died.'

'The Uí Duach never won back the rulership of the Osraige?'

'They did not. But, by all accounts, Uí Duach clan lands were once rich and fertile and no one went hungry, which is as things should be.'

'Is Cronán related to Tuaim Snámha, who is Prince of Osraige?' Eadulf asked.

'That is something we must find an answer to,' intervened Fidelma. 'The question is whether Cronán is a rebellious chieftain or whether Tuaim Snámha, the Prince of the Osraige, is supporting him? Again, I think we shall find an answer in Durlus Éile.'

'Back to Durlus,' sighed Eadulf. 'We seem to be travelling in a circle.'

'I would have thought you would have grown used to long journeys on horseback by now,' Fidelma replied cheerfully.

'I was never meant to be a horseman,' he said gloomily. 'Yet it seems that ever since I left my people in Seaxmund's Ham, to follow the New Faith, I have continually travelled. Is there no place in this world where I have not been? I have been to Rome, to Autun, to Gaul, Burgundia and to Armorica; across the Kingdoms of Angles and Saxons and Britons, and all over these Five Kingdoms of Éireann. I have been sea-sick many, many times. Is there such a malady as horse-sickness? If so, I have had it.'

Gormán chuckled and slapped his thigh in appreciation. 'And yet, my friend, you will not quit until you have reached your goal. That is a sign of perseverance in the pursuit of truth, which anyone should be proud of.'

'If we resolve this mystery, Eadulf,' Fidelma, riding alongside him, leaned over and laid a hand on his arm, 'I guarantee that we shall not move out of sight of the great Rock of Cashel for a long, long while.'

'If I recall, our journey started by the finding of a body almost under the shadow of your brother's palace. Now see where we have been led.' Eadulf gestured across the flat boggy plains.

'Then the sooner we start for Durlus, the sooner we will arrive.'

'Which leads me to suggest, lady, with the sun being high, not having broken our fast this morning, we might usefully stop at the next tavern we come across,' suggested Enda.

'I doubt there are many taverns within this country,' replied Fidelma sceptically. 'Nevertheless, I think you have made a good suggestion . . . if we find one. It is always good to pick up any local gossip. We might be able to find out more about Cronán.'

They continued onward in silence through the almost desolate countryside and then started to notice slight changes as more trees began to grow and the ground became firmer. The distant mountains were becoming clearer as they approached. They forded several streams before they came to one which was quite wide but not so deep that they could not cross it on horseback. This was undoubtedly the Black River. On the far side, Gormán let out a grunt of satisfaction and pointed. Among some thinning trees ahead they could see some cabins and hear the sound of a hammer striking an anvil. Then they saw movement of animals and people.

'A small settlement,' Gormán announced unnecessarily. 'Let's hope they have a tavern rather than asking hospitality from farmers.'

A shout from the woods told them that their approach had been spotted and they were aware of several men taking up farm implements – scythes, rakes, hammers, whatever came to hand. They moved slowly forward to what appeared to be the entrance of the small settlement while women were gathering the children who had been playing and drawing them back towards the shelter of the cabins.

'They seem a nervous set of folk,' murmured Eadulf.

'Don't touch your weapons,' Fidelma ordered, noticing that Gormán and Enda's hands were near their sword-hilts. 'Let me go first.'

As they trotted up the track, they saw that trees encircled a dozen cabins, almost as if planted as a protective wall. One of the huts was obviously a smith's forge; smoke was lazily circling from the fire before it.

'Halt there, strangers!' instructed a strong, firm voice. The speaker was a tall, well-muscled man, who held a blacksmith's hammer across his chest in a ready position. His leather apron and sleeveless jacket proclaimed his profession. Not only was his face cleanshaven, but his head as well. Fidelma brought her horse to a halt and her companions followed her example.

'Peace and health to you, smith,' she greeted.

The man's eyes narrowed with suspicion. 'You know me?'

Fidelma laughed in amusement. 'It would take someone with no sight in their eyes to mistake you as other than a smith. Or do you often put on that garb and take up a smith's hammer to mislead passing strangers?'

One or two of the men standing close by smiled at this. The smith shifted uncomfortably. Obviously he did not want to appear a fool in front of his fellows.

'What do you want here?' he demanded gruffly.

'We were looking for a tavern to refresh ourselves on our journey to Durlus. If there be no tavern, then we would seek some hospitality; that is all.'

The group of men looked at each other and there was a perceptible loosening of their grip on their weapons.

'You seem very nervous, my friends,' Fidelma continued. 'Is there a reason why you would treat travellers in this manner which contravenes the laws of hospitality?'

Only the smith had not made any indication of changing his suspicious gaze.

'Who are you?' he demanded.

'I am Fidelma of Cashel, sister to Colgú, and these are my companions. Eadulf of Seaxmund's Ham, and Gormán and Enda of my brother's bodyguard.'

The names effected an immediate change on the smith and his companions. At once they put down their makeshift weapons and the smith came forward with his head lowered respectfully.

'Your pardon, lady. These are worrying times. You are welcome to the Baile Coll, the township of Coll of the Uí Duach. I am Coccán. As you rightly say, I am the smith here. I am also the tavern-keeper and many other things beside. Please, step down and let us offer you refreshment, as poor as it is.'

He turned and signalled a young boy to come forward to hold Fidelma's horse as she dismounted. The boy then gathered the reins of the four horses and led them towards a fenced paddock.

Already the atmosphere had changed and become relaxed and normal. The women had released the children back to play, although most of them came over to stare at the strangers while the womenfolk returned to their various chores.

Coccán led the way into a building next to his forge which turned out to be used as a tavern.

'Why the suspicious welcome, Coccán?' Fidelma was saying as she seated herself.

'Merchants passed this way yesterday, lady, coming from Durlus, across the river. They spoke of large armies riding out of the west, burning and destroying.'

Gormán glanced at Eadulf. 'Perhaps they were the same merchants who were in Durlus Éile the other day,' he muttered.

'We too have heard such stories,' Fidelma assured him. 'But we were informed that these so-called armies are just bandits. They are far to the west of here and not likely to threaten this area.'

'Perhaps it is a question of each time a merchant tells a story, the numbers multiply and thus increase the wealth of the tale,' Enda said cynically.

Fidelma had noticed that the smith still looked uncomfortable.

'You are not telling me the entire truth, Coccán,' she went on quietly. 'Is there some other threat that worries you? As you are of the Uí Duach, I can only presume that it is due to the tales we have heard of the enmity of Cronán?'

'And you would not be wrong, lady.' The words were spoken by a large woman who came forward with jugs of ale and mugs, and some meats, bread and apples.

'Cronán of Gleann an Ghuail is not well disposed towards our people, lady,' shrugged the smith.

The woman who had been serving the ale gave a sniff. 'Why not tell her?' she said to the man in a harsh voice.

Fidelma glanced from the woman to the smith. 'I am not only the sister of your King, but I am a *dálaigh*. You need have no fear of me.'

The woman placed her large hands on her hips. 'There you are.' She addressed her husband. 'What better protection could you seek than that? Speak, man!' She turned apologetically to Fidelma. 'My husband only hesitates because he is fearful for our people here. Our clan has suffered much of late.'

'So what troubles you, Coccán? Who threatens this place?'

The smith sighed. 'It is as my wife says. This little settlement of ours could be wiped out in the blink of an eye. We have no one to protect us. That is why I feared to speak.'

'You have my word that no one will harm you so far as I can speak on behalf of my brother the King.'

'A township due south-east of here was destroyed only a few days ago. One of the survivors came here to tell us.'

Fidelma's eyes widened a little. 'An entire township destroyed? Are you saying that Cronán did this?'

'His men were responsible,' Coccán told her. 'Several people were slaughtered. The rest were carried off to his fortress. One of the survivors was my own cousin. He and half-a-dozen other men escaped and are now seeking shelter at the rath of the chieftain of the Uí Duach, or rather what remains of his rath, which is not far from here. My cousin told us that the township was summoned by a group of strange religious. The leader of these religious told them that the settlement must provide all able-bodied men to join them in a great crusading army. That they must gather with weapons within two days and swear an oath to fight in the name of the True Faith. In addition, the women and children were to gather all their goods and treasures and bring them with them. They had two days only, otherwise retribution would be levelled against them.'

'So what happened?'

The smith gestured unhappily. 'The chieftain of the settlement laughed outright. He told them that only Tuaim Snámha, the Prince of Osraige, had the power to summon the clans for a hosting, and only then in time of dire need. He had seen no fiery cross summoning any of the clans of Osraige, so by what right did a religious have to do so and call down retribution on them if they did not obey?'

'And then?'

'The religieux, who was cowled the whole time, as were his companions, simply said that the word had been given. If the trumpet was sounded seven times, then they should beware. How the people responded to it was up to them. If they made a wrong choice, then the word of their example would be spread across the land of Osraige, and it would serve the religious just as well to inspire others to join them.'

'Are you saying that it was these religious who fired the township?' asked Eadulf.

'They allowed the people two days, as they warned, but those in the township just thought they were crazy and dismissed the threat. On the third day, the township found itself surrounded. Out of nearly sixty people, ten were killed and the others taken prisoner. That is, except my cousin and some friends who escaped, as I have said, and that was because they had left the settlement to tend to their traps in the wood, thus were spared the fire and sword that their companions suffered. Those young men have now sworn blood vengeance and taken up arms as warriors. It will do them no good. Six against the hundreds that Cronán has to command.'

There was a silence and then Fidelma asked: 'You said that they were ordered to present themselves with weapons in two days and the women and children were to bring goods and treasures. At which spot were they meant to gather?' She had a feeling that she knew the answer before he gave it.

'To the Abbey of Liath Mór.'

Fidelma was not surprised. 'Liath Mór,' she said heavily. 'I have given my word that my brother will free the Uí Duach hostages there. What was the name of the township that was destroyed?'

'It was called Eirc, and it is due south of this place in Uí Duach country.'

'And was your cousin able to identify any of these cowled religious who first issued the threat to the township?'

'Indeed he was. He recognised the leader as Cronán's nephew Anfudán.'

Fidelma was thoughtful for a moment and then she asked: 'The words that your cousin used – are you sure he said, "If the trumpet was sounded seven times"? Or did he speak of the "seventh trumpet"? This is important.'

Coccán raised a hand to his forehead as if to massage his brow.

'It might well have been as you say. I heard this story from my cousin. He might have confused the words but I am sure the figure seven was used in it.'

Eadulf glanced at Fidelma. 'That is not the first time we have heard about a seventh trumpet.'

'It was what Brother Ailgesach was raving about in his delirium,' Enda put in. '"Beware the seventh trumpet."'

'It is from the holy writings,' Fidelma explained. Then she sighed deeply. 'There is something dark and evil in these matters. Something that I . . .' She addressed the smith. 'When did Cronán first start to raid the Uí Duach?'

The man spread his hands helplessly. 'The best of our warriors have been taken or killed over several years as the fortress of Cronán and his roadways have risen to dominate the Osraige lands to the south.'

Coccán's wife added: 'It began many years ago. Cronán started to raid the Uí Duach lands and take prisoners to use as labour to build his fortress. Some of the hot-headed warriors of the Uí Duach marched on Cronán to demand reparation. He defeated them easily and seized them as well. He declared most of them as *daer-fuidir* to work in his fortress.'

'It is amazing that no word of this has come to my brother in Cashel,' Fidelma said.

Coccán shrugged. 'This is an isolated territory. Just bog land. No one cares about this place or its people. We get few travellers, for the highways pass around our lands and not through them. Anyway, people have become too scared to speak. Those that do speak out disappear.'

'Tell me more of this Cronán. Does anyone know his purpose?'

The smith actually burst out with a sharp laugh. 'Lady, he is Cronán of Gleann an Ghuail, Lord of the Hills of Sliabh Ardachaidh. His purpose is conquest and power. He simply marched into the buildings of Liath Mór several years ago, threw out the community, declared himself Abbot and forced men to start building a great fortress under the guise that it was an abbey. He now controls all the northern marshland of Osraige.'

'Well, whether chieftain or abbot, the religious are not above the law of this land,' Fidelma said angrily. 'Surely your own prince, Tuaim Snámha of Osraige, would bring the man to order? Has no one made representations to him?'

'Cronán claims the support of the Prince of the Osraige and so we must accept his authority.'

'No one has contacted Cashel and told the King how matters fare here?'

'What would distant Cashel care about a few poor people in a bog land of no worth?'

'Even the poorest in our society have rights and will receive protection from any despot, be he King or Abbot.'

'That may be so in an ideal world where people respect the law,' interposed the wife of Coccán with a bitter smile. 'In our world, lady, it does not happen. I know it is so written in law, but that does not mean it is so done in practice. To stand up against the wishes of King and Chieftain, who calls himself an abbot, is like trying to flood your field by throwing stones in the nearby river.'

Fidelma's frustration was apparent by her sharp exhalation of breath.

'Well, my brother, the King, shall hear about this and there shall be an accounting. I promise you that, as both the King's sister and as a *dálaigh*.'

She suddenly realised that Eadulf was dozing and recalled that none of them had slept during the previous night at Liath Mór. Gormán and Enda also looked exhausted. They had to move on, but sleep must come first. Even a short nap would help before continuing their journey. Coccán's wife interpreted the situation and led them to a side room, promising to rouse them to give them time to cross the river and reach Durlus before nightfall.

To Fidelma it seemed that her head had hardly rested on the pillow when there was a sudden shouting and the sound of a horse approaching at a gallop. At once Gormán and Enda were up, swords at the ready. But Coccán the smith appeared in the doorway and told them: 'Put up your weapons. It is only my cousin. He is the very person that I have spoken of from the township of Eirc.'

They returned to the tavern room and a moment later a young man strode in. He was covered in dust and there was blood on his forehead. He looked exhausted. 'Water, I pray you,' he gasped.

He was handed a beaker of water which he drained at once.

'What is it?' demanded Coccán.

'I came to warn everyone,' the man said breathlessly. 'They must be prepared for an immediate attack from Cronán.'

'An attack?' repeated Fidelma, moving forward.

The young man glanced at her in surprise and then, seeing her in the company of Coccán, nodded. 'An attack from Liath Mór. My chieftain sent half a dozen of us to attempt to speak with Cronán this morning, to ask why he had attacked a peaceful township . . .'

Coccán interrupted hurriedly: 'I have told them about the attack.'

'We had not ridden far south when we heard a band of men riding hard in our direction. I told my men to disperse and string their bows. It was then I saw that those approaching wore the dress of Cronán's cowled murderers. I was going to let them ride by when I saw that son of a she-devil, Anfudán, at their head. In my mind's eye I saw the burning township of Eirc. I could not help myself, but I loosed my arrow straight into his throat! Some of his men had their swords out but my companions let loose a shower of arrows. Some fell and the rest appeared unnerved and fled the ambush. They left three dead including Cronán's nephew. I have no regrets for them.'

'Are you sure that Anfudán is dead?' asked Fidelma.

'I am sure,' the young man confirmed grimly. 'Now we will have stirred up a hornet's nest. Once Cronán learns what has happened he will unleash his hordes against us. That is why we are riding in all directions to warn our people. Everyone must be prepared to abandon their homes and settlements and move towards the mountains. You know what Cronán did to our township of Eirc. He has brought fire and sword to many other Uí Duach settlements. His vengeance will now be merciless and total. You must prepare to fight or to flee for your lives.'

CHAPTER SIXTEEN

A short time later, as they continued their journey westward towards Durlus, Eadulf turned to Fidelma.

'The matter becomes more complicated as we progress,' he observed. 'Added to everything else, we think we have found an abbey and uncovered a fortress run by a merciless warlord who thinks nothing of destroying an entire township.'

'You realise that Anfudán and his men were probably chasing after us or Torna when they encountered those Uí Duach men?'

'Yes, that is true. When we get to Durlus, will you send on to Cashel to inform Colgú?'

'That is my intention,' she assured him. 'The sooner he can send warriors here to protect the Uí Duach, the better.'

'That is one thing that bothers me,' Eadulf reflected.

'Only one thing?' responded Fidelma with a ghost of a grin.

'Cronán is obviously increasing his labourforce. Why? Why does he want these workers?'

'It takes a lot of labourers to build the causeways and roads,' replied Fidelma.

'There is something else,' Eadulf went on. 'I presume that most of the people in Osraige are of the Faith?'

Fidelma was puzzled. 'Of course.'

'Why then do you suppose a condition was made that the townsfolk of Eirc were to swear allegiance to the *True* Faith and not just to serve Cronán?'

Fidelma was about to respond when she realised the emphasis that Eadulf had placed on the word, and found that she could not answer him.

The journey to the edge of Éile country before the River Suir was made without incident. They had decided to walk their horses slowly, resting now and then, just in case of the need to call upon them for sudden bursts of energy to take them out of danger. So there was a feeling of chill in the air from the oncoming autumnal evening darkness by the time they approached the river.

'It will be sunset soon,' Fidelma said, glancing up to the western sky. Perhaps they had stayed too long at Coccán's village of Baile Coll. But they had needed to rest.

'We will still reach Durlus well before dark,' Enda told her, seeing her anxious gaze and thinking she was worried about arriving in darkness.

The river, when they came to it, was not as broad as its lower reaches and it was easily fordable. They moved across on horseback in comfortable fashion as the passage of the shallows was clearly visible under the translucent waters in spite of the lateness of the day. Even the darting brown trout caused Eadulf to think that all he had to do was dismount, bend down and catch them with his bare hands. They splashed up on to the far bank and took a moment to rest again. It seemed absurd that he could think such incidental thoughts in the dark atmosphere of the last few days.

To the south stretched the flat plains that reached down to Cashel and, for Eadulf, they were familiar and reassuring compared to the countryside through which they had just ridden. To the north was the long dark ridge of mountains stretching westward. Then he frowned as he spotted a peculiar indentation in the silhouette of the mountain range.

'What's that?' he asked Fidelma, pointing towards it.

'They call it Bearnán Éile,' she replied immediately. 'The Gap of the Éile. In olden times, it was where warriors defended the route into Muman when the hosts of the Northern Kingdoms tried to invade.'

'A curious gap,' observed Eadulf, still looking at the silhouette of the dark table-top of the mountain.

Enda, who had overheard the conversation, interrupted with a chuckle. 'A curious legend has originated here. I heard it from the mouth of a merchant of the Éile. He was trying to belittle Cashel. The story is this: local people say that the devil was flying over this land and decided to take a bite out of the mountain-top. The people of the Éile were so pure and unblemished that it was reflected in the clean and unpolluted taste of their green fields and mountains. The devil didn't like the taste and so, further on, he spat it out. The piece he spat out, which landed on the plain further south, was the Rock of Cashel.'

'A silly story and one not worth its repeating,' Fidelma said dismissively. 'However, it is a ride south to Durlus, so let us not waste time.'

Enda grimaced at Eadulf. It was clear Fidelma did not share their sense of humour.

They moved on, proceeding at a comfortable pace down the track along the riverbank. The road was well-kept, according to law, and it was clear that the Éile were keen to impress visitors from the north when approaching their principal fortress and capital. The road was wide enough, allowing, according to law, for two large wagons to pass one another in opposite directions with ease. Hedges, weeds and brushwood were cleared or cut back and tended. Where the road passed over soft, muddy ground, planks were laid, resting on trestles so that they did not sink. It was a technique used for causeways and crossing bog land, as they had witnessed in the lands of the Osraige. Eadulf knew that, according to the *Book of Aicill*, which contained the laws on the subject, each local chieftain had to see that these highways were maintained in a proper manner.

Large sections of the way, which moved directly south, did not follow the course of the Suir but passed through a forest.

Gormán had been riding a short distance ahead of them as he had done almost since they had left Cronán's fortress early that morning. He had volunteered to do this in order to give them warning in case of any attack. But now he suddenly turned his horse, almost rearing it on its hind legs, and came galloping back to them.

'Take cover!' he ordered sharply. 'There, down there!' He pointed to a gap between thick bushes of gorse and blackthorn which led into a depression sheltered from the roadway.

'What is it?' demanded Fidelma, as she and the others instantly obeyed.

'Warriors! Coming up the road.'

They followed his instruction quickly, moving down an incline into a deep hollow and finding themselves completely hidden in a thicket reinforced with closely growing trees. They were able to halt there and sit quietly on their horses. Within a few moments the sound of cantering horses vibrated along the track and continued quickly by. Gormán had, in fact, swung off his mount and, crouching low, had moved out of the hollow to a spot where he could observe the passing of the riders without being seen. They heard the receding sounds of the party and began to relax as Gormán returned.

'Mounted warriors, lady,' he reported. 'I felt it better that we do not encounter any strange warriors while we are outside the protection of Durlus.'

'Did you see who they were?' Fidelma asked.

'They bore the standard of the Éile. But until we know who our enemies are, it is best to take precautions.'

'I would agree,' she said. 'You saw no sign of any religious emblems carried by them?'

Gormán immediately shook his head. 'These looked like the warriors who guard the Princess of the Éile.'

'And they were riding north towards the Gap of Éile?' Fidelma mused. 'If any danger threatens Muman, that is where one would expect it to come from. I wonder if Gelgéis has already heard news from Osraige.'

'You think that there is some threat to Durlus? Some connection with what is happening among the Osraige?' asked Enda.

'Until we can find out what is at the core of these matters, we have to proceed with caution. I suggest that we wait until darkness before we enter Durlus, and then proceed directly to our friend Gobán the smith.'

Eadulf looked surprised. 'Why go to the smith and not to the fortress of Gelgéis?'

'We don't know yet where Gelgéis stands in these matters. I think she has lied to me about Torna. It was in one of her store sheds that my abductors left me for dead with the body of the poor ferryman's son. Even though she expressed horror and denied knowledge of this, I want to see if Gobán can provide any more information for us before we go to see the Princess of the Éile again.'

'Very well, lady,' Gormán said. 'Remembering that Gobán's forge is on the far side of town, do you want to ride through the town or swing around it and approach from the west?'

'Can we do so?'

'It is not an easy route, lady, as we would have to travel on lesser roads than this one, perhaps those of the *tuagrota* category.'

Eadulf knew this was a small track usually called a 'farmer's road', since farmers used these tracks as a right of way to an adjacent main road. But Fidelma was shaking her head.

'With darkness coming on, I think we should stay on the main road. In this case it is a matter of better the path that we can see rather than go in darkness along byways we do not know.'

Gormán glanced up at the sky. 'Then, perhaps, we should wait here for a while before proceeding. We can then move through the town after dark.'

Eadulf knew that Fidelma was not the most patient of people when there was a purpose to be fulfilled. But she could sit still for long periods when she began to meditate as the ancient priests in her country were wont to do. It was called an act of *dercad* in which the body and mind were still and rested. Fidelma slid from the back of Aonbharr, securing the beast's reins over a bush before choosing a dry spot to be seated, cross-legged and hands in her lap. She closed her eyes.

Eadulf dismounted, following the example of securing the reins of his own horse. As if by an unspoken agreement, both warriors went to separate places where they could watch the road, while Eadulf moved to take a seat on a fallen log. Eadulf always found it hard to do nothing, merely awaiting the passing of time. He could never master the ancient *dercad* technique that Fidelma had tried to teach him. He tried to sit still but instead of closing his eyes, he let them wander around the small clearing. There was a slight breeze and he was aware of the rustling of the leaves of the hardy rowans, whose white blossoms had now trans-formed into bunches of red berries. Among them were their almost inevitable companions, the slim trunks and grey-white bark of the silver birches, with their hanging branches. The whisper of the trees distracted him a little.

He turned to the area of thicker growth which concealed them from the roadside. Here, dense blackthorns, with their cruel thorns, provided a basic defence, interspersed with the yellow flowers and curved spiny leaves of a gorse species that also provided evergreen cover. Eadulf suddenly caught sight of a small brown furry creature scuttling at his feet. It was no bigger than the distance between the first and second knuckles of his forefinger. A tiny shrew in search of insects for its food. A faint fluttering noise then captured his attention and a bird with a long stiff tail, down-curved bill and a distinctive stream of white around its eyes, landed at the foot of one of the nearby rowan trees.

Eadulf watched with mild interest as it suddenly started to ascend the trunk, uttering a shrill 'tsee'-sounding call. It climbed in a spiral, in jerky fashion with sharp talons around the trunk. Now and then its bill would strike at the tree as it found its prey: weevils, beetles, earwigs, woodlice and spiders that hid in the cavities of the trunk. Eadulf frowned, trying to recall what sort of bird it was. Was it a *meanglán*? He tried to think of the name in his own language. The tree-creeper – that was it! The name exactly described what the bird did when it went in search of its food.

Eadulf was not aware that he had made a noise of satisfaction when he remembered the name. The slight sound drew an exasperated sigh from Fidelma.

'Can't you *ever* relax?' she complained.

'I thought I was,' protested Eadulf.

'I swear I could hear your mind working from here,' she replied. 'The purpose of the *dercad* is to empty the mind of thoughts, not to fill it.'

'That's impossible.'

'It is difficult to begin, but never impossible.'

'I was merely looking at our surroundings.' Eadulf was irritated. He thought he had been occupying his time meaningfully.

'Indeed, and you were being distracted by the sounds and vision of the world about you. The idea of the *dercad* is to see into the internal and not be distracted by the external.'

They fell silent again and this time Eadulf closed his eyes and tried to let his mind drift. It seemed only a second later that he found Gormán halting before him and realised, with a feeling of guilt, that he had nodded off. He was aware of Fidelma asking: 'Is it time to be moving?'

'We can reach Durlus at nightfall if we start now,' the warrior confirmed. 'There has been no other movement on the road.'

'Very well.' She glanced at Eadulf, who was blinking and yawning. She smiled and shook her head. 'You were supposed to be meditating, not sleeping.'

He sprang hastily to his feet, brushing the leaves and twigs from his clothing. The others were mounting and he went to untether his horse, thinking he would never get the hang of this meditation. His mind was either too active or he emptied it so much that he fell asleep.

Led by Gormán they once more set off south along the road to the township that surrounded the fortress of the Éile.

Gormán was right. They reached the outskirts of the township when darkness had begun to engulf it and when tiny flickering lights began to spread from building to building. The main square was lit well, and there was a brazier in the centre around which a few people still congregated. Above the town was the dark outlines of the fortress of Gelgéis, the Princess of the Éile. The road to it was also well lit so they could see that the gates still stood open, with warriors pacing up and down outside.

Gormán took them straight through the square and along the road to the southern outskirts where Gobán's forge was situated. Although it was dark, the fires at the smithy were still ablaze and the ring of metal against metal could be heard, showing that the smith was still at work. As they came to the entrance of the forge, they saw him bent over his anvil.

Gormán raised his voice to greet the smith.

Gobán turned in surprise, lowering his hammer.

'So, you have all returned safely,' he greeted them. 'Did you discover what it was that you set out to find?'

Fidelma dismounted. 'Partially,' she replied. 'But once more we come to you seeking hospitality . . . and some information if you have it.'

The smith grinned. 'Well, I suppose I should now end my day's toil. I was trying to sharpen a plough-share for my neighbour, Lorcán. But it can be finished in the morning. Bring your horses in and we'll put them out to grass in the back field again. There's water there for them as well. As for hospitality, there is ale and meat enough, but the sleeping accommodation will be cramped, as well you know. I can sleep in the forge . . .'

'As can Enda and I,' said Gormán immediately.

Gobán asked Enda to keep watch on the forge fire to make sure that it didn't spark but died gently. There was always a danger of fire at a smithy's forge. Then he organised the leading of the horses into the field, and providing fodder and water for them. Before long he had also arranged ale and platters of food for his guests in the cabin behind his forge.

'So, Gobán?' asked Fidelma, after they had settled to their meal. 'We are anxious for any news. Has anything been happening since we left?'

'They found the body of the ferryman's son where you said it would be,' he replied soberly. 'Then Bishop Daig took the body downriver to the young man's father, Echna, the ferryman.'

Fidelma nodded sadly. 'Justice has already caught up with some of those who took his life,' she murmured.

The smith gave her an uneasy glance but did not press for details.

'Tell me,' she went on, 'what have you heard of Liath Mór?'

'The old Abbey of Liath Mór? Apparently it has been rebuilt. Have you seen it, lady?'

'We have, but what have you heard about it, other than it has been rebuilt?'

Gobán shrugged. 'I have only heard from travellers that it is now more of a fortress than an abbey. I was also told that it is an unfriendly place that denies hospitality to passing travellers.'

'Have you heard anything about Cronán?' asked Eadulf.

The smith scratched his head. 'All I know is that Cronán of Gleann an Ghuail is a warlord, related to the Prince of the Osraige, Tuaim Snámha. He declared himself abbot and started rebuilding the abbey. I gather it is completed.'

'Anything else?'

'Only that no member of the former community remained there after the rebuilding started. There was even a story that the real abbot, Cuanchear, had been killed by Cronán. These were rumours,' he said heavily. 'No one knew the truth.'

Fidelma sighed. 'What you say does not surprise me,' she said. 'What happened to the rest of the brethren there?'

'I think the remaining brethren fled into Laigin. In truth, lady, it is a place to be avoided. At least it is isolated in the bogs and wastes, so we are not much concerned with it.'

The smith went outside to fetch water and Eadulf gazed thoughtfully at the smouldering fire. 'It is Cronán's intentions that I want to know about,' he said at last.

'Intentions?' Gormán stretched on his seat. 'That's simple.' Fidelma and Eadulf stared at him in surprise. 'Think like a warrior intent on warfare. You saw the work they are doing, laying the new roadways across the bog land. Then we have evidence of Cronán trying to increase his strength in labourers.'

'You are right.' Eadulf turned suddenly to Fidelma. 'It is a highway system into Éile where none expect it. Think of horses being able to move rapidly over what was impenetrable bog land. He means to send raids into Éile. Most important is the question – how long will it be before an attack is launched along the new roadways?'

'From what I saw, it would take only several days before it is completed,' said Gormán.

Fidelma was shaking her head. 'Raids? I don't think he is going to all that trouble just for raids.'

Gobán had come back with the water and overheard the last remarks. He stood bewildered. 'I don't understand. Are you saying that the Osraige are going to attack us?'

'Perhaps not just the Osraige,' replied Fidelma grimly. 'Cronán's roadways stretch to the east as well as the west, and I agree that I do not think he means them for friendly trade.'

'But it is over in the west that we hear of attacks, raids and battles,' protested Gobán.

'Battles?' Fidelma picked out the word. 'We have heard of raids in the west but not of a battle.'

'There has been news of one,' Gobán told her. 'The King's warriors clashed with the raiders.'

'Who was victorious?' Gormán asked anxiously. Both he and Enda were friends as well as comrades of Dego, who had been sent to track down the raiders.

The smith held up a hand in a helpless gesture. 'It was only yesterday when a merchant came to the tavern in the market square. He was bursting to tell his news. I will try to stick to the basic facts, so far as I can claim them to be facts, because I swear that with each telling he grew more colourful in his account.' He paused and took a sip of his ale. 'Do you know the place in the Land of the Uí Fidgente called Muine Gairid? There is a large religious community there.'

'I know it well,' replied Fidelma.

'That was to be the target of these raiders. However, as they were gathering for the attack, they were surprised by your brother's warriors. They engaged them and caused them to withdraw back to the western hills. They saved the community from destruction.'

'It is a large community,' Eadulf said with a frown. 'How on earth did the raiders think they could destroy it?'

'According to the merchant's tale, their numbers could match the religious there man for man.'

'But that means—' began Eadulf.

He was interrupted by Enda. 'That means that a single *ceta*, a company of one hundred of our warriors, drove hundreds of raiders from the field. If that is true, there will be no approaching Dego for his vanity and boasting.'

The smith had not finished. 'According to the merchant, the King's men did have help. They were reinforced by warriors led by Donennach, the Prince of the Uí Fidgente himself.'

'Then these raiders were not Uí Fidgente?' Gormán said. 'So, who were they?'

'Everyone is talking about them but this merchant could offer nothing but speculation.'

'Are you telling us that the raiders have been defeated?' Fidelma said.

'The merchant had much more to say but little of relevance to fact,' lamented the smith. 'However, I did gather that the battle was fierce and the raiders finally retreated, leaving many dead and a few wounded behind. However, they moved into the western mountains, and the pursuers lost them.'

'Was nothing learned about who they were or who commanded them?' Fidelma asked.

'The merchant only knew that they claimed to be fighting for the True Faith.'

Fidelma and Eadulf exchanged a startled glance.

'What did they mean by that?' Eadulf wanted to know.

The smith shrugged. 'What can I say? I am only repeating what this merchant said and can add nothing of my own. As I said, I doubt whether he was in possession of all the facts himself.'

'You are right,' Fidelma agreed. 'Anyway, tomorrow I shall go to the fortress for there is much I need to discuss with Gelgéis. Eadulf will come with me, while Gormán will see what gossip he can pick up in the market square.'

'And what of me, lady?' asked Enda.

'At first light you, Enda, will ride for Cashel and inform my brother what is happening here and especially of the need to launch an attack to free the Uí Duach in Liath Mór.'

'Do you really think that there is a threat to Éile from the Osraige?' Gobán asked. 'Is Cronán definitely going to attack us?'

'I am sure of it, but I can't say when it will happen,' replied Fidelma. 'However, I think it will take place soon. We know that new roadways are near completion. Events have already started to occur in Osraige that bear similarities to events in the west. They must be connected.'

Eadulf had never seen her as agitated before. She tried not to show it but he knew her well enough to spot the signs. Usually, even in the most difficult circumstances, Fidelma looked upon problems as a challenge that brought a sparkle to her eyes as she took them on. He realised that she was frustrated because none of the facts that they had gathered seemed to fit into any coherent pattern.

'Perhaps we should get some rest,' he ventured.

She looked at him with anger flickering in her eyes. He waited for the inevitable barb of sarcasm, but then she seemed to relax and even smile.

'I suppose I am being tedious, Eadulf. I fear that I have repeated my frustration about this matter many times of late.'

'Of course not,' he said. 'You have always told me that it does not do any harm to reassess what facts are known.'

'I have also told you that there should be no speculation without information,' she replied.

'I do not hear you speculating,' he said gently. 'What I hear is the enumeration of the facts that we have gathered which seem related but in such a manner that can make no sense.'

Fidelma chuckled in approval. 'You are right, of course. It is the mysterious relationship of these facts that vexes me more than if I had no facts at all.'

'We have come a long way – and in just four full days since the body of the envoy was discovered,' Eadulf said.

'Except that he was no envoy.'

Eadulf was just about to demand an explanation when the sound of a distant trumpet made them all start.

Góban was first upon his feet. 'That is the sound of some person of rank announcing their approach to the fortress of Gelgéis.'

'So long as it is not the seventh trumpet,' Eadulf half-joked with dark humour.

Fidelma rose to her feet. 'So late in the evening? That is unusual.'

'Sometimes it happens, lady,' replied Góban. The smith had opened the door to his cabin. 'Nevertheless, there are horses coming this way,' he added, as he placed his head to one side in a listening attitude.

'Horses,' muttered Gormán. 'Several horses. It sounds like warriors.'

'Wait here,' Fidelma instructed. 'I will go to the entrance of the forge and see who they are as they pass by into the town.'

'But . . .' Eadulf began.

'Stay here,' she insisted, and moved quickly to the front of the forge. She hid in the shadow of the building and peered towards the roadway which led past into the town. A dozen riders, carrying torches to light their way, followed by a wagon drawn by two horses, also with lanterns on it, were moving slowly by. Her mouth opened slightly in astonishment as she recognised them.

Her companions waited apprehensively in the cabin for her return. Gormán and Enda had their hands on the hilts of their swords, although what they expected to do if this was some enemy at the gates, Eadulf was unsure. The tension in their bodies was obvious. Judging from the sounds of the horses' hooves on the road, there was a whole column of riders. It seemed a long time before the clatter of the horses and wagon began to fade into the distance.

Fidelma wore a thoughtful expression as she returned and resumed her seat.

'Were they more of Gelgéis's warriors?' asked Gormán.

'Not this time,' she replied simply.

'Then who were they?' prompted Eadulf.

'From the banner they were carrying, they were warriors of the Osraige. I saw it in the light of the lamps they carried.'

'Osraige? You mean they are Cronán's warriors!' Gormán exclaimed. 'Are they going to attack Durlus?'

'And how many warriors are there?' demanded Enda at the same time.

'About a dozen, I should say,' Fidelma told them, adding, 'But I do not think they come as enemies. At their head was none other than Drón.'

Eadulf took some moments to register who she meant. 'Drón of Gabrán? Do you mean the father of your brother's wife-to-be?'

'The very same,' Fidelma affirmed heavily. 'Drón – and his daughter Dúnliath is with him. At the end of their column was a wagon containing their belongings. Now what on earth are they doing here? And why have they left Cashel?'

CHAPTER SEVENTEEN

A s Fidelma and Eadulf rode up the slope towards the gates of the
fortress of Gelgéis of Éile, they could see that this time they had
been recognised. One of the guards had disappeared inside, apparently
to alert the steward. The other guard greeted them respectfully as they
trotted through the gates into the courtyard, and two attendants came
forward to hold their horses' heads while they dismounted. The atmosphere was friendlier than at their first arrival at the fortress – was it
only two days ago?

The sallow-complexioned steward, Spealáin, appeared on the steps
of the Great Hall, then came forward to greet them with a wary smile
of welcome on his dark features.

'Greetings, lady, and to you, Brother Eadulf. We did not expect you
back so soon, especially with the news from the west.'

'And what news would that be, Spealáin?' Fidelma asked.

'Have you not heard, lady? It is bad news, indeed.'

'I have heard that there has been some battle near Muine Gairid,'
she said, glancing at Eadulf, 'and that the bandits were dispersed.'

'That is old news now, lady. Apparently there is to be another and
bigger battle expected any day now. Your brother, King Colgú, has led
his troops out of Cashel to meet the rebel force. I am told that he has

led an entire *cath*, a battalion of three thousand warriors, into the land of the Uí Fidgente.'

They heard his words in amazement and Eadulf began: 'But if the bandits had fled after being confronted . . . ?'

'The raiders apparently rode back into the western mountains where, it is reported, they have regrouped and were joined by many others. Now a large rebel force has gathered.'

'How did you come by this news?' Fidelma wanted to know as the steward conducted them into the Great Hall of Durlus.

'We heard the news only last evening, when Drón of Gabrán and his daughter arrived from Cashel. Your brother had sent them hither for safety in case the day does not go well for him.'

'They brought this news to you?' Her tone was slightly incredulous.

'Indeed, they did, lady.'

'And they are still your guests here?'

'They are. They came with an escort of Drón's bodyguard.'

'We would like to see the Lady Gelgéis,' Fidelma said after a brief pause.

'I will take you to her chambers immediately.'

They followed him across the Great Hall which, for the time being, appeared to be empty. Eadulf could see that Fidelma was as astonished by the news as he was. It was astounding to hear that a band of raiders had grown overnight into a large rebel army. However, it seemed unlike Colgú to send anyone away from Cashel for safety. The great Palace of the Eóghanacht was one of the strongest fortifications in the country, rising 200 feet above the surrounding countryside on its base of limestone rock; its walls had never suffered a defeat since the great King Corc had first kindled his fires on it and proclaimed it to be the seat of the Kings of Muman many centuries before. Not even when Colgú had led his troops against the rebellious Uí Fidgente some years before at Cnoc Áine, had there been any necessity to abandon Cashel. This was strange news indeed. She wished that she had not let Enda ride off to Cashel at dawn if all was not well there.

Spealáin accompanied them up a wide stone stairway on the far side of the hall to the next floor, where the senior members of the fortress had their living quarters. At the end he asked them to wait while he knocked respectfully on the door of what turned out to be Gelgéis's personal reception room. He entered and closed the door behind him, only to reappear a moment later and beckon them in.

Gelgéis had risen from her chair in token of respect to Fidelma. Eadulf, behind Fidelma, saw her body tense a little. Then he realised that Gelgéis had been closeted with Drón, the emaciated-looking noble of Gabrán. He had also risen, and there was something close to a sneer on his thin, red lips. Unattractive as it was, Eadulf knew from past experience that this was the closest the man could come to a smile.

'It seems that my small fortress has become a place of refuge for the Eóghanacht and their kin,' greeted Gelgéis dryly.

Fidelma took a deep breath. 'I am not seeking refuge . . .' she began.

'Then you have not heard the news?' It was Drón who intervened.

'The steward has told us a story which we can hardly believe,' she replied. 'I find it curious that my brother, the King, should advise you, Lord of Gabrán, to seek refuge away from Cashel whose walls have never once been breached since the Eóghanacht made it their capital. I am told that a rebel army has suddenly materialised as if by magic out of the western mountains.'

Eadulf was sure that the twitch at the corner of Gelgéis's mouth was one of amusement. She indicated that they should be seated and resumed her own seat.

'We were just discussing the matter,' she said. 'Of course, your brother would be concerned with the safety of his bride-to-be but I think Drón was about to answer this very question when you arrived.

If I understand matters correctly, Drón himself made the suggestion that they come here.'

'I was concerned,' admitted Drón. 'I suggested that we removed ourselves from Cashel until this matter of rebellion in the west is resolved.'

Fidelma turned to him. Her expression brought a faint colour to his pale cheeks.

'I have my daughter's safety close to my heart, lady,' he continued defiantly. 'It was not of myself that I was thinking. I would stay and draw my sword in defence of the King if it were necessary. I have tried to keep Dúnliath out of harm's way ever since her mother abandoned her. Were it not for my daughter, I would gladly volunteer to join any of the King's hosting.'

'Of course,' agreed Gelgéis in a sweet tone of voice. 'No one is questioning your loyalty to the King. Yet I perceive no danger to Cashel. You have told me that Colgú is leading an entire battalion of his warriors out to face these rebels . . .'

'And yet,' Fidelma intervened with emphasis in her voice, 'my understanding was that these same rebels, whoever they are, were just a band of raiders, bandits who had already been defeated by a single company of my brother's warriors. How have they now grown into a great rebellious army?'

'The survivors of these rebels were driven back into the western mountains and there they were joined by many others,' Drón said immediately. 'That certainly was the story that merchants brought to us and why I decided to hasten here for safety when Colgú left to confront them.'

'With my brother gone from Cashel, who was left in charge of its defences?' asked Fidelma.

'Why, his heir-apparent, I suppose. Finguine.'

'So Finguine has returned from the Cenél Lóegairi?'

'He returned a few days ago. However, with rebellion abroad I felt that we should seek protection in a more neutral territory.'

Fidelma's eyebrows rose slightly. 'A neutral territory? Éile is still part of the Kingdom of Muman,' she pointed out.

'Well, whatever the cause of your coming here, Drón,' Gelgéis said quickly, 'be assured that you and your daughter are welcome to share the safety of these walls from any enemy, be they foreign or domestic. The freedom of our fortress is yours, Drón. I shall look forward to your company at the midday meal?'

It was clear that Drón was being dismissed. He did not look happy but rose reluctantly to make his exit with formal etiquette. However, as he passed by Fidelma, he paused and whispered: 'There is a matter I wish to speak with you about. Urgently.'

'Then I will find you later,' nodded Fidelma.

When the door had closed behind him, leaving Gelgéis alone with Fidelma and Eadulf, the Princess of the Éile seemed to relax.

'I cannot forget that Drón is of the Osraige and I find it difficult to trust him,' she confided. 'So now, Fidelma, you seem sceptical of the news he brings. You do not believe that there is a full-scale rebellion in the west of the kingdom rather than just a series of bandit raids?'

'What do *you* believe?' countered Fidelma.

'I think Drón is more timid than he likes to admit.' Gelgéis smiled. 'I believe he came here fearing more for his own safety than that of his daughter. But I can't see him inventing the idea of your brother having to lead an entire army to the west if he was just going to put down a few bandits.'

Fidelma was thoughtful for a moment.

'I could understand the matter of a western rebellion more readily if the Uí Fidgente had joined it. For a long time they tried to overthrow Cashel, but the defeat of their warriors at Cnoc Áine some years ago saw an end to such ambition. Prince Donennach, who rules now, is a wiser head than his predecessors. He has brought the Uí Fidgente to a peaceful and productive state of affairs. And, of course, we have heard that these western raids were as much against their settlements as anyone else.'

'Added to the fact that the bandits have never been large in number,' according to reports, it seems curious that an entire army has suddenly emerged to frighten Drón,' Eadulf said.

Gelgéis was nodding slowly. 'I cannot disagree with your observations.'

There was a tap on the door and Spealáin came in, looking anxious. He hurried over to Gelgéis and murmured in her ear. She visibly started and her expression matched that of the steward. Then she rose.

'You will have to excuse me,' she said. 'Some urgent matter needs my attention. I shall be busy for a while but I trust you will join me for the midday meal. We shall talk more then.'

Fidelma and Eadulf rose in surprise at this brusque dismissal.

'We were hoping to put some questions to you,' Fidelma protested.

'The hospitality of Durlus is yours, lady,' replied Gelgéis. 'I hope, before long, that I may fully explain my situation. But, like you, until I can understand certain things and who is involved, I can trust no one . . . not even the sister of a King.' She turned to Spealáin. 'See to the wants of our visitors,' she instructed him.

As Spealáin was ushering them from the chamber, Fidelma saw that Eadulf about to speak, but she shook her head in his direction to stop him making any remarks in front of the steward.

'How may I be of service to you?' asked Spealáin.

'Where is Drón at the moment?' Fidelma enquired.

'He went to the stables where some of his men are tending their horses.'

'His Osraige warriors are at the stable?'

'Some of them. Others are playing *buanbaig* in the courtyard.'

Buanbaig was, like *fidchell* and *brandubh*, a popular board game.

'Do you have a good garrison here?'

Spealáin appeared to realise what her question implied.

'Enough to protect Durlus,' he replied distantly. 'But I fear that your question is inappropriate. I can answer only to the Lady Gelgéis on matters of detail of the security of this fortress.'

'Inappropriate or not,' Fidelma said steadily, 'I would be on constant alert, with warriors from the Osraige being allowed unhindered access to this fortress.'

The steward stared at her for a moment and then gave an eloquent shrug. 'You share my lady's concerns. Don't worry. They will be watched – as will all the strangers within this fortress.' The last sentence was added softly, almost as an afterthought.

They had come to the main door of the Great Hall where the steward halted and said apologetically, 'If you will forgive me, I have other duties to attend to. But you can see the location of the stables from here. Unless you have specific need of me, I will let you find Drón by yourselves.' With a swift nod of his head, he vanished into the hall.

Fidelma was thankful, for she did not want the steward present when she spoke with Drón. She was about to proceed down the steps to the courtyard when she saw Eadulf looking puzzled. As he was about to speak, Fidelma gave him one of her rare mischievous grins. 'I swear I shall scream if you say that you have no understanding of these matters, Eadulf.'

'I wish I could say it were otherwise,' he sighed. 'It is clear that Gelgéis is not being open with us. What does she mean, that she cannot trust you? Whose side is she on?'

'Fidelma!'

The call of greeting was almost gushing with good will. They turned to see the slender figure of Dúnliath emerging from the Great Hall behind them.

'Why, Fidelma, and Brother Eadulf . . . how wonderful to see you both here! I thought I was going to be so bored. Now I am happy.'

Fidelma suppressed an inward groan. 'It is good to see you so well, lady,' she replied pleasantly. 'I had heard that you came here with your father.'

The girl pouted. 'Oh, indeed. He is a dear person but such a dullard – always busy with affairs of state and law and wars and all those silly things. He insisted that we must come here . . . and for why?'

Fidelma's expression was solemn. 'He did not tell you?' she queried.

The girl frowned. 'Something about being safe until affairs in Cashel were cleared up. I don't know what affairs. Do you?'

Fidelma ignored the question and asked: 'How did you leave my brother?'

'Colgú? He was well when I last saw him.'

'When and where was that?'

'Yesterday morning at Cashel, when he left.'

'Where was he going?'

'He said something about having to ride off with some of his warriors. I don't understand it. We were going to have such fun with a feasting and entertainment, and he suddenly changed his mind and said he had to leave.'

Fidelma regarded the girl with disapproval. She wondered how on earth her brother could be attracted to such a . . . the word that came into her mind was *óinseach*, which described a foolish, giddy young woman. How could she become Colgú's wife when she had no thought for anything other than pleasure?

'So Colgú left Cashel before you?' Eadulf interrupted her thoughts. 'Did he expect you to leave as well? Or did your father decide to leave after he had left?'

'Oh, I don't know. Anyway, it is good that you are here, lady.' The girl was chattering on, oblivious of their serious expressions. 'Maybe we can persuade Gelgéis to organise a feasting and entertainment? I heard there is a travelling band of gleemen in the township.'

Eadulf had to think before he was able to translate the word *crossan* as gleemen. Dúnliath caught his frown and said quickly: 'I mean jugglers, buffoons and entertainers.'

'Perhaps you should speak to Gelgéis about it.' Fidelma forced an icy smile. 'We have some serious matters to attend at the moment.'

Dúnliath pouted once more. Eadulf half expected her to stamp her foot. 'Everyone, it seems, has serious matters to pursue. Does no one find time to enjoy themselves here? At Cashel there was always business that called Colgú away. As King he should instruct others to carry out his orders and not have to do things himself.'

'Lady,' it was Eadulf who spoke softly, 'it is in the nature of kingship to be the servant of the people.'

'A king is not a servant!' The girl giggled as if he had made a joke. 'You speak nonsense, Saxon.'

'Angle,' corrected Eadulf mildly, but the girl ignored him.

'My father is Lord of Gabrán and this being so, people hurry to carry out his will. If they don't, they know they will incur his displeasure.'

'The sign of good kingship is wisdom and the ability not to ask of others what you cannot do yourself.'

'A king may do what he pleases, Saxon,' she said airily. 'He is higher than the people and they must obey or be punished.'

Eadulf's smile was fixed. 'When I came to this country, I found a question in the law text known as the *Crith Gablach*. It asked: *what makes a king higher than the people*?'

'And did you also find the answer?'

'The answer was that it was because the people ordained the king and not the king who ordained the people.'

For a moment the girl stared at him in incomprehension. It was

Fidelma who felt that she had to try to explain. 'No one is above the law, Dúnliath, not even a king. A king is there because the people appointed him, and he can only remain king as long as he has their approval. He is there by the will of the people.'

The girl shrugged, saying, 'I have no understanding of such things. But I find Brother Eadulf speaks in amusing fashion. In truth, you must come to a feasting and entertain me with tales of your strange land. You will be better entertainment than a simple gleeman.'

Eadulf looked outraged but Fidelma gave him a warning look.

'We must be off,' she said coolly. 'Doubtless, we shall see you later.'

She turned and walked down the steps to the courtyard and Eadulf hurried after her. As they walked over the flags towards the area of the stables, he could not restrain himself.

'It is not my place to criticise, but—' he began.

Fidelma cut him short. '*De gustibus non est disputandum*,' she said. The words literally meant 'about tastes there is no disputing'. She felt a little guilty as she said it because it was her brother's tastes to which she was referring.

Eadulf thought for a moment. 'I suppose that it is better not to argue about matters of personal preference, but I have no understanding of the attraction apart from the physical.'

They came to the stables and found Ailill. The handsome young warrior hailed them with a broad smile.

'Greetings, cousin Fidelma. I did not expect to find you here. When did you arrive?'

'We have only just come,' returned Fidelma. 'I observe that you still travel with Drón and his retinue?'

'You sound disapproving, cousin,' the young man said. 'But he was my fosterer and raised me as a warrior, and so I am beholden to him. I command his small bodyguard.'

'I did not mean to sound critical of your motives. We do not seem to have had much time to get to know one another.'

'Doubtless we shall see more of each other, cousin, after the Lady Dúnliath marries your brother.'

'Doubtless,' she echoed, trying to keep the lack of enthusiasm for such an event from her voice. 'We are actually looking for Drón and were told that he was in the stables.'

'He was here earlier but left.'

'Do you know where he has gone?'

'I regret I do not, cousin. But I do not think he has left the fortress. Perhaps he is resting in his chamber. Is there anything that I can help you with?'

Fidelma thought for a moment and then told him: 'I was surprised that you left Cashel in case of attack from the band of raiders. You must know how strong the defences of Cashel are. I would think that it was the safest place in the kingdom. That was why it perplexes me, to see you here seeking shelter at Durlus.'

Ailill sighed. 'If the truth were known, cousin, I think the suggestion came from Drón himself. I agree that we would have been safer in Cashel than here, but Drón seemed to get it into his head that there was some rebellion against Colgú. But, after all, what need we fear of a band of religious fanatics, raiders out of the Glen of Lunatics, led by a crazed old woman? However, Drón is a father and is fearful for his daughter's safety . . .'

'Lady!' One of the guards from the gate came trotting up, apparently looking for her.

'What is it?' She turned, distracted for the moment.

'A man has left an urgent message for you at the gate.'

'A message – for me? Is he at the gate now?'

'He left it a short time ago, lady.'

'Why was I not informed before?' she asked crossly.

The warrior flushed. 'Because you were then with the Lady Gelgéis and I could not disturb you. It is only now that I was told you were in the stables.'

'Very well,' she said in a conciliatory tone. She glanced back to apologise to Ailill but found that he was already walking over towards the main buildings. She turned to the guard. 'What is this message and who left it?'

'The message was simple, but he made me repeat it. It was that you should go to the shed where you were left and meet with him. The man said that he would wait there until midday and no longer. You should go there by yourself if you wanted to learn the secret of Liath Mór. He emphasised that part – that you should come alone, otherwise you would learn nothing. Those were his words and beyond that I have no understanding of them.'

She was examining the guard carefully. His features were without guile. He had delivered the message woodenly as if reciting it by heart.

'And did this man have a name or a description?' she prompted.

'He was man of medium height, clad in a long grey cloak and a cowl over his head that made any close description impossible.'

'Had you seen this person before?'

'Not to my knowledge, lady. That is all I know. Is something wrong? Should I report this matter to Spealáin, the steward?'

'You have done your duty,' she replied. 'That will be all.'

'This is a trap if ever I heard one,' Eadulf said when the guard had returned to his position. 'It is one of Cronán's men.'

'It could also be one of the *daer-fuidir* who has escaped with some information; although it does sound more like a trap. On balance, there is enough bait to make the chance worthwhile.' Fidelma made her decision. 'Come – let's find Gormán,' she said. 'We shall go and meet this person, but on our own terms.'

*   *   *

Gormán was easily found, in a tavern at the corner of the market square.

'What do you intend, lady?' he asked after she had explained the situation.

'You said that this shed was directly across the river, opposite the wooden quays of the town?' Fidelma asked. 'I am afraid I have little remembrance of such details when you rescued me.'

'You are right, lady. That is probably why this man, whoever he is, has chosen the spot. From that shed he will see you coming across the river and will thereby ensure that you are alone.'

'Is there any other place where I could cross unseen?'

It was Eadulf who pointed out that where they had recrossed the river and taken Fidelma back to Gobán's forge, was at the south end of the town. Here, the river curved so that any boat crossing there would be obscured from the hut.

'That settles it,' she announced. 'I shall get a boat and cross from the jetty directly to the hut. I shall be alone.'

'Alone? That's inviting trouble,' Eadulf protested.

'You two must already be across the river and come up on the hut through the trees that surround it,' she said. 'Then I shall cross. We do not want our friend to be able to slip away. Understood?'

'How long will you give us to get into position before you cross?' Gormán was ever the practical strategist.

'I'll wait on this side of the river until I hear two short blasts from your hunting horn, Gormán. Don't sound it too near the huts so as to alarm our friend. I want him to think that you are just someone hunting in the forests beyond.'

The warrior agreed. As they rose to leave, Eadulf leaned forward and placed his hand on her arm. 'For Alchú's sake be careful, if not for mine.'

She looked back at him. 'I'll be careful for *all* our sakes, Eadulf,' she replied solemnly.

*   *   *

It took Fidelma a while to explore the quays along the river of the township before she discovered a boatman who had a suitable little craft carved out of a single piece of oak. The owner made no fuss about letting her borrow it. She rowed downriver to the spot nearly opposite the collection of huts on the other bank and pretended to be checking something in the bottom of the boat. Thus she was able to delay until she heard the two short blasts from a horn somewhere in the woods behind the huts. Then she began to row across the river, judging its flow so that she was not swept too far downstream. She was near the bank, her eyes focused carefully on the huts, when it happened almost too quickly to follow.

As she neared the bank, the door flew open and a figure appeared. The man had a drawn bow in his hands and, had she not bent to take up the boat's painter to make it fast, the arrow would have caught her full in the chest. As it was, it skimmed so low across her back that she could almost feel its passing. There was a cry as Gormán appeared suddenly at one side of the hut with Eadulf running up on the other side. The bowman, his grey robes flying, had taken in the situation in a moment and turned, running down the side of the hut. Eadulf tried to stop him but the bowman, using his bow as a weapon, struck out, causing the wood to crack into two pieces and Eadulf to stagger back and lose his footing from the impact of the blow. Then the bowman, with Gormán following, disappeared from sight.

Fidelma ran forward to help an embarrassed Eadulf to his feet. He was bruised by the blow but otherwise unhurt, and angry that he had been unable to stop the attacker. They heard the whinny of a horse and then the crashing of undergrowth. It was not long before Gormán returned, his expression furious.

'He escaped?' There was hardly any need for Fidelma to ask the question.

Gormán was clearly annoyed with himself. 'He had a horse ready behind the hut and sprang on to it like a veteran warrior. He'll be halfway back to Liath Mór by now. But I recognised him.'

'You did? Who was it?'

'The hood of his robe fell back and it was our friend Brother Sillán.'

Fidelma sighed deeply. 'Well, at least that does not surprise me. But why try to assassinate me now? Cronán must know that I will have passed on the knowledge we gained and, if not I, then you would have shared that knowledge.'

'Maybe Cronán wants revenge for the death of his nephew, Anfudán,' offered Eadulf.

Fidelma turned to her companions. 'Tonight I shall request permission to stay in the fortress. Now, Eadulf, I think we should have that word with Drón.'

She and Eadulf recrossed the river without incident. Gormán left them and went to take the other boat back and go to Gobán's forge to collect his horse and their saddle-bags. The warrior who had given Fidelma the message from Sillán greeted her with an anxious look as they approached the gates of the fortress.

'Did you see the messenger, lady?' he asked nervously. 'Is all well?'

'I saw him,' she confirmed with dry humour as she passed him. 'However, he had to leave in a hurry but his message was clear enough.'

As they were crossing the Great Hall, Ailill was coming down the stairs from the guests' quarters.

'Are you looking for me, cousin?' He greeted her with a smile.

'I am still looking for your foster-father.'

'I am sure that he is resting in his chamber.'

'Do you know where that is?'

'Up these stairs, turn to the right and his chamber is at the end of the passage. Shall I come with you?'

'There is no need,' she replied.

The young warrior raised a hand to his forehead in a vague salute and left them. They ascended the stairs and turned into the passage. Eadulf rapped sharply on the door at the far end. There was no answer, but some sound caught Eadulf's ear.

'There is someone in there,' he said, raising his fist and hammering on the door. Moments passed without any answer so he grasped the ring-handle and twisted it. It opened easily and they stood on the threshold peering in. The room was well lit from a tall window.

Drón was lying on his back on the floor just under the open window. His chest was covered in blood, and blood was still bubbling from the side of his mouth. He was coughing a little. While there was no sign of a weapon, it was clear that he had been stabbed several times in the chest just below his breastbone. Fidelma stood back to allow Eadulf to kneel down at the man's side. A cursory glance told Eadulf enough. He raised his face to Fidelma and shrugged eloquently.

'He's still alive, but . . .'

Fidelma bent down. 'Drón, who did this to you?'

The pale eyes tried to focus but the effort was too much. Between coughing and choking on the blood, Drón strove to form words.

'Too . . . too late,' he managed to articulate. 'Ét . . . Étain . . .'

Then blood spurted like a fountain from the corner of his mouth, and a strangled sound came from him as his body convulsed in its death throes. Then he lay still.

Eadulf's expression was stern. 'Do you think that Sillán has been here before us? He kills Drón and then attempts to kill you.'

Fidelma did not respond immediately. Instead she rose and walked to the chamber door and closed it. Then she walked back to the window and glanced out.

'Sillán might have come to the gate to deliver his message for me, but he then went to ambush me on the far side of the river. This killing was but recently done. There was no way he could recross the river and accomplish this deed. This looks like the work of a separate hand.'

'If so, it is surely a curious coincidence,' replied Eadulf. 'Anyway, we must inform Spealáin, the steward, at once.'

Fidelma put out her hand to stop him. 'Did you hear his last words?' she said.

'I did. It was Étain. Wasn't that the name of one of his wives?'

'Ah, so it was,' she said thoughtfully.

'Maybe his last thoughts were of her?'

'Maybe.'

'At least we know that *she* did not kill him,' added Eadulf as an attempt at dark humour.

Fidelma peered around the chamber. There was no sign that Drón had struggled with his assailant before receiving the fatal blow. Everything was neat and tidy; even the man's bed had not been disturbed.

'Go in search of the steward,' she said finally. 'I'll see if I can find anything else here. The only thing we can be sure of is that the killer came in by the door. The window is too high above the ground outside. Oh, Eadulf, tell the steward to ask Gelgéis to break this news to Drón's daughter.' She frowned suddenly. 'Her life might be in danger too. Spealáin should have a care for her welfare.'

'That is, if Gelgéis and her household are not mixed up in this matter,' Eadulf pointed out. 'How can we trust anyone?'

'You are right to remind me of that fact.' Fidelma was serious. 'I am convinced that many answers to our questions will be found here.'

'Here and not Liath Mór?' Eadulf was surprised.

'Here,' Fidelma repeated firmly. 'Find Spealáin while I see if I can find anything that will help us.'

Eadulf hurried off on his errand.

Fidelma returned to the body and examined it carefully. All she could tell was that Drón had been facing his killer at the time when he had been stabbed. His dagger was still sheathed and there were no other weapons to hand. She noticed his sword standing in a corner near the bed. She went to look at it. It was obviously where he had placed it when he came to the room. It was now clear to her that he had let the killer come inside and there was no suspicion of any impending attack until the person struck. That indicated that he knew his killer. Nothing else provided any other clue at all. She went back to where the body lay under the window, feeling baffled and frustrated. Another mystery or part of the same mystery – and nothing to provide a link!

As she stood there, a sound came up through the open window. It was a soft footstep on the flagstones below.

She leaned out and glanced down into the small passage that ran under the window. A figure was moving quickly by. It took her only a moment to recognise the young man. She gave a gasp.

He heard the sound and turned, looking up to see where it came from. His eyes widened in astonishment as they met her own.

'Torna!' she exclaimed.

CHAPTER EIGHTEEN

G elgéis greeted Fidelma and Eadulf with a worried expression as
they entered her chamber. Spealáin, her steward, stood to one side
with Bishop Daig of Durlus. They obviously shared her anxiety. She
waved them to seats without rising herself. That she had forgotten the
etiquette of greeting the King's sister was a token of her concern at
the recent news.

'This is a bad business,' were her first words.

'Have you informed Dúnliath?' Fidelma asked.

'I have indeed. Bishop Daig has tried to give her comfort but she
has withdrawn to her chamber with her grief.'

'And has Ailill been informed? He is commander of Drón's
bodyguard.'

'He has, and is making preparations.'

'What preparations?' Fidelma was puzzled.

Gelgéis looked at her in surprise. 'Why, to take the body of Drón
back to Gabrán for the *aire*, the watching, and the funeral obsequies
due to a chieftain of Gabrán. Dúnliath intends to join them as soon as
she has composed herself.'

It was custom that a day and a night were usually given over to a
vigil for the corpse of a noble before burial at midnight on the next

available day. Fidelma knew that it would take a few days to reach Gabrán.

'She cannot leave,' Fidelma said quietly but firmly.

Gelgéis's expression now was one of bewilderment mixed with irritation. 'Who is to say she may not?' she demanded aggressively. 'I have agreed to her request to do so.'

'With respect, lady, the matter is not in your hands. It is a matter of law.'

'Law? May I remind you, lady, that you are not in your brother's court now, to dictate what is or what is not the law! This is Durlus Éile and I have my own Brehon by whom I will be guided.'

Fidelma's eyes narrowed; a sign of warning to those who knew her. 'I am acting by commission of my brother, the King of all Muman, and believe this is—'

'Your belief is no concern of mine, Fidelma. My own Brehon will determine the cause of Drón's death and who is responsible,' snapped Gelgéis, unnerved by events.

'Your own lawyer . . . who is he?' asked Fidelma mildly.

'He is named Brocc. He is well-qualified to handle this matter.'

'Ah, I think I have heard of him. But I am told he is qualified only to the level of *cli.*' There was a pause and Gelgéis's brow furrowed. She sensed what Fidelma was about to say.

'I suppose you hold higher authority over his qualification?'

Fidelma smiled tightly. 'I am qualified to the level of *anruth*, as well you know,' she said.

Gelgéis sighed with resignation: 'So, are you assuming authority over this matter?'

'I am.'

'Then we must await your orders.' She glanced at her steward and Bishop Daig, saying with faint sarcasm: 'We must all cooperate with Fidelma of Cashel.'

The two men shuffled uncomfortably but said nothing.

Fidelma did not even look at them. 'My orders are firstly that Dúnliath and her retinue must remain at Durlus until my investigation is concluded.'

'And secondly?'

Fidelma held Gelgéis's eyes with her sharp gaze as she spoke. 'Secondly, you will now produce the man called Torna.'

It was Bishop Daig who answered her. 'I think that you have asked once before about a man called Torna and were told that no one in Durlus knows anyone by that name.'

'Then perhaps you know him as Tormeid? By whichever name you know him, I want him produced.'

She saw Gelgéis's eyes widen at the sound of the name. It was only a slight movement before her features tightened into a mask. This time it was Spealáin who spoke. 'I am confused, lady. When you were here a few days ago I recall that you told us that this person, Torna, had been taken against his will into Osraige. Why would he now be here?'

'He was taken to the Abbey of Liath Mór across the river in Osraige and made prisoner there. However, he managed to escape. I saw him a short while ago in the passage that runs below Drón's chamber, just after Eadulf and I found the body of Drón. So please do not waste time playing word-games with me, nor pretend that he is not in this fortress!'

Gelgéis was silent, staring at the floor. The others waited uneasily for her response.

'The time for prevarication is over, lady,' prompted Fidelma. 'I speak not only as sister to the King but as a *dálaigh*, and there is little need for me to remind you that there are penalties for one who ignores the request to speak the truth. Torna, as I know him, or Tormeid, as I think you know him, is one who, by whatever name he bears, has suffered the events that I have told you about – abduction, imprisonment at

Liath Mór, escape and arrival here in your fortress. Do you deny knowledge of him?'

She caught sight of Bishop Daig's glance towards Gelgéis and said, 'I see that some spark of memory is now awoken in you, Bishop.'

'I know of no one called Torna,' he muttered stubbornly.

'That was *not* the last question I asked,' snapped Fidelma. 'As a Bishop, you will recall that you should not bear false witness. That is part of the Faith as well as our law.'

Bishop Daig flushed. 'I do not think you need lecture me about matters appertaining to the religious, Fidelma of Cashel. As I recall, you have formally renounced your vows in this matter.'

'My vow is to uphold truth and the law, and that was made long before I entered a religious community and found it as corrupt inside its walls as the world is outside! So I ask you again – and please consider my question before you answer it.'

Bishop Daig flicked a tongue over his dry lips.

Gelgéis intervened before he could reply. 'Are you accusing this man, Tormeid, of the murder of Drón of Gabrán?'

'How can I decide that until I have questioned him?' Fidelma replied, sensing that she was finally breaking through the barrier of denial.

Gelgéis then said: 'Can you tell me something of what you know about Tormeid?'

Eadulf groaned inwardly as he recognised another prevarication. Nonetheless, Fidelma stretched almost lazily in her chair.

'Let us concede that the real name of the man I know as Torna is Tormeid of the Uí Duach. He pretended to be a poet and knew Torna was the name of a famous bard. Tormeid, however, was a warrior. I saw, even in the darkness on the riverbank, how he attempted to fend off the abductors that night.

'Not everything he said was a lie when we camped with him by the river, and so I have interpreted what he said using some of the information that we have gathered recently. I believe I can recount his background. Cronán is not well disposed to the Uí Duach clan and had asserted his authority over them. Tormeid told me that he had been taken prisoner during warfare between his clan and a powerful chieftain. That powerful chieftain was, of course, Cronán. Cronán had seized many of the Uí Duach and made slaves of them – *daer-fuidir*.'

She paused. There was a quiet tension in the room as everyone waited for her to continue the story. Gelgéis cleared her throat a little and motioned to her to go on.

'So there was Tormeid, a prisoner – a slave – in the fortress of the Lord of Gleann an Ghuail . . . a *daer-fuidir*. There he fell in love. The girl was called Muirne. Unfortunately, Muirne was Cronán's daughter. They were about to be betrayed by a fellow prisoner whom Tormeid had consulted and so they eloped. They were crossing a river, which I believe was the Suir, when the girl was drowned.'

Eadulf leaned forward eagerly and added: 'Hence, when Cronán's project for the rebuilding of the Abbey at Liath Mór as a fortress was coming to fruition, he insisted that it would be renamed Dún Muirne in his daughter's memory – even though it was his action that caused her death.'

Fidelma observed from Gelgéis's expression that she was right. 'Tormeid reached the far bank in safety. He came here in the land of the Éile but was unable to return to his own clan, the Uí Duach. So he took service with you on this side of the river. Am I correct, thus far?'

The ruler of the Éile blinked rapidly and blushed.

'You tell a good story, Fidelma,' was all she replied.

'I hope it will get better,' said Fidelma. 'I have told you that Tormeid was abducted. I was also taken because the abductors thought I was his companion. This was not Muirne, of course, since she was dead. Then who did they mistake me for? I was left for dead by these abductors when they realised I was *not* Tormeid's companion. Thankfully, I was rescued by my friends, who had tracked our passage. Tormeid was taken on to the Abbey of Liath Mór. My companions and I followed the abductors there. At Liath Mór, another old friend arrived. This was the person who had called himself Brother Biasta, the man who had murdered Brother Ailgesach. In escaping from Liath Mór, Torna killed Biasta. I had not seen Torna since our abduction until a short while ago when I saw him from the window of Drón's chamber. In this very fortress.'

Gelgéis's face was white and strained.

Fidelma smiled without humour. 'Am I coming closer to an under-standing with you, lady? Do you still say that this man, Tormeid – by whatever name he is now called – is not here? He may wish to know that five of his friends and cousins were executed by Cronán as venge-ance for his escape and the death of Muirne. I wonder how many will be executed now that he has escaped a second time?'

There was a shocked silence. Gelgéis finally turned to her steward. 'Spealáin, you had best go down and give the order that the Lady Dúnliath and her party are not to depart until I, or Fidelma, have given permission.'

Spealáin bowed his head without comment and left the chamber.

Gelgéis sat staring at the floor for some moments, tapping her foot absently. Bishop Daig stood shifting his weight from one foot to the other, as if awaiting her decision.

'This puts me in an awkward situation, Fidelma,' the Princess said after a while.

'No situation is so awkward that recourse to truth will not remedy it.'

'Yet the truth is not entirely mine to share.'

'That needs a better explanation,' replied Fidelma.

'I wish I could provide one immediately, but I would ask that you give me some time before I answer you.'

Fidelma raised her brows slightly. 'Time? When is the telling of truth dependent on time? Anyway, time is not in a plentiful supply at the moment.'

'If you give me a short time, you shall have your truth. That I swear. And I also swear this: I am a loyal defender of this Kingdom of Muman and of her legitimate Kings. Everything that I have done is in support of that conviction. I am your brother's truest ally, lady.'

Fidelma searched the woman's face, seeking any sign of guile or deceit, but found only anxiety.

'Very well,' she agreed at last. 'But I need a response. When you have discussed the matter with Tormeid, or whatever you call him, I hope he will come and supply me with clear answers to my questions.'

Gelgéis met her gaze and held it, realising that Fidelma knew exactly why she was prevaricating. Then she dropped her gaze and indicated her acquiescence with a nod.

It seemed that she was about to say something when a distant shouting came to their ears. Gelgéis rose from her chair and went to the window. Fidelma and the others joined her, looking down towards the main gate of the fortress. Some riders had arrived in the courtyard and one of them had dismounted and was speaking volubly to Spealáin, the steward. They saw Gormán emerge and greet the newcomer.

'What is this?' muttered Gelgéis.

As they watched, Spealáin was leading the newcomer and Gormán towards the main building. In expectation, Fidelma and the others turned to the door, and within a few moments there was a quick knock and Spealáin entered, followed by his companions. The first thing Fidelma noticed was that the newcomer wore the gold collar of the Nasc Niadh, the élite warriors of Cashel.

'A messenger from—' began Spealáin.

'I know who this is,' interrupted Fidelma. 'I remember Aidan very well from when he helped us rescue Eadulf from the evil intentions of Abbess Fainder of Ferna.'

The young warrior cast a smile at Fidelma, pleased by her recognition, but he was obviously still very agitated. As one of her brother's élite bodyguards, he was certainly no fool, and it was clear that he had grave news.

'My companions and I have ridden from Laigin. We bring news of serious import for King Colgú, lady. The southerly routes to Cashel have been cut off, so we have had to make our way north across Osraige territory to reach here.'

Fidelma was surprised. 'Cut off? In what way are they cut off?'

'By armed bands of Laigin warriors, lady,' replied the warrior. 'We had to take the lesser known paths from Laigin through forests, bog lands and remote places of Osraige to reach here.'

'What news do you bring that causes you to be so disturbed?'

The warrior visibly braced himself. 'It is bad news, lady. Muman will soon be under attack from Laigin.'

There was a silence as his words registered. Then Fidelma asked: 'How do you know this, Aidan?'

'Fianamail, son of Máele Tuile, the King of Laigin, has issued a call to arms. We saw the *crois tara*, the fiery cross, being carried from settlement to settlement. His main force has marched from Ferna to gather at Dinn Rig on the west bank of An Bhearú . . .'

'That's on the border with Osraige,' put in Spealáin, seeing Eadulf's baffled frown.

'The fortress of Dinn Rig is just north of Gabrán,' muttered Bishop Daig, with a meaningful look at Gelgéis.

'You say the Laigin army has crossed the river of An Bhearú?'

'His main army is on the west bank,' repeated Aidan. 'They are not yet crossed into Osraige.'

'Do you know this for a fact and not from hearsay?' Gelgéis demanded of him.

'My companions and I saw Fianamail's troops gathering there – and they were not there to look at the sunset over the mountains.' Aidan's response was cutting.

'How long ago was this?' asked Fidelma.

'Only two days ago, lady. As I say, we managed to cross into Osraige and travelled by the use of new roads that have been built across the bog lands. If Fianamail gives the order for Laigin to march on Cashel, those new roads are going to allow his army a quick passage across Osraige into Éile and Muman.'

Gormán was grim. 'I cannot believe it. Muman is at peace with Laigin. It has been centuries since Laigin incurred the wrath of the High King by making an unprovoked attack on a neighbouring kingdom. Have they not learned a lesson from the *bórama* yet? And why attack at this time?'

'I don't grasp the meaning of that.' Eadulf had not understood the reference that Gormán had made.

It was Gormán who explained to him: 'Centuries ago, when Tuathal Techtmair was High King in Tara, the avarice of Eochaidh, who was then King of Laigin, caused a great warfare. It resulted in the death of many, including the two daughters of Tuathal. For that crime, as well as others, Tuathal faced Eochaidh with a large army, defeated and killed him. Then the High King imposed a tribute on the people of Laigin, called the *bórama* – the cow tribute. Five thousand cows had to be paid to Tuathal and to his successors if Laigin ever broke the peace again. The legitimacy of the tribute remains. If Laigin ever breaks the conditions and attempts to go to war with a neighbour, unless that neighbour is invading Laigin, the High King has the right to march his army into the kingdom and demand the *bórama* fine.'

'But we have heard that Moling, the Bishop of Ferna, and adviser to Fianamail, King of Laigin, was sent by Fianamail to Tara some weeks ago,' Bishop Daig said. 'We were told that he was sent to persuade the High King and his Chief Brehon to declare the tribute as no longer applying.'

'It might have been a ruse,' added Gelgéis. 'We expected as much.'

'You expected this!' Fidelma exclaimed. 'You had knowledge that Fianamail and Laigin were preparing for this invasion?'

'We had word of a conspiracy,' said Gelgéis. 'It was mostly suspicion, but suspicion is not evidence. We needed evidence. We—'

'"We" meaning you and Tormeid?' Fidelma's voice was sharp. With this latest news from Laigin, it was even more important that Gelgéis admitted what she knew. The very matter that had caused Fidelma to start out on this journey was the murder of a young man who bore the symbol of an envoy from Laigin. She was slowly beginning to see how the pieces in this complex puzzle fitted together.

She turned back to Aidan. 'Is there anything more you can tell us?'

The young warrior shook his head. 'With respect, lady, we should ride post haste for Cashel and warn the King.'

Fidelma compressed her lips in thought for a moment. 'I agree. Except that we are unsure where my brother is now. We are told he has raised a battalion and marched to face some rebels in the west.'

Aidan's expression was one of dismay. 'Then it means our border is undefended.'

'Did you pass by Liath Mór when you came here?' Eadulf asked suddenly.

'We came within sight of it, but knowing that the Osraige has too many connections with Laigin for my liking I decided to pass to the north of it, using the woods for cover.'

'A wise precaution,' replied Eadulf. 'Did you see any activity in Osraige?'

'We did see some deserted townships and farmsteads in Uí Duach territory.'

Fidelma had walked to the window and was gazing down into the courtyard again. She was deep in thought. Gelgéis went to join her.

'What shall we do?' asked the Princess of Durlus.

Fidelma turned to examine her, gazing long into her eyes. Then she spoke quietly so that the others would not hear.

'I think the first thing would be for you and Tormeid to tell me what you know. I need to be able to trust you fully, now Muman is under threat.'

'We suspected that there was some plot involving Cronán and the raiders to the west. We hoped to find some answers from Ailgesach: that was why we went to see him. I swear it.'

The Princess of the Éile seemed badly shaken at the news that Aidan had brought. Fidelma felt confident that the young woman was going to help rather than hinder her, but that was not enough. There were important matters to be considered. She swung back to address Aidan.

'My brother must be warned, if we can find him. Aidan, you and your men have ridden long and hard to reach us. You need rest. If Gelgéis can provide you with a fresh horse, can you, or one of your number, ride to Cashel and relay this news?'

'I will do so, lady,' replied the warrior without hesitation. 'My men can rest.'

'Then bear this news back to Cashel. If you can't find Colgú there, as we have heard, then seek out my brother's heir-apparent, the *tánaiste*, Finguine. He should be able to send messengers to alert my brother as well as raise new *cath* to defend Cashel from any attack from the east.'

Aidan was already through the door, before she had finished speaking, with Gormán following to ensure Aidan's wants were provided for. Fidelma turned back to Gelgéis.

'I presume you have good horses and good riders here in Durlus?'

'Of course,' the Princess replied immediately.

'Then choose your best rider and horse. They are to set out immediately for Tara . . .' She paused as Gelgéis motioned Spealáin to come forward to take notice of the instructions. 'He is to ride for Tara and inform the Chief Brehon, Sedna, and, indeed the High King Cenn

Faelad himself, of what is taking place here. Say that we are threatened by Laigin who are in some conspiracy with Cronán of Gleann an Ghuail and perhaps others in Osraige. We can say no more except that we entreat the High King and Chief Brehon to demand the withdrawal of Fianamail's army from the border of Muman.'

Gelgéis was shaking her head. 'Even our best rider and horse, travelling through the night, will not make Tara before midday tomorrow. And if the King and Chief Brehon were to intervene, it will be a few days before they can contact Fianamail.'

Fidelma glanced at Spealáin. 'Tell, whoever you pick, to do their best,' she said, adding to Gelgéis as he departed, 'I do not expect this will save us from attack, but at least we will have the satisfaction of knowing that the High King and Chief Brehon are alerted to the Laigin threat.'

'But what are we to do?' demanded Gelgéis.

'As soon as Spealáin returns, you must post sentinels around Durlus so that we can be warned when Osraige and Laigin start to move against us.'

She suddenly realised that only she, Gelgéis and Eadulf were left in the chamber

'Now, lady, I think—' began Fidelma, when the door was flung open without warning, and Dúnliath stormed in, Ailill following anxiously behind her. She addressed Gelgéis directly.

'I have just been informed that I and my retinue are not allowed to leave your fortress, lady. We were to accompany the body of my poor, murdered father back to Gabrán for Christian burial. What means this discourtesy to his mortal remains?'

In the excitement of the last few moments, Fidelma had almost forgotten about Dúnliath. Obviously, Spealáin had been distracted by the new arrivals and had not delivered an explanation.

'The Lady Fidelma will tell you why it is not possible for you to leave Durlus at this time,' replied Gelgéis.

Gelgéis was clearly waiting for Fidelma to exert her authority as a *dálaigh*. But Fidelma realised that she now had a better reason for stopping Dúnliath from leaving.

'You have doubtless heard the recent activity in the fortress, Dúnliath,' she said mildly. 'We are under threat and it is not wise that anyone travel east, especially not towards Gabrán.'

The childlike features of the girl's face seemed to be unusually harsh. Before she could speak, however, Ailill interrupted, his expression one of perplexity.

'I am not sure that I follow you, cousin,' he said. 'We have heard nothing except the coming and going of horsemen. Then we were informed that we could not leave the fortress.'

'We have just had news that a large army under the King of Laigin is now encamped on the west bank of the River Bhearú, a short distance from Gabrán. They appear on the verge of invasion. The news is that they will start crossing into Osraige soon. Osraige may join them. They mean to invade Muman.'

Ailill's features were set firm but the girl was blinking in bewilderment.

'What does that mean?' Her voice was whiny as she looked up at Ailill. 'I want to go home to Gabrán.'

'It means that Laigin's warriors will soon be sweeping through Gabrán, if they have not done so already,' Gelgéis explained testily. 'Now, I suggest you return to your chamber, lady. We will keep you informed if we hear any further news.'

Ailill swallowed hard. 'Is Cashel in danger, cousin?' he asked Fidelma. 'What of this rebellion in the west? You have only to call on my service, although I feel that I should be rallying the men of Gabrán for I am . . . was . . . the foster-son of Drón.'

'You understand that even if the attack does not materialise, you are to remain here until we have determined how Drón came by his death? I have taken charge of this matter.'

There was a slight tension of the man's jaw and then he nodded. 'Of course. But shouldn't we have more concern for the threat to the kingdom?'

'Do not be concerned. Both matters will be dealt with.'

Ailill took the miserable and still-complaining girl by the arm and ushered her out.

Fidelma turned back to Gelgéis. 'I think time is running out, don't you?' she said.

Gelgéis obviously knew what she meant and, without a word, turned to a curtained alcove, drawing back the drapery to reveal a wooden door beyond. She opened it and gestured for Fidelma and Eadulf to follow. A steep wooden stair led below. Oil lamps lit the depths into which they descended. They came to another wooden door. Gelgéis paused and rapped on it.

'It is I,' she called softly.

There was a movement from beyond and a bolt rasped in its metal holder before the door swung inward.

Whoever opened it was standing back and Gelgéis led them into a chamber which was surprisingly filled with natural light as one side seemed to open on to grounds at the back of the fortress. Fidelma had a glimpse of a vegetable and herb garden beyond. Then she turned to face the person who was just shutting the door behind them.

'Well, Torna? Or should I say Tormeid?' She smiled thinly. 'We meet once more.'

Tormeid, whom she had last seen briefly under Drón's window, stood before them. He looked at Gelgéis with a question in his eyes.

'Events are fast moving,' she told him. 'Fianamail of Laigin has gathered an army to invade Muman. I had to bring Fidelma to you.'

The man they had known as Torna turned back to Fidelma and Eadulf. 'It is good to see you alive and well,' he said. 'I feared for your safety when we were captured on the riverbank.'

Gelgéis indicated some chairs. The room was apparently an ante-chamber to the garden, filled with numerous tools, plants and boxes. Neither Fidelma nor Eadulf spoke.

'Forgive my receiving you in these conditions,' the erstwhile poet continued. 'Once you saw me from the window, I suspected that it would not be long before you found me.'

'I have been trying to track you down since Cronán's men took you. We followed you to Liath Mór.'

'So I heard. Gelgéis has told me who you thought I was. It was well worked out, lady.'

He sank into a chair, and only then did Fidelma and Eadulf seat themselves as well.

'Was I right?' enquired Fidelma.

The young man smiled again. 'Your reputation has not been acquired for nothing, lady. You were right in most particulars. I am Tormeid of the Uí Duach. I may also add that I was one of a group of so-called hot-headed young warriors who went to demand reparation from Cronán of Gleann an Ghuail. I was captured and deprived of my liberty along with others.'

'And all else was correct?'

'It was.'

'But it leaves many questions to be answered.'

'Of course it does.'

'These questions might have been answered more rapidly had you both been honest with me from the start,' Fidelma observed sharply.

Gelgéis was shaking her head. 'We could not answer your questions before we knew if we could trust you.'

Fidelma's eyebrows arched a little. 'If you are loyal to Cashel, as you claimed, why couldn't you trust me?'

'The fact that you were the sister of King Colgú,' Gelgéis said simply. 'You might have been part of the conspiracy to overthrow him.'

For the first time, Eadulf saw Fidelma rendered speechless for a few moments. Finally she said: 'I think an explanation is in order. Why should I be planning to overthrow my own brother?'

'All in proper order, lady,' Tormeid replied. 'Your actions have now shown that you are to be trusted. We are satisfied that you are not part of this conspiracy.'

'Well, that is something,' she replied dryly. 'Very well. All in good order as you say. Let us finish the story of how you came here, Tormeid. You escaped from Cronán's fortress together with his daughter, Muirne. Is that correct?'

There was a slight tightening at the corner of his mouth but he nodded.

'You have just escaped a second time from Cronán's fortress of Liath Mór,' said Eadulf. 'By the same method?'

The young man nodded again. 'Indeed. Both times it was by the same method.'

'Through the underground vaults you yourself helped to construct?'

'When I was a prisoner, a *daer-fuidir*, I was set to work on the vaults of Cronán's fortress. I think you will have seen enough of it to realise that it is a massive construction. Those of us who were forced to build those cellars and fortifications made sure that we created a means of exit unbeknown to those overseeing the work.'

'It was by that method that some of the *daer-fuidir*, the Uí Duach slaves, also helped us escape,' Eadulf commented.

'We were helped by a girl called Ségnat,' Fidelma added. 'She told me that it was Tormeid who had escaped with Cronán's daughter, so then I realised your true name. I tried to persuade her to escape with us. There were reasons why she stayed.'

Tormeid's face was a white mask of guilt. 'Gelgéis has told me. Believe me, I did not know until now that I had cost the lives of five of my good friends and cousins. When I escaped with Muirne I knew the secret way in and out of those dark vaults,' he said softly. 'I did not think Cronán would be so cruel and vindictive to punish others for my actions.'

'So you escaped with Muirne and were trying to cross the Suir. But the river was in flood and she drowned, just as you told me. Is that correct?' pressed Fidelma.

The young man lowered his gaze. 'It is.'

'How did you come to Durlus?'

'Gelgéis and Spealáin happened to be passing along the river road, north of here. They found me more dead than alive on the riverbank. They also found the body of Muirne. They brought me to the fortress where I was nursed and revived. I told them my story and Gelgéis gave me shelter and promised not to inform Cronán. The body of Muirne was buried by Bishop Daig.'

'How long have you sheltered here in Durlus?'

Tormeid actually forced a smile. 'Ever since that day I was dragged from the river. I now serve among the warriors of Gelgéis here in Éile.'

'How did you learn about this conspiracy? From Brother Ailgesach?'

Tormeid and Gelgéis exchanged a glance.

'You seem to know much,' Tormeid remarked softly.

'And deduce much,' Fidelma smiled confidently. 'Brother Ailgesach, when he came to Durlus, told Gelgéis that while he was an attendant to those afflicted in the Gleann na nGeilt, the Glen of Lunatics, he had come across some frightening information. The years he had spent there among the insane had driven him to drink; but even with his drink problem he had learned something that he needed to tell someone, hadn't he? He had learned about a conspiracy.'

Gelgéis spoke quietly: 'When he left the Glen of Lunatics, Abbot Ségdae appointed him to run the chapel at Fraigh Dubh. But he came here first. He had discovered that someone was being paid to persuade people to join a band who would attack religious communities and isolated settlements in the west. This person was a religious fanatic who had been recently incarcerated in the Glen of Lunatics because of their religious madness. Ailgesach kept the name of this person a secret because he wanted to gather more information. He told me that a relation of this person was due to visit the latter at the Glen of Lunatics. Ailgesach had contacted this relative, who had promised to find out what information they could uncover.'

'So you and Tormeid arranged to visit Ailgesach at Fraigh Dubh when this person returned from the Glen of Lunatics with the information. Correct?'

'We did.'

'Brother Ailgesach had already told you that the conspiracy concerned a noble of Osraige. That person was none other than Cronán, and presumably that was why Tormeid was an enthusiastic ally in this venture. You both went to stay at Brother Ailgesach's cabin, waiting for the man with his information.'

'He did not show up,' Tormeid said. 'But while we were waiting, Brother Ailgesach did reveal his name. It was Bran Finn, the Prince of the Déisi Muman.'

'So the fact that he did not show up was worrying to you both. Gelgéis had to return to Durlus to host the big harvest festival that had been arranged. That was why you parted company.'

Tormeid agreed. 'We had gone a good way back to Durlus when I decided that I should return to Imleach, even to the Glen of Lunatics, to find out if I could get some news of Bran Finn. We met a merchant who told us about a place where I might get a boat back downriver. I thought I would travel that way in the guise of an itinerant bard. This would allow Gelgéis to take the horses back to Durlus. Alas, the ferry, with the tavern and chapel, had been destroyed. That spot was where you met me.'

'What you did not know was that Bran Finn was already dead,' Fidelma said sombrely.

Tormeid's astonished expression confirmed it all.

'His body lay not far from Fraigh Dubh,' she went on. 'He had been travelling there when he encountered his killer. The conspirators had learned that Bran Finn had visited his relative and was planning to take some evidence to Brother Ailgesach. They knew that this information – evidence of their conspiracy – would be passed on, so they had to make sure of two things. One, that Bran Finn would not supply the evidence he had discovered and, two, that Brother Ailgesach would pass on nothing else of what he knew about the Glen of Lunatics. Biasta was sent to Fraigh Dubh to ensure that Ailgesach's voice was silenced. He succeeded, in spite of our being there, and he escaped with final instructions to the conspirators in Laigin.'

'How did Cronán's men find us on the riverbank and abduct us – and why did they think you were Gelgéis?'

'Durlus is not isolated, my friends. Doubtless there were people willing to pass information on to Cronán. Spillán came here and was told that you had both gone south to Fraigh Dubh. He was riding south. In fact, you had turned off the main highway to get to the river and he nearly missed you. Sillán was told by the same merchant who had directed you where you had gone. The same merchant misinformed us about the location of the tavern by the river. Sillán did not know that you would part company with Gelgéis, who would go back to Durlus with the horses. But he did know that you would have to camp by the riverbank at that point because there would be few boats downriver until the next day. Sillán rode directly to a place where he had left some of his men and instructed them to abduct you and Gelgéis. They were to bring you to the sheds in Durlus where he waited. They were then to return with the captives to Cronán. The men were looking for you, whom they knew, and a female companion. They made an obvious mistake when they found us.'

'It sounds complicated,' commented Tormeid.

'Events in life can be complicated,' Fidelma sighed. 'But this became simple once we found the thread to unravel it. Sillán's men just made a mistake.'

'Bran Finn was bringing proof of a conspiracy,' Tormeid said. 'Of a rising against Cashel – but by whom?'

'By someone able to start a minor uprising – something that would distract attention away from what would eventually take place here in the east.'

'When Bran Finn did not appear on the appointed night, Gelgéis had to return to Durlus otherwise questions would be asked, rumours would be spread,' agreed Tormeid. 'I decided to turn back to search for Bran Finn. When I met you, I was aware that the only other thing that Brother Ailgesach had told me about the conspiracy was that whoever was involved in overthrowing Colgú was someone close to the King. That was why I lied to you about who I was and, indeed, that was why Gelgéis did not help you at first.'

'We needed to know who was leading these raids in the west and the links between them and Cronán. All Ailgesach could tell us was that a strange religieux from Osraige had been reported in the Glen of Lunatics,' Gelgéis said. 'He thought this person had brought gold to help recruit the raiders.'

Fidelma exhaled slowly. 'That makes sense. And so this religieux, who was doubtless one of Cronán's men, perhaps even his son, Sillán, supplied money to help start the unrest there.'

'But all Brother Ailgesach could tell us was that there was some religious involvement. Sometimes, when he was in his cups, he said things which did not make sense. He talked about someone who had been chosen by the seventh angel to drive the impure of Faith from the land. He spoke much about the seventh trumpet, until we finally realised that it was a password among the conspirators.'

'Why did he not reveal the name of the person who would lead the rebellion in the west?' Gelgéis asked.

'We did not even know at that time that Bran Finn was the person who would bring us information. We were not told by Brother Ailgesach until we went to Fraigh Dubh,' said Tormeid. 'As I say, that is why I lied to you and why Gelgéis was unhelpful, because you were the sister of King Colgú.'

Fidelma felt almost amused. 'And you both suspected that I might be involved in this conspiracy?'

'You would not be the first sibling to covet the other's power and position,' replied Gelgéis.

'Why did you not go directly to Colgú with your suspicions?' asked Eadulf.

'And give warning to the conspirators who were trusted by him so that they had time enough to hide their tracks?' Tormeid replied scornfully. 'We needed more information.'

'Now that you have confirmed that it was Bran Finn whom you were due to meet, I can tell you why he was involved,' Fidelma announced.

They all regarded her with surprise.

The moment was interrupted by the sound of footsteps hurrying down the stairs. A voice was calling for Gelgéis. The door burst open as Tormeid sprang to his feet, but it was Spealáin the steward who entered, followed by a breathless Éile warrior.

'It's one of our sentinels,' gasped Spealáin. 'He comes bearing alarming news.'

'What news?' snapped Gelgéis and Fidelma, rising in unison.

For a moment the man hesitated, glancing from one to another in surprise.

'Speak, man!' prompted Spealáin.

'There is an army heading in this direction,' the man gabbled. 'I came to warn you.'

'An army . . . from the east?' demanded Gelgéis. 'From Laigin?'

The man shook his head, rushing on: 'Not from the east, lady; from the west. We think it is the rebel force that we have heard so much about. They will soon be in Durlus – and at the gates of the fortress.'

CHAPTER NINETEEN

It was not the rebel force that was approaching Durlus. It was a small company of warriors, no more than a *ceta*, 100 men, with Colgú and Caol, the commander of the King's élite bodyguard, at their head. Enda and Aidan rode immediately behind, followed by the Chief Brehon of Muman, Brehon Áedo, together with Abbot Ségdae, the senior cleric of the kingdom.

As the column of horsemen trotted up to the gates of Gelgéis's fortress, Gelgéis, Spealáin and Bishop Daig went forward to receive them as protocol demanded. The escorting warriors waited patiently on horseback outside the fortress while Colgú with his immediate entourage dismounted. Gelgéis welcomed the King first before stepping back to allow Fidelma to come forward to embrace her brother. Colgú acknowledged the assembly with an encompassing smile.

'Enda and Aidan have told me the news,' Colgú said immediately, before any questions were asked. 'Dego and his warriors have gone to confront Cronán of Glean an Ghuail. Is there any more news of Fianamail and his Laigin men? Have they moved into Osraige yet?'

'Not that we have heard. I have sent to Tara to alert the High King and his Brehon,' Fidelma replied briskly.

'That is good,' said Colgú, wiping some of the dust of travel from his brow.

'I don't think that Laigin is our immediate worry,' she continued. 'Fianamail knows that he must have a good excuse to invade Muman if he wishes to avoid retribution from the High King. Laigin is already under the restriction of the *bórama*, the cow tribute. If he acts precipitously, he will find himself having to pay tribute to Tara, which is not what he wants. I think he wants to be able to claim that Laigin warriors entered this kingdom legitimately to resolve a civil conflict in Muman that made it unstable as a neighbour.'

'We can agree on that,' Gelgéis added. 'We have been discussing this and conclude that Cronán was trying to construct some civil conflict and is in a conspiracy with Laigin to use it as an excuse for Fianamail to enter the kingdom.'

'That's right.' Fidelma nodded. 'And the purpose of that conspiracy is to replace you as King with some Laigin lackey.'

'Well, the rebels in the west have been defeated, as will Cronán be shortly. We have captured their leader,' Colgú said wearily.

'You have captured Étain of An Dún?' Fidelma asked quietly.

Colgú's eyes widened a little. 'So you already realised that she was their leader?'

'I had worked it out. The young noble who was killed near Cashel was Bran Finn of the Déisi Muman. Had I met him when he visited Cashel I would have recognised his body and resolved this matter that much more quickly. Bran Finn had visited Cashel on his way to Imleach and then the Glen of Lunatics, which is looked after by members of the abbey. He was taking money for the upkeep of a kinswoman being held in the glen. It was in that same glen that Brother Ailgesach spent those years looking after the inmates; the same place which drove him to drink, to deal with the horrors of that task. There was only one noblewoman of the Déisi who had been recently incarcerated there.'

'You are right, sister,' Colgú confirmed. 'The so-called rebel army was a ragtail of bandits, thieves and misfits, and a smattering of those who will serve anyone for money or loot. They were the dregs who fled almost as soon as Dego's warriors confronted them. But when he saw who was leading them, he sent for me. She and some of her more fanatical followers had fled into the mountains. I left Cashel with a few warriors to join him and we quickly flushed them out of their lairs.'

'So you have taken her captive?' pressed Fidelma.

'We have her captive,' confirmed Colgú. 'But from what Enda tells us about Cronán's fortress, I estimate that it will need more than a full *cath*, a battalion of three thousand, to tackle the task of reducing that place. The longer the siege, the more justified Fianamail will be in claiming a right to intercession.'

Tormeid moved forward. 'It is no use attacking against the gates and the walls. But I can make it simple for your men to take the fortress with the minimum loss of life.'

Colgú turned to him with a questioning look. 'And you are . . . ?' he asked.

'This is Tormeid,' Fidelma explained. 'He is a warrior of the Uí Duach who was held prisoner in Cronán's fortress where he was forced to help build it. He knows underground passages that will lead our warriors into the very heart of Cronán's fortress. He escaped and now serves the Lady Gelgéis.' She smiled at Tormeid and told her brother: 'You may trust him implicitly, Colgú.'

'And you will also find Uí Duach prisoners in the fortress who, given the chance, will turn on their captors,' added Tormeid.

Colgú regarded the young man for a moment. 'Are you prepared to take my men into the fortress through the underground passage?'

'I am,' Tormeid answered resolutely.

'Then Muman and I will be ever in your debt,' Colgú said, holding out his hand to the young warrior. A moment later, he threw off his fatigue and became filled with new energy. 'Enda, accompany Tormeid here to join Dego and our men. They are south of the Suir and marching towards Liath Mór even as we speak.' As Enda and Tormeid left without a further word, Colgú turned to Gelgéis: 'Lady, forgive me, but I must request your hospitality of Durlus for my entourage while we await news and while these matters are resolved. I shall also need a secure place for my prisoner.'

'Then you shall have it,' Gelgéis replied, turning to relay these orders to Spealáin.

There suddenly came a high-pitched cry and Dúnliath came pushing through those who surrounded Colgú. Ailill followed at her shoulder.

'My lord! Oh, my lord! Have you come to rescue me?'

Colgú appeared slightly embarrassed as the young woman threw herself into his arms.

'Dúnliath! What are you doing here?' he asked in surprise, disentangling himself from her embrace. 'What rescue do you need?'

'After you had left Cashel, my father brought me here for safety. He said it was for the best.'

Colgú seemed puzzled for a moment. 'I do not understand why. There was no threat to Cashel, and the bandits were already defeated to all intents and purposes. I thought that Drón knew that before I left. Where is your father?' he demanded, looking about him.

It was Fidelma who explained. 'Drón was murdered here a short while ago.'

Colgú barely had time to register his astonishment before the girl almost wailed, 'I wanted to take his body home to Gabrán for burial but I was not allowed to leave. Please, my lord, you will escort us home now, won't you?'

'I am responsible for stopping her leaving,' Fidelma said hastily, before her brother could respond. 'Firstly, there was news of the Laigin army only a short distance from Gabrán and, secondly, I had to take charge of the investigation into the murder of Drón.' She lowered her voice. 'I believe his death is related to the conspiracy which confronts us. In the circumstances, I could not allow Dúnliath and her escort to leave until the matter was resolved.'

Colgú gave a smile of reassurance to Dúnliath.

'I must agree with my sister. It is not the time to be travelling east through Osraige, with the threat of the men of Laigin gathered almost within sight of Gabrán. I still don't understand why you are here. You would have been much safer in Cashel. No harm would have come to you there.'

Fidelma intervened. 'I can take it that you did not suggest that Drón bring his daughter and his entourage here for safety?'

Colgú looked at her in astonishment. 'Why would I do that? Cashel is impregnable.'

The girl gave a tearful sniff and said, 'It was my father who thought it best to come here and cross into Osraige.'

'Well, no matter. I am here now.' Colgú smiled, as if comforting a child. 'And have no fear, my sister will discover who assassinated your father.' He turned and saw Ailill for the first time. 'Greetings, cousin. You should have persuaded your foster-father to remain at Cashel.'

The young man grimaced. 'I did my best but Drón was a man who was difficult to shift, once his mind was made up.'

Colgú said gently to Dúnliath, 'There are things that I must do – important matters that need attending to. You go now and I will join you shortly.'

It was a hint but the girl was not one to take hints. Instead, it was Abbot Daig who came forward and ushered the unwilling girl back inside the building. Ailill paused for a moment but, sensing his presence was not wanted, turned to follow them.

A sudden tiredness spread across Colgú's features. At the same time he became aware that his companions were still standing waiting for his orders. He looked about and, with growing guilt, realised that those warriors of his escort who had not accompanied Enda and Tormeid were still patiently mounted and also awaiting instructions. Colgú turned to Caol. 'Deploy the men, then bring our prisoner, Étain of An Dún, into the chamber to which the Lady Gelgéis's steward will conduct you. Make sure that she is secured, for in her distempers she may harm herself, let alone others. Also ensure that you post sentinels at the crossing-points along the river to await news from Dego as to how matters fare at Liath Mór, and quarter the rest of our men as best you can.'

Caol raised a hand in acknowledgment and hurried away without further ado.

'With Gelgéis's permission,' Colgú announced, 'I suggest that we all repair to her reception chamber and you can tell us all about this matter.'

To his surprise, Fidelma shook her head. 'There are still many strands of this mystery that need to be pulled together, brother. Before we begin to understand this conspiracy, I would like to speak with the Lady Étain.'

Colgú grimaced dourly. 'I have no objection but I must warn you, the lady is not right in her mind. Probably she has not been sane in years. I doubt whether you will get any sense out of her.'

'Indeed. She was not in her right mind the last time we encountered her,' Eadulf reminded them.

'Nevertheless, it is important that I try to speak with her,' insisted Fidelma.

'As soon as Caol has brought her into a safe chamber, we shall go to see her,' Colgú acquiesced. 'Now, perhaps I can prevail on the Lady Gelgéis for some refreshment, for it has been a long and dusty ride and I can tell you how we defeated the so-called rebellion in the west.'

*　　*　　*

'What I want to know is how you managed to capture Étain of An Dún after the stories we had heard,' Fidelma said, when refreshments had been served to her brother, Gelgéis, herself and Eadulf.

'It was not difficult. She and her band of wretches attacked isolated settlements, travelling merchants and also small religious communities. From each they looted and increased their wealth to be able to extend their numbers,' said Colgú.

'But there was no big battle?' Gelgéis asked. 'We heard there was a battle and you had to take reinforcements from Cashel.'

Colgú guffawed. 'No more than a skirmish before Étain and her followers ran away, chased by Dego and his hundred warriors. Where did you hear of such a thing?'

'So Dego could have overtaken and captured her?' queried Fidelma, not answering his question.

Her brother shook his head. 'Dego was so surprised by the size of the band and the poor quality of the bandits that he thought their flight into the western mountains must be a ruse; a means to lure him into a trap – especially when he identified Étain of An Dún as their leader. I confess that I would have thought the same. So he sent a messenger to me and suggested that he would take his men into the trap if he could coordinate with me – asking me to bring a company of warriors round against the rear of her band. That way, if it was a trap, she would be the one that would fall into it. Brehon Áedo and Abbot Ségdae came with me and we took no more than a company.'

'Only a company of warriors, not a full battalion?' asked Eadulf. 'How many men did Étain have?'

'Hardly any at all, and when we had a final encounter, most of those fled at the sight of trained warriors – as they had when they first encountered Dego and his men.'

'So what of these stories that we heard, of a mighty army . . . ?' Gelgéis was baffled.

'It was either in the frightened minds of those telling the stories, or else they were lies deliberately spread to create panic,' concluded Colgú.

'So the mighty army turned out to be nothing but rumour?'

'Isn't there a saying that a bad rumour is stronger than good news?' Colgú grinned. 'It only needed a hundred trained warriors to disperse the rebels. Most of them were simply there for the loot they'd been promised. Only a handful of acolytes following Étain were possessed of her fanatical religious zeal and remained with her until the end.'

'But surely they could see that she was insane?' Eadulf said.

'Insane? Yes. But she has strength of purpose, a commanding attitude, and was ruthless with both friends as well as enemies. Those sorts of people often command loyalty, whether from fear or avarice, in those who follow them. They spread their own insanity like a disease.'

'It is hard to believe that she could attract any following at all.' Gelgéis shuddered.

'From my dealings with her, I have to admit that she is an amazing woman in many respects,' Fidelma said. 'It is true that Étain is a fanatic. She believes in the teachings of the Faith to which she has been converted. It was her own arrogance, her egotism that produced this madness. She truly believes that she, and she alone, holds the key to the truth and can protect the integrity of the Faith in this land. That became clear when we confronted her in Lios Mór. And there are always conscience-free sycophants who will be lured by orators of false passions who promise them the wealth with which they can purchase power.' There was a pause before Fidelma asked her brother: 'So what happened when you caught up with her?'

Colgú said wearily, 'She had a few remaining followers. Those whose loyalty she had purchased had already fled. Most of her band had been killed during her quest for power. As I said, Dego and his men had managed to deal with them. I and my warriors were barely needed. So how on earth did these rumours spread of great battles and me leading a full *cath* from Cashel?'

'It is the story that Drón told us,' replied Gelgéis.

'How did Aidan come into contact with you?' Fidelma asked her brother. 'I had sent him south to Cashel to warn you of Fianamail's actions.'

'We were on our way back to Cashel with Étain when I met Caol and Aidan with a full *cath*, a battalion of a three thousand warriors, moving north. Enda had joined them. Finguine, my *tánaiste*, had sent them in good faith, having heard news from Aidan. He decided to hold another *cath* ready to guard the southern approaches. He thought the Laigin army might attack across the fords of An Ghlais Alainn straight westward to Cashel. But Finguine is cautious. He considered the possibility that they could attempt to come through the territory of the Éile as they had tried years ago. So we joined with Caol and his warriors and came here. The rest you know, and you are telling me this is all part of some conspiracy?'

'A curious one, indeed,' said Fidelma. 'I believe that if we can stop Cronán and his plan, then Fianamail and his Laigin army will be denied an excuse for invading Muman.'

'Let us hope you are right.'

'Did you try to question Étain of An Dún?'

Colgú uttered a short, dry laugh. 'There is no means of conversing with her, sister. She has been raving some curious words, almost as if she were quoting some Scripture and calling on God to vanquish her enemies. It was quite unnerving. When we captured her she had some kind of religious banner.'

'So she has offered no coherent explanation nor given you any clue as to her part in this conspiracy?'

'Our physician attempted to calm her with some potion, but . . . well, you will see for yourself.'

'There were no other prisoners; no one of intelligence who could explain the reasons for these actions?'

'Only three remained alive, and they were seriously wounded. We left them behind to be tended to.'

'I just want to be sure about one thing,' Fidelma said. 'You left Cashel with only a hundred warriors to support Dego?'

'Correct.'

'And you made no suggestion to Drón that he would be safer coming here than remaining in Cashel?'

Colgú sniffed in disgust. 'I have already said so. I do not understand how that impression was put about. He and Dúnliath were totally safe in Cashel. You are not saying that he was lured here as part of this conspiracy? Lured here to be killed? I think it is high time you told me what this so-called conspiracy is all about, and who is involved.'

'That I shall do shortly,' Fidelma replied. 'But perhaps we can now see the Lady Étain first?'

Gelgéis reached for her hand-bell to summon Spealáin.

'You'll excuse me if I do not accompany you to see this madwoman?' she said. 'I do not know her and have no wish to do so. She is responsible for so much evil, and I would rather not look upon such madness.'

Spealáin entered with Caol behind him, who confirmed that the prisoner was locked inside a chamber below in the fortress. They conducted Colgú, with Fidelma and Eadulf, to a stout wooden door outside which one of Spealáin's own men stood on guard. Before throwing the bolts, Caol said softly for Fidelma's benefit: 'She is restricted for her own benefit as well as yours, so do not be shocked at her appearance.'

'That is understood,' Fidelma acknowledged.

The chamber was certainly no cell. A shaft of late-afternoon sunlight came through the window, and it would have been a pleasant room had it not been for the solitary occupant. A large chair stood in a corner and in it was seated a figure. Rather, the figure was strapped to the chair with manacles of iron restricting her wrists and ankles. Her hair was matted and tangled; there was blood on her face and on her clothing, which was torn and soiled.

Fidelma's breath caught in her throat as she viewed the pitiful creature that huddled before her. Her mind went back to when she had first met Étain of An Dún. Was it only a few months before at Lios Mór? Then she had been a tall, imposing figure with traces of her former youthful beauty. The sharp blue eyes, which once were like gimlets, piercing into their minds, were now pale and without lustre. Now there were telltale marks of age around them. A few months ago it was only by peering closely that Fidelma had seen that the woman used berry juice to darken her brows and hair, which had been braided and elaborately dressed; held in place with gold circlet pins. Now her hair was dishevelled, dirty-grey – even white – and caked in places with blood and dirt.

Fidelma glanced with a frown at Caol. 'Can she not have been allowed to bathe and have a little dignity?'

Caol stiffened at her rebuke. 'She is quiet now, lady, but this mood does not seem to last for long. She can become like a hound out of hell itself. I have never seen her like for ferocity. I would not place you in such harm's way.'

Fidelma knew Caol well enough to accept that he did not act without a good reason. She took a pace forward and cleared her throat. 'Lady Étain, do you know me?'

There was scarcely any movement, hardly even of natural breathing, but Fidelma became aware of the eyelids flickering and then those pale eyes were trying to focus on her.

'It is I, Fidelma of Cashel,' Fidelma said softly.

The woman tried to raise one of her manacled wrists in salutation but she could not lift it very far. She gave a deep sigh. There was an elaborate dignity in the gesture.

'I regret that I have to receive you thus, lady.'

'Are you able to answer some questions?'

'Questions? There are no questions to be asked. Just believe and all will be well. *Caeli enaran gloriam Dei!*'

'Indeed, the heavens do bespeak the glory of God, but we must also ask questions that are unrelated to matters of the Faith. I would speak about your cousin, Cronán.'

Colgú and Eadulf both started at the information. Eadulf dimly remembered that Cronán had said something about a cousin of his marrying a noble of the Déisi, but . . .

'He is your cousin, isn't he?' asked Fidelma.

The woman was almost whispering now. 'He is a grand abbot. He told me the truth about the seventh angel. I shall soon mount to the throne of this world, for it is my destiny to ensure that all see the glory of God and the truth of His message.'

'I would like to know how you and Cronán set about this task,' Fidelma said.

A sudden flash of recognition crossed the woman's face, and her eyes changed from pale to bright blue. She was staring malignantly at Fidelma as if seeing her for the first time.

'I recognise you, Whore of Babylon!' Her voice grew harsh and venomous. The malevolent face then turned to Eadulf, causing him to take a step backwards. 'This woman is responsible for the death of the Prophets and Apostles!' she shouted. 'She is a dwelling place of evil, a cup full of iniquities.'

Caol made to go towards Étain as she writhed and twisted against her bonds. Fidelma reached out a hand to stay him.

'She is quoting from Scripture,' she explained quietly. 'It signifies nothing.'

'Nothing?' Étain was slobbering, the spittle on her lips. 'And their dead bodies shall lie in the streets of their great city . . . and the people and the clans . . . they shall see the dead bodies . . . but they will not be able to put the dead into graves, for there will be so many.' Her voice rose to a croaking crescendo. 'The seventh trumpet sounds; the kingdom of this world will become the kingdom of our Lord.'

'The seventh trumpet,' muttered Eadulf. 'So that was the code of their conspiracy?'

Fidelma glanced sadly at the woman who had collapsed back in the chair after her violent tussle against her bonds. She was muttering and weeping. But there was nothing else they could do. They left and went outside. When Caol bolted the door, there was a troubled look on Fidelma's face.

'Is there nothing we can do? No balm that will keep her quiet?' Her question was directed at Eadulf.

'For such a state as that woman is in, it is hard to say what will help her. We could try lily of the valley, maybe fennel, or a mixture of both in an infusion.' He spread his hands almost helplessly. 'Perhaps the best thing is to induce sleep.'

'I am sure Gelgéis has an apothecary here,' Colgú said, turning to Caol. 'Go and ask for such potions as Eadulf suggests. But ensure that the woman remains restrained.'

'I have seen enough not to be reminded of that duty,' muttered Caol as he left them.

'And now we must have some answers, Fidelma,' Colgú said briskly. 'You started off with the death of an unknown Laigin noble outside Cashel. How has it developed to this . . . ?' He spread his arms to encompass everything.

'That I believe I can now answer. Let us see if Gelgéis will allow us to meet in her personal reception chamber again, this time with her advisers and with Brehon Áedo and Bishop Ségdae.'

The chamber seemed crowded. It was not made to accommodate the nine people who filled it. Gelgéis had vacated her usual chair of office for Colgú to sit in while she had taken a chair close by Áedo, the Chief Brehon of Muman. The latter sat next to Gelgéis's own Brehon, Broce of the Éile. Next to him was Abbot Ségdae and Bishop Daig. Spealáin stood by the door which he closed after attendants had brought refreshment for everyone.

'So where shall we start in unravelling this mystery?' Colgú asked the question directly of his sister.

She said: 'Let us start with the decision of Brehon Áedo . . .'

The Chief Brehon of Muman glared at Fidelma. 'What do you mean?' he growled. 'What have I to do with this conspiracy?'

Fidelma answered with a reassuring tone. 'Let us hope that you have nothing to do with it, except indirectly. But cast your mind back a few months. We were all at the Abbey of Lios Mór, investigating a particularly gruesome murder. I presented the case. You will recall?'

The Chief Brehon uttered a curt, 'Of course! It was shown and judged that the Lady Étain of An Dún was guilty of the murder of her own son and, indeed, of others.'

'Exactly so,' agreed Fidelma. 'It was a bizarre case and the Lady Étain was so deranged that you agreed that she was a *dásachtach*, suffering the worst condition of madness. She was sent to Gleann na nGeilt, the Glen of Lunatics, which is under the authority of the Abbey of Imleach.'

'Lady Étain was the leader of the uprising in the west. Are you saying that was a continuance of what happened at Lios Mór?' demanded the Brehon.

Abbot Ségdae shifted uneasily on his chair. 'I hope there is no reflection on how my abbey oversees its duties in the matter of Gleann na nGeilt?'

'As we understand it,' continued Fidelma, 'because of Lady Étain's rank and position, one third of her lands were used to provide for her upkeep and care during her lifetime. Two thirds were reverted to her family and to the payment of compensation to her victims and for fines.'

'That is the law,' agreed Brehon Áedo.

'And her family were . . . ?' prompted Fidelma.

It was Abbot Segdae who answered. 'You know well, Sister . . .' He paused, remembering her previous rebuke. 'You know well, Fidelma. She was of the Déisi Muman, the widow of a prince of that clan.'

'And thus related to the late Bran Finn, Prince of the Déisi?'

'Of course.' His eyes narrowed. 'Are you saying it was Bran Finn who brought the funds so that she could employ her mercenaries?'

'Not at all. He went to the Glen of Lunatics to discover who was involved in this plot. The funds actually came from Cronán, the Lord of Gleann an Ghuail, who was Étain's cousin. He had inadvertently told me that he had a cousin who married a noble of the Déisi.'

Eadulf nodded slowly. Before Fidelma had questioned Étain, he had entirely forgotten the exchange at the meal in Liath Mór.

Light was beginning to dawn on their faces. Colgú leaned forward in his chair. 'So this unrest in the west – Étain's raids against farms and settlements, particularly religious houses – they were master-minded by Cronán?'

'Those who were at Lios Mór will bear witness that the Lady Étain's crimes were inspired by a religious fanaticism. It was that which motivated the murder of her own son. When Cronán was devising his plot, he played on this. He sent to Étain, pretending that he was speaking as an abbot, and telling her that the seventh angel, a figure from the Holy Scriptures, had appeared and said that she was to lead an army to cleanse the land of the impure of faith.'

'But she was supposed to be confined in the Glen of Lunatics. How would she get the money to pay her band of cut-throats and escape?' Brehon Áedo stopped at a gesture from Fidelma.

'The Glen of Lunatics is no prison, and while the most dangerous are closely watched by the religious of Imleach, it would be easy for someone aided by outsiders to escape. Her own cousin, Cronán of Gleann an Ghuail, sent her money and support, probably via his son, Sillán, or one of his men like Biasta. I shall come to them later. Brother Ailgesach had become aware of the conspiracy during his last days working among the unfortunates in the Glen of Lunatics, and he warned Gelgéis – is that not so, lady?'

Gelgéis immediately confirmed it.

'Ailgesach promised her that he would try to get some proof of the conspiracy and find out what was behind it,' Fidelma went on. 'Unfortunately, he did not name Étain – and only at the last moment mentioned Bran Finn. He arranged with the latter to get that proof and bring it to him, at the same time arranging for me and Tormeid to meet with Bran Finn at his chapel. We were there at the appointed time but Bran Finn did not appear.'

'That is because he was already dead,' Eadulf told them. 'It was his body that Tóla found at the stream bordering his farm. The fellow was killed on his way to the rendezvous.'

'But I thought the body bore the emblem of the Uí Máil, the Kings of Laigin?' Colgú frowned.

'That was part of the proof to show the alleged involvement of Laigin. It was what was inside that brooch that was the real evidence,' Fidelma said. 'But whoever killed Bran Finn had removed the paper inside the brooch yet neglected to take the evidence of the brooch itself.'

'So Fianamail was waiting to hear that Cronán and Étain were rampaging through the kingdom,' Colgú said. 'Then he would use the excuse to enter the kingdom to stop civil strife. But Étain has been captured and Cronán must soon surrender or be destroyed.'

Gelgéis sighed deeply. 'So close and yet so far.' There were frowns from several who had gathered there. 'If Bran Finn had reached us, he would have brought proof of the conspiracy and told us who was involved. We waited in vain at Ailgesach's place. When he did not appear, I returned here to Durlus. Tormeid decided to go to the river, intent on travelling to Imleach or the Glen of Lunatics to see what he could discover about Bran Finn.'

There was a silence for a while.

'There is one thing that mystifies me,' Abbot Ségdae said slowly.

'Only one thing?' Fidelma smiled.

'We know that Étain suffered from extreme religious zeal. I can accept that was what inspired her madness, sent her riding forth to murder and pillage under the banners we have seen. Are we to understand that Cronán, who has declared himself to be an abbot, is similarly cursed?'

'His purpose and that of Étain, his cousin, were not the same,' explained Fidelma. 'He was simply prepared to allow her to be the distraction in the west of the country. True, he had his warriors carry out some similar raids under religious banners against the Uí Duach. That was in order to fool people into thinking it was all part of a general unrest to provide the excuse for Fianamail. But Cronán's goal was power. Power and pure avarice. He was waiting until he knew the warriors of Laigin were gathered on the border before he unleashed his main assault. His belief was that the conflict would bring Laigin in on his side and precipitate him to power.'

Colgú shook his head with a smile. 'For the first time there is a flaw in your argument, Fidelma. You have overlooked the most important point, sister. Cronán is no Eóghanacht. As powerful as the Laigin men could make him, he would never be able to claim the throne of Muman as a legitimate King. The *derbhfine* of the Eóghanacht have to make that choice according to law, not only from the most worthy to govern – the best able, if you like – but also from the bloodline. Cronán is of the Osraige. He is not of the Eóghanacht bloodline. Anyway, he is answerable to Tuaim Snámha, the Prince of Osraige.'

Brehon Áedo was puzzled. 'This is complex. Are you saying that Tuaim Snámha is involved?'

'I cannot prove that, but I suspect that he is not. I believe that Cronán's conspiracy with Fianamail of Laigin would be that Tuaim Snámha would be displaced and that Cronán would be made ruler of Osraige.'

'Then what of Muman?' demanded the Brehon. 'If this conspiracy was to overthrow Colgú, surely that means there is someone else involved?' His eyes widened. 'There is only one who can succeed in Cashel. Finguine, son of Cathal Cú-cen-máthair, your *tánaiste*, your heir apparent. He is of the bloodline. And he has been left safe in Cashel with an army at his command.'

All eyes turned to Fidelma. 'Finguine is—'

She was interrupted by a sharp rap on the door and when Spealáin opened it, they could hear Caol's voice outside whispering urgently. Spealáin turned back into the room with a shocked expression. He seemed unable to articulate for a moment and Colgú looked to Caol, who stood framed in the door behind the steward's shoulder.

'What is it, man?' he demanded testily.

The commander of his bodyguard took a quick step into the room, glancing round awkwardly.

'The guard I left outside the prisoner's room – one of the Éile warriors – has been killed. The Lady Étain has escaped. She is nowhere to be found.'

CHAPTER TWENTY

Fidelma and Eadulf entered the chamber where they had recently tried to question Étain of An Dún. Outside, in the passageway, the body of the warrior who had been left on guard lay in a crumpled and bloody heap. It looked as if he had been stabbed several times in the neck and chest in a frenzied attack. Inside the chamber, the bonds that had secured the woman lay scattered around. Eadulf gave them a cursory glance.

'Someone has released her from those chains,' he said, stating the obvious.

Caol and Gormán had entered behind them with the agitated Spealáin.

'Cathchern was a good warrior,' the steward grieved. 'He would never have allowed a stranger to approach and strike him without even attempting to draw his weapon.'

'That is the only explanation,' agreed Eadulf. 'Whoever killed him and released the prisoner was known and trusted by him.'

'Then there is a traitor here.' Gormán's expression was grim. 'It could be anyone of the Éile.'

'There are no traitors among the Éile,' snapped Spealáin.

'You have every right to protest,' agreed Eadulf calmly, 'but we must consider logic. The guard was attacked by someone he knew, or whose rank he had to respect.'

'We can discuss this later,' Fidelma said. 'It is more urgent to find where Étain of An Dún is hiding and who is hiding her. Now she is free, in her current state of mind, she will doubtless be bent on vengeance.'

'There is one point to consider,' Eadulf said quietly.

'Which is?'

'You know how her mind was when we saw her . . . well, the person who released her had the ability to do so without her raving or crying out and alarming anyone. That person was well known to her, able to quieten her.'

'A good point, Eadulf.' Fidelma turned to Caol. 'I want you to go to my brother and persuade him to return to the chamber Gelgéis has allotted him and await the outcome of our search for Étain. Do not leave his side, even if he tries to insist. Do not leave him alone until I say otherwise.'

Caol hurried off while Fidelma turned to the steward.

'Spealáin, you must alert Gelgéis and the guards. There must be a detailed search of the fortress for this woman and anyone else behaving suspiciously.'

'Are you sure you can trust me and the guards of Durlus?' the man said bitterly.

Fidelma answered with a thin smile. 'Trust must be earned, Spealáin,' she replied. 'I suggest you set about earning it.'

He bit his lip and then hastened after Caol.

'Do you think Étain is going to attempt to assassinate the King?' asked Gormán anxiously.

'She is crazy enough to try,' Eadulf said heavily. 'With the way her mind is working, I do not think she would even be able to find her way to the King on her own and do the deed.'

'That's just it,' Fidelma interrupted. 'She is not capable on her own. Someone has released her and may even now be leading her to my brother.'

'Then . . .' Gormán was white-faced as he turned to the door.

'Wait! We can leave Colgú's protection to Caol,' called Fidelma, halting him. 'Our task is to find Étain and her companion.'

Outside in the corridor, ignoring the crumpled body of the warrior, they paused, uncertain of their direction. Then Gormán sucked in his breath and pointed. There were smudge-marks of blood on the stone floor. Someone, either Étain or her rescuer, had trodden in the blood of the guard and moved on, not noticing.

Gormán eased his sword out and led the way, following the trail. At the end of the passage, the trail turned down another short passage and ended before a stout wooden door. There were no locks on it. The young warrior motioned them back and reached forward. The door pushed open easily. A flight of steps led down into what was obviously a cellar or small vault. They could see a flickering light at the bottom.

'Wait here!' whispered the warrior. 'I'll go down first.'

They knew better than to object. Gormán moved noiselessly down the stone steps, his sword held ready in front of him. Then he disappeared from their sight. There was a long silence and Eadulf fidgeted uneasily. Fidelma was about to call down when Gormán's voice came up to them.

'It's all right, but you had better come and see this.'

Eadulf went first down the steps and into the cellar, which was lit by an oil lamp. Gormán was standing before what seemed to be a mound of clothing on the floor in front of him.

'What is it?' demanded Eadulf.

Gormán stood back and gestured to the huddled figure at his feet.

Fidelma let her breath escape in a long deep sigh. 'It's Étain,' she said softly.

'A single stab wound in the heart,' confirmed Gormán.

Eadulf took the oil lamp from its resting-place and held it above the figure so that they could see better.

'Did you . . . ?' Fidelma looked up at Gormán.

'God forbid, lady. I am no killer of old women,' protested the warrior. 'I came down here and saw this bundle of clothing, or so I thought. I discovered it was a body and made a quick search, but there is no one else here.'

'The wound is still bleeding, the body warm.' Eadulf had peered closer. 'And . . .' his voice rose sharply, 'she still lives!'

He gently thrust Fidelma aside, handing her the lantern, and knelt beside the woman. Even as he did so, he realised that it was too late. The Lady Étain of An Dún was breathing her last but, in that moment, she was conscious and her pale eyes became wide and staring. A strange understanding entered them. She was trying to speak. Eadulf raised her head a little with one hand behind it, and bent his ear to her trembling lips. Words came as a painful breath followed by a long rattling sigh and she was dead.

Eadulf laid the woman's head back on the bloody flags, then slowly rose to his feet.

'Did she say anything?' Fidelma demanded.

'I believe she was thinking of her family in her last moment.'

'Why do you say that?'

'Because she said two words – "my daughter" – that's all.'

Fidelma stared at him and he saw comprehension dawning in her eyes. Then she quickly addressed Gormán. 'Find Spealáin and inform him of this matter. He can remove the body. I will let my brother and Gelgéis know.'

Eadulf followed her as she hurried away.

'What is it?' he demanded as they raced back towards the guest quarters.

'I have just realised that my brother is still in danger,' she panted.

They found Caol standing outside the guest chamber which had been assigned to Colgú.

'Didn't I tell you not to leave my brother's side?' Fidelma's voice was raised in anger.

Caol was shocked, for he had never heard her sound so angry or upset before. 'It's all right, lady,' he protested. 'The King is not alone. He told me to wait outside.'

'Did I not make my instructions clear? Not alone? Who is with him?'

'Why, the Lady Dúnliath.'

To his surprise, Fidelma physically pushed him aside and hurled herself at the door. It was secured from the inside.

'Break it in!' Her agitation galvanised Caol into action.

Caol threw himself at the door. The wood around the lock cracked and splintered and gave, precipitating him into the room, followed a moment later by Fidelma.

Dúnliath had been wrapped in an embrace with Colgú and now she spun away and stared at them with cold fury on her face. Colgú himself stepped back in utter astonishment.

'By the . . . !' he roared. 'What does this mean, sister?' His voice was low and ominous.

'I am thankful to find you unharmed, brother.' There was relief in her voice, but she knew that Colgú was possessed of a temper equal to her own.

'Of course I am unharmed!' he snapped. 'There are boundaries that even you may not trespass across. What do you mean by this outrageous behaviour?'

'I gave specific instructions to Caol not to leave your side until I said so.'

'That's not his fault. I ordered him to leave as I was not alone.'

'And I instructed him not to leave your side, no matter who was with you,' replied Fidelma with equal firmness.

'I was with my betrothed, Fidelma. How dare you . . . ?'

Dúnliath had controlled her shock and anger now. Her features had resumed their usual benevolent expression.

'Come, beloved,' she said to Colgú, 'don't be angry with your sister. That she is so concerned with your welfare is much to be praised. She was worried for your safety.'

'Yet your worry was unnecessary,' Colgú ranted at Fidelma. 'Caol was outside and Ailill is in the next room. I had but to call, and either of them could have reached us if it were necessary. And why would it be necessary? The only way to surprise me in here would be an attack through this window, and that is a long climb from the courtyard. I doubt anyone would risk it. So now we have a splintered door as the result of your concern, and that must be repaired. You will have to apologise to Gelgéis and to her steward.'

Fidelma did not reply but stood looking around the chamber. She tried to keep her expression neutral as she examined the features of the fair-haired girl.

'Alas, lady, I have some sad news for you and that precipitated my anxiety for my brother.' She saw the girl's face tighten, but she said nothing.

'What sad news, Fidelma?' Colgú asked curiously.

'Dúnliath's mother has been found dead.'

Apart from a further tightening of the girl's face, she remained silent, immovable.

'Dúnliath's mother?' Colgú was puzzled. 'Found dead? Where? How do you know? I have no understanding of this.'

'In a vault in this fortress,' replied Fidelma.

Colgú remained bewildered. Then he looked at the girl. 'Who is your mother, Dúnliath?'

The girl did not reply. She had become as rigid as a statue. It was left to Fidelma to supply the answer. 'Étain of An Dún,' she said quietly.

Colgú's gasp of astonishment was louder than that of Eadulf and either Caol or Gormán.

'I thought your mother had died a long while ago,' he said to Dúnliath. Fidelma did not take her eyes from the girl.

'Dúnliath told me some time ago in Cashel that her mother's name was Étain. Drón of Gabrán married twice. His second wife was the mother of Dúnliath, who left him. Dúnliath was then raised by his *dormun*, a concubine.'

There was a growing noise along the corridor and Spealáin and his guards were crowding at the door. Fidelma turned to Eadulf, who was the only one unmoved by the revelation, and asked him to assure them that Colgú was well and to wait at the end of the corridor. When he had done so, she found Colgú was staring incredulously at Dúnliath.

'Is it true?' he finally asked. 'Why didn't you tell me?'

She spread her arms as if in surrender. 'I cannot be blamed for who my mother was,' she replied. 'In truth, I had little knowledge of her except her name. She left when I was a baby.'

'Did your father ever divorce Étain?' pressed Colgú.

'As your sister says, I was brought up by his *dormun*, my father's concubine,' the girl said defensively. 'For many years I even thought she was my blood mother.'

'But Étain had been married before she married your father, hadn't she?' Fidelma pointed out.

The girl nodded. 'It was only a few days ago that I was told that my real mother had originally married a noble of the Déisi Muman, by whom she had two sons. When he died, my mother married Drón. Then, when she deserted my father, she left me behind and I understood she returned to the Déisi fortress at An Dún where she raised her sons. She never acknowledged me.'

'When did you last see your mother?' Colgú asked.

'I saw her once some years ago when she passed through Osraige on her way to Gleann an Ghuail.'

'You had not heard that she was condemned to incarceration in the Glen of Lunatics earlier this year after she had murdered one of her sons?'

'I did not.' Fidelma found there was little to learn from the fixed expression on the girl's features.

'You did not know that she had escaped and was leading a band of rebels in the west?'

'As I did not know she was there in the first place, then I could not have known that she had escaped,' replied Dúnliath flatly.

'You did not know that she had been brought here, to Durlus, as a prisoner this very day?'

'I did not.'

'This is all hard to believe,' sighed Colgú, having exhausted himself with his rapid questioning.

The girl's chin came up defiantly. 'I can only tell you the truth.'

Colgú suddenly remembered what Fidelma had said first of all. 'You say that Étain is dead?' he asked his sister. 'How? Did she refuse to surrender?'

'She was murdered.'

The King's eyes widened a little. 'Murdered? I don't understand. She escaped from her confinement and . . . ?'

'She did not escape: she was released. I suspect that whoever released her tried to persuade her to come here and murder you. They failed because Étain had become hopelessly deranged. She was impossible to control and more of a hindrance than a help to the conspirator, and so they had no choice but to kill her. I will speculate, although it is not in my nature to do so, that they hoped that her body would remain undiscovered until they could come to your chamber and kill you.'

All eyes had turned on to Dúnliath. The girl was trembling.

'It is not so. I did not . . . it is all a fabrication!'

Eadulf spoke quietly. 'You will be interested to know that when we found your mother, she was not quite dead. She said two words before she expired.'

'She identified her killer?' Colgú asked.

Eadulf regarded Dúnliath sadly. 'Your mother had two sons by her first marriage. That we know. How many daughters did she have?'

'As far as I know, I was her only daughter,' the girl replied, puzzled.

'The two words that she spoke were – *my daughter*.'

Dúnliath staggered and would have fallen, had not Colgú caught her and lowered her to a chair.

'Get water quickly,' he ordered as he tried to massage her hands.

Eadulf handed him a goblet from the side table, but Fidelma suddenly struck it from his hand. She smiled apologetically.

'Let us take all precautions,' she advised and then asked Gorman to go for fresh water.

The girl was moaning and coming back to consciousness by the time Gorman returned.

'Are you charging her with being part of this conspiracy, Fidelma?' asked Colgú in a hollow tone.

To everyone's surprise she replied, 'Not yet. It is late now. I suggest that we ask Áedo, as Chief Brehon of Muman, and Brocc, as Gelgéis's Brehon, to convene a court in the Great Hall tomorrow so that they may judge my explanation of these events.'

'Very well,' Colgú agreed, almost in relief.

'Tonight, my brother,' Fidelma said softly, 'you must heed my advice and be very well-guarded.'

The morning heralded a bright, crisp and clear early-autumn day. There were no clouds in the azure sky but the sun was weak and high and there was a chill in the air. That morning, the news arrived that Fidelma had been waiting for. It came in the persons of Enda and Tormeid. Spealáin conducted them directly to Gelgéis's personal reception chamber where she and Colgú were breaking their fast with Fidelma and Eadulf. It was clear both newly arrived warriors were excited.

'Well, it seems that you have good news for us,' Fidelma observed as she welcomed them.

'Good news, indeed, lady,' Enda confirmed with a smile. 'Cronán is dead and Spillán is among the prisoners, and all the Uí Duach that were forced to serve Cronán have been released.'

'Including Ségnat?' Fidelma asked immediately, and then relaxed with a smile at Tormeid's affirmative.

'Were there many casualties?' Colgú asked after the murmurs of satisfaction subsided.

'Very few, considering. A company of us entered the fortress—' began Tormeid.

Enda interrupted immediately. 'We followed Tormeid's plan. We were to sneak into the fortress through the underground tunnels and then open the gates for Dego's men.'

'I merely showed the way through the tunnel that led into the bowels of the fortress,' Tormeid said modestly.

Enda interrupted again: 'No – Tormeid commanded us. We were joined by some of those Uí Duach whom Cronán had kept as *daer-fuidir*. We surprised the defenders. They were watching from the walls, observing Dego's main force, who had lit fires and taken up positions to act as a distraction while they waited for our signal. We came up into the courtyard and a group, led by Tormeid here, fought their way to the gates and opened them. Then Dego and his men rushed in.'

Tormeid was looking embarrassed. 'It was almost too easy,' he said. 'Surprise was on our side.'

'Tormeid came upon Cronán and bested him in a single combat,' added Enda.

'I gave him the opportunity to surrender, but when he saw all was lost he ran on my sword and even with his dying strength tried to take me with him to the Otherworld. I would have liked to have captured him alive,' Tormeid added ruefully. 'As soon as they saw that their leader was dead, the others began to lay down their arms. Sillán among them preferred surrender to death. Once he surrendered, the fortress was ours.'

Colgú rose smiling and held out his hand to Tormeid. 'Then this was well done, my friend. You have saved the lives of many of my warriors and, I hope, have restored peace to this kingdom.'

'There are other matters to be resolved before peace can be declared,' Gelgéis reminded them.

'Oh . . . you mean the Laigin army gathered on our border?' Colgú asked.

'I do not think that we need fear them,' Fidelma pointed out. 'As I said before, I doubt they will attack now that both Étain and Cronán have been defeated. Laigin has no excuse to invade us now. But Gelgéis is right: there are other matters to be resolved.'

'We know that Étain was in league with Cronán to create disturbances in this kingdom and that the King of Laigin was awaiting his chance to interfere. What more do we need to know?' demanded Colgú.

Fidelma knew that Colgú was not usually so obtuse. She guessed that he was trying to protect Dúnliath. It had been a shock for him to learn that she was actually the daughter of Étain of An Dún.

'We need to know who killed Drón and who killed Étain,' she returned. 'We also need to know who killed Bran Finn of the Déisi – and why. It is the enemy within that we must identify.'

'Are you blaming Dúnliath for these deaths? Come now.' Colgú's voice was tense. 'I am beginning to think that your dislike of the girl has led you astray in this matter, Fidelma. You surely can't believe that because she was the daughter of Étain she—'

'You have never done me an injustice before, brother,' Fidelma interrupted. 'Nor me, you. Last night I promised that today I would reveal everything before your Chief Brehon. I trust that you will allow him to judge what I say before you condemn me?'

Colgú's face coloured a little as he said, 'True. You have never let me down before, sister. Very well – you must do what you must.' He then left the chamber with Caol. It was clear that he was angry, but was making a conscious effort to control himself. Enda and Tormeid appeared discomfited, but Fidelma did not bother to enlighten them. Instead, she turned to Gelgéis, who also appeared uncomfortable at the King's departure.

'Last night I sought your permission to use your Great Hall, lady. Can we call all the relevant parties together there at the time of the midday bell?'

Gelgéis inclined her head. 'I have already made the arrangement.'

'Then you will excuse us until then.' Fidelma rose and went to the door, followed by Eadulf and Enda. Gelgéis and Tormeid watched them go with troubled expressions.

The Great Hall of Gelgéis of Durlus, Princess of the Éile, was abuzz with excitement. It had never been so crowded. There was, however, only a small proportion of the inhabitants of Durlus present, compared with the warriors of both the Éile and Cashel. At one end of the hall was a raised platform on which stood a central chair, occupied by Colgú. Next to him sat Gelgéis, while on the other side of the Princess of Éile sat her Brehon, Brocc. Bishop Daig of Durlus sat alongside him. By the King's other side sat the Chief Brehon Áedo and Abbot Ségdae, as senior bishop of Muman. Spealáin, as steward of the fortress, stood ready behind Gelgéis. To one side of the platform, Tormeid was stationed with half-a-dozen warriors of Éile; at the other side were Caol, Gormán and Enda, with several Cashel warriors.

Fidelma and Eadulf had already taken their places facing the King, having made sure that Dúnliath was present in the hall. Ailill, commander of what was now her bodyguard, stood close by. Fidelma noticed that even their erstwhile host, the smith Gobán, had deserted his forge to become an interested spectator at the back of the hall. It was apparent that Colgú's mood was restless, a sign of his irritability. The Chief Brehon of Muman opened the proceedings by asking Fidelma to speak.

'I do not wish to take up much of your time,' she said. 'Much of what has happened in these few days has already been explained. But I must reiterate some matters so that we may come to a better understanding of them.'

She paused and waited for a signal from her brother for permission to proceed in her own way.

'Some days ago, the body of a noble was found not far from Cashel, and it was on that matter I was sent to investigate. At first it was thought that the dead man was a Laigin envoy. Eventually, he was revealed to be Bran Finn of the Déisi Muman. The discovery of his body began to unravel a conspiracy against this kingdom. To make it simple, there were four leading conspirators. These were Étain of An Dún, Cronán of Gleann an Ghuail, and the King of Laigin, although we can only infer his participation by his actions rather than be able to prove it with the evidence which was destroyed by the murderer of Bran Finn. That murderer was the fourth conspirator.'

Colgú heaved a tired sigh. 'And you will of course name that conspirator?'

'Of course.'

'And you will prove to us beyond doubt that person's participation in this conspiracy?'

Fidelma was aware of a suppressed sob from Dúnliath.

'That I shall,' she answered determinedly. 'Everyone knows that

Étain was declared a *dásachach*, having been found guilty of murdering her own son as well as others. She was removed to the Glen of Lunatics. It was there that her cousin Cronán manipulated her religious madness to his own ends and was able to persuade her that she should embark on a religious crusade. In his pretence to be Abbot of Liath Mór, he told her that she had been summoned by "the seventh angel" to drive the "impure of faith" from the land. He provided her with money to gather a small band of mercenaries to attack clergy and churches in the west. She did so with relish.

'As I said, Brother Ailgesach, who was from Durlus, was one of those who attended the unfortunates of the Glen of Lunatics, and his work among the insane had driven him to alcohol as a means of compensating for the traumatic effect of that experience. He had discovered what Étain was planning, but was unable to get information about the extent of the conspiracy. He knew she was being visited by emissaries from Cronán dressed as religious, so he contacted Bran Finn of the Déisi Muman. As you know, Étain was of the Déisi and had been married to a member of Bran Finn's family, and so it was his family that were responsible for her. Therefore, according to law, it was up to Bran Finn to ensure that she was cared for, after having her property confiscated when she was declared insane. Bran Finn agreed that he would visit her in the Glen of Lunatics, ostensibly to see that she was lacking nothing in her care, but also to try to find out more about the conspiracy and bring the facts to Brother Ailgesach.

'Brother Ailgesach told Gelgéis about the arrangement. Gelgéis, knowing that Cronán had recently built a fortress less than a day away across the Suir, was worried. She also knew that Brother Ailgesach in his condition would scarcely be a credible witness if anything developed, so she arranged that she and Tormeid would go to see him. He failed to turn up. He had been murdered before he could bring the evidence to Ailgesach's cabin. When Eadulf and I searched the place, we found a note signed by the initial *B*. The writer said he had evidence of the conspiracy and would arrive with it to show Ailgesach about the time of the third quarter of the moon.

'As I say, he was the young noble whose body had been found in the stream near Cashel. Bran Finn had said in his note that the best place to hide something was in full sight. The connection was therefore simple.

'A brooch bearing the emblem of the Uí Máil of Laigin was pinned on his cloak. This had a hollow niche inside it where a message could have been hidden. I do not doubt it contained the proof of the conspiracy. The killer removed the incriminating message but left the brooch, probably not realising it could be identified as belonging to the Royal House of Laigin. That was also evidence that Bran Finn carried in full sight. However, the killer did know that the wand of office that Bran Finn carried had the emblem of the Déisi on it, which would identify Bran Finn. That evidence was snapped off at the top and the telltale emblem discarded.'

She took up her *marsupium* and from it she removed the brooch with the emblem of the Uí Máil on it, then the piece of paper with Bran Finn's note and, finally, the broken bottom half of the wand of office and gave them to Brehon Áedo.

'Sometimes in these matters, not all details can be discovered. We know that warnings about Brother Ailgesach were sent to Cronán. Who sent them, whether Étain or the person I shall call "the chief conspirator", we will probably never know. We do know that Cronán sent Biasta to kill Ailgesach. And we know that Cronán's own son Sillán was sent to Durlus disguised as a religieux. Perhaps some word of Ailgesach having visited there had reached Cronán.

'This was the complicated part. Still worried about why Bran Finn had not appeared, Tormeid went to meet Ailgesach and Bran Finn. When Bran Finn still failed to appear, they decided to return to Durlus. Tormeid later chose to go to Imleach to try to find him. Gelgéis took their horses back to Durlus while Tormeid attempted to get a boat on the River Suir. Sillán found this out and sent some of his men to abduct Tormeid and Gelgéis, not knowing that Gelgéis had already reached the safety of Durlus. Unfortunately for me, the abductors thought I was Tormeid's companion. I have already explained that part. I do not want to confuse things by going into that matter again . . .'

'But I *am* confused,' Tormeid said, stepping forward. 'May I speak?'

Colgú glanced at Fidelma and she signalled her assent.

'You said Biasta was on the road south to Fraigh Dubh in order to kill Brother Ailgesach. How could he be, when he had already killed Bran Finn to prevent him meeting with us at Ailgesach's chapel?'

'I did not say it was Biasta who killed Bran Finn,' Fidelma replied. 'The killer was our fourth conspirator. In fact, he was the man who orchestrated the entire conspiracy.'

For the first time Colgú became alert. Craning forward, he stared at his sister.

'Did you say – *man*?'

'I did,' she confirmed. 'Everyone would be led to believe there was some religious turmoil in this kingdom. Then, Colgú, you would be assassinated. That would be the point when Fianamail would seize the opportunity to march his warriors through Osraige and against Cashel on the pretext of securing peace. He would then place a new ruler – who would be his puppet – on the throne of Cashel.'

'We have spoken of this before,' Colgú said with a frown. 'And I told you that such a successor had to be of the Eóghanacht bloodline to gain approval. Finguine, our cousin, is my *tánaiste*. He is the one who would succeed me.'

'That was not the idea.' Fidelma was grim. 'Finguine would be disposed of; probably he would be made to seem responsible for the plot to overthrow you, so that the real conspirator could grasp power.

Finguine would be declared unworthy by him. So Fianamail would place a new person in Cashel as legitimate ruler, someone the Eóghanacht *derbhine*, the electoral college of the family, would deem suitable. That person would have to be another Eóghanacht.'

Gelgéis was nodding in agreement. 'That was why Tormeid and I were not forthcoming with you, Fidelma. You could easily have been in a conspiracy against your brother. Such things have been known.'

Colgú was trying to follow the logic. 'The succession is clear . . . If Finguine were to be ousted as my heir apparent, then who would have any legitimate claim?'

Fidelma paused for a moment and then spoke slowly. 'Our father's nephew, Máenach, succeeded to the Throne of Cashel and ruled wisely and well for over twenty years. He died eight years ago. *But he had a son.*'

There was a sudden and complete silence in the hall as many eyes turned on the figure standing behind Dúnliath.

It happened very abruptly. With a cry of rage Ailill sprang forward, drawing his sword and swinging it around his head to clear a path. Using this method, he fought his way towards the doors. With the hall crowded, however, he did not stand a chance. Many voices were calling on him to surrender and he was forced to halt. His sword in one hand, no one noticed that he had also drawn a dagger in the other. Giving one more desperate glance around for an avenue of escape, he drew himself up, uttered a harsh laugh and drove the dagger straight up under his chin. Blood spouted and sprayed from the wound and he fell backwards without a sound.

The profound silence of shock was broken by a shriek of grief as Dúnliath half-rose from her chair and then collapsed senseless on to the floor.

It was a while before those crowded around were brought to order. The body of Ailill mac Máenach was carried away and Dúnliath escorted to her chamber. There was a quiet in the hall.

'Ailill by his action seems to have confirmed your accusation, Fidelma,' Brehon Áedo said gruffly. 'However, it would be best if you explained how you came to your conclusions.'

Fidelma sighed as she spoke. 'I never thought that he would kill himself,' she confessed. 'However, *potius mori quam foedari* – better to die than to be dishonoured. But the death of any member of our family is a matter of sadness. In this instance, the sadness is intermingled with shame as we of the Eóghanacht claim our true descent from Eibhear Foinn, son of the incomparable Míle Éaspain who brought the Children of the Gael to this land at the dawn of time. We are proud of our lineage and our honour. The fact that our cousin could be party to such a conspiracy against his own family is a grievous blemish on our honour.'

She turned to her brother and those gathered with him.

'Having discovered the conspiracy, and realising that the death of Bran Finn played a central role in the matter, I come back to that very point. Bran Finn had travelled from the land of the Déisi Muman to visit Étain in the Glen of Lunatics, to ensure that she was adequately provided for and to get information for Brother Ailgesach. Being a noble who believed in protocol, he first came to Cashel, to pay his respects to you. While there, he saw Drón and Ailill – or, rather, they saw him. He must have said something which alerted Ailill to the risk that knowledge of the conspiracy might be obtained by the Prince of the Déisi. Bran Finn went on to see Abbot Ségdae at Imleach and then on to the Glen of Lunatics. By what means I cannot know, he discovered that Étain possessed a Laigin locket containing a message which was evidence of the complicity of Fianamail, King of Laigin. Finn was making his way to keep that rendezvous with Ailgesach at Fraigh Dubh when Ailill came upon him or, indeed, was lying in wait for him.'

'How was that possible?' demanded Colgú. 'Ailill was a guest at Cashel.'

'You will remember that on the day before Bran Finn's body was discovered, our cousin Ailill went hunting? He was late back with nothing to show for his pains, but boasted of a near-miss with a red deer. It is possible that a warrior of Ailill's ability could have a bad day at the hunt, but I doubt that he was hunting for deer. He was hunting for Bran Finn and found and slew him. He took the contents of the locket but, stupidly, he left the locket itself which bore the emblem of the Laigin King.'

'What was inside the locket?'

'As I said, we shall never know exactly. I should suspect either an assurance from Fianamail or a message to him. Whatever it was, it would be evidence to implicate Fianamail which we now, alas, lack. With Bran Finn dead, Ailill returned to Cashel. We saw tracks of a horse further along the stream.'

'But surely Bran Finn was riding a horse?'

'He was, but Ailill led it away after he had done the deed and turned it loose upon the heath at Fraigh Dubh. The carpenter, Saer, told us that he had seen a horse running wild on the Black Heath that morning.'

'Are you saying that Ailill killed Drón as well?' demanded Gelgéis.

'Dego had requested reinforcement because he was suspicious that the raiders might be laying a trap. Once Colgú had left Cashel with his warriors, it was Ailill who persuaded Drón to bring his daughter to Durlus for safety. I presume the purpose was to meet up with Cronán and await the arrival of Fianamail. This was where Ailill made a mistake. He tried to throw the blame for the decision to come here on Drón. This would have made Drón look guilty. At that stage no one outside the conspiracy knew the raiders were led by Étain or of her religious fanaticism. But Ailill knew. When we spoke at the stables here, he said, "What need we fear of a band of religious fanatics, raiders out of the Glen of Lunatics led by a crazed old woman?"'

'Why kill Drón?' asked Brehon Áedo.

'To keep him quiet before he could speak to me. Drón had become suspicious; he had asked to see me. When Eadulf and I went to his chamber we passed Ailill coming from that direction. We arrived in Drón's chamber to find him dying. His last word misled us. He simply said "Étain". Maybe he had heard that she was leading the raiders – she, who had been his wife and the mother of his precious daughter. I am not sure if there was anything else. Anyway, Drón was dead.'

'And what of the murder of Étain? Was that Ailill again?'

'Now that was a great mistake on Ailill's part. He thought he could release the old woman and guide her to Colgú's chamber where she could be persuaded to attack him in her frenzy. Then his plot could proceed as before. Colgú would be assassinated and Cronán and the King of Laigin would enter Durlus. Ailill would be declared the rightful heir to the throne of Muman. The problem was that Étain had her moments of sanity as well as insanity. She refused to cooperate. Her enemies were the religious, whom she saw as betraying the True Faith, or her own conception of the Faith. It was not with Colgú. She resisted Ailill and he killed her.'

'But Eadulf swears that her last words as she was dying were "my daughter". That implied her attacker was Dúnliath,' pointed out Colgú.

'That was my misinterpretation,' Eadulf admitted. 'In fact, she was expressing her fear *for* her daughter not *of* her daughter.'

Colgú's features lightened. 'A fear because Étain knew that by marrying me, her daughter, Dúnliath, would be in danger from Ailill?'

There was a moment's silence and then Fidelma raised troubled eyes to her brother. She wondered whether he knew the truth. Then she said, 'In her last moment of sanity, I think Étain feared for her daughter's safety if Ailill's ambition was fulfilled.'

CHAPTER TWENTY-ONE

It was several days later when Fidelma and Eadulf were seated in Gelgéis's reception chamber alongside Colgú and Tormeid. There was a lighter atmosphere in the room than there had been on previous occasions. Dúnliath had been allowed to depart from Durlus with the body of her father for burial at Gabrán. Ailill had been buried without the ceremony which, in other circumstances, would have been his due as an Eóghanacht prince. His grave would remain unmarked for he had forfeited those rights. All the Uí Duach hostages at Liath Mór had been released and Sillán and the survivors of Cronán's men had been taken under escort to the fortress of Tuaim Snámha, the Prince of Osraige, for him to mete out justice. It was accepted that he had not been involved with Cronán in his conspiracy with Fianamail of Laigin.

Colgú, however, was looking tired and careworn as he told them that he had just received a message from the Chief Brehon of the Five Kingdoms, Brehon Sedna.

'Brehon Sedna is now in the Laigin capital of Ferna,' he told them. 'The threat of warfare between Laigin and Muman has entirely receded. He sends us news that Fianamail of Laigin has withdrawn his army from the borders of Osraige and disbanded it.'

'And Fianamail's excuse for massing them on the border in the first place?' asked Gelgéis with a cynical smile.

'It was the excuse that we expected. Fianamail has assured the High King that he only assembled his warriors and marched them to the border as a means of protecting his kingdom when he heard reports that Muman was erupting into civil war.' Colgú pulled a face. 'Fianamail adds that he is delighted that this has turned out to be false information.'

This was greeted with a hoot of laughter from Tormeid.

'So I don't suppose the Chief Brehon is proposing to punish Fianamail for his role in this conspiracy?' Fidelma asked dryly.

'As there is no proof that any warrior of Laigin entered Osraige with hostile intent, or any other part of the Kingdom of Muman, the Chief Brehon felt there are no grounds to impose the *bórama*. Laigin does not have to pay the tribute to Tara for breaking the peace,' confirmed Colgú.

There was muttered disapproval from Tormeid but Colgú did not seem upset.

'You might say that there was punishment enough for Fianamail.'

'How so, brother?' Fidelma was surprised at Colgú's easy attitude to the decision.

'The recent entreaties from Laigin and her eloquent ambassador Moling, the Bishop of Ferna, for the *bórama* to be withdrawn have been totally rejected. The tribute will remain in force and will become payable for the foreseeable future. Laigin's territorial ambitions will continue to be held in check.'

There were some sounds of approval at Colgú's news, but everyone seemed clear that they would have preferred Fianamail to have received a harsher punishment for his territorial ambitions.

'So we can declare that Laigin's threat to Muman is no more . . . Well, at least for the time being?' Fidelma conjectured.

'With Cronán dead, his fortress is also to be destroyed, levelled to mere ashes by order of the Prince of Osraige.'

'But can we trust Osraige?' Tormeid demanded. 'Tuaim Snámha must accept some responsibility for allowing Cronán of Gleann an Ghuail the freedom to build his fortress and construct those roads . . .'

Colgú raised a shoulder and let it fall in silent eloquence.

'Tuaim Snámha and I have exchanged envoys and he has agreed that, as ruler of Osraige, he must accept some culpability as to what has happened. He has agreed to pay compensation to the Uí Duach for what they have suffered from Cronán of Gleann an Ghuail. He will also allow the religious to rebuild Liath Mór as the community origi-nally intended, if they wish to return there. I shall also have to consider what compensation is due to the communities and settlements that Étain destroyed. But peace has returned.'

When Tormeid had finished thanking the King on behalf of the Uí Duach, Fidelma asked him: 'Will you return to the territory of the Uí Duach now, Tormeid?'

The warrior shook his head.

'I cannot ignore the fact that, had I not escaped from Liath Mór that first time, my comrades and cousins might still be alive. I cannot face my clan . . . yet.'

'You cannot be blamed for that,' Colgú assured him. 'But if you will not return to the land of the Uí Duach, what then?'

Tormeid glanced towards Gelgéis. 'I shall remain here in Durlus,' he said, adding softly, 'that is, if I am allowed?'

Gelgéis's happy smile needed no interpretation.

'Then,' commented Fidelma approvingly, 'we shall look forward to returning to Durlus soon . . . as guests at your wedding feast.'

It was on the following day that Colgú was riding at the head of a column of horsemen proceeding southwards along the highway to

Cashel. Behind him rode Fidelma and Eadulf, and behind them came Caol, Gormán and Enda. Fidelma, with a whispered word of explanation to Eadulf, galloped forward so that she was riding alongside her brother, out of earshot of the entourage. For the first time in her life Fidelma felt nervous about raising a subject with him.

'So, Dúnliath decided to leave for Gabrán to bury her father?' She did not ask why Colgú had not gone with her.

'She was determined to bury her father in the tomb of his ancestors,' Colgú said gruffly. 'I gave her my permission.'

'What then for you and her, brother?' Fidelma asked hesitantly.

There was a tightening of the muscles of the King's jaw. 'What now?' He repeated the question but knew well what she meant.

'I do not wish to intrude but it is a matter which concerns not merely the kingdom but also our family,' Fidelma said gently.

Colgú's smile seemed more of a painful grimace. 'I did not think it merely a prurient enquiry.' He paused for a few moments and then sighed deeply. 'She will remain at Gabrán. There will be no wedding at Cashel, if that is what you mean.'

Fidelma regarded her brother sadly. His shoulders were slightly hunched as if a great weight had descended on him.

'Is it because her mother was Lady Étain that you felt you could not go through with the marriage?' she asked. 'The madness that she was possessed of is not necessarily something that would be inherited.'

Her brother regarded her for a moment as if trying to peer into her innermost thoughts. Then he said, 'It is not her relationship with Étain of An Dún that was the problem.'

'Not that? Then what? From what we have discovered, it seems that she was not in the conspiracy with Ailill.'

'We shall never know for certain,' Colgú replied. 'However, it was in your mind, wasn't it? When Eadulf told us Étain's last words – "my daughter" – she was expressing her fear *for* her daughter and not *of* her daughter . . . I think you knew.'

'But I said it meant Étain feared for her daughter's safety if Ailill's ambition was fulfilled.'

'That was said to spare my feelings,' Colgú said. 'I am not as stupid as you think, Fidelma. Étain was afraid because she knew Dúnliath was in love with Ailill.'

Fidelma had suspected this; however, she had hoped, for the sake of her brother's happiness, that Colgú was unaware of it. Fidelma had wanted to spare him more hurt and bitterness.

'We shall never know,' she said now. 'You are rejecting her merely on the basis of suspicion.'

'A suspicion I could live with. But I would not be able to ignore the fact that she is bearing Ailill's child.' The words were spoken flatly.

For the first time in her life Fidelma felt a sense of utter shock. She swallowed hard. 'I had no idea,' she whispered.

'Now you do surprise me,' Colgú commented, trying to regain a sense of grim humour but sounding only more bitter. 'My astute, sagacious sister, I thought you knew everything. I thought that you were infallible. How could you, so shrewd, have missed that point? Remember this, sister, that the child she gives birth to will also be an Eóghanacht. Ailill's father was Mánach, King of Cashel, after our father died. One day, who knows, we may have to watch Gabrán for gathering stormclouds if ambition stirs in the child.'

Fidelma felt a wave of sadness for her brother and did not rise to the taunts he made. He was like a small child, striking out from his hurt emotions.

'Were you that much in love with her?' she asked softly. When her brother did not answer, she said: 'I thought so. Then out of that love, could nothing be repaired?'

'And the child?' His voice was harsh.

'Fosterage is the tradition of our people,' she pointed out. 'A child's love and affiliation is nurtured.'

Colgú answered her with a bark of angry laughter. 'Truly, sister, you are known for finding a saying to match every occasion. I'll give you one. Don't our hunters say – *what do you expect from a pregnant wolf but its cub?*'